He turned and stumbled towards the window . . . Behind him, the obscenities he'd seen in the walls were breaking free of their shackles; the soft thumps they made as they dropped to the floor quickened his step. He only stopped short when he saw the face peering in at him through the glass.

It was a face he knew, or thought he knew, except that it looked composed of rain. At first he was sure it was weeping, since the eyes overflowed with water; but so did its streaming hair and the rest of its features. Pleadingly, the intruder opened its mouth to speak, and more water gushed forth. 'You —' he lip-read, 'you don't know what you've unsealed.'

Somewhere a rock and roll drum-beat pulsed . . . Then, as the figure raised a hand to rap the pane he recoiled, expecting the glass to shatter. Instead it was the hand he saw disintegrate; there was the briefest impression of blood and serrated flesh spraying up, and the face contorting in anguish. Seconds later it was hardly a face at all . . .

Dark Brigade

Chris Westwood

First published in 1991
by HEADLINE BOOK PUBLISHING PLC

A HEADLINE FEATURE paperback

10 9 8 7 6 5 4 3 2 1

ISBN 0 7472 3479 5

Typeset by Medcalf Type Ltd, Bicester

Printed and bound by
HarperCollins Manufacturing, Glasgow

HEADLINE BOOK PUBLISHING PLC
Headline House
79 Great Titchfield Street
London W1P 7FN

Wendy –
This tale of grace and danger is for you
– with all my love

Prologue

On Providence Street, 1977

For I know that nothing good dwells in me, that is, in my flesh; for the wishing is present in me, but the doing of good is not. For the good that I wish, I do not do; but I practise the very evil that I do not wish.

— Romans 7:18–19

At that time of year the tide would be in by late morning, and across the water the small fishing vessels rolled and bobbed, the beat of their motors gradually fading until only the sound of the waves remained. Then, at sunset, the sound would slowly rise again — with the thin, hairdryer-drone of cheap motorbikes — and the small boats would grow larger, returning to the harbour on the south side of the bay.

Whenever he watched their progress from the front, Jim Doherty would stand, hands pocketed, and wonder at the stirring of dread in his bones. It came to him often, this thrill, this calm certainty that sooner or later something disastrous would overtake the vessels and all who sailed in them. It was a feeling of dark premonition, one he'd never been able to explain to himself or to anyone else. Perhaps it was to do with the sight of the clouds that came in with the boats; clouds of a deep thunder grey which eventually broke and scattered as the boats neared the harbour, clouds which became once again what they'd always been — ravenous flocks of gulls, crying for carrion. The instant the clouds became gulls again, the feeling left him.

And kids like gulls flocked to the harbour and gathered there when the nights were fine. Some came to greet their fathers, home from the range; others came in boredom for something to do. They stood, faces blushing in the sunset, breathing the smells of raw fish and salt air, seeing the vessels unload with the same fascinated eyes that saw the unloading every night. *One day, son, all this* — the men's eyes promised, their brows lobster-red from the salted air — *all this will be yours, if you want it.*

On the day of the storm, though, there were no small boats on the water, and only the occasional trawler idling on or about the horizon. Most of the fishermen were finishing up at the pubs before closing, or at home in front of their radio sets, grumbling and cursing the shipping forecasts, and by mid-afternoon the waves were climbing the promenade walls like steeplejacks. By then the sky had grown so dense and so angrily loaded it was impossible to tell where the seas began and the heavens ended; the trawlers had vanished into a horizon as pale and blank as a whitewashed wall.

Jim was in the arcade with Colin Schofield before the worst of it broke. Behind them, coins chimed, bells rang, and a black-hatted Westerner entered the saloon firing both Smith & Wessons at once. At the entrance a group of leather-jacketed rebels struck poses, and each other, while the Pistols charged through 'Pretty Vacant'. In one corner, Jim could see Terry Mack converting ten pence pieces into fifties, grafting lumps of silver foil on to coins and then filing the edges into shape. His hands made quirky little movements while he worked, and every now and then he would wander across to the change machine, feed in his loaded coin, collect the five tens that came chinking out from the return slot, and wander back to his corner near the Check Your Heart-Rate machine and begin again.

'There's a belter on the way,' Colin was saying, staring from a window which faced out on to the promenade. He'd been watching transfixed for almost five minutes while the storm gathered, inside and out. 'Do you want to stay or brave it?'

'Brave it,' Jim said, not even thinking.

'Then how about heading up to McGonnigles and grabbing a coffee and watching the storm from there until it passes?' Colin turned, swept away from the window, and started to tug on his brown corduroy jacket all in one motion, as if to make up for lost time. As they stepped outside he said, 'Doesn't it strike you as odd?'

'Doesn't what?'

'That Terry Mack never plays the machines with all that money he makes. What do you suppose he does with it all?'

'How should I know?'

'If you ask me, he's sticking it in his arm or up his nose,' Colin said. 'Didn't you notice his eyes just lately?' And he immediately broke into a run, inviting Jim to give chase.

The front was barren. All along the promenade, amusements were holed up behind shutters and cross-hatched metal grilles while the wind tossed last week's fish and chip papers at their doors. The Hippodrome towered above the small shops, the cinema, the abandoned Fantasy Fair with its ghost train and Miracle Mirror Maze, and with its domes and reaching spires it might have been a slowly decaying fairy-tale castle while last summer's Max Jaffa posters peeled from its walls. They ran towards the south cliffs, beneath which extended the empty pitch and putt course and the Crazy Golf, and at the end of the prom, Colin turned right on to Seaview Road.

Here, small gift shops closed for the season rose in a sharp incline towards cafés, flatlets, more gift shops. The rise was impossibly steep, and often caused Jim to wonder — and wonder now — how all those shops ever avoided collapsing down the street and into the sea, one after another, like lemmings. They were half-way up the slope when Colin went on, 'I'll tell you what though. If that's what Terry Mack wants to do with himself, that's his business. So much for anarchy in the UK. Not me though. *I'm* going up and out; I'm clearing out of this. You watch me, Jim!' And he broke into a sprint which drained the last of the spring from Jim's legs and left him lagging, like a faithful but very ancient dog, far behind.

He dropped gears and began walking instead of running and finally caught up outside McGonnigles, where Colin was jogging briskly on the spot. 'God, just breathe that air,' Colin said, and demonstrated, expanding his chest. 'Fill up those lungs.'

'I can't breathe.'

'The air's so clear, and it's going to be clearer after the storm. Just you wait. Isn't it something, Jim! I could go all day!'

Then he set off from McGonnigles and turned left at the corner on to Providence Street, an even steeper assault than the one they'd just made. For a moment Jim faltered in the doorway, thinking about the warmth inside and the storm about to break, but when he realised Colin wasn't about to turn back he followed.

Providence Street rose acutely, almost to cliff-top level. This was a narrow cluster of small tea-rooms and fortune-tellers' houses, of brightly coloured shutters and hand-painted plaques above doorways. Like most of the gift shops, the prophets were closed for the season; no doubt burning their summer profits on holidays abroad in the sun, Jim thought. *Madame Echo, Clairvoyant; The House of Everlasting Light; Rose the Seer,* announced their signs in glaring, flaking yellows and reds; *Palms Read, Futures Told, Destinies Divined*.

Colin had slowed, finally stopping beneath a sign with

6

black stencilled letters which read, obviously enough, Jim thought: YOUR FUTURE NOW. Below that, a simple flourish added, *Pay Later,* and an arrow gave direction to a side entrance. The small bay window at the front of the house was all tiny square sections of glass dwarfed in painted-black frames, from which it was probably no easier to see out than in.

'Did you ever go into one of these?' Jim wondered.

'Once or twice,' Colin said. 'Never this one though. I don't remember passing this one before. It must be new.'

'But the paint looks so old.'

'And the window's so grey and so grimy you can't even see through it.' Colin wiped at the pane with a fist bunched in the sleeve of his jacket, and then backed away sharply as if a face had appeared at the window, staring out. 'Let's go in,' he decided at last. A fine rain was beginning to spot and sparkle upon the pavement. 'It'll be a laugh. Just until the storm passes.'

'I thought we were going to McGonnigles,' Jim protested, in no rush to find what awaited him in the future, let alone in the house.

'We will — right after this. How much money you got?'

'Enough for McGonnigles.'

'So put your lunch on the tab.'

'I don't have a tab.'

'Then start one,' Colin said, and breezed around the side of the house, into a narrow alley where red-brick buildings faced one another across piles of refuse, their walls daubed with current new wave names: The Damned, X-Ray Spex, Wire. All along the alley plastic dustbins were posted in doorways like sentries, rusting fire-escapes spiralled towards darkened upper floors, made darker by the sky now squeezing between the roofs, angry and grey.

The fortune-teller's was the first on the left. Again the

promise, YOUR FUTURE NOW, on a hand-painted plaque screwed to the door below a square of bevelled glass impossible to see through. On the wall beside the door was a small white button, which Colin began thumbing until chimes sounded indoors, a voice muttered something in reply, and a smeared shape moved behind the door. Then the door swung open, and a man's face peered out.

At least Jim assumed it was a face, since it couldn't reasonably be anything else. Bruised and mottled by years, it looked like a sketch that had been crossed out and redrawn several times. The man wore a beard, a wiry gingerish tuft of a thing like a goat's, but his eyes were a child's, clear and blue as an Indian summer sky. He looked first at Jim, without interest, and then his gaze settled on Colin.

'Well?' he said.

Colin cleared his throat. 'We saw your sign, mister, we thought — '

'Name?' the man said.

Colin gave his name.

'Well, come inside, Colin Schofield. Bring your friend — if he wants to come too.'

He turned then, and padded indoors. After a moment's hesitation — Colin nodding, Jim shaking his head resolutely, Colin seizing Jim by a sleeve — they followed. There was no light inside; the windows in the narrow kitchen they passed through were either too small or too filmed over with grease to allow any in. A few cracked and stained saucers and cups sat on a drainer, and there was a faint smell of stagnant water beneath other kitchen smells — cooking oil, gas. In one corner, blind potato eyes were bursting from holes in a sack; in another lay a tray of turquoise rat poison. 'Where did he go?' Jim wondered, before he saw the curtain settling in a doorway beyond the kitchen.

The curtain gave into a spartan front room which faced the main street. When Colin and Jim entered, the goat-bearded man was already seated in an upholstered armchair by a tiled open fireplace, gesturing for them to sit. There was a small wood-framed sofa opposite him, and a threadbare pile rug drawn up to the hearth. A layer of lime-coloured carpet underlay covered the rest of the floor.

Following Colin's lead, Jim dropped on to the sofa, crossed his legs, stared at the fireplace. No fire burned in the grate, and judging by the cold and damp air no fire had burned here for weeks, if not months. There was a battered portable two-bar electric heater beside Goatbeard's chair, loose wires sprouting where the plug had been ripped from the cable. Damp patches marked the ceiling and walls and, here and there, the red and gold floral wallpaper was beginning to peel loose in strips. How long had the house been degenerating about him? Had he begun to notice yet, or care?

'So, then,' Goatbeard said wearily, 'how can I help you?'

'I was about to ask you that,' Colin said. 'We were just passing, you see, and we saw – and we thought – '

'And *you* thought,' Jim corrected him.

'And so *I* thought, why not?' After a pause he added, 'This isn't exactly what I expected.'

The fortune-teller laughed, or made a sound quite like a laugh, and then with nicotined fingers took out a snipped, half-smoked cigarette from a pocket and put it to his lips. 'You mean you're wondering why there's no crystal ball, no candles, no cards, no smell of incense; and you're wondering why I don't have my windows curtained to shut out the light.'

'I was wondering that,' Colin said. 'I expected – more a kind of gypsy woman with bangles and beads, and a

9

circular table or something. Doesn't this work better in the dark?'

Goatbeard leaned back in his chair, struck a match, inhaled smoke. Behind him, rain tested the small square panes of the window like prying fingers. 'The dark works for some, not for me. I can't see your eyes in the dark, and I do like to be able to see your eyes; that's where your future lies.'

'So what do you see in mine?' Colin ventured, in a wavering voice that seemed suddenly to have lost its confidence.

'I see you're not so sure you want to go through with this,' Goatbeard told him. 'Do you think it's just a lark, Colin Schofield? Do you know what you're asking me to do?'

Colin and Jim exchanged glances: Jim's said, Let's go, Colin's said, Wait — Not Yet, No Hurry. There was a moment where silence seemed to permeate the room, to seal it; and then thunder descended outside, its after-echoes meditating in the chimney's shaft, and Goatbeard said, 'Most people come here for reassurance: they want to hear that everything's fine, everything's all right, or will be, and of course I can't tell them that. There's lonely people wanting to hear that they won't be lonely forever, and I can't tell them that either. If you want your future now, I always say, stay put, here it comes. If you want reassurance then go next door, stop wasting my time.'

He paused, smoked, watched the smoke rise in a blue lambent spiral to the ceiling. 'What you're doing is asking me to open a door, Colin Schofield — a door with Restricted Access on it; and this door, it stands there like an elemental law, and once you enter the room behind it, you're on your own. It's out of my hands. I opened the door myself once,' he said, 'and believe me, once opened, it never closes.'

Obviously the man was half-insane — which explained why his ranting made no sense, why his gaze flitted anxiously about, unable to settle on any one thing.

'So what did you find when you opened the door?' Colin asked.

'Isn't it obvious?' Goatbeard replied. 'I hoped for the same things we all do; I hoped for many treasures I never found. Look around you; look at what's happening, if you want to see what I found there.'

Jim did. He looked around at the unfurnished room — at the ghost-mark on one wall where a mirror had been, at the floor-space a chest of drawers might have occupied, at the drab carpet underlay, tack-marked along its periphery.

'Piece by piece they're taking it all away from me,' the fortune-teller said, and Colin said with astonishment, 'What? You're being repossessed?'

'Who are *they*?' Jim wondered; but Goatbeard gave no reply, perhaps hadn't heard the question.

'Shit, he can't even afford to keep furniture,' Colin said righteously. 'Is that what you saw in your future? You were going to lose everything you owned?'

'That and much more, everything I owned and very much more — ' Goatbeard said, and then stopped, perhaps at a thought or a sound. A shadow had crossed his face, one hand gripped the chair's armrest, knuckles whitening.

Somewhere in the room there was movement. At the edge of his vision Jim could see wallpaper peeling, sagging lower, drawn down the wall as if by the sheer force of its weight — or will. Above the curtained doorway they'd entered by was a slight but unmistakable shifting of paper down wall. Suddenly the light had thickened, making the doorway appear further away than before. Briefly he considered taking his chances and escaping without further delay; but was held by a still briefer vision of Colin mocking him, later, when the cold light of day had shed sense over what he was seeing.

'You're not lonely, Colin Schofield,' the fortune-teller declared. His yellowed fingers picked the butt from the midst of his bearded mouth and shied it towards the hearth. 'You have friends who trust you and even look up to you, isn't that so?'

'I suppose — ' Colin cast a sheepish glance towards Jim; perhaps modesty restrained him, for he took several seconds before stammering a reply. 'I — I suppose so.'

'And you're gifted — in academics and sports, wherever you turn your mind or your hands you excel.'

'He does,' Jim said promptly, when Colin, flushing, said nothing.

'And secretly you plan to break out — from this town and the many things you despise here. You despise its smallness, and how deadly it is in its sameness, year after year; the way nothing changes, and the way no one thinks beyond here and now. It all makes you burn inside.'

'Yes,' Colin said.

'But you won't go as far as you think, and you won't climb as high as you hope.'

Colin flinched. 'How do you mean?'

'I can't tell you that; I can only tell you what I see, what's inevitable.'

A brief silence elapsed then, and there was only the patter and gossip of rain beyond the still of the room. The storm was almost directly overhead now, the rain consolidating; the cloud cover had moved over the streets, quenching the light. That, Jim thought, was why

Goatbeard had receded to a propped-upright blur, his features so indistinct. But what he was saying was equally blurry — you could have applied it to any coin-slot junkie down at the arcade and been close to correct. Yet the fortune-teller's words, or the way they were spoken, disturbed him. It was the calm assurance of the old man's tone, as if instead of prophesying things to come he were reciting phrases from a history book.

To Jim he looked practically shapeless where he sat, almost indistinguishable from the swollen grey mass of his armchair. In the poor light, denser than fog, his eyes were the only brightness.

'People expect a lot from you, and you expect a lot of yourself,' he said to Colin.

'Yes,' Colin agreed, without hesitation.

'You hope that your academic gifts will raise you above the shit-pile. Your school and your family hope for this too.'

'Yes.'

'There are dreams of university places and honours degrees and a life after that which will set you apart — a life of prosperity, of sweet suburbia, a career in Law or perhaps Education.'

'Well,' Colin said.

'But these dreams are not yours; they're imposed on you, they're dreamed by others. And sometimes you rebel and you toil against the grain. Your interests are not *their* interests; you think your talents will lead you elsewhere — towards making, creating, doing — '

'I don't — ' Colin faltered. 'I don't follow.'

'You're destined to lose something,' Goatbeard said. 'Something's about to cross your path, Colin Schofield, something — ' He trailed off.

Colin looked nonplussed. His face tautened, his mouth

13

quivered open. 'What am I supposed to lose then? What's supposed to cross my path?'

'I can only tell you the inevitable, I can only describe what's there – '

The man was ranting, his blue eyes had turned opaque. Jim wasn't at all sure where all this was leading, but a growing unease made him want to be free of this room and this situation at once. Why then did his limbs restrain him when he tried to stand? He felt drained as if by a long and arduous journey through dreams, his body failing to co-operate. Would he be breaking some unwritten law if he managed to upright himself while the man was speaking – the elemental law that Goatbeard described, broken as soon as the door was opened? He looked at Colin, who was perfectly still, inanimate even – who might have been stuffed if his eyes hadn't seemed so alive, so troubled.

'Colin?' he said, but Colin said nothing. 'Oh Christ,' he muttered, at the sound of wallpaper renting itself from a wall nearby. 'Can't you hear it? Can't you see – ?'

'Hear what? See what?' Colin said, and turned away, clearly irritated by the intrusion.

The storm was here, the light was dwindling, darkness hadn't so much descended on the room as formed out of it – thrown up as an unhealthy secret. It belonged here, as much an essential part of the room as the old man himself, as the wallpaper.

'You shouldn't have pried,' the fortune-teller was saying, in a voice which was harsh and sibilant and not entirely his own. 'You really shouldn't have come, you're not welcome down here. Why did you have to disturb us like this? Don't you know there's a price to be paid for what you've done?'

'We'd better leave,' Jim said; but neither Colin nor the goat-bearded man seemed aware of him. Something had

14

changed for the worse here – didn't they sense it at all? If they did they weren't showing it. They seemed quite oblivious to the way that the room had succumbed to shadows, to the commotion of swift, small movements about the walls.

'Colin,' Jim said, louder. 'Don't you think you've heard enough?' But his pleas were falling on deaf ears – his own as well as Colin's: no sound escaped him, only a murmur. Either terror had stolen his tongue with his strength or the old man was casting some kind of spell over him – and over Colin too, if Colin's vacant-eyed stare was anything to go by.

He managed to force himself to his feet, but the effort of working his limbs seemed tremendous – they felt clasped by hands he couldn't see. If he could drag himself as far as the doorway, the vision would end, he'd be able to rouse Colin out of his torpor. And then through the gloom he saw that the doorway was no longer there; instead, wallpaper covered it, a blundering mass of red and gold flora, its patterns redrawn as horrors. One thriving sunflower had an open wound at its centre, and below it, maggots boiled feverishly on a leafy stem; from the midst of a tangle of foliage slithered a white limbless newly-born, eyes blind, mouth sealed. As far as he could tell there was nothing even remotely human about it.

Jim screamed, or at least felt the rise of a scream. It never emerged, and its pellet of sound only lodged in his throat, choking him. Colin never so much as looked up. He was listening to the fortune-teller and nodding his head in agreement. What a pseud, Jim thought, pretending he understands this nonsense. Let him perish, if that's what he wants; let him stay and face the consequences alone.

He turned and stumbled towards the window. If the door was sealed off, then at least he could force an exit through

15

here. Behind him, the obscenities he'd seen in the walls were breaking free of their shackles; the soft thumps they made as they dropped to the floor quickened his step. He only stopped short when he saw the face peering in at him through the glass.

It was a face he knew, or thought he knew, except that it looked composed of rain. At first he was sure it was weeping, since the eyes overflowed with water; but so did its streaming hair and the rest of its features. Pleadingly, the intruder opened its mouth to speak, and more water gushed forth. 'You – ' he lip-read, 'you don't know what you've unsealed.' That was as much as he could make out, as much as he'd want to.

Somewhere a rock-and-roll drum-beat pulsed, perhaps in a neighbouring street. It gathered in Jim's head, a relentless protest against something or other, tuneless and violent, a song of the age of revolt. Then, as the figure raised a hand to rap the pane he recoiled, expecting the glass to shatter. Instead it was the hand which he saw disintegrate; there was the briefest impression of blood and serrated flesh spraying up, and the face contorting in anguish. Jim blinked, and incredibly the face was dissolving. Seconds later it was hardly a face at all. Then it was rain.

'Good Christ,' a voice said, loudly enough to make him start. The illusion gone, rain drummed the glass as before, a steady tattoo. 'Good Christ, he's the one – '

He turned and saw the fortune-teller and Colin staring gone-out at him, their faces full and clear as new moons, now that the clouds had lifted. The room was itself again, filled by a splendid and almost artificially crystalline light.

'Jim?' Colin said. 'What are you doing by the window, Jim? Didn't you hear us calling?' He was wearing a look of grave concern which was still there five minutes later

16

when they stepped back outside on to Providence Street.

The sky still brooded, but the rain had lessened to a mild drizzle. It had sweetened the pavements and returned a freshness to the air, and on Seaview Road a few stranded pedestrians were beginning to unfold themselves from shop doorways. A man soldiered past, face blued, lips cursing, a dripping newspaper held tented over his head.

'So much for that,' Colin huffed, and pocketed his hands. 'Two quid for my future, and he tells me everything I already know.'

'What did he mean,' Jim said, 'when he said you were going to lose something?'

'Oh, that? He has to put something like that in for effect; it's part of the show – and not such a bloody good show either, eh? He made it sound so convincing, before, but he wasn't talking about me at all.'

They went up towards Hawthorne Drive, where the road levelled out past a spare auto-parts place, a junk shop, a sex emporium which local residents were petitioning to close. In recent months its flesh-filled windows had been bricked through twice by the moral minority, Jim had heard.

'Jim?' Colin said suddenly.

'Yes?'

'Did you see something in there, at the fortune-teller's?'

'Like what?' Jim said, and instinctively bit into his lip. He mustn't say anything yet, not yet, not until he could be clearer about whatever the vision had meant.

'I don't know . . . You didn't pay any attention when I called you. You didn't seem to hear me at all. And, Jim, when you were staring out through the window and slamming it with your hand – I thought . . . What did you see?'

'Nothing,' Jim said, thinking that might close the topic.

17

At least he'd hoped it might; but perhaps it wasn't closed yet. Colin had stopped and was staring back down the street, one hand puzzling the back of his head. 'What do you make of that? I never saw anything like it before.'

It took a second before Jim could register what it was he was supposed to be seeing. Under the paled sky, a shadow trailed over the kerb behind them, extending perhaps ten or twelve feet down the slope, as far as the Kodak billboard girl, smiling outside a newsagent's door. It was his own shadow, rooted at his feet; and yet Colin, beside him, cast none.

On another day, Jim would – they both would – have explained it away as a trick of the light; an apparition thrown down by belts of cloud which were gradually shifting inland while occasional sunlight filtered through. The atmosphere in disarray, there was no telling how many tricks might deceive the eye.

But for Jim the clincher was when, after giving a brief but vigorous wave, his shadow turned and slipped into a side-street without him.

I

The Future Now

The heroine in the story must wear gloves of steel
Her violence must be real
It is her act of glory that for love she'll kill
When Death comes flying sad and sweet;
It is my angel

— Doll By Doll

I believe in the r'n'r dream,
R'n'r as primal scream

— The Fall

one

A cargo of bodies tumbled out of the foyer.

Some had their lights out and were unable even to stand of their own free will; some wore haircuts exploding like brains from their heads in red and green waves. Others, lips black, cheeks rouged, eyes dimmed in hollowed-out sockets, looked to have been buried and born again. So the fun was over for one more night; it was time for death to walk the streets.

The rebel stepped amongst them, elbowing his way forward, and continued up a dozen stone steps to the Psychic Dance-hall. It was the newest, most decadent place he knew, a Lyceum of the Lost, wall-to-wall with part-time revolutionaries most nights of the week. But he wasn't here for the music, thank God, that had been finished an hour ago. He was here for a simple business transaction, and his heart was in his mouth.

At the top of the steps a poster peeled from a wall haunted by ghosts of old groups. A reggae turn: The Dread Zone. And inside, beyond the swinging doors, punters cupped reefers in their hands like clubs of schoolboys behind the school gym or the bicycle shed.

Here one customer slid, presumably against its will, down a wall. There another slept standing, leaning back against a door beneath a sign which said EXIT, blocking

21

whoever was trying to push through from the other side. Yet another lolled cross-legged on the foyer's burgundy carpet, meditating.

Nearer the side exit a monkey-suited man was trying to disperse a group of Rastafarians, parting his hands like Moses before the Red Sea, sweeping tides of consumers towards the door with a midnight goodnight: 'You paid up, saw the show, heard it all, had your money's worth, now get the fuck out.' Watching him, the rebel shook his head and clucked his tongue. He'd heard the place employed men with histories of violence. Perhaps a record was prerequisite to the job here. He turned away in search of the stairs.

'See how they run!' another in a suit remarked. This one was standing beneath a screen-printed poster, a glaring mauve and yellow, which prophesied names from a forthcoming ultra-violent sickpunk festival – The Implants, The Running Sores, Dog Babies, Snatchnasty, The Criminals. 'The Fuck Off and Die Show', they had wanted to call it originally – so, at least, the rebel had heard – until the rock press refused the advertising, until venues, promoters, and finally the participants themselves, it seemed, lost faith in the idea.

It was, the rebel considered, a cosy rebellion: the spirit of '76 and '77 distilled beyond belief, made safe as a sideshow. They didn't live it or feel it, these people, they simply wore it one night a week, their badge of anger. It was all on the outside for them. Certainly it was one stop better than the current crop of sugar-coated chart pills, but one stop wasn't worth a hell of a lot.

Half-way up the stairwell to the balcony he passed a Johnson & Johnson jacket engaged in heated discussion with a red-lettered Kill Me T-shirt. The T-shirted youth was rolling against the stair rail, both hands clasping his midriff, eyes partially closed, seeing nothing. 'You keep your hands off of her, gobshite, or else,' the Johnson & Johnson jacket warned as the rebel brushed past. At least they were talking real life here: none of your r'n'r posturing.

But there was something in the face, in the eyes of the T-shirted youth to short-cut the rebel's breath. Later he'd remember it as a lack of light, a grey, blank despair which saw nothing and yet saw all. The boy was afraid for his life, or worse. Seconds later, when the rebel looked back, the T-shirted youth had doubled himself, as if gripped by a sudden convulsion, and the Johnson & Johnson jacket was gone.

Upstairs was thankfully less hectic. The rows of seats nearest the balcony's precipice had been removed, tables and chairs arranged in their places. From each table radiated a dulled yellow candlelight around which hovered, like moths, the faces of press agents, record company executives, journalists. The rebel moved forward, straining for features in the gaudy light. Wine was flowing, slightly inebriated laughter rising lightly to the high domed ceiling like smoke. Judging by the numbers of empties scattered about their tables, they had all been here for the duration, ignoring the show.

Hardly the place, the rebel thought, for a traditional rock business lig; surely they'd all be far happier on the nightclub circuit, down at the Groucho, or Stringfellow's. Then he thought that perhaps they came here, to this morgue, in search of credibility. Rock was long dead, if they did but know it. Its message had melted, its legacy now was a million flickering video images; but these people still hung their careers from its corpse − it was in their interest to preserve the illusion of life. Otherwise they were finished.

Well, whatever it was they were celebrating, he wanted no part of it.

He found Max Beresford seated alone and drinking sake near the front-right of the balcony, directly below a red neon exit sign. The man's eyes were hidden behind rectangular-rimmed mirror shades that reflected the rebel's image back at him. 'Danny,' Beresford said as the rebel approached, and immediately offered a hand, moist and yet cool to the touch. 'Danny, do have a seat.'

He was greyer and leaner than Danny remembered from their one previous meeting – a midsummer's bacchanal staged by Beresford for the newsworthy signing of Cora DeVille to Monolith Records. Cora, of course, had failed to attend. A personal appearance would have been more than anyone dared expect. Now that he thought of it, Danny remembered talking incessantly, drunkenly, for most of the evening while Beresford nodded and patiently listened; he remembered the promise Beresford had made as the evening drew to a close. Yet for all of that he couldn't recall getting home after, or how.

'So you found me,' Beresford said, and Danny said, 'Yes, but why here?'

'Oh, I don't know,' Beresford said. 'Perhaps I have a thing about graveyards. I think we'd both like to see something positive happen, wouldn't we, Danny? You know, the phoenix rising out of the ashes, that kind of thing. What publication did you say you were from?'

'*Killzine*,' Danny said. 'We call it *Killzine*.' But to call it a publication was flattery, it was more a radical bog-roll.

'And what does that stand for, exactly?'

'A very angry fanzine,' Danny said, and Beresford laughed. Perhaps the formalities were over now, perhaps they could come to the point of this meeting. Beresford's easy manner and mild, accentless voice were only making

Danny more and more anxious. 'When we talked before, you mentioned an exclusive, Max, an interview.'

Beresford licked his lips, the brief jut of tongue a shocking pink riding over his colourless flesh. 'At a later stage, perhaps. Cora isn't ready for that yet, not for the small press, and I have to support her wishes. You see, Cora – ' he was about to go on when a sudden rush of feedback from below silenced him.

Down on the dance-floor – a disaster area of crushed plastic glasses and stubbed-out smokes – roadies were tugging wires from walls and drums from a lightless stage; a long haired tour manager skidded over a slick of someone's vomit and cursed towards anyone willing to listen.

'Cora *is* the business right now,' Beresford said. She's the name on everyone's lips, and the first interviews will be strictly mass circulation. It has to be handled sensibly, a phenomenon like this. Later, perhaps, we can help you out, but I'm sure you'll understand.' He broke off then, until a tour-jacketed PR from Virgin had finished striding past to the exit, and then added, 'Listen, Danny, even the dailies want to know what she's about; they all want to see her, meet her, discover her. Even the Pistols didn't have this when they started.'

So there was no exclusive, after all. He should have expected as much. 'Why did you bring me here, then?' Danny said. 'What are you offering?'

'That depends on what you're prepared to give in return. I'm looking for someone who's in touch with what's going on, someone like you. There's a world of hungry punters out there, Danny, and I'd like to give them a little something in advance.'

'I don't quite follow,' Danny said, and Beresford said, 'You will.' He was producing a smart tan briefcase from under the table, laying it gently on the table's surface. 'Take it,' he said, 'but don't open it yet, not here.' When he saw the look on Danny's face he explained, 'Keep the case if you like. You can keep one of the cassettes for yourself as well; that's your exclusive, you can write what you like about that. The rest of the tapes I'd like you to distribute.'

Danny inched forward in his seat. 'Tapes of what? Of Cora?'

'Of course.'

'Why?' It made no sense: sessions for the début *Dark Brigade* album had been conducted in utmost secrecy; no one had even heard the voice of the starlet as yet. Incredibly, Cora had become legend before her first cut or the first live date; by shunning publicity she'd become massively public — a mystery the world craved an explanation for. Why then, was Beresford pushing out bootlegs of such an important official release? Anyone would have thought he was running a non profit-making organisation.

'It seems an unusual way to conduct your business,' Danny said after a moment.

'It's an unusual business to conduct,' Beresford said affably. 'What you have there are pre-mixes. They're intended to whet a few appetites, not to replace the real thing. The mood on the street, Danny, is one of frustration; the masses are praying for action, for something dangerous and new, and Cora believes the time is now right. The people are ready for her, and she's ready for them.'

That much at least was credible. Certainly the frustration out there was real enough; it was a growing rage Danny had himself expressed in the pages of *Killzine*. True revolutions, he'd said, came in ten or twelve-year cycles; and this one was long overdue.

'Do you know any good people in the press?' Beresford wondered now. '*NME*, or *Alter-Image*, or *The Face*? Well, I'd like you to land a copy with each of them. The rest are to go underground, to the people you meet at parties, at ligs, wherever you happen to hang out. Circulate, get it to anyone who matters. Do you think you can do that?'

'I can do it,' Danny said. 'I just don't understand what you're up to, Max, but I'll do it. And later, you'll give me a shot at an interview?'

'Later,' Beresford agreed, with a barely discernible smile.

And later, descending the stairwell from the balcony, the rebel caught sight of Cora's name, large lettered, plastered above a toilet door in dark, dried blood. Or perhaps it was only aerosol paint; it seemed far more likely it was that.

Many times recently he'd found himself wondering whether Cora just might, after all that had gone before, be a hype; and each time he thought of it, he realised he needed her not to be. Well, even if she were nothing more than a myth created for media, he was part of that myth; and if her mission were truly subversive, he was part of that too.

The briefcase and its priceless secret keeping time against his leg, the rebel crossed the foyer, fending off a glare from one of the suited strong arms waiting there, and went out to meet his audience.

two

In the late afternoon, Jim Doherty began opening the mail. As usual, it brought the expected flood of abuse, a scattering of intelligent thought, and too few surprises. *You bastard, Jim Doherty*, were the first words he read, neatly typed on a slick sheet of paper the same day-glo green as its envelope, which was postmarked Poole, Dorset. *I know that's hardly a constructive way of tackling you, after your demolition job on Morrissey's London concerts; I know that calling you deaf, blind and cretinous will hold no water at all. But the next time you sign your name to such tosh, to such utterly misguided, misinformed tosh, I'll be forced to drop in where you work and put you straight.*

There was more, but he needn't go on with it. Still slightly glazed from today's liquid lunch, he couldn't even afford the letter's author a smile. He might have done, if the tone hadn't been so self-consciously intense. *I never read such bollocks as*, another letter began, and he crumpled it at once in both hands.

Every two months or so − at least that was how the rota worked out − it came Jim's turn to edit the *Alter-Image* correspondence page. This time, again, it seemed that the best of the copy would be that which he'd have to invent.

He turned to another, this from Hounslow: *Doherty's so-called 'review' of Morrissey's London appearance was,*

*to put it mildly, a wank. I know so, because I was there,
and in my opinion –*

Jim thrust the letter aside. Incredible as it seemed – and
as the anonymous, typewritten death threat he'd received six
months ago went to show – words on paper, in print, were
apt to provoke the most vicious responses. Better the hate
mail than nothing, of course. But of late, unless he was much
mistaken, there had been a slowly ascending note of hostility,
a note so strong that it sang. There was genuine hurt in the
hearts of these readers. It was as if they were personally,
physically slighted if one dared tear strips from the wallpaper
they worshipped. Where would their fury end?

Beyond the windows of the open-plan office, three
storeys high over Long Acre, the sky at the roof-tops was
turning a serene, cloudless, Prussian blue. It would be fine,
if he could only begin to breathe. In all this time he'd still
not grown used to the city's humid summer, or the filth
its heat summoned.

The office was nearly dozing today. A few yards from
him, a couple of subs were poised over their lay-out sheets,
shielding their work like boys in a mathematics exam. And
nearer, Nina Fowles, the raven-haired gossip writer, sat
with her long sleek legs curving up to her desk whilst
caressing a trimphone receiver with hands and tongue. She
was whispering sweet nothings across the Atlantic by the
sounds of it: he didn't, he never did, did he really? Now
and again, Jim picked up the edges of names she was
dropping, or words she was mispronouncing, and had to
restrain himself from groaning aloud. Above the clatter
of obsolete typewriters, even above the unanswered shrill
of editorial telephones, Nina talked; and above her talk
the office CD player hammered out rap to the street. In
here, in his head, it felt like the din of factories.

He noticed now that one or two items in the mail pile on

the desk were marked for his personal attention. Someone had managed to muddle them in with the letters file. The first, when he tore it open, was the latest issue of *Killzine*, number eleven. Sellotaped to the front cover was a giveaway cassette, no label, and a brief covering note from the editor, Daniel Zero. *To Jim with compliments*, it read. *I hope this means as much to you as to me*. Whether Danny meant the tape or the issue wasn't too clear. He was about to skim through the magazine's photocopied pages when the phone at his elbow clicked twice, then rang.

Jim caught it up. 'Hello, *Alter-Image*.'

'I'm just calling to remind you,' Elaine said. 'You're supposed to be leaving early today. Can you still make it?'

Good God, he'd almost forgotten about the flat. While he'd been drinking his lunch hour away, she'd been supervising their things to South London. 'I'll be there by five,' Jim told her. 'We're going to press soon, and I have to get this done. Can you cope until I get there?'

'The worst will probably be over by then. The removal men just dropped a box of your records down the stairs, and half of my clothes are missing, but apart from that were doing fine. Watch what you're doing with that,' she pleaded with someone out of Jim's range. Her muffled voice sounded exhausted. 'Jim, I'll try and call you back,' she said, and rang off, leaving him stranded.

It had been a friend of Elaine's at the bookstore on Charing Cross Road who first suggested the place in Catford: south of the river, hardly fashionable, no underground stations, but a very good rent for the whole upper floor of a house. Just this morning he'd left Elaine with the keys to the flat and bundled their crates of belongings to the doorway of the room in Finsbury Park in readiness for the removal men. How could he have let it slip through his mind?

He should have taken the day off as well, except there were no volunteers to rescue the letters page out of his hands; and no wonder. Well, if the readers insisted on writing abuse, they could read it for once. He'd better dash off this page in a hurry.

There was one more item of personal interest here, the envelope unstamped and addressed in a careful, looping hand: its sender must have dropped it in at reception or in through the office door this morning. He prised the envelope open, unfolded the doubled scrap of ruled paper torn from a spiral bound notebook, and read:

Jim. I'm going to ruin your life as you ruined mine.

XX

That was all. The note was unsigned, its brevity startling. He stared at it, unblinking, for fully ten seconds, seeing only an arrangement of black letters on white ruled paper, feeling his mind unclouding itself of booze and snapping sharply back into focus. At the edge of his desk the phone was ringing again: his fingertips brushed the receiver blindly, not lifting it.

Earlier today he'd put in his eighth or ninth call to Monolith, in the vain, mad hope of a Cora exclusive. For bait he'd been able to offer a full colour front page, a large lead feature. So too, he imagined, had a hundred other journalists sharing the same vain, mad hopes of the same exclusive. But it was too soon to expect a return call from the hectic Beresford office; they'd been stalling the world for weeks there.

More likely this was Elaine calling back, but he couldn't answer her yet. He couldn't think what he might say if he spoke to her now. He would in a minute, though, just as soon as he knew why the handwriting, looping across the faint-ruled page he was grasping, looked so familiar.

three

'At last,' Elaine said, as soon as she had the door open. 'You're just in the nick of time.'

Then she smiled, and smiled with some degree of relief, Jim thought, as if for the first time today she were actually breathing out. There were smears of dirt about her forehead and arms, smears of dirt caking the folds of her faded blue dungarees where she'd wiped her hands, which were chalky with dust. Her pale green eyes looked drained by a day of physical graft, her dark blonde hair was tied back in a pony-tail too tight and too short to flatter her face. The sight of her now made him feel doubly guilty for having left her alone to the task.

'Just in time for what?' Jim wondered.

'To rescue me,' she said, and promptly ushered him in from the doorstep to the hall. The heavy, paint-peeling door swung to, shutting out the small thatch of sun-beaten, overgrown front lawn, the crowded dustbin without a lid, the sepia houses across the street.

'We've company,' Elaine said in a whisper, and before Jim could speak she touched her lips with a forefinger and pointed upwards, directly above her head, to the ceiling. 'If you're very discreet she might leave.'

She turned and thumped her way upstairs ahead of him. The air here seemed cloying and stale, and the stairs and the landing above were thick with darkness. Must requisition a lightbulb or two, Jim thought, one hand tracing the stair rail to steady himself; and throw a few windows open for good measure. The narrow landing had a narrower strip of loose carpet trailing towards two small bedrooms on the right, and on the left towards a kitchen, a bathroom, a small furnished living-room. 'Mind your step,' Elaine said as he reached the top. 'The carpet slips.' After clearing her throat she said, 'Jim, I'd like you to meet Carolyn.'

At first he couldn't imagine who she meant. Hard streaks of barred light fell across the walls where the upstairs doors had been left ajar, but the rest of the landing stood in shadow. When one of the shadows stepped forward, hand proffered, to greet him, he nearly bolted.

She must have been six feet tall, or more – a tall, angular woman in a red bandanna and an ankle-length print dress whose design had grown over with sunflower heads. So hippies were not consigned to extinction, after all; this one was truly larger than life. Even her hand felt far larger and firmer than his when he took it.

'Now that we're neighbours, I thought I should say hello,' Carolyn said. 'You're Jim, aren't you?' Before he could answer she quickly pressed on. 'Well, I'm pleased to meet you, I do hope we'll get along. I'm downstairs with Derek – I'm sure you'll meet Derek sooner or later. We've had the ground floor a couple of years now, and before that we were up here. I've been helping Elaine with all the unpacking.'

'And cleaning,' Elaine said. 'Whoever was here before us left the place in a hell of a state.'

'That would have been the students,' Carolyn said. 'A noisier, messier lot you wouldn't wish to see. But the landlord doesn't care, as long as he gets his rent. Elaine

34

tells me you're a writer or something,' she said as they entered the living-room. Paperback books and records occupied most of the furniture — a three-piece suite which looked relatively well kept, a cheap teak veneered dining-table. Mounds of unconnected cable for the hi-fi trailed over the floor from a coffee-table heaped with separates. An obsolete gas fire sat on the hearth in front of a bricked-in chimney.

With the strong evening light streaming across Laleham Road and in through the large front windows, Carolyn looked suddenly far older than before, perhaps in her early forties. Now she was breezing about the room, absently brushing her hands across chair backs, shelves, trailing her fingers over the grim floral wallpaper as if touching memories. 'You write about music, don't you? I expect that's very exciting.'

'Not too exciting at the moment,' Jim said. 'But something's about to give, just as it did in seventy-six.'

'Seventy-six? Oh yes, I think I was there, but I didn't really care for it much. Give me Jim Morrison any time.'

'It's late,' Elaine said; her pale face was exasperated. She glanced at her watchless wrist. 'Are you hungry yet, Jim?'

'A little,' he managed to say, before Carolyn said, 'Tell me, who have you written about? Have you interviewed anyone I might know?'

'On Thursday he's meeting Peter Gabriel,' Elaine volunteered, though the mention of Gabriel's name caused no ripple with Carolyn. Perhaps she had never heard of him, or perhaps she never heard anything beyond the closed world of her thoughts.

'Do you think that what's happening now, Jim,' Carolyn was saying, 'is really so good? I mean, the punks were a very negative thing in some ways; surely they did more for

35

the fashion industry than the music industry. And they brought so much anger and unpleasantness. Isn't whatever comes next going to make matters worse?'

'I don't believe things could be any worse than they are right now,' Jim muttered. He was groping around in his clothes for a cigarette, only to discover he'd smoked the last. Instead, rolled into an inside pocket was the copy of *Killzine* he'd brought home, and the free cassette that came with it. He set them down on the dining table, atop a stack of outdated *Alter-Image* issues. 'At the moment, everyone's talking about Cora,' he said. 'It could be that she'll be the start of something, but until we see more of her we won't really know.'

'Oh, *Cora*,' Carolyn exclaimed. 'Haven't I heard her?' It was as though a cloud had lifted, as though she'd finally discovered a common ground she could stand on. 'Yes, I think she's tremendous. I think I heard one of her records.'

'She hasn't released any,' Jim informed her.

'Really?' That seemed to confuse her, but not for long. 'Then it must have been a tape – yes, a tape, that's it. Someone brought it to one of our parties, and I had to ask what it was, I was so impressed. Sounded just like the Velvets with Nico, only different somehow. It was just so, oh – what's that phrase?'

Carolyn was clicking her fingers for words, Elaine was growing impatient, arms crossed, in front of the door. Even without looking, Jim knew what her face must be saying: help, get me out of this, give me a break. 'Are you sure it was Cora you heard, and not something else?' he wondered.

'No, it was Cora right enough. I remember because that was the party where the trouble began. Usually they're such mellow affairs: a few friends, a few drinks, a little mushroom punch and a white line or two, *you* know.'

'I can imagine,' Jim said. It sounded like a record company's promotional launch; a wake for the respectably stoned. While Elaine fumbled the door open he guided Carolyn gently, in slow motion, towards it. 'Did you say trouble?'

'Well yes, there were a couple of gatecrashers, and things started to get a little – heavy, I suppose. One of Derek's friends got a wine bottle in the face and I had to call the pigs. It isn't usually like that, though, it's the only time the scene turned ugly.'

Then her gaze fell on Elaine, on the void beyond the living-room, the landing, the top of the stairs, and the penny dropped. 'Are you sure there's nothing more I can do?' she said to Elaine, but she was already past the threshold, padding reluctantly out to the unlighted landing, across the extended tongue of shabby carpet. 'No, I suppose you'd like to take stock, settle in for the night. If there's anything I can do, though, just hammer on the floor, the sound does tend to travel. And come for a drink sometime – maybe tomorrow. Come have dinner. I have to be going now,' she finally announced with a sigh, a heave of defeat.

'I'm sorry about that,' Elaine said as soon as she'd gone. 'I wanted it to be just us.'

'She isn't so bad, I suppose,' Jim said. 'At least she's sociable. Did she stay long?'

'Only all afternoon. I was starting to think she'd moved in.' Linking arms, Elaine walked him through to the small linoleum-floored kitchen where cardboard boxes and cans and packets of foodstuffs were tipped across all available surfaces. A small square window above the sink was so thickly layered with grease it seemed to look out on a world of blurs. 'I think she really did come to help, though, but for the last two hours I've been listening to her life story. How she met Derek, how and why they dropped out of college. And Carolyn grows marijuana in her window boxes, don't you know! But I'm sure she means well,' she added, laughing. 'Maybe she's lonely.'

'Maybe so. I'm only sorry I couldn't be here to help.'

'No need to apologise,' Elaine said. 'I know how it is with those music biz buddies of yours. God, what a glamorous life you lead, Jim Doherty.'

'I know; all that sex and drugs and rock and roll. Doesn't it make you feel sick?' He grinned, and she landed him one in the chest, rocking him slightly on his feet.

'I thought you might like to eat out tonight,' Elaine said now. She was tugging an elastic band from her hair, vigorously shaking her head as she reached the kitchen doorway. 'That's another way of saying you'll do the cooking if we stay in.'

Jim said, 'I'd love to eat out.'

'Just as soon as I've freshened up, then. Fix yourself a drink and give me ten minutes. I have to get rid of this grime first, I feel like death.'

While Elaine began twiddling the bath taps he browsed through the other rooms, imagining how they might be with a few coats of paint in a few weeks' time. In the living-room, the day had collapsed to dark, and beyond the windows thick clouds were blundering in over the roof-tops. He switched on the light, which stammered a little before coming alive, and then crossed the room to draw the curtains.

In one of the houses opposite a domestic argument was in full swing: voices rendered incoherent by loathing were trading threats and abuse. But the sounds of disintegrating crockery he half-anticipated hearing never came. Instead

38

a dog, perhaps part of the household, commenced howling as if it were being slowly flayed.

In Elaine's handbag, abandoned on the sofa, he found the pack of ten Rothmans she'd been withholding to help him cut down. This latest purge was as futile as all the rest. He took one out, lit it, and for a while tried to concentrate on the issue of *Killzine* he'd brought home. It was the best of the independents, if a little relentless for his taste. Here was a retrospective on Throbbing Gristle and Psychic TV, an interview with the cult electronic group, A Scanner Darkly. But the poor electric light was distracting him; it tended to make the wallpaper shift at the edge of his vision. He was straining to make sense of the words.

From the bathroom drifted the echoes of water drumming into the tub, the somehow reassuring sound of Elaine stepping into the water and settling, the water lapping about her, and the mild falling, rising lull of her voice as she began to sing to the tiled walls. It was a melody he knew, yet couldn't quite place. The words were just vowel sounding noises she was inventing as she went along.

Here on page twelve was Daniel Zero's editorial – the usual primal scream, God bless him, Jim thought. The usual monthly dispensation of vitriol: rock is dead, or whatever. But that was before he'd read what Danny had written. He'd written that he'd seen the future of rock and roll, that the name of its future was genocide.

Ridiculous. The word he'd used was Cora, not genocide. What on earth had caused him to think of genocide? He'd seen the future of rock and roll, whose name was Cora: even a faulty electric light socket couldn't excuse his misreading of that. Outside, the family row was receding – not before time – and a car door was slamming, an engine revving. Knuckling tiredness from his eyes, Jim read, *If there were means to convey the power of this music*

I would certainly use those means. The choc-stock rock business day jobbers are worried; the major record companies are worried; as are the DJs, the journalists, the politicians, the boneheads. And small wonder they're worried. In all our dreams and in all our hearts we've been waiting for The Dark Brigade *to arrive, for this moment to come –*

Absolutely, Jim agreed, though he wished the light would stop drawing his eyes, that the shadows it cast in the room's four corners would cease their small, almost imperceptible movements. His vision was blurring, his head beginning to pulse. *Sooner or later*, Danny had written, *this had to happen, the tide had to turn and it's all been coming to this, it's always been coming to this but jim the dark brigade is a dangerous beat it grows on you and grows in you it does things to you i wish jim i wish i could say what it's doing to me god help me god help god help –*

Jim thrust the magazine down and stood up abruptly. The editorial said nothing of the kind; it was merely a rave preview of the Cora LP, which in all likelihood Daniel Zero had never heard. Now he could hear Elaine stepping from the bath, the bath water draining, normality returning, Elaine's damp footsteps heading along the landing to the bedroom. Why had he imagined the magazine had said that? Surely the letter he'd torn open today hadn't upset him to that extent? It couldn't really say what he thought.

Then he noticed the cassette he'd put on the table. In the uneven light, its plastic shell seemed to be glowing, to be grabbing for his attention: Play me, it hinted, play me.

Cora, he thought, suddenly aware of his heart racing too fast to keep up with, of his hands turning cold with sweat. It couldn't reasonably be anything else. Cora was everywhere – on the streets, on the toilet doors of rock venues, on the grubby walls of underground stations, and now here she was in the room with him.

Five minutes work and he had the hi-fi hooked up, the Aiwa connected to the Naim, the Naim to the Royds, the cassette from Daniel Zero balancing in the palm of his hand. The printed page had only deceived him; he was exhausted, that was all, he'd only imagined he'd read such nonsense. But this was something solid, and if he couldn't trust his eyes, then at least he could trust his ears. Before he could set the tape deck in motion, though, Elaine was behind him in the room, sniffing the air and tutting.

'You've been pilfering cigarettes from my bag again,' she scolded, arms sneaking round his midriff, fingers busily investigating his pockets, absently brushing against his penis. 'That's out of tomorrow's allowance. Ah, now this is encouraging. This is very encouraging. I think you can afford to pay for the meal tonight.'

'So what do I get in return?'

'The tab. Here, zip me up.' Elaine swivelled round on the balls of her feet. 'And pick up your comic book.'

In the time it had taken her to enter the room she'd made everything real again. She so often did, which sometimes gave him the feeling that she was all that held him together, the one small voice that cut through the bullshit he tolerated for a living. From the inside, the business of rock and roll seemed a very large, very serious world indeed; to Elaine it had never been anything but a microcosm.

He put the cassette down on the tape deck for later audition. It didn't matter, it wasn't really so urgent; it was just that his curiosity had been piqued, nothing more. His eyes were in need of relief from words in print, not from lightbulbs or wallpaper patterns. Perhaps a complete break from the business would pull him together again, make him less jumpy.

Shit, though, to imagine what a moment ago he'd imagined. Of course there was nothing at the peripheries of the walls, or behind the bricked-in chimney's façade; and the cassette housing hadn't glowed, it was only the way the light had struck it. Naturally there was nothing of consequence in the xeroxed pages he'd thrown to the floor, not even the one which had earlier said, *God help me Jim*. It certainly didn't say that now.

No, it wasn't the thought that he might be slipping which bothered him; it was the crystal clear memory of things he knew he could never have seen.

42

four

Elaine devoured her meal with an appetite, but at last she had to concede and lay down her fork, when the portions of beansprouts and rice began to outdistance her.

'How can I feel so pigged and have more on my plate than when I started?' she wondered with genuine bewilderment, but the problem was beyond solving. She pushed her plate to one side and rested her elbows informally on the table. 'Anyway, I think we did the right thing, moving here. Don't you agree, Jim?'

Jim skewered a segment of mushroom and popped it into his mouth and nodded.

'I mean, there's so much extra space, and the landlord doesn't care if we give the place a face-lift, so long as it's within reason. There's the spare room you can use for your work when you work at home — and we're so far from the rat-race here. We're away from your so-called scene. Down here, it won't come between us.'

'You think it does? Come between us?'

'Sometimes it does, sometimes.' She was blushing at him across the hot-plates, or perhaps that was just the restaurant's lighting. 'But it won't always be like that. Soon you'll move into a real occupation. You won't be thirty and too old and too bloated and only in it for the money and the kicks, with the love all gone out of it. You

43

remember what you said about that, Jim, don't you?'

He could barely contain his amusement at that; for some reason she'd made him think once again of Charles Foster Kane's Declaration of Principles. 'I said when the love went out of it, so would I.'

'And has it?'

'More or less, yes.'

'Then why keep with it?'

You'd make a far better journalist than I ever did, he thought. You know how to work people into corners, and then how to hold them there, all escape routes blocked. 'I suppose it's because of what's happening,' he said. 'What's about to happen. I'd hate to think I was walking out on the game just a moment before the action started.'

For a second she looked as though he'd lost her; then a cloud cleared from her face. 'Cora, you mean?'

'Yes. I really think she might signal the start of something. Just like the Pistols did; just like − '

'She really has you out on a limb, Jim, doesn't she? But how do you know she's worth waiting for, and not just some − some great new rock and roll swindle?'

'I don't know,' Jim had to confess. 'That's why I'm waiting.' After a beat he added, 'In the meantime, it's a living, ain't it?'

Elaine seemed to brighten at that, and leaned back in her seat, hands folded across her stomach. 'Just don't say I didn't warn you if she turns out to be Malcolm McLaren in drag, then.'

She had an easy, contented, cat-like quality about her at times, and this was one of them. At such times, too often fleeting, a peace would descend on her, and on him, and he'd know that the on-rushing flow of the world could be stemmed and its trials and intrusions forgotten, at least for a while. He'd make his customary proposal of marriage and Elaine, thank God, knowing he could never be serious, would flatly refuse. And at last the real world − whatever that was − would appear through a crack, and the moment would end, as it ended now.

They talked for another hour or so, until the wine thickened their tongues and Jim had smoked one more cigarette from his ration while comparing the tab with the contents of his pocket. Towards the end they loitered like children in a toy shop, wanting to savour what remained of the evening, wrap it up, keep it, carry it home like a takeaway.

As soon as they were outside, though, Elaine fell silent, and quickened her step towards Laleham Road. The air had a surprising chill after the warmth of the restaurant, but that wasn't why she was hurrying. Lowering his head to the cold, Jim tried to keep pace with her. Now, especially, he was glad not to have mentioned the letter he'd received at the office today; there was really no point in reopening old wounds.

The letter was probably nothing, of course. All of that was behind her, mostly forgotten, and there was no reason why Elaine shouldn't feel perfectly safe here, miles from Finsbury Park. Wasn't that why she'd leapt at the chance to move south in the first place? It wasn't the generous rent or the size of the place that attracted her, but the distance the move put between Elaine and what had happened before.

High above them, the night sky was a vast grey canopy waiting to collapse over the suburbs. The streets were slumbering − or trying to, though The Jesus & Mary Chain were crashing away at an upstairs window where a party was already well under way. Cars were double-parked outside the house: some were abandoned half on, half off of the pavement. Several crushed beer cans lay in the gutter.

Further on, a shackled dog barked at the sound of Elaine's heels clicking past. A number of streetlights were out here, either faulty or vandalised; the houses on the streets seemed nothing more than crude blocks of darkness, as though they'd been hurriedly painted in with a too-large, too-cumbersome brush.

Just as they neared the point where the side-street met Laleham Road, Elaine stopped with a start, her bunched fist wrenching Jim's coat sleeve. 'What's that?'

The sudden dig of her fingers made him look up sharply enough to crick his neck. At the front door of the house, directly beneath their lighted window, something had just bolted for cover among the shadows. If he hadn't quite seen it, he'd certainly caught the after-burn of its movement.

'Jim?' Elaine said; the involuntary pressure of her fingers briefly increased, then relaxed. Her free hand must have gone to her mouth, since her cry when it came sounded muffled and indistinct.

It can't be, Jim thought, and long before he knew it he was running, Elaine forgotten, his rushing steps landing like deadly silences across the tarmac. Streetlights towered above him, miles high, mere streaks of blurred, sourceless light, blurred in his vision as if by tears. Some distance behind him Elaine was calling, imploring him to turn back as she tottered forward across the street to the gateway. He'd reached the gate and turned on to the path before grasping what it was he was running towards. Too late, he thought; he can't have, he thought, as a shadow not his own rose up to full height against the front door. Surely he can't have found us so soon.

Jim faltered half-way between the gate and the house;

a cartoon character applying the breaks for balance, rearing dust. The shadow had merged with shadows again, and he'd barely regained his footing when the lidless dustbin, shedding its load, came skittling towards him along the path. It gave him no time to react — a brief hesitation was all it took. The laden bulk connected with his leg, its gaping mouth vomited refuse, and Jim reeled sideways into a puzzle of untended grass.

As he hit the ground, palms first, he could feel the eager greeting of nettles, could hear the night bear down on him with the force of a man's hand. Deep in the grass, something soft and moist — a discarded and decaying apple core perhaps, or worse, something living — burst and collapsed at his touch. Now, raising his head, he caught sight of Elaine moving in at the gate, into the cast of light from the upper window.

'Stay where you are,' he shouted in protest. 'Don't come any further.'

Lights were blinking on in houses across the street and dogs were beginning to chorus. The disturbance must sound hysterical, Jim thought, if he could only stand outside it for a second. He scrambled himself up and to his feet just as a man's outline cleared the wall and dropped down to an adjoining garden.

Seconds later Elaine reached him, heels scraping the path, her voice wavering between small gasps and swallowed tears. 'He knows where we are already,' she told his chest.

No, he wouldn't have that, he wouldn't have her believing that. 'It could have been anyone,' he said. 'Just a prowler; someone trying to break in, that's all.'

When, after a minute, she'd calmed, and her breath had grown even again, he righted the dustbin — a deadweight: the bastard must have infinite strength — and then let her

47

indoors with his Yale key. 'I won't be far behind you,' he said, and stood at the doorstep, watching the street, until her footfalls had finished climbing the stairs to become dull, solid thumps above his head.

Outside there was no sign of life: houselights were being doused once more, dogs were being threatened into silence. Whoever had been here would be streets away by now. It was doubtful whether they'd risk coming back.

Upstairs, a beat began – a churning of guitars and drums thickened by the walls. Elaine had found Cora's tape, and now she was drowning her thoughts with it. He'd be surprised if it turned out to be sedative in its effect, but still.

He closed the door and stepped into the hall, vaguely aware of something his foot was scuffing aside from the mat. He stooped, groping for it in the dark, and picked it up. As he followed the stale smells upstairs to the landing he felt a thrill of relief – relief that, in spite of herself, Elaine had run in ahead of him, without stopping, without pause for thought.

Relief that he wouldn't now have to explain that their visitor had been posting a letter.

five

Something had been growing in him for years now, and at last he was close to becoming one with it. Sometimes this thing, whatever it was, felt like a friend, a pet, something he could only partly control and which more usually controlled him. Perhaps it was only a feeling — a welter of feelings, which might placate him for a while or might pain him deeply. Sometimes, he knew, it was the very thing that drove him on, that caused him to do what he had to. Sometimes he felt nothing at all, and even that would be feeling of a kind — of release.

The jinxed man emerged from a side-street and hurried into the greenish glow of traffic lights near Lee High Road. He'd been running hard, almost lost his way once or twice, and his body was stiff and there was heat in the crooks of his arms and the seat of his pants. Some way ahead there were buses; surely one would be able to take him where he needed to go.

He had enough in his pockets to get him to Soho, and once he got there enough for the price of a whore; perhaps not enough for a good one, but tonight that was hardly the issue. He did know one, since he thought of it, who frequented a bar near Rupert Street — an evil bitch, though in the past she'd seemed willing enough. And none too fussy: tonight she might even take her fee in punishments.

Doherty though, Doherty was the one who ought to be punished, the jinxed man reasoned. Somehow, at some time, it was Doherty — he knew without measure or proof it was Doherty — who had made him like this, who had sold him out. He'd hardened himself, though, over the years; he'd learned how to deal with the sickness. He had done time for acts he had never committed, and if time had taught him nothing else it had taught him patience.

The letters, he thought, were a sign of limitless patience. Enough to keep Doherty screaming in silence somewhere deep down in his mind, he hoped. But that was only a part of the régime, the outer circle. What he'd done to Doherty's girlfriend had been the business — what he'd attempted to do. No doubt she'd been in a state of shock for weeks after; perhaps she still was.

He'd followed her from the underground at Finsbury Park, keeping his distance, musing over graffiti on a wall if she happened to glance back. He'd been as thorough then as he had been tonight while tracing Doherty across London to the south, from Charing Cross as far as Lewisham, then beyond. He'd followed her into the alley beyond the twenty-four hour radio cab office, beneath the blind gaze of boarded-up windows, to a spot where the crumbling brown tenements had rushed back memories of prison walls, of thousands of desperate eyes staring out.

But it hadn't been rape — they couldn't pin that one on him, even when he'd been forced to shortcut her screams with a fist. He'd come off in his pants before he could put it anywhere near her: she'd sensed his arousal just as he'd sensed her fear, which was when she'd begun to scream.

And later, although the papers claimed rape, he knew it wasn't so, and he knew that both Doherty and the girl knew it was not so. It was a knowledge they shared, the three of them. In its way, it was a knowledge that connected them inextricably. Perhaps they even shared with him a greater knowledge still − of fear, and how it felt when your life became fated to the point of ruin.

I *am*, he thought now, the shadow of the bastard himself. The dread in his eyes, the spirit of his past come to revisit him. At Waterloo, the bus jerked him upright, shocking his senses as if he'd been slapped awake from a dream.

He couldn't be sure it was Doherty, of course; he had no way of knowing it was. On occasion he actively doubted it. Then he must trust to instinct, the flow of the spirit, for it was instinct which told him which course to take, which path to follow, and as long as he kept faith the pain would subside and the sickness would leave him. Now he needed a place in the city in which to take stock. He squinted from the grubby bus window, at the lights balanced precariously on the blackened river, and wondered how many others there were out there, like him.

When the night bus dropped him at Trafalgar Square he strolled towards Soho, stopping here and there outside all-night kebab places, relishing the hubbub of sights and smells. He wished he could hold down his food these days − make a glutton of himself as these others were doing − but the feel of the stuff in his stomach only caused him discomfort and nausea. He could have loitered an hour, watching the glossy dead meat revolve in a window off Leicester Square, but a spasm somewhere about his midriff drove him on towards where he must go.

He hurried across the Square, nursing his ribcage. It hardly mattered how many sanguine faces turned towards him or how many prying eyes stared. They were nothing to him, he was light years ahead of them. They were riding high on easy pleasures, spirited along by the cool summer night with heat in their veins which the booze had put there. They didn't know what the world could do to the human soul, turning it inside out, making it terrible. They hadn't discovered it for themselves yet, so why should they care?

It took him two minutes of casting about in the bar near Rupert Street before he laid eyes on the whore, and by the looks of things she was free, as he'd hoped. A few men browsed past her or happened to glance her way now and then, but it seemed that none had attached himself. Most likely she wouldn't be here if anyone had.

She was perched on a stool at the crescent-shaped bar, legs crossed left over right at the knees, a filterless cigarette dangling from her pudgy white fingers while her lips mimed the song on the jukebox. She wore an unbelted, unbuttoned, gaberdine raincoat, and beneath that a knitted dress of a modest, not too glaring pink. She looked in better shape than his mental image of her – a clearer complexion, less of the slapdash make-up and dangling beaded bracelets; it occurred to him then that she might be off-duty, if a whore like her ever was. She was too filthy a cunt to be caught cleaning up her act, for sure. He could but make his approach and find out.

'Can I get you a drink?' he asked, sidling in at her elbow.

'Do I know you?' the whore said abruptly, and seemed to stiffen.

'No,' he lied. He held a ten pound note to her nose, wafting it this way and that. She inhaled his money, then softened, smiling at him, or perhaps at someone behind him. 'Smells dirty. All right then, a small vodkatini,' she said, and held a forefinger and thumb two inches apart.

By the time the drinks arrived the whore was loosening up and starting to talk a little. She hadn't remembered him, or she would have remembered who had put the scar in the cleft of her chin. It had faded now to a whitish smudge

— another customer would probably never have noticed it. 'Are you working tonight?' he said at last.

'Who told you I work nights?' she wondered, as the bearded man behind the bar turned away to wipe glasses, shaking his head. 'Yeah, well. I work when the work's there to be had,' she confessed.

'And where *do* you work?' he said, although he already knew. He had passed the place many times only to stare up at her window, to imagine and lose himself there.

'A few minutes walk from here,' the whore told him.

'Do you have a — a manager or something? Someone I have to see first?'

'Shit, no. I couldn't afford to live if I had that. This is a strictly private enterprise, bub.'

He forced a laugh; that should be enough to keep her off-guard. Again, he'd fooled her, he'd known what her answers would be before she'd so much as opened her mouth. He should have been a journalist like Doherty.

He took a swallow of whisky before saying, 'Well, then, how about me? You think you might like to do me a little part-time?' The whisky burned him, and he set down his glass on the bar and pushed it aside. He had to be casual about this; he couldn't risk putting her off having come so near to the act.

'OK,' she said at last. She wheeled away from the bar, giving his forearm a gentle pat. 'Just give me a minute. I have to fix my face.'

Good luck with it, the jinxed man thought.

She lived around the corner, one flight up above a sex boutique, which if nothing else was appropriate. Overripe breasts and behinds jostled for priority in the window display, beneath a winking set of red and blue neon lights which alternated between *Sex* and *Aids*. In the gutter in front of the shop, the vegetable remains of a day's market trading were beginning to stew and turn liquid.

'Do you think you can manage it?' the whore said as they climbed the stairs to her rooms. 'It's just that you look a little scrawny to me. You might be a junkie for all I know.'

'Don't worry about me,' he said, and thought, worry about yourself. Even a junkie riddled with diseases too numerous to mention she'd probably welcome with open arms. But he said nothing more as he followed her pendulum walk to the top of the stairs, where the lime-green walls looked spongey with damp.

'In that case,' the whore said, 'there are house rules. I might as well clear that up right away. I'll take it in the mouth or the arse if that's what you like, but I can't tolerate freaky stuff, no watersports or shit like that. And there are always people I can call if — ' She broke off, breathless after the stairs, her fingers at the handle of a door to the left. 'I guess you're all right though, I guess I can trust you. Sometimes, though, the types you pick up, you wonder how they cope being round other people at all; beats me how they ever slipped through the net.'

Her room was a dive. Psychedelic posters yellowed by dirt and by sunlight crawled from the walls where their corners had fallen away; articles of snagged and discarded clothing were strewn across the threadbare carpet, over the backs of chairs, across the filthy bed. The bed-sheets themselves looked like soiled permanent fixtures. A book of yoga positions and a copy of *Zen & the Art of Motorcycle Maintenance* cohabited a dusty table-top where a travel-alarm had stopped at six-twenty. A balloon made of paper depended overhead from a single sixty-watt bulb.

All this he glimpsed through a strobing light, the room filling with alternate washes of blue and red neon. Nothing had changed since the last time. The bitch apparently didn't care how customers saw her, whether or not they judged her by how she lived. In this, the slowly spoiling refuse heap she called home, she was truly naked.

'You want music?' the whore said, and before he could answer she'd clicked on a portable ITT radio-cassette at the bedside and tugged off her coat. 'I don't know what this stuff is, someone gave it to me,' she explained.

He watched while she sat on the bed to begin peeling a stocking from her leg; her legs were fine and tapering, the best thing about her, he thought. 'When the music stops you've had your time,' she said.

'Like musical chairs.'

'Kind of like that.'

The music began, and he knew it intimately: to hear it was almost like coming home. It was a music to make his blood charge and his palms to grow clammy in anticipation, and when the vocalist intruded, his belly to blaze. It had always been in him, this music, it had always done something for him.

Finished unravelling her stockings, the whore was easing herself off the bed and to her feet. The deepest, hardest bass notes were causing the tape player's plastic casing to vibrate. Whatever it was inside him was beginning to glow like a beacon; now he could imagine its radiance spreading outwards from the extended tips of his fingers, from his eyes, going out to the world, almost blinding him.

It had to be the light, not the rhythm, that was causing his head to thunder, forming a ball of blood beating pressure behind the eyes. Surely it was the light that afflicted his vision, making the whore's features appear to reassemble themselves until they no longer belonged to her but to someone else. 'Well, do you or don't you want to?' she sighed. 'Are you just going to stand there all night?' She stepped free of her garments and ran one pale hand back through her mop of dyed blonde hair. 'You're not going to waste my time, are you?'

In that moment he could no longer be certain, he couldn't respond to her or the situation. The whore's eyes had the hopeless, plaintive expression he'd seen in the eyes of Doherty's girl five or six months ago. Indeed, in every sense he could think of *she* was Doherty's girl: she deserved to be punished for the sins Doherty had visited on him, for every one of the lost and despairing nights he'd spent alone, hanging on — as if there were something worth hanging on for.

She deserved to be punished, severely punished, because as she stepped towards him and the neon moved across her features, he realised the whore was not Doherty's girl but Doherty himself. But of course! That's what Doherty was, and had always been — a rock-and-roll whore, a seller of dreams to the young and the vulnerable, the worst kind of parasite there was.

'Get out of me,' he said then, with such violent suddenness he surprised himself and brought a frown to the whore's face. She took one more cautious step towards him and faltered. 'What are you talking about?'

'Nothing.'

At first he couldn't be sure why he'd said such a thing; he was only aware of the deep-seated pain, deeper and worse than before. Then he began to see, as if a mist had lifted itself from his thoughts. Doherty was innocent. The whore was the monster from inside, the thing that had flourished within him for too many years, driving him to do what he must.

'Listen,' she was saying. 'I don't have to do this for a living, you know, but I want to. If you're nervous, I'll help you. Here, let me do that.'

She began to unbutton his shirt while he stood, arms
dangling at his sides, hearing and feeling the distant beat,
and beyond that the howl of a further distant cop siren
somewhere off in the night. The whore had opened and
half removed his shirt when she stopped and drew back,
her eyes trained on the lower region of his stomach.

'What's that?' she said. She allowed her fingers to flit
briefly across it, and again recoiled. 'What's wrong with
you?'

The jinxed man laughed, and that was enough for her.
Either she'd seen something in his face as the red neon
caught it, or the memory of his earlier visit had returned.
She stumbled awkwardly for the door, but his arm was
hooked tautly around her throat before she'd taken three
paces. 'Get out of me,' he spat at her — the whore in his
arms, the whore in himself.

As he dragged her to the floor he was thinking, please
don't let me go on with this, please don't let me go on.
There were tears in his eyes, his whole body ached. It was
something he wanted not to do, but had to, because now
he understood almost everything. The thing which had
been growing in him was not only his master but his enemy;
and must perish. It was a thought which returned to him
time and again as he worked, until the blue and red neon
saturated the night to become his only reality; and until
the music stopped.

six

Peter Gabriel was as courteous — and as nervous — as he had been during their last encounter, almost two years ago. Jim himself was as tense as a watch spring this afternoon, which did nothing to improve the flow; perhaps that was what had set Gabriel on edge, unless it was just the excess of office coffee his bloodstream was having to cope with.

To Jim's final question — did Gabriel believe that the visual media had destroyed music, making it secondary to the image? — Gabriel replied, 'I think you'll find you've already asked me that.'

Jim groped briefly for another topic to round this off neatly, but none was forthcoming. The revolving cassette spools were carrying his mind along with them, giving him no time to think. At five he was to meet Elaine on Charing Cross Road; from now on, he mustn't allow her to travel home alone to an empty flat. Perhaps the time was right to contact the police again, this time with the intruder's handwritten notes as proof: the police might be able to offer Elaine protection if nothing else.

In the end it was Gabriel who shut off the recorder. 'Something bothering you, Jim? You know, you shouldn't expect miracles when you've only half an hour of a person's life to play with. I think you'll do well with what you have there. If I were you I'd loosen up a little, try not to take any of this too seriously.'

The publicist's outer office was traffic-jammed with journalists by the time Jim packed up to leave. Interviews had been programmed end-to-end throughout the day in thirty-minute slots while Gabriel occupied the inner sanctum, an oracle in constant demand. Already they were running an hour and three-quarters over schedule, and when Jim stepped out to the street it was almost four. He still had time to collect his mail and messages at the office before meeting Elaine.

He rushed clear of Soho and clear of the plastic lobsters in restaurant windows, hardly aware he was doing so. Whatever misfortune had touched his life, whatever force, it had returned him to the feeling of dread he once felt at the sight of thunderclouds rolling in from the sea. Why Elaine, though? Of all the people he knew or could think of she was the least deserving of this. If someone had a vendetta with him, why make her part of it?

They had met at a Muswell Hill party almost a year ago to the day, and he'd immediately balked at the way she'd deflated what he did, making it seem less important than he'd thought. Later he'd realised that was exactly what he needed: a conscience, and someone to be it. What it was she'd seen in him he couldn't imagine. Clearly it wasn't the glamour associated with his profession — he only pretended it was glamorous for the sake of those who wished to believe that it was. Perhaps, he'd reasoned, Elaine was just his good fortune. He'd never felt he deserved her.

She'd moved into his bedsit from the house she'd been sharing in Highgate with three girl students, and hadn't objected to the cramped room, or to Jim's Italian cooking, or the disenchanted moods he brought home from work.

In every sense, confinement had brought them closer together. When the death threat arrived during the sixth month it was Elaine who'd torn open the envelope: in the light of what had happened since, she must feel she'd opened far more than a letter that day.

While he walked to Leicester Square, clouds freed themselves from the sun: another humid late afternoon made worse by the city's taut skin of smog. Tempers would flare if it went on like this for much longer. In some cases tempers already had. At a newsstand an *Evening Standard* board screamed, CALL GIRL MURDERED. The headline dominated the racks themselves, but it was Cora's face − this week's front cover of *Sounds* − which called his attention.

He'd already seen the feature − with its tag-line, *The Last Great White Hope*? − which had proved to be nothing more than conjecture, the usual peppering of quotes from Max Beresford and from people who knew people who claimed to know Cora. But as always it was the image which mattered. The shock of auburn hair, the porcelain features whose sensual mouth and narrowed, livid eyes might blister a hole in a man's heart. It was a definitive portrait which made him think of Garbo, even James Dean; she was really as unattainable as that. Even the grubbied print couldn't diminish the image's power. Jim stared hard and long, forgetting the time, until the newspaper salesman glowered him on his way.

She was everywhere now. There were posters at underground stations, and on boards and on fences as far removed as Portobello Road and Drury Lane: '*The Dark Brigade Cometh*' they said − a message as clipped and oblique as a Tory election slogan.

Already, T-shirts bearing a similar promise were on the racks of Kings Road boutiques, and on the backs of consumers mulling like walking billboards outside a crowded Our Price record shop. A peroxide punkette trooped past, a Walkman plugged into her skull. Could she, too, be listening to Cora's pre-release? More posters filled the window display, obliterating Michael Jackson and The Hothouse Flowers from view. She was poised to shift units in their thousands, more probably millions, on the basis of this cultivated mystique. If not quite The Last Great White Hope she was surely becoming a name now, as common as a public awareness of war.

Jim had scarcely been at the office long enough to reach his desk and flop down when he saw Martyn Sheppard, the *Alter-Image* deputy editor, approaching.

'How did it go, then?' Martyn said. His determinedly set expression gave nothing away, as if he were a lush playing sober. But he neither swayed nor slurred as he levered himself carefully on to a cluttered desk corner. He was wearing a faded Madonna T-shirt with his crew cut and jeans. 'Well?' he prompted.

'How did what go?' Jim frowned.

'The Peter Gabriel thing.'

'Oh, that.' What could you say after thirty minutes cooped in a boiling room, eyeing the clock, fixedly watching the progress of cassette spools while your mind betrayed your tongue? 'It went.'

'Fine,' Martyn said, 'then at least we have something. See if you can transcribe it and hack it out by tomorrow. We're at the printers a day early next week.'

'I'll do what I can,' Jim said and if that sounded slightly complacent Martyn's face didn't show it. Instead he smacked his lips and looked away towards Nina Fowles, who was holding open a dictionary over her typewriter and prodding the keys with one finger. Did Martyn have something to feel nervous about that he couldn't come straight to the point?

'There was a phone call while you were out,' he said finally.

'That's hardly out of the ordinary, is it Martyn?'

'Decide for yourself. This was a phone call from Beresford's office.'

'Really?' Jim straightened, his swivel chair creaked. A call from the Beresford office, after months of blocked and buffered and unreturned calls, of excuses made and promises broken? 'I'd say that's out of the ordinary.'

'So would I. Especially when they specifically asked to talk to you.' Martyn drew the back of one hand across his sweatless brow, lowering his voice to a whisper. 'Jim, I know how easily you make enemies; you have a particular attitude − a point of view that people love to hate, and if you want to make a career out of pissing off the music industry that's up to you. But don't, please, whatever you do, make an enemy of Max Beresford.'

'You think I'd do that?' Jim said, hand on heart.

'He may be a nobody, and even Cora may prove to be a nobody before we're finished, and Monolith Records may be nothing more than a six-month-old one-shot indie, but we can't afford to take the risk. This is just too goddamned important a chance to waste.'

'Let's see what he wants first,' Jim said, and seconds later he was telling the switchboard girl, 'Line, please.' He waited until the clicks and stutters had subsided and the dialling tone begun and then tapped out the sequence of numbers, vaguely aware that editorial eyes were upon him, that Nina had ceased her one-fingered prodding.

The connection sounded compressed by static, like a far-distant, out-of-phase radio station. Foreign, indecipherable voices broke in and dropped out, cross-talking. Could this really be what he'd been waiting for? − surely it shouldn't be so easy, or Beresford suddenly so accessible. But the ringing had stopped after ten or twelve pulses, the receiver was being lifted, he was being transferred to the Beresford office.

'I think you'll find what I have to say quite pleasing,' Beresford volunteered without delay. 'Jim, I assume you're aware of our latest signing – I should say, our only signing: Cora DeVille.'

'Are you kidding?' Jim almost told the receiver; but instead he said, 'Yes, yes, I'm very much aware of her.'

'I gather you've taken a personal interest in her case.'

'Yes.'

'Well – ' Beresford's voice was slick and treacherous as a greased pole. 'I'm now in a position to offer you what you've been looking for.'

A voice which may only have been static had begun a breakneck poetry recital at the limits of Jim's hearing; perhaps it was only his own inner voice, racing incoherently ahead of him at the news. 'You're talking interviews here?' he managed to say.

'That's correct, Jim. An interview, and a personal appearance of a kind – what you journalists refer to, I think, as a secret gig.'

'Where?' Jim wanted to know. 'When?'

'I can't tell you that, Jim, it's a secret gig. Nearer the time you'll have all the information you need, but right now I don't even want you to hint of it, especially not to your News editor.' A crackle, a rush of static, and then Beresford went on. 'Your review of Cora's live show will not be an exclusive, of course – we can't promise you that. We feel that the rest of the press are at least entitled to *something*, but no more entitled than Cora's public. The interview though will be yours and yours alone.'

Jim cleared his throat, buying himself time to think.

'Just a minute,' he said while he searched his clothing for cigarettes he did not have.

It was the proverbial offer one couldn't refuse. Barely ten minutes ago, playing this scene through in his head as fantasy, he'd known precisely how he'd react. Now, the prospect was daunting, the office appeared to have frozen inanimate about him. He was vaguely aware of Martyn silently urging him on, of subs having laid down their rulers to await the outcome, of traffic beyond the open windows receding. He could imagine how Elaine would greet this news, but she couldn't be expected to understand; she'd never appreciate how much this meant.

'Go on,' he said finally, and Beresford said, 'I'd like you to think of this as a peace offering, a small concession. It isn't that we're hostile towards the press, it's just that we believe in a selective approach to promotion and publicity. Too much exposure, the wrong kind of exposure, can have a harmful and cheapening effect.'

'Publicity isn't a one-way street, Max,' Jim replied. 'We'd be doing each other a favour.'

'That's as maybe. Do try to understand, though, that the transaction will be strictly on our terms. You won't be using a photographer; we'll take care of the image. And we'll reserve the right to veto your final copy. If you've any objection to any of this – '

'I've no objection,' Jim said, 'as long as you don't insist on conducting the interview yourself.'

There was polite laughter on the line, distorted by static. 'Then I think we have a deal. We'll contact you again, Jim, as soon as everything's finalised.'

He was about to sign off when Jim said, no longer able to suppress it, 'I want you to know I'm grateful, Max. I don't know why you should come to *Alter-Image* rather than the *NME* or the dailies or whoever, but – '

'Oh it has nothing to do with *Alter-Image*,' Max Beresford said. 'I thought you would have realised that by now, Jim. It's you.'

'Me?'

'Indeed. It was Cora's wish.'

At first Jim was dumbstruck, his knuckles whitening as he clenched the receiver more firmly, his heart throwing a punch within his chest. 'Max, I don't understand,' he finally managed, and then he was speaking to a severed connection, listening to a gaggle of foreign radio voices, none of them Beresford's. By the time he'd cradled the receiver the static had become an atmosphere of Long Acre traffic, and Martyn Sheppard was standing over him, fingers crossed.

'Well?' Martyn said. 'Do we hold the front page or what?'

seven

The chaos began just before midnight.

It began as two factions of armed and war-painted youths emerged from underground stations at Bond Street and Tottenham Court Road, wielding clubs and iron bars and, in one instance, a medieval mace. Within minutes their chants filled the streets and the flow of traffic became a jam. They broke towards Oxford Circus from subways, from backstreets, from the doorways of nightclubs and art-house cinemas; and all at once it seemed that the city's black heart had emptied them out, like the voiceless dead from their graves, to answer its beat. For the beat was in the air tonight, in all parts of the city, and the beat was a madness and the madness was all. The city's tortured soundtrack was slowly resolving itself into one perfect, clearly defined rhythm.

It was an innocent bystander — a telephone sales girl; this wasn't her war — who became the first of the night's many casualties. She'd chanced the wrong moment to step clear of her taxi, which had pulled to the kerb near the 100 Club. Somewhere beyond her the first shop windows had gone through, and department store security alarms were beginning to shrill. Closer still, fifty or more bodies were clashing outside a window displaying blind, reaching mannequins in this summer's flimsies. Before the girl had taken ten paces from the gutter, the first wave engulfed her.

The mob came dressed in the colours of rage, in scarlets and purples, their hair cropped close to their tattooed skulls. She scarcely had time to register more — a glimpse of someone's lapel badge, a pale expanse of forearm inscribed with an icon, a swastika perhaps. But that was all. She could not run, for the course was blocked and their hands were upon her.

Within seconds — perhaps fractions of seconds — of stumbling into their path, the telephone sales girl had been seized from both sides, her clothing snared, her left arm wrenched from her body.

At first she couldn't tell whether the sound she heard was anything more than a parting coat sleeve. Certainly the pain didn't register, it had all come upon her too quickly. It wasn't until she raised her eyes — to see the coat sleeve raised aloft like a prize, her limb still within it — that the blackness descended. Seconds later she was under their feet.

Further along Oxford Street, two cars had been overturned and set alight by the rioters. Slick yellow flames were beginning to kindle and the smell of petroleum to spread. Pedestrians, panicking, hurried into the road as the lights turned green. Motorists, forced to swerve and stall as they tried to avoid the disturbance, were being systematically dragged from their vehicles to be brutalised. One man had been set alight before he stumbled, arms flailing, towards New Bond Street.

In Brixton, the police were out in numbers within the hour. A wall was being built there formed of riot shields, a wall which would rapidly be broken down by missiles the protesters were hurling. Stones were landing, and bricks and bottles and darts which they'd stolen from public house dart-boards were landing. In Handsworth, Birmingham, a Molotov cocktail landed, burning to white the lens of an ITN video camera.

They were seeing it all at Carolyn's.

'That's heavy dub,' Derek said calmly as he switched off the television. 'That's just too fucking much.' He settled back in his armchair, waiting until the screen's blue-white dot had receded to nothing before dragging on the reefer his fingers held at the tilt. His eyes looked sunken almost to sleep, and his shoulder-length hair was shiny with grease. He stared at the ceiling, shaking his head, slowly releasing a grey plume of smoke from his nostrils and mouth. 'I told you this was coming, Cal. It's going to spread like a cancer. This time they're going to tear everything down.'

Flutter-fingered, Carolyn was stacking and clearing the plates from her table while Elaine sat uncorking the wine she'd brought. Carolyn's every movement seemed tainted by panic, and had seemed so all evening, even before the bulletins started. Knives and forks rattled free of her grasp like living things. Derek's portion of nutloaf remained untouched on his plate, and now she was looking at him, exasperated. 'Do you have to start skinning up before everyone's finished?'

'You're all finished now, aren't you?' Derek glared. The chinks of cutlery sounded painfully brittle with the TV turned off, conspicuous as sound-effects in a low budget film. 'What do you think, Jim?' Derek said. 'Do you think the ruling class are about to get what's coming to them? What do you think's going on out there?'

'Whatever it is it ain't the summer of love,' Jim said. 'And I really don't know about the ruling class; most of the people in the thick of it were just window shopping. That man — ' He faltered, thinking again of the motorist they had torched like an effigy of Guy Fawkes: though the news report hadn't shown it, his mind's eye had caught every last and atrocious detail. 'What they did to him and the girl, that's nothing to do with anything: it's just mindless and sick.'

Derek considered. 'It is a sickness, Jim, you're right about that. What you're seeing is proof that the human soul has a terminal sickness.' The air in the downstairs flat was becoming acrid with his marijuana, the primal colours of its psychedelic posters were beginning to glare. Derek was slurring, 'Whatever we've been holding inside is finally coming out. I tell you, that's what's going on out there. The fucking power-heads are losing their grip, it's time for the real people to take over.'

Carolyn was looking ready to burst. 'Can't we talk about something else? It's horrible.' Her gaze fell on Elaine and then Jim; she was pleading for moral support. 'Would you like to help with the dishes, Elaine? And, Jim, why don't you tell Derek about what you do for a living?'

'You told me yourself what he does,' Derek said as she tottered away from the dining-table, arms loaded. Apparently the only voice he wanted to hear just now was his own.

'I really don't know what it is with him,' Carolyn said to Elaine as soon as they were safely kitchened, the door closed behind them. When the plates cut the surface of the foamy water and slid vanishing from sight underneath, she added, 'He's been terribly arrogant just lately, and talking such nonsense – well, you heard him. I really must apologise.'

'Don't,' Elaine said, squeaking her hands into a pair of yellow rubber gloves. 'Perhaps it's just the dope talking.'

'Usually it quiets him down. Or at least it used to; not lately. Lately he seems to be changing somehow.' For a moment the pale discs of her eyes looked frantic, unable to hold Elaine's gaze. There was, Elaine noticed, a suggestion of bruising low on her neck near the collar bone; or was the bruising just shadow? 'Do you ever smoke it?' Carolyn wondered.

'No, it always seems to put me to sleep and leaves me hung over the next morning. I can't see the value in anything that does that.'

'Maybe you're more the amphetamine kind.'

Elaine almost laughed, but managed to cover it with a cough. 'I really wouldn't know about that.'

A silence elapsed then – an uncomfortable silence, Elaine felt. It was as though the riots on TV had burned a hole in the evening for all of them. It was too close and too current to shut out. They couldn't do that, not even with the TV switched off. But what Derek was doing was worse: his behaviour might explain why Carolyn looked so edgy tonight. The disturbances hadn't shocked him at all; he seemed to be actively welcoming them.

Elaine was wondering where the evening's downward spiral would end, and whether it would end at all, when Carolyn said casually, 'Have you been long in London, you and Jim? Your accents – you're both from the north, aren't you?'

'Jim grew up in a spa town on the east coast,' Elaine explained. 'Before London I was living in Washington; I'm originally from Harrogate. My father is Irish. That's why my accent's a bit of a muddle.'

'I think it's a rather nice accent,' Carolyn said. She seemed to be taking an age over the pyrex tureen she was wiping before setting it down on the drainer. 'And you seem so well matched, you two.'

'We share the same nightmares.' Elaine laughed. 'In many ways we're complete opposites – positive and negative poles, if you like.'

'Which is which? I know how you mean, though. Derek's my opposite too — he's a meat eater, I'm a vegan. There are so many differences. In fact I think we're more opposite than we used to be.' She was smiling now, without much humour, at a memory. 'I often wonder if that's why our daughter turned out as she did.'

'I didn't know you had children.'

'Just the one. Zoe, we call her. She'd just turned twenty when we saw her last and she was having her nipples pierced. I told her, "Well, it's your body." '

'She's living away now?'

Carolyn gave a nod. 'But I wouldn't know where. She was our love child, you get me, but she was so full of hate when she left. We were both seventeen when Zoe got born. Most of the time we were high as kites on acid: they were crazy times. Derek was even tripping the night I went into labour, and he held my hand all the way through it.'

'Why did she leave?' Elaine asked. 'Or is that a moot point?'

'Not really; she left because she wanted to, and because we couldn't hold on to her any longer. Well, it's her life too — we did with ours as we wanted. It's just that later on she developed this — well, this rage, I suppose you could call it. She grew so negative about everything, and I really couldn't tolerate that in anyone.'

They were talking around whatever subject Carolyn was trying to avoid, which was fine by Elaine. If the subject was Derek, she'd rather not discuss it anyway: his arrogant display tonight had left a bitter taste in her mouth. Now that she thought of it, she couldn't help feeling that Carolyn, too, had changed since their first meeting, when she'd been sociable to the point of suffocating. Now she was defensive, jumpy even, as fragile as the crockery she was wiping dry with a checked towel. If Derek had changed

72

as she claimed, then Carolyn had surely changed with him.

Now she was moving the towel in stiff rhythmic swipes, back and forth, sending a gleam around the rim of an already polished plate. It took a moment or two before Elaine fathomed what Carolyn was doing, that she was keeping time.

While they'd been talking a rhythm had begun in the next room. Elaine recognised it instantly. She was beginning to know it well — the familiar wall of sound which Jim had described as 'Sister Ray' with even less polish; Cora's voice, as cool and glassy as Suzanne Vega's, with a truly exhilarating range. Jim had been playing it often of late, and even Elaine had found herself putting it on in absent moments. She still couldn't see the attraction or understand why Jim had pinned so many hopes on this music, but in spite of herself she'd returned to it.

'Has it taken hold of Jim as well?' Carolyn was saying now. 'The way it's taken hold of Derek?'

She probably meant the music, Elaine decided. 'It has in a way,' she said, 'but it goes with the job. He still believes rock and roll has something to offer, and Cora's his way of proving it. If a new wave is coming, he wants to be there when it happens.'

'Is that what you think?' Carolyn's face was expressionless, her towel kept pace with the backbeat. 'You think Jim got hooked because it's his job?'

'I — I think so,' Elaine faltered. 'Why else would he?'

'You never thought there could be more to it than that?'

What was the woman trying to say? Why were her arms still quivering, now that the last of the plates had been dried and stacked? For a moment her hands continued to beat the air; their involuntary nerve dance made Elaine think of headless chickens. Then she cast aside the towel as though it were a boiling poultice in her grasp.

73

'Listen to me,' she said sharply. She gripped Elaine by both rubber-gloved wrists. Suds drooled over the drainer to the floor. In her eyes, the panic had returned. 'There *is* more than that. You have to stop him before he goes any further. She'll do to him what she's doing to Derek.'

'She'll do what?' Elaine barely had time to say, but then there was movement across the kitchen, a Hendrix poster was swinging inwards with the door, Cora's voice was rising from a whisper to a shout.

Jim was in the doorway. 'I was just explaining to Derek,' he began and then stopped abruptly. By the looks of him, by the way his syllables combed themselves awkwardly from his tongue, he'd been hitting on Derek's joint. 'I was explaining we ought to be crashing out soon.' A slow confusion crossed his face as he looked from Elaine to Carolyn and back again. 'What's going on?'

'Just having a heart to heart,' Carolyn said dimly. She unlaced her fingers from Elaine's wrists, wiping the damp on the front of her smock. 'How are you getting along with Derek?'

'Fine.' He looked at Elaine. 'And you?'

'Fine,' Elaine said.

'Get me the hell out of here,' she said seconds later in her best American accent, Derek and Carolyn safely out of her range. 'The place is a madhouse.'

They trooped up the stairs and into the lounge, where the net curtains breezed away from an open window, where Cora's cassette gleamed like silver the moment the light came on. The telephone had been installed earlier today. It sat, a candlestick design which Elaine had chosen, atop one of the stand-mounted loudspeakers. It was ringing as they entered: rang twice, then rang off as Elaine snatched it up.

'Probably because the connection's new,' she said, and cradled the earpiece. Then, 'Why did you do it, Jim?'

'Do what?'

'You know.'

He could only shrug. 'Why did I smoke dope with Derek? I was trying to be sociable, Elaine, that's all.' But he sounded as though he didn't believe it either.

'You said you wouldn't,' she said quietly, collapsing beside him on the lumpy sofa. The upholstery had worn through to the thread in places; she scratched at it, absently, with a fingernail. 'You're supposed to have tried it and hated it and rebelled against it. You even said in *Alter-Image* that it was strictly for people with holes in their lives; holes they were trying to fill with – '

'I know what I said,' he said, but there was impatience in his voice – the voice of a schoolboy grown weary with reprimands. He recognised the tone straight away, and wished it were something he could see and touch, that he were able to tear out of himself.

'I'm not trying to lecture you,' Elaine said. She'd been reading his thoughts again, as she constantly did. 'You know I'm no puritan. It's just that you've been through it before, and you don't need people like Derek to drag you back where you were.'

'You sound like your father,' Jim said before he could stop himself. He could tell by her face that the remark had stung like a slap. Her father was a deeply religious man, but a bigot for all that. 'You'll be quoting me Scripture next: the dog returneth to its own vomit.'

She stood up sharply. 'I can't talk to you while you're like this, I'm going to bed. We'll discuss it tomorrow.'

'What's to discuss? Have I fallen short of your standards?' He was almost shouting now. For an instant he stood outside himself, ashamed of his spoiled child's petulance. 'Would you like to tell me what was going on before, with you and Carolyn?'

'Nothing was going on.'

'What was that bitch saying about me?'

'Nothing that made any sense,' Elaine sighed. She went to the door and half opened it, hesitated there, peering back at him with her reddened face. 'Nothing that made any sense until now.' There was no trace of anger or malice in her at all as she said, 'We'll talk tomorrow. Let's not make tonight any more of a flop than it already is.'

In that moment, as she stood there, he found himself hating her. It was a blind, aimless hatred, in need of an object to fasten on. She ought to be furious with him, but that was beneath her.

After she'd gone he sat — he couldn't be sure how long — trying to scorch a hole in the sofa's variegated pattern with his glare. His limbs felt twice their usual weight, as heavy as sacks filled with soil. The rhythm pounded steadily in his head while his fingertips tapped it out on his knee.

Why had he tried to hurt Elaine? He was certain that, at some point, he'd wanted to. It was just one of those things, he should have said, and left it at that. It was not a great sin to share dope with Derek while Derek blethered endlessly on like a prophet of Armageddon; nor was his behaviour something to feel proud of. His first year in London had been the usual spree of drugs and drink, the usual indulgence of a wide-eyed yokel let loose in the city for the first time; and he'd very quickly tired of it. The only sin was that he'd lapsed — he'd forced something out of his life only to usher it in again.

In a minute he'd stop seething and apologise to her. He couldn't remember the last row they'd had, or whether they'd ever had one at all. But he never apologised, for

Elaine was already asleep when he came to their room.

In bed she turned away from his touch: even from the depths of her sleep she was snubbing him. He probably deserved it. Tonight he'd been directing his frustrations and energies in all the wrong places.

Now he settled, head pillowed on his hands, and peered towards the square of moonlit window. They must buy curtains for this room as a first priority, he thought. The silhouetted limb of a dead birch tree scraped the pane like a clawed, prying finger. He had never been able to watch it for long, he'd found. It was trying to remind him of something he couldn't quite place, something he was almost afraid to remember.

As sleep began to seduce him the scratching transported him back, back, towards something, some place and time, some event, he'd rather he never returned to. He fended it off and turned on to his side, so that his face was pressed close to the coffee and cream slope of Elaine's shoulder.

At least her breathing was reassuring. Nothing else seemed to be, lately. Where had his rage come from; and why had he subjected Elaine to it? It was a stranger in him — part of a far larger, deeper fear whose source he couldn't locate. Suddenly he was horribly afraid — for her, for himself, he could not tell.

The man who had sent the threatening letters: he had started this fear, but surely he wasn't the centre of it. The centre was vast, it reached back and back, it hadn't a shape or a form as the prowler had had.

It had nothing to do with the riots, Jim told himself now; and then wondered why he should think that at all. The dead tree's branch had extended its skeletal outline across the pale sheets to the down at the nape of Elaine's neck. Its shadow trembled there, and he let his finger stray to touch it, and it danced away from him, mocking him.

No, whatever disturbed him had nothing to do with the riots. The riots were something outside him, images of war trapped in a TV's cathode-ray tube. They concerned other people, not him. They belonged to another world. Yet in a way he couldn't quite define, the news reports had made him feel personally threatened; they hammered ferociously at his door. The torched man, the telephone sales girl the mob had crippled; even now, in his mind, they were suffering. If these atrocities didn't concern him, why should he feel so responsible?

eight

'Jim, what are you doing?' Elaine said.

The first time she spoke he could barely distinguish her outline from shadow at the doorway. As he tugged off the headphones she repeated what she'd said. It was well past three in the morning — he had no idea how well past. The living-room was in darkness but for the greenish glow of the amplifier's pilot light and the steady red pulse of the cassette deck's VU meters. His eyes had grown as accustomed as a cat's to this gloom, but he wasn't prepared for the blast of the sixty-watt bulb as she turned it on. Feeling his pupils stop down like shutters, he threw a protective hand in front of his face.

Just as quickly, Elaine switched it off again. She crept across the room, lowered herself to kneel at Jim's feet, and Jim could still hear Peter Gabriel whispering secrets into his palm. Elaine peered up at him, her hands on his knees.

'Can't sleep,' he said very softly, as though afraid of waking someone. 'Too much to think last night. I'm transcribing an interview.'

'I missed you,' Elaine said. 'When I woke and you weren't there I felt — afraid.'

'You're crazy, that's all.'

'I know.' She laughed, then settled again. 'It was only

79

a feeling, very brief. Perhaps I was dreaming. Will you come back to bed in a minute?'

'In a minute,' he said. 'I wasn't really transcribing anyway. I was just looking for something to fill my head with, instead of my thoughts.'

'Your thoughts?' Her voice sounded taut, but he did not reply. 'Jim? I'm sorry about earlier.'

'So am I.' At first that was all he could think of to say. A confusion of feeling welled up in his throat. 'I behaved like a shit and I'm sorry for that,' he managed. 'It wasn't so much what I did as how I reacted to what you said. Why should you be sorry?'

'I don't think you'd understand why,' she said.

'Try me.'

'I'm sorry because,' she said, and supported him to his feet while Peter Gabriel, still whispering, tumbled to the floor and landed beside the armchair with the softest of thumps. Together they switched off and unplugged the hi-fi, said goodbye to the dancing coloured lights and the whispers. Then Elaine went on, 'Because I half believed something Carolyn told me. I believed it without understanding it.'

'What did she say?'

'Something and nothing. She thought you might be going the same way as Derek, because of this obsession,' – she stopped herself there, perhaps because she'd seized on the first word that came to mind, however appropriate – 'this fascination you both have with Cora.'

Jim stood, his hands resting on Elaine's shoulders, his breath suspended. Beyond the curtains, Laleham Road was almost preternaturally quiet, especially so after last night's news items. 'I don't suppose she explained which way Derek *is* going?'

'Since you mention it, no.'

'Then you're right: I don't understand why you're apologising.'

Again she laughed, but softly, soft as a murmured prayer. 'She did say in passing how terribly arrogant he's been lately.'

'Thank you very much.'

'But now I'm beginning to think she's as crazy as Derek – perhaps it might be contagious.'

'Perhaps so.' And perhaps both he and Elaine were dancing this futile dance of apologies because it was all they had. Perhaps whistling past the graveyard was the only way of denying the prowler his existence, or his letters their power. Good God, if Elaine had only seen the letters for herself! In here, together, they were safe – at least for a time – from the world, its charms and its poisons. It wouldn't dare come near her. He wouldn't let the world tear them apart.

Saying no more he drew her towards him, discovering her again with his touch, tasting the scented freshness of her hair and her skin. He lowered his face, very gradually, to caress her breasts through her nightshirt. She responded and he held her close, as if for the last time. The last time: the thought crossed his mind in a trice and was gone. He couldn't believe it was so.

As they walked to the bedroom, Elaine wondered in a casual and matter-of-fact voice, 'Jim? If I asked you to give up the exclusive, if I asked you not to pursue it any further, would you do it?'

The question surprised him and yet failed to surprise him. In a way, he'd been rehearsing the answer for days. But after a matter of seconds when he did finally stammer a reply, he couldn't be sure he believed it.

nine

Now that his eyes were burning, there was only the pain to keep him alive. Like a fire that has outgrown its kindling, it lived in him now according to its own rules, its own customs, its own insatiable hunger. What began as a craving, nothing more than a common heat rash, had quickly become a fever. He shifted on the bed, hands clawing at his face in an effort to tear loose the discomfort.

His room didn't help; a small box room — twenty cubic yards of stale air — had grown hotter and more humid than ever. Although the window was thrown open as far as it would go, the air failed to penetrate. He had vomited twice in a matter of hours and had been too exhausted to clean up after himself. He'd collapsed on the bed and remained there since early evening, unable to budge.

Now the burning had spread to his chest, to his lifeless arms. This was always a crucial time: it meant either that the craving might pass, or completely consume him.

He threshed and turned and, after a moment, panting, lay perfectly still. His body was matted and oily, and he could no longer distinguish between the sheets and himself, or between his sopping clothes and his hopeless, boneless limbs. His tongue tasted of charred paper. At least that was something — one of his senses he still had control of. He'd hold on to it as best he could, if only for sanity's sake.

Vaguely, as if watching through frosted glass, he saw himself shift to the edge of the bed and sit upright. The bedsit rotated, dragging its postered walls through his sights. A once-white sheet slithered to the floor in a mass, collecting at his feet. The craving was worse now: it was going to peak, not trough, as he'd feared.

He lay, hands raised, studying his arms as if they belonged to a stranger. Minute tics jumped across the paled flesh, each tic a flying spark from the mother-fire. He pumped his left arm from wrist to elbow, bloating the vein, making it ready. Love is the drug, he thought incoherently; revolution is the drug, revolution is the opium of the masses. If they could see him now, the boneheads, the pus-heads, those cogs in the music-machine big wheel, they would rock and roll themselves to death, laughing.

Above the miniature sink of unwashed cups, a crack in the plaster rose to the ceiling, finer and more intricate than a spider's weave. Last night or the night before that, he had dreamt the crack wider and deeper, and through it something had been oozing into the room. What will tonight's dream bring? he thought; which of my songs would you like to hear next?

Beside the sink was a two-ring gas burner. Instinct carried him through the routine without further delay, firing the gas, steadying the hypodermic. He hoped the routine might bring pleasure this time, but more than that he hoped it would finally finish him.

He pumped the vein, pumped the vein again. His eyes were on fire, the insides of his lids felt seared. Why didn't he just reach into the flame and let it consume the rest of him? Nearby, on a stool topped with a red PVC seat, he caught sight of his copy of *Exile On Main Street*. That would be his nostrum tonight: the Stones at their finest, before they began the down-slide. He reached, black-veined, to pick it up. He lowered it carefully over the heat, watching the vinyl soften and distort and gradually melt. He steadied the hypodermic.

Daniel Zero woke to the sound of light rain drumming against his window. His first thought, once he'd regained what was left of his senses, was one of relief. He'd woken, but only just in time. Although he was dreaming impossible dreams, he was sure they would kill him the first time he failed to escape them.

He stared about the room, at the dozens of Cora posters bearing the '*Dark Brigade cometh*' legend, packed so densely around the walls that their edges overlapped. He looked at the two-ring burner where he did not stand, hypodermic poised; he didn't even possess a copy of *Exile On Main Street*. The fine line crack he'd dreamt of was there, curling up to a corner of the ceiling, but it was nothing more than a harmless flaw. None of this reassured him. The beat was still with him, even though it was only the blood rushing to his ears, the pattern of rain on the window sill.

The digital alarm clock at his bedside told him he was late. Soon he would have to go out. He felt trapped into going, when all he wanted to do was curl up and wait for the revolution to pass. To think he'd wanted it though, summoned it with all his will! He must have expected it to change everything but him.

Swinging himself off the bed, he crossed the room and looked out on a world of charred chimney stacks and fire escapes grown useless with rust. The window was open, and the rain spattering in through the gap looked muddy. Puddles were forming on the carpet, on the edge of the folding table he kept under the sill where the light was truest. The hours had mounted up into days and then weeks while he'd worked at this table, pasting together issues of *Killzine*. Now he couldn't think of a word worth writing.

He tugged the window shut, though its swollen wood frame resisted and required forcing, and looked down at the table. All its clutter had been swept to the floor except for the briefcase. It sat there, sleek and mysterious, its contents incredible. As he stared at it, he began to perspire.

At last he thumb-dialled the combination, clicked open the locks, raised the lid. Inside were the sixty-four cassettes, white labelled, just as he'd known he'd find them. A matter of hours ago, when the sickness first took him, the case had been empty.

He had lost count of the times he'd emptied it, or the times it had obligingly filled again, though he'd long ago stopped caring. Each time the equation was complete the craving grew more acute, forcing him out to the streets. And each time he went out he sensed he'd discovered his true vocation: he was neither prophet nor sage of the Underground, but gravedigger.

Once while crossing Waterloo Bridge he'd even considered tossing the case, open, to the river, and standing above it in the darkness as the water coiled it greedily down. But he hadn't been able to do it, not yet. He could never be sure if his life depended upon it, or what price he'd be paying if he ever dared let go.

Instead he'd left it stuffed with loose papers overnight, and in the morning the papers had been on the floor and there, inside the case, were the blank white spines of the sixty-four cassettes, perfectly ordered as rows of teeth. Now here they were again. And they bite, he thought wearily. Each time they bared themselves they were sending him out with a message: Go forth and spread my word, take my songs to the people.

Deptford was more than an hour's walk away, his body

sagging over most of the distance. The rain had stopped early: it would have been pleasant to stroll, face upturned, to feel its cooling touch on his skin, but instead the small hours were humid and dry. Daylight was still some way off, and the air was sealed out with the light.

The pubs were closed and there were no discotheques here that he knew. As he walked, he had to keep reminding himself that the beat was not around him in the streets but within him, in his step, in his gasping breath. He made his way past the Albany, past a pub which he'd never dared enter. The walls outside were decorated with National Front slogans, swastikas, a variety of charming pronouncements − *Coons Repatriate* was the first he saw, and enough to send him on his way.

African chants, Latin-American sambas drove him forward across the wide empty streets and into an alley between silent factories. The light here had been sucked out completely: the alley seemed as long as a railway tunnel and its darkness as final as a tomb's. But there was light at the end, some distance ahead, and he bolted towards it, the briefcase jarring against his leg. As he gathered speed, so did the footsteps behind him.

Danny stopped, looked round, saw nothing. What did he expect to see in this darkness anyway? The footsteps subsided immediately. There was an angry, familiar, prickling sensation breaking across his chest and his stomach as he turned to move on. The footsteps were ghosts of his own, he reasoned − echoes bandied about between the brick walls like gossip. But to reason was easy − reason was something he hadn't been blessed with for days, even weeks; just lately it seemed as elusive as a vital phrase to an author.

Ahead the decaying light opened up into a road, the lanes intersected by misshapen bollards. He crossed towards an estate in which multi-storey blocks of council flats reached for the sky. Saplings were planted at intervals along the pavement, most of them deformed or broken under the constant weight of swinging and clambering children. In the communal forecourt, a car was stranded without wheels or windscreen, its doors stacked neatly beside it. Scraps of litter flitted across the gravel from a skip which stood in front of the nearest block; it was surrounded by swollen black bin liners, many of which had burst open. Switching the loaded briefcase from right hand to left, Danny hurried in for his meet.

Two small girls sat on the concrete steps outside, their blotchy legs splayed before them. They watched him approach and then pass, whispering and elbowing one another into hysterics. As he reached the doors, the elder girl — a redhead of perhaps seven or eight — shouted, 'Mister, you can fuck my friend if you like.'

The other girl snorted back laughter and covered her face, but the redhead was perfectly serious. She was trailing him indoors through a lime-green corridor which smelt of urinals, dragging at Danny's sleeve. 'Did you hear what I said?' the girl demanded. 'For a fiver she'll fuck anything that moves.'

'Back where you came from,' Danny hissed at her over his shoulder. Clasping the briefcase more firmly between both hands, defying the girl to come near it, he approached the lifts. He fired the button twice and again, and waited. Much of the graffiti on the walls was visual — the usual cartoon cocks and CND symbols, Cora's name writ large above a doorway in aerosol. As the lift doors opened, just a fraction, and then shuddered closed again, the redheaded girl called helpfully, 'It don't work, mister. The thingy don't work.'

Leaving the opening, closing door to its tantrum, he took

the stairs. This time the spare set of footsteps went before him. Four flights brought him out to a narrow balcony overlooking the forecourt. As he reached it, a sleeper train trundled over a bridge, almost level with his face. Its stream of lights signalled empty compartment after empty compartment rushing by; was anyone driving? Tonight, for some reason, it seemed perfectly likely that no one was.

Danny moved along the balcony, checking for the door with no number. Even this far above ground level he could hear the two girls on the steps braying laughter to the air − laughing at him, he supposed. And with good reason too. Any outsider could see that both he and his situation were laughable.

The door he was looking for was the fifth along, but there was no sign of life here. The lights were dimmed, so whoever he was supposed to meet had either given up on him or else − But no, why should they wait for him in the dark? He was contemplating turning away, turning and running, when he realised the craving would never allow him to. If he couldn't unburden himself tonight, he might never have the chance again. Dry mouthed, he knocked at the door and waited.

After a short delay the door opened partly, then opened fully. A figure too dark for him to see clearly stepped quickly aside to let him through.

Tonight's delivery was to be marked Export Only by the looks of it. Seated in front of him was a mustachioed Japanese in a powder-blue suit. His eyes were deep set beneath a brow that loomed forward like a warning. As the door closed he looked at Danny as if he were something that had crawled from a toilet, then looked quickly away. Behind him, Max Beresford was adjusting a dimmer switch on the wall. The man who had opened the door − a respectable up-market punk, Danny could see now;

platinum blond, in a grey leather jacket and black leather tie — strode past him to an adjoining room. For a time there was silence. The Japanese forced a cough into his fist. Then Beresford said, 'Danny boy, so nice of you to come at last.'

'I didn't expect you,' Danny said. He looked around the unfurnished room, at the carpetless floor, then at the Japanese. 'You slumming again, Max?'

'Now, now,' Beresford smiled. 'I was just explaining to Mr Oshima how we intend to extend our market abroad. I was suggesting that couriers of your calibre are likely to prove very valuable in the future.' Beresford's face, the skin drawn tight across the bones, looked paler and more skeletal than ever. It was a parody of a death mask, the skull too large for its surround. Were there eyes behind the infuriating mirrored shades he wore? Danny suspected not.

'So.' Danny moved further into the room, feeling suddenly more than a little vulnerable. Something told him he might not leave this place again now that he'd entered, but in this too he was beginning to feel too exhausted to care. 'What's the game plan, Max?' he said. 'I guess I don't get to meet Cora after all, right?'

'You never know, Danny. No doubt you will in good time. But first we have this arrangement with Doherty. You know him, of course?'

Danny shrugged. 'We've met. He's OK.'

'I believe he's very much like you,' Beresford said. 'That's why we chose him out of all the contenders, because he's been searching for something that matters. We're convinced he'll give it everything he's got.'

'And me? What do I do in the meantime?' Danny glared at Beresford. 'Do you expect me to stay on as your errand boy, is that what you think?'

'I don't think you have much choice in the matter, do you?'

Suddenly Danny was seething, his heart thumping the roof of his mouth. He crossed to the Japanese, setting the briefcase down at his feet. 'Perhaps your Mr Oshima would like to know what this stuff does to people.'

'I can assure you, Danny,' Beresford said, 'Mr Oshima already knows all there is to know. But none of it really concerns him; he's a marketing man.'

'The master recording is analogue,' Oshima said. He had the case on his knee and was testing for the combination. With seemingly minimal effort he found it. 'It's our job to digitally remaster, that's all. We have a large and increasing home market for DAT format recordings, and Monolith don't have the capacity yet. This is where I can be of service to Max.'

But Danny was turning on Beresford as if Oshima had never spoken. 'I don't care what you're doing in Tokyo or New York or fucking Timbuktu, Max. You let me think I was doing you a favour by keeping my side of the bargain. You didn't tell me what I was getting into, or what I was carrying. You didn't say you were poisoning me.'

Beresford took a pace towards Danny, his thin lips working without sound. Past him, Danny saw that two figures had appeared in the adjoining doorway – the punk, together with another, larger, man whose face in this light looked oddly incomplete.

'Poisoning? Frankly, Danny, I'm disappointed,' Beresford said. 'I thought you of all people would have welcomed the change. Was it just lip-service when you were ranting about apathy and anarchy? Maybe they were just words you picked out of old songs.' He was smiling, but there was something more than a little troubling in the smile. 'You used to think of yourself as a rebel, Danny.

91

Why do you run for cover as soon as the true liberation begins?'

'What liberation?' Danny thought of his ripening veins, the thrill of the rhythm which coursed through his blood, the needle, his too vivid dreams of r'n'r suicide. He glanced at Oshima as if for help, but there was no help forthcoming. Oshima was busily transferring cassettes from the briefcase to a Tokyo Airlines' flight bag. Danny said, 'All I know is that this − this thing you've put inside me is trying to kill me.'

'It's doing nothing of the kind,' Beresford assured him. 'If you could only be patient and wait for the change to be complete, you'd see how glorious the new state can be. Don't resist, is all.'

'I have to resist. I'm a rebel, remember? And I know what they're saying on the news. I've seen what the rioters are doing to each other, they're defeating whatever common cause they had to begin with. You've poisoned them too, Beresford.'

But Beresford was unmoved. He drew a Moré from its slender pack and calmly set light to it. 'Whatever's inside will out,' he said. 'That's something you've still to learn, young man: the meaning of revolution. The spirit of the thing will always build and build up within. Eventually it will surface − sometimes with ugly consequences. Sometimes it will involve the mind, sometimes its effect may be purely physical.' He paused, trapping Danny momentarily in the mirrored lenses. 'What happens then will vary from individual to individual; but what we're discussing, Danny, is a million − *millions* of private revolutions. Know what you're opposing before you oppose it, that's all I'm saying.'

'And that's all you have to say?'

'That's all.'

'You're dicking off, Max,' Danny decided. He started for the door at once. 'You're a murderer, and I'm leaving.'

Before he could clasp the door handle, the platinum punk emerged from the next room, striding towards him. This was it, then. It was to end with him in this shabby interior, beating his fists against a numberless door, his voice raised for one final primal scream which no one would hear. Strangely, the prospect hardly unsettled him at all – it was almost comforting in its way. Then Beresford raised a hand, halting the aggressor in his tracks. The punk hesitated, but held his ground.

'It's all right,' Beresford said. 'He can go. He still needs us.' To Danny he said, 'Aren't you forgetting something?'

The Japanese stood, smart as his suit, and proffered the briefcase like a peace offering. 'Very good to do business with you,' he said. 'I'm sure that Cora will be big in Japan.'

Reluctantly, Danny accepted the token. 'But this time I won't keep it,' he told Beresford. 'I'll burn it or throw it away.'

'We'll see.'

'I won't keep doing what you've been making me do.' But he had the briefcase tucked under one arm, pleasantly weightless now, and the craving was receding in small, regular steps. 'I'm going to let people know what Cora is really about.'

'How can you do that,' Beresford wondered as Danny went out, 'when you still haven't discovered it for yourself?'

Outside, first light had almost reached the balcony. The sky above Deptford was a sublime pinkish, greyish mural. Somewhere – in a ghetto several streets away, or perhaps elsewhere in the building – a man and a woman were screaming. It was the first discordant note of the day, the first of many, Danny suspected. Could he help it? He thought that in some way he could.

He was a well which never ran dry and would never run dry; if only that were a blessing instead of a curse. There must, please, surely, be something he could do. He moved to the edge of the balcony, looked down at the forecourt, the vandalised car. It wavered uncertainly four flights below him, but the thought only made him nauseous, and he turned away. He'd always believed suicide was the out of the coward; but it really required great courage.

Half-way down the concrete stairwell he met the redheaded girl coming up, and wished he had jumped. At first glance he'd wondered why his shadow should rise up the stairs to meet him, when he knew that it couldn't possibly – but the shadow was hers.

'There's a man wants to see you,' the girl said. 'He's been asking questions about you.'

Danny clutched the briefcase in front of his chest in a purely defensive gesture. Had his heart skipped a beat, or did some small, solid weight rattle inside? 'What does he want?'

'You'll find out,' she said, trooping past him. 'He's right behind me.'

Danny froze. His mind wanted to run, though his anchored legs prevented him. In any case who could he turn to? – not the girl, not Beresford and his goon squad. But the fear relented the instant he saw who was climbing the steps. The man looked too pathetic to worry about, as faded and spent as an old crumpled photograph. Yet there was loathing in his eyes; loathing and something far worse.

'I think you owe me an explanation,' the man said, and stepped nearer. 'You can start by explaining exactly what it is you've done to me.'

ten

The air was alive the night *The Dark Brigade* came to the Psychic Dance-hall. All through the day, and through the previous day and the day before that, the grapevine had hummed with the news that this was the venue, however bizarre a choice it seemed. A call came in for Jim Doherty from one of Max Beresford's minions, confirming the rumour: there would be no complimentary tickets, but instead, a guest list as long as an Egyptian scroll. Jim bartered long and hard for a Plus One, and got it. There were others less fortunate.

'What makes you so special?' Nina Fowles had whined at him soon afterwards, upon finding the Monolith switchboard jammed. 'Were you born with a silver coke spoon up your nose or what?'

It was a comment which came back to Jim later as he watched the hundreds of punters lingering and pacing the street outside the gig, some spilling over the kerb and into the road and into the face of the traffic as it crawled back and forth on The Strand. They stared, betrayed, as he guided Elaine up the steps and into the fray. They'd journeyed here to worship their goddess, only to be turned away, ticketless.

The entrance was blocked, as was the foyer beyond. Gangs were storming the doors, boot heels scuffing up the rise. Those nearest the front, shoulder to shoulder like rush hour commuters, were arguing heatedly with a bouncer, who seemed uncertain whether the doors should be open or closed. 'We're full,' he explained to one. 'If your name's not on the list there's nothing I can do.' 'You can take your list and shove – ' a blue-haired Mohican was replying, until the bouncer's look silenced him.

'Can't you just take two or three more?' said a girl whose voice was close to tears. 'Really, we won't take up much space.' She looked around anxiously for support, and when Jim found her eyes meeting his, he looked away.

Elaine shifted her weight nervously from foot to foot. Firecrackers were going off in the street, and directly below the Psychic Dance-hall a litter bin which hung from a lamp-post was beginning to blaze. Perhaps he'd been wrong to bring Elaine here when she hadn't wanted to come, but the alternative would have been to leave her at home, alone in the flat. He'd never considered forgoing the occasion himself.

'Isn't there another way in?' Elaine said impatiently. Several steps above them a scuffle had broken out between two young skinheads and a dark-haired man in an emerald-green dress. A hand flashed upwards above the spiked and permed heads, its knuckles glinting with silver rings. As the hand came down again Elaine stiffened, and Jim realised that what he'd glimpsed on the hand were knuckle-dusters.

Someone screamed, the crowd parted; a many-armed mass tumbled out of control down the steps. Perhaps, Jim thought, this was rock's own Judgement Day, or something like it: hundreds seized by panic, afraid above all else to be shut out from the revelation. A girl wearing DMs and braces launched herself at the door, mouthed an obscenity at the bouncer, and beat a hasty retreat.

'Jim, please – ' Elaine began, but he was already ushering her to the entrance. 'Are you seriously telling me this is what you've been waiting for?'

Just ahead, a thoroughfare had opened near the foyer where the man in girl's clothing lay crumpled and bloody. One of his high heeled shoes lolled point-upwards two steps below him. Either side of him the numbers were dispersing, some cursing, some shaking their heads in grim acceptance; there were shouts of Cool It, That's Enough. At the doors, the bouncer glowered a warning at Jim, and Jim made a gesture through the glass, a mimesis of writing.

The door parted, just a fraction. 'You're on the list?' the bouncer interpreted, and when Jim nodded he said, 'You better hurry in then. You won't be so popular out here; if I were you I'd take the rear exit when you leave.'

'So much for the new thing,' Jim heard Elaine whispering, possibly to herself, as they stepped inside. In the distance a police siren rose and fell. 'Meet the new boss, same as the old boss,' she added disconsolately.

Bass notes ricocheted like muffled bombs in the foyer while a thin-faced man scanned the slithering folios he was holding for names. Jim's was amongst the first on the list, which looked as long as a novel. As the thin-faced man crossed him out, Jim said, 'How many people did Monolith invite?'

'One thousand eight hundred,' the man said after a moment's thought. 'Maybe a little under two thousand; that's capacity.'

'No paying guests?'

'No, it's free, everything's free.' The man appeared faintly incredulous. 'Everything but the beer and the tokens.'

'If it's free, then why are so many locked out?' Elaine wondered. Her eyes were on the souvenir stall, where three

Boy Georges, a Bono, and a doll-faced girl in a black latex dress were haggling for posters and sweatshirts.

'It's free,' the thin-faced man said at last, 'to anyone with their name on the list.'

Elaine took Jim's arm as they strolled to the doors which led on to the dance-floor. To their left a lurid print poster announced a punk revival-revival festival which had already been and gone. As they neared the doors Elaine hesitated. 'Don't lose me,' she said with an urgency he didn't at first understand.

'Just keep hold of my arm,' he told her.

But Elaine was indignant. 'No, what I mean is – don't lose me.'

A sudden twist of nerves inside him, not amusement, made him laugh aloud. 'Elaine, it's only another rock show.'

'Is it?'

Inside, the thunder of warm-up House tracks had ended; now the thunder was more immediate – a ripple, then a gathering of applause which was soon bedlam. Pop celebrity doppelgangers came running, alerted, from the souvenir stall, the sagging arms of sweatshirts trailing behind them. The girl in latex fumbled half-way to the dance-floor, losing her change, not stopping. Her coins were still turning circles in the foyer as she pushed past Elaine at the doorway. 'Are you ready?' Jim said and, before Elaine could reply, stepped inside.

His first thought was that the houselights had not been dimmed for the show; but the brightness emanated from the stage. He tugged Elaine through the heat and the sickly-sweet tang of marijuana and past a line of staring faces he couldn't name. Some were familiar – a *Melody Maker* journalist nodded in his general direction before turning beck to the light; another face, chops blued by stubble, shied quickly away just as he thought he might recognise it.

Either side of him, ring pulls exploded spray from beer cans, massed bodies threw themselves to the air, arms upreaching. They landed, leapt, landed again simultaneously, shuddering the boarded floor to the weight of a giant's tread.

As the crowd surged forward, a space opened near the bar at the back of the auditorium. Elaine marched towards it, fending off elbows. A pall of smoke swirled above the ghosted heads of the audience. To each side of the stage, PA stacks towered to balcony level beneath the domed ceiling, their electrical drone on the edge of cold, hard feedback. As the fog rose further, enveloping the uppermost sections of the stacks, Jim was able to make out the source of the light.

All at once a heaviness lurched in his stomach. Had the audience really known what they were coming to worship when they came here to worship this? The stage was empty, yet they seemed neither to notice nor care. At centre stage, where perhaps an elevated drumkit should have been, or a bank of Marshall guitar amps, a screen the size of a cinema's was gradually unfurling. Its surface blazed white, the light strobing over the sea of heads and hands like a series of film frames. Instinctively Jim raised his sights to the balcony: the heavy form of a video projector depended from there, sturdy as a tank.

'Is this it?' Elaine was shouting to make herself heard. 'Is this all there is?'

Jim could only shake his head, uncertain. There must be more — surely they hadn't come here to bow down to a video idol's image. He watched the whiteness expand and brighten, and for a second was forced to turn his face from the screen as the light became blinding.

Elaine was shouting somewhere outside his crowded

head, a lone voice among thousands. Her fisted hand tugged at his sleeve. Whatever she was trying to tell him must be significant, but for the moment he couldn't imagine why. The rhythm was all that mattered now. It grew from the stroboscope's pattern: dancers moved in slow motion to a beat which could only be sensed, not heard. It belonged to the people, he understood that now. And it came from the people. It had gathered inside them for years like a slow-burn, like a core of spirit the world had for years failed to quash.

Some short distance behind him a fight had erupted in front of the bar. Several youths in motorcycle jackets were forcing a young man in army peripherals to the floor. It was only a stupid distraction, something he shouldn't let bother him; even when he saw the lighted cigarette butt being ground out in the victim's face it seemed hardly important, nothing to do with him. 'Stop them!' someone was shouting. 'Please!' As the music started and Jim turned back to the stage, he found himself looking directly into Cora's eyes.

Her face hovered over the dance-floor, filling the screen. It was a face as familiar as a friend's: the dark and ferocious eyes, the alabaster skin, the full lips parting slightly as she peered across the dark. The hint of her smile took his breath away. Everything was forgotten. How many times had he dreamt of this vision, of being so near to it?

Hands groped upwards and towards her like the crests of waves, shadows pressed forward to crush the ones nearest the front against the stage. Did they believe the image would make them immortal if they could only reach out and touch it? Perhaps so; or perhaps they sensed this was as near as they were ever going to be to the legend.

Before he knew he was doing so, Jim set off, dragging

Elaine with him as he worked his way forward and into the thick of the crowd. At first she resisted, but he shouldn't expect her to share his enthusiasm. She'd set her heart firmly against Cora from the start. He must make allowances for that.

'What are you doing now?' she gasped, but her words were lost to the noise. 'You're really no better than the rest of them; it *is* an obsession.' Then she seemed to give in, her pace quickening as the beat forced her on.

As the crowd closed around him, Jim felt the temperature rise unbearably. Perspiration rolled from his brow, his eyes were streaming from the smoke. To his right a man whose face appeared only half-formed collapsed back into shadow; next to him, Jim saw the gleaming head of a bald girl, safety pins decorating her shaven scalp. None of this seemed to mean anything. Nothing would until he'd drawn close to the image, perhaps even touched it. He'd almost reached the centre of the dance-floor beneath the great dome when a voice from the screen said quietly, 'Hello, Jim.'

Jim halted a little uncertainly, heels skidding across the slime. Had the voice spoken from the screen, or only in his mind? Surely not the screen, for Cora was singing, *Pleased to meet you, guess you know my name* – cruising through a cover version of 'Sympathy for the Devil'. The sound was incredible, the Stones by way of middle period Talking Heads – seemingly countless strands of percussion were interweaving, at war with each other; there was really no way a small quiet voice could make itself heard above that. He turned to Elaine, who was watching the light, apparently having heard nothing outside the song.

'Hello, Jim,' the voice repeated, and this time he knew it belonged to Cora. He'd always known she would sound like this, breathy and slightly husky. But there was something in her tone which seemed to mock him as she added, 'Pleased to meet you at last. Guess you know my name.'

'Who are you?' he managed to say, but she was already lost in the song.

Up on the screen, vast as a Big Brother billboard, the image was slowly dissolving. Cora's flesh was a turmoil of minute living things, writhing about her like meal worms. Then the dissolve carried through and Cora was gone, and the living things were no longer fish-bait but the threshing arms and heads of an audience. It took a second before he realised the on-screen audience were here, now, surrounding him in the Psychic Dance-hall. He saw himself amongst them, Elaine somewhere to his left. Strobes made the movement of limbs appear jerky and vaguely comic, like the movement of actors in old silent films.

Almost immediately the image changed, and another audience appeared. Elaine's fingers brushed lightly against his. These were the disenchanted hundreds who waited in the street beyond the Psychic Dance-hall. Some were casting lighted fireworks into the road and into a convenient litter bin. Others charged up the steps to the blocked foyer doors, their faces set for battle.

Jim felt a calm settle over him. Cora was transporting him towards something – a place and a time – he'd never been able to approach alone. With Cora to guide him he knew he could go there. He was standing out on the steps with Elaine. It must have been less than an hour ago. The heat and smoke of the Psychic Dance-hall no longer existed, or at least he felt no longer connected to it. He'd betrayed Elaine by bringing her here; he'd told her the event was just a formality. She was too vulnerable, too precious to take for granted. He imagined he'd make it up to her later.

But the song was over; a guitar sliced out the intro to one of Cora's own anthems, 'The Shadow out of Time'; the pictures were changing too quickly before his eyes. Vague pale shapes flitted into focus and then out again. The rapid fire of a snare drum pumped his system like a rush of amphetamines.

Who was Elaine, anyway? Of course, he had never met her, and if he had she had made no lasting impression. But that was because he was someone else at some other point in time, before the intruder had entered their lives with his threats. He was younger now than he had been for years. He'd yet to enter the city, to discover love, to flirt with death. Before he could fear the fear of losing Elaine, he first had to meet her.

The walls of the room he was in were the colour of oysters. They had painted it this way, he recalled, to make the most of the inadequate light which reached here. He was in Seaborough, in the small attic room above the Georgian guest house his parents kept open through the summer season. In July and August and then September, the streets would fill with holidaymakers, and guests would descend on the house from distant places in the north and south. They blundered through the rooms, sometimes meeting him on the narrow stairs, lost for words, their breath thickened by whatever they'd bought in the downstairs bar. They commented on the ozone and the view from their rooms; asked him what he planned for a future without once sounding interested in the reply.

Until October the attic room remained out of bounds to him, the guests preferring to stow their children there. After they'd gone he'd quickly lay claim to the place. It would be where he slept and studied, rising from his studies once in a while to stare out through the small porthole window set into the sloping roof.

Behind him, his bed crawled with darkness; he was blocking the light from the window. The oyster-coloured counterpane was neatly spread, spoiled only by the ruffled patch where he'd rested himself to put off his shoes. A bookshelf above the headboard bulged with required reading: *Fantasy & Science Fiction*, *Monty Python's Big Red Book*, which promised a free gas cooker with every other copy; a pile of *Record Mirrors*. Between the bed and the window, a small stripped pine table supported his typewriter. A blank white sheet was rolled into the platen.

The sheet was supposed to be covered with words: a thousand at least — that was the number this weekend's English assignment specified for the story they had to write. This one, he'd decided, was to be called 'The Change'. It would tell of a multi-limbed, multi-eyed creature which killed and consumed a young girl in a forest clearing and which later discovered the girl to have mystical powers which would gradually humanise it — would, if he ever managed to force himself past the title.

But today something was making concentration impossible. Something for which he had no name, and which gnawed like a toothache. Downstairs, his father was putting up shelves in the bar and building an extension at the back of the house — a double room with shower en suite to be ready for guests in the Spring season, he hoped. His patient hammering and sawing filled the morning with rhythms as it filled every Saturday morning; but Jim knew it well, it wasn't the thing that distracted him.

He looked out over Seaborough, but could see nothing to help him there. The porthole window faced out on a world of washing lines in back yards and tangled TV aerials above smoke-toned slate roofs. Past the roof-tops, past the chalk-white hotels clustered above the town, the streets declined sharply to the promenade. Today, a mist was unfolding from the sea, causing the trawlers and small fishing vessels to vanish. The minute blobs which were people in the streets were raising smaller blobs — umbrellas — above their heads.

Why did the incoming storm make him feel worse? For some reason storms always had. He turned from the window, took a pace into the room and stopped. Something or someone was slowly dragging the counterpane from the bed.

That was impossible, he knew. There was no one here but himself, and in any case an intruder would have to climb the last flight of stairs to the attic, stairs from which his father had stripped the carpet and underlay. The wooden risers would creak to a tread, and the creaks would rebound as echoes between the upstairs walls. No one could reach here without his knowing. The movement of bedclothes was only his shadow flitting across them as he stepped clear of the window.

Except that the shadow was far larger than his, not shrinking as he took one more pace towards it. Instead, rolling silently from the bed, it flitted to full height up the wall.

Jim glanced tentatively at the door, but that was no use. The shadow would be around and across it, quick as a spider, before he could move. A cry for help would be even less use: how could he expect his father to hear him above the chipping and hammering of work tools? 'What do you want?' he asked, as the shadow extended a hand and began to advance.

'You, of course,' he thought it replied, but he couldn't be sure what he'd heard. He stumbled backwards, one hand seeking purchase, thumping out rashes of meaningless consonants on the page in the typewriter. The shadow strode forward, darkening the bookshelf above the bed, darkening a poster of the Queen with a safety pin worn through her nose. Droplets of whatever composed it fell from the limbs, patting the carpet like fresh minted coins. For an instant he thought he could see the face, weeping and smudged as though bound in polythene, as though straining the limits of its form.

A chair went over to his left. Momentarily its legs tangled with his, and he almost fell. 'Please leave me alone,' he tried to say, but the uninvited guest had no ear for advice. The sloshing noises it made as it moved towards him were worse, he thought, than any appearance darkness could conceal. 'Please,' he repeated. Please don't – '

'If you won't come to us we'll come to you,' it said. The voice sounded waterlogged, almost a gargle. Downstairs the hammer had been traded for a drill. The shape loomed larger, feeling its way along the walls. What law had he broken to deserve this? Whatever it was, this silhouette, it existed in more than two dimensions, and had stepped from a fourth to claim him. It had gathered its strength from the four corners of this room; from places beneath the bed and the closet set into one wall where daylight never penetrated. Soon it would fill the room, it would reach him at the window, blot out the day; what would he be then?

If only the undersized window were vast and its light dazzling! Then the visitor would never have discovered places to hide and multiply strength. It stepped closer, increasing its size, clogging the oyster wall behind the small bed, which now looked the colour of pale, dead flesh. Now he could smell its breath – not fetid and death-filled as he might have expected, but salty, ancient. 'Come here,' it beckoned.

Coldness prickled the back of his neck. He'd retreated as far as he could, until his shoulders were lodged against the roof's acute slant. The first specks of rain were drumming above his head and against the glass of the half-open porthole. So the storm had arrived at last; even in here, in this retreat from the world, it had found him. 'Come to us,' the figure reiterated.

All at once there was no other course to take. Whatever reason he'd ever possessed had deserted him, his thoughts were as jumbled as the garbage he'd put on the typewritten page. If he stayed where he was the visitor would smother him, take him whether he resisted or not.

Hands outstretched, he ran directly towards it.

It disintegrated around him at once; rain hammered into his face as he felt the power dissipate. It gave with a sigh, a sound of escaping air. It drenched him, cascading across walls and across the surfaces of furniture. As the storm-coloured light returned to the attic he landed face down on the bed.

For a long moment he lay as still as he could, face pillowed, listening to the storm. Then he turned on to his side, raising himself with an elbow, hoping for normality, and finding it. The air was fresh and autumnal and salted; moisture glinted on the walls and dripped from a corner of the table on to the carpet. Above him the rain on the roof was a maddening staccato. That, and his father's drill thrilling through the walls, made him think for some reason of Cabaret Voltaire – phased electric instruments squeezed through Space Echoes.

More than this, he was reminded again of the ocean. She – why did he think of the ocean as she? – had been sending him storms for years now; and now this. He'd escaped this time, albeit narrowly, but what of the next time, or the time after that? He'd given up running long ago, for there was nowhere left to run; now he could only sit and wait.

Outside, the rain thrashed hard and thrashed angrily

down in the yards where the washing lines hung. As the downpour thickened across the roofs he knew precisely what it reminded him of. The applause of a thousand and more hands clapping; clapping in darkness, like the thousands of hands which applauded beneath the great dome in the Psychic Dance-hall.

eleven

She didn't regain her senses until she realised they were being stolen from her. If not for this sudden awareness, reaching her like some dim inner voice as she floated beyond the grey, she would have been finished. With an effort that rocked her whole body, she snapped back to herself. For an instant she was weightless, her lungs airless, her strength sucked out by the eyes. But no one would look twice when they saw the way her head jerked, the way her arms twitched: they'd probably think she was dancing.

Were they trying to do it to Jim as well, coax him out of his head without his knowing? Above her the huge screen flickered; twenty-five frames per second rushed past, too quick for her eyes to register. But her mind caught atrocious fragments: the shrivelled head of an infant; a man whose flapping limbs looked composed of roots; a dark burning city. No wonder the idiot dancers flung themselves about like neurotic drinkers. Their nervous systems were under siege. They were dancing for their lives.

The beat, she thought. The beat was poisoning them all. It couldn't control the chaos it caused, it didn't know how to stop as the bands had stopped in the film she'd once seen about Altamont. She remembered that someone had died there, at Altamont: as the music crashed to an impromptu close a young man had crossed the path of a blade. What must he have thought when he realised that the last thing he'd hear was the beat? Did this audience foresee the same violent and glorious end? Perhaps so Elaine thought; perhaps they'd inherited whatever legacy the dead man had left.

She was hemmed in by darkness, by the smell of the threat of further aggression. Only days ago she'd watched with dismay while the riots played out on the news; now she couldn't even feel dismayed, only numb.

'Jim!' she cried. It was important that he hear, but how could she expect him to when she couldn't even hear herself? He was glued to the screen like a TV addict in front of a soap, head nodding back and forth. Either side of him, boys and girls collided, airborne. Spray flew up from their brows and their plastered hair and froze in the greyish light. It wasn't until she began pummelling his shoulders with both fists that Jim turned and looked at her. At first he seemed hardly to recognise her, his expression one of distracted annoyance. 'Jim,' she mouthed, voiceless this time, touching his face.

Thank God, she thought then, at last. A flicker of recognition in the eyes meant something – meant he was fighting whatever held him. 'How long,' he shouted, 'has this been going on?'

'I don't know, Jim, but we've seen enough, both of us.'

He nodded. 'I was wrong, I shouldn't have brought you,' she lip-read. An elbow jutted between them, cutting him short, and for an instant she saw intolerance cross his face. 'Do you think you can find your way to the exit now?'

She was about to turn when she noticed the crowd parting some short distance beyond him. A handful of youths in black leather had fallen awkwardly aside as though they'd been pushed. Another disturbance, her instincts told her; she could only hope it was nothing so serious as she feared. She pictured spiked knuckle-dusters, Bowie knives, skewers: good God, where would it end? What she'd seen already tonight would haunt her for weeks, no doubt about that. Then she saw the three suited men picking their way across the dance-floor, between the dancers. They came forward purposefully, like bouncers intent on trouble-shooting, and something in their manner made her want to cry out. Perhaps it was what she glimpsed in their faces as the light washed across them.

She looked at Jim, saw him frown, saw he was unaware of what moved behind him. If only she had the strength to reach out, drag him clear of trouble, or the voice to make herself heard. 'What are you waiting for?' she lip-read, and before she could answer he was surrounded.

Jim looked at the men and then looked sheepishly at Elaine. He shrugged as if to apologise, but what did he have to apologise for? It was the gaunt-faced man who spoke first. 'Now's the time,' he might have been saying, but his moist pale lips worked like worms – impossible to decipher. His hand rested lightly on Jim's shoulder: a comrade's touch, but how easily might those fingers clench and rent like talons?

While the man talked, Jim responded with nods. He still hadn't emerged from his dream, by the looks of it. Finished speaking, the gaunt-faced man looked at Elaine and Elaine recoiled. Reflected in his mirror-shades she saw both herself and her double. Why did she feel his stare had marked her for something?

And what were these men to Jim? The blond-haired punk was gaping at her as if she were a prize he couldn't wait to carry home. 'It's time we were going,' she called to anyone willing to listen, and then realised the others already were.

Now the houselights were rising to a dim glow. The last song had ended, the party was over. Shoulders pressed into her, forcing her back towards the exit while Jim was escorted in the opposite direction. From where she was he looked diminutive, quite pathetic, but the fleeing crowd prevented her from following. She saw hands and arms reaching, whitewashed faces with nothing, no light, behind the eyes.

She was trying to resist the crowd, but had no more control of herself than a novice might have on an ice rink. A hand lodged between her breasts and shoved, and she narrowly avoided falling to be trampled. There was light in the foyer and the narrow space between the doors was bunching with fans; their mindless struggle making her think, briefly, of zombies she had seen in an all-night film show near Leicester Square.

She struggled to look back for Jim. He was far away now, and now even further away and very small. He was trying to tell her something — 'I'll meet you at home'? — but a hand restrained him. As the darkness blotted him out, one of the men, the one without a face, turned to glower after Elaine. That was her first impression. It took several seconds, long enough for the crowd to skittle her out through the doors to the foyer, before she realised the man had been smiling.

At least there was space in the foyer, though the entrance was as congested as when she'd come in. While a mass of red and green and blue heads dispersed, she paced a patch of wine-coloured carpet under the punk revival-revival poster. The carpet was all faded vomit and blood stains and made her stomach churn. Perhaps in a minute she would be unpleasantly sick; fair comment on what she'd just witnessed.

Now: she must think and think quickly, decide what to

do about Jim. If he was in trouble, then why had he bothered to apologise to her? Would the men have dragged him away if their business was wholly innocent? Maybe she should call the police, she thought, and then thought more of it: the streets were full of mercenary eyes, the cops wouldn't give her the time of day for something like this. Their hands would be full tonight.

Were the men something to do with the Cora exclusive? She wondered whether to wait until the dance-floor emptied and then follow. Nevertheless, she found herself heading in the opposite direction, towards the main doors. Better the street, the world of impatient traffic, than the darkened hall and whatever waited beyond.

Half running, half falling, the mob carried her out through the doors. From here there was no turning back: if she struggled, it would be with the wasted effort of a non-swimmer caught out at high tide. Their elbows buffeted her ribs, and she felt the keen scrape of bootheels about her shins, snagging her tights. At the bottom of the concrete steps she ran free just as, across the street, an emergency-stopping car sounded its horn.

Someone had run out in front of it – an angry young man wearing equally angry ripped and torn jeans. The driver shouted abuse, to which the rebel responded with a kick, leaving a dent in the car's offside door. When some of the crowd began cheering and the rebel raised his fists to the air for glory, Elaine turned away. She'd had enough of this scene for one night, and for ever.

The blaze of neon signs and passing car headlights on The Strand seemed as unworldly as the strobes in the Psychic Dance-hall, their brightness forcing her to squint as she ran, smearing the colours like flames. Soon she'd adjust, if she could ever adjust to anything in the real world again.

The pavement felt all uphill, making her legs ache mightily. It didn't help that she had no idea where she was running, except that she knew the Psychic Dance-hall must have a rear exit nearby. That's where Jim would be, if he hadn't already been ushered away. A dull pain made her glance down to a bloodied shin; a lamp-post rushed towards her, and she almost collided with it. Shooting out both hands, she managed to grasp its coldness to steady herself.

Behind her she heard football chants merging with traffic noise – Cora's name repeating itself over and over like a war cry. She was free of the audience now, although she felt little or no relief. Further on, where The Strand met Southampton Street, she stopped on the corner while the sleek dark outline of a limousine whispered past. The huddled shapes inside were indistinguishable as people, nor could she tell how many there were. She stood for a while, watching the limo into the distance on The Strand until its tail-lights grew soft as watercolours. Then she turned up on to Southampton Street.

As she rounded the corner, a figure advanced from a doorway some distance behind her. She did not see it, or she'd have spared Jim Doherty no more thought; she would have been sprinting in spite of herself. But she was far too preoccupied with her aching legs, with the ache which had spread to her chest and stomach, now to her head. She knew the back of the Dance-hall must be close, and she would crawl to it if she had to.

twelve

The Charing Cross platform was in darkness, the lights in the waiting train subdued. The compartments nearest the unmanned ticket barriers were a hubbub of private parties – fans from the Psychic Dance-hall, hymn-singing football supporters whose faces pressed the glass, staring out. Their smeared features made Elaine think of melting wax doll heads; none of their parties tempted her.

She had to walk the length of several carriages before finding a compartment to suit her. A meek-eyed college girl and her boyfriend, the slumped figure of a man dozing under a newspaper were all she could see: the many empty seats drew her in. Her heels had covered as much ground as she could face tonight, and now she needed to sit and take stock, let her body calm down.

The compartment looked like the scene of a brawl, with its cigarette-burned seat cushions and stubs on the floor, its crushed cans and plastic cups; even a discarded Lil-lets pack tucked half in, half out of an ashtray. Elaine took a seat at a window from which, if she happened to look up, she wouldn't see the young lovers embrace. Their closeness would only make her feel alone and neglected, no matter how sternly she reminded herself she was not.

She let her eyes close as a shudder ran through the train and the train wheezed clear of the station, but there was little chance of sleep before home. Sleep wouldn't come for hours, not until she'd heard from Jim, probably not for hours after that. He'd phone if he could, since he'd know her well enough by now to know she was worrying. Her fruitless search for the back of the Dance-hall had cost more than half an hour, but for all she knew Jim's had been one of the featureless heads in the limousine on Southampton Street. Who was to say he hadn't been spirited away to one of his after-gig ligs, that this very minute he wasn't plying himself with white lines and alcohol? Wouldn't that be just like him?

Between her closed lashes the city faded to grey, a thousand points of light swirling like motes of dust towards a vacuum. There was something hostile out here; something hostile and wild and unforgiving, from which she was running and had always been running.

'Sooner or later it will catch you,' a memory stirred, her father's voice boomed. 'As you make your bed, so you must lie in it. It isn't done, Ellie, not in this family. Not when I think of the years I spent trying to lead you right, trying to – ' He was talking about her decision to live with a boy, in London, with Jim. She'd never have mentioned it if she'd known it would cause such bitterness, but at the time her confession had seemed the fair thing to do. If she'd kept the news to herself he would never have known, since he'd always refused to visit the city, had talked of it often in hysterical terms: it was the centre of vice and lost souls and rottenness, all that was wrong with the world could be found there. 'If you must do this thing,' he boomed again, 'you won't come crawling back as soon as it all goes wrong. The wages of sin,' he was about to go on when the train lurched and brakes pierced her eardrums. I am not you, dad, she thought; if I sinned I'll take penance for my sins, I'll pay in my own way, but I won't take penance from you. Be damned if I will.

She opened her eyes, looked dreamily out on to Waterloo Station. A group of Rastafarians were sharing a joint and a joke in front of a timetable, their dreadlocks bunched up into red, gold and green woollen caps. Above their heads, rigor mortis had set the clock's hands at three-twenty. To the rear of the train some of the football fans were hurling cans and drunken abuse from their windows, much of it aimed at the Rastas, who only laughed louder. Safety in numbers: was that the only way to conquer this fear and uncertainty?

Waterloo drifted away to be replaced by a further tangle of lights and tall buildings. She settled, letting the train's rhythm soothe her, letting her fingers tap out its rhythm on the armrest.

Was this her penance then – the uncertainty, the fear of the nightmare which began in Finsbury Park and had refused to release her ever since? 'The wages of sin,' her father repeated, booming. No, it couldn't be, it wasn't as he'd have her believe. If she'd sinned at all, it wasn't her sin which had brought this upon her. The terror had been there before she ever met or agreed to move in with Jim, before she even came to the city. She'd known it before she knew sin, before she grew to understand she had once been innocent.

A tattered paper cup rolled towards her, making her start when it settled against her foot. At the far end of the compartment the young college girl sighed, and it occurred to Elaine how similar were the sighs of fear and of pleasure. Was that how death might sound; like an exchange between lovers?

What was she thinking of? First her father's counselling, now this. Why must she always suspect the worst? Stop slouching, back straight, chest out! She forced herself to sit upright, one hand brushing off crumbs from the seat like unwelcome thoughts.

Paranoid, Jim had called her, only days before the derelict traced her to the alley near their flat; and she'd replied that if paranoid meant knowing someone was out to get her, then that's what she was. After all, paranoia was perfect awareness, some said, with good cause. But there were perils in every town and city, and no reason to believe that it was her they were all conspiring against; or that any such peril had followed her on to the train at Charing Cross.

London Bridge arrived and promptly departed, as did the meek-eyed girl and her boyfriend. Nearer home the train began to swagger drunkenly, its rusted metal beat losing tempo. All along the track, houselights glowed in squat grey same-looking buildings, trees bristled forward from the blackened banks. As New Cross sailed past, a clattering impact made Elaine look up from her hands, which were folded firmly across her bag.

At first she thought nothing of it – a simple complaint of unoiled machinery or a frisson between two connecting carriages, a sound from outside. When she heard it again, however, she knew she'd been mistaken. It hadn't been a clatter so much as a breathless thump, a rustle of clothing. And it wasn't outside the carriage. 'The wages of sin,' her father boomed, but she quickly willed him to silence again. No one had followed her from the city. Nothing had accompanied her but her own pitiful imagination and the souring aftertaste of the evening.

In spite of herself, Elaine stood and rounded the seats for a clearer view of the aisle. The sliding partition door at the far end was locked open, the toilet sign above unlighted. All the seats were apparently empty. No one waited, nothing moved. She shivered, feeling a draught, and had taken one step back to her place when something came scuttling along the floor towards her.

It was a newspaper – the newspaper the man had been wearing while he slept. Perhaps he hadn't been sleeping at all, only pretending to. Where was he now then, since she hadn't seen him leave? She'd only half assembled the answer to that when the newspaper reached her feet and she glimpsed a headline on the front page.

SECOND CALL GIRL MURDER, it said. POLICE SUSPECT – but that was as much as Elaine saw before the pages scattered past her, turning over and over and into themselves before vanishing under a seat, out of sight. She could guess without reading what the police suspected. That the killer was punishing the sinful, he was coming for those who had fallen from grace.

All at once the panic flooded over her, bringing her close to tears. It had been threatening to do so all evening. Yet her eyes were too dry for tears; they were as dry as her mouth, dry as her swollen throat as she tried to choke up a scream. Who would hear it though, above the oblivious backbeat of carriages over tracks? The man had been hiding and not sleeping under his newspaper headline because he hadn't wished to be recognised; because he intended to finish what he'd started.

A sudden motion of the train threw her sideways. Elaine barely managed to keep her footing. Her chafed shin struck the base of a seat, returning a thrill of pain she'd nearly forgotten. She clutched at the headrest to steady herself. As she found her balance the lights faltered, went out. Jim, God damn you! None of this would be happening if you hadn't sold out to Cora! Couldn't you have told them, just once, where to shove their exclusives?

But it was too late for recriminations. Heat glazed her

vision as the lights came back on, throwing a veil over everything: the luggage racks, the opaque windows, the steady ascent of a shadow not her own. Across the compartment, near the locked-open door, a figure was rising to its feet.

She should have seen it coming. So much for perfect awareness. He'd kept such a low profile through the journey he'd made her forget she wasn't alone, and now he was going to finish her. He was going to make her regret it hadn't been over in Finsbury Park, where his breath had been stale and acrid in her face and had wafted the heat of cheap alcohol; where the broken street light above her had seemed, for a second, the last thing she'd ever see.

She mustn't let him come nearer, even if she had to jump from the train to prevent him — would the risk of injury be so great, anyway, compared to this? If she stayed where she was she'd be dead meat, no question.

The train lurched over an uneven section of track, prompting her into moving. Blind instinct swung her around and towards her own end of the compartment. Here, the connecting door was solidly closed. It seemed not to want to open as her hands tore at the handle; the rubbered buffer thumped shut several times before she squeezed through to the corridor.

She was facing the exit door now, and beyond its darkened glass was the world she'd so long been afraid to be part of. She'd gladly be part of it now, broken limbs and shattered ribcage and all: anything was preferable to this. A red warning reminded her not to open or lean from the window while the train was in motion. Ignoring it, she flung one hand into the rushing air, groped for the cold metal feel of a handle. Any minute now the partition would open and there he'd be, there he had always been, the man she'd been born to fear.

She closed her eyes as if for a last, hurried prayer. No time to apologise, only to beg for release: she'd have to get right with God later and God would have to take the offer or leave it. Her heart was in sync with the train, her closed eyes were briefly dazzled by strobing lights. There was the sound of a door some way behind her as she twisted the handle, took her first step towards oblivion. When she opened her eyes she was looking out on Lewisham Station.

The next door along the carriage was also half open. Elaine didn't wait to see who emerged. She stumbled down to the platform before the train had stopped fully, and set off. Her heeled, gripless shoes were as good as useless, trying to keel her over as she ran. She clattered across the asphalt with the shriek of brakes and slammed doors behind her, attacked concrete steps, trailed fingers across frozen bricks, felt bruising hands clench tight about her lungs, stealing her breath.

She mustn't look back, she wouldn't give the killer the satisfaction of seeing her fear. She staggered forwards while instinctively – stupidly, she realised – searching her bag for a crimped season ticket. It was a needless effort under the circumstances. No ticket collector waited to pounce at the empty barrier; there was no obstruction.

Footsteps, party chants, drunken war cries chased Elaine from the station. Outside, where the pavement declined sharply to the busy main road, a twenty-four-hour radio cab office glowed as warmly as a rustic inn. Salvation, she thought – either that or total hallucination. Two vehicles were drawn to the kerb in front; a gunmetal-grey Escort and a jade-green Datsun. A man perched half on, half off the Datsun's bonnet, smoking. As Elaine fell inside and slammed its rear door behind her, the man looked up, astonished. With a flick of fingers he sent the cigarette's orange beacon spinning away down the slope, and climbed in behind the wheel.

'Seen people in a hurry before, but not this much of a hurry,' his outline informed her. 'Where to, miss?'

Elaine told him, and waited for the reassuring kick of the engine. As the driver pulled out she shuffled around to peer through the rear windscreen. The rest of the passengers were leaving the station in one huddled group, some clapping out beats above their heads. She'd outdistanced them, but she needed all the leeway she could get.

'Someone you're trying to avoid?' the driver said, his indicator ticking off seconds on the dashboard. A convoy of HGV vehicles thundered by, moving air.

'You could say that,' Elaine said.

'I'll put my foot down if that's what you want.'

'If you would.'

She said no more. She was still preoccupied with the crowd of travellers; one man had broken the ranks and was jogging half-heartedly down to the radiocab office. Of course, he needn't rush, why on earth should she think he would? He knew the street where she lived, wherever she went he would find her. She'd never outdistance the killer, only forestall him.

The driver swerved out into traffic. A sequence of lights washed over Elaine as she turned back to face the road, green and amber and blue. She watched illuminated shop windows sail past, but they were meaningless to her, whatever they were selling belonged to another world. There was nothing more to be done: she'd reach the flat, call the police at once, and after that she could only wait out the inevitable. The cab driver accelerated from Lewisham. A red light came and went, and she began to think of Jim.

Far back in her mind she couldn't help resenting him. It was only this present crisis, of course, which made her do so; she wasn't seeing anything clearly. But she couldn't escape the feeling that he, no one else, was the cause of this jinx, this terror. He'd tempted her into his life — and she'd gladly entered it — but he hadn't been there when she needed him; not that night in the alley just streets from the North London flat, certainly not now when so much had come to a head. A part of her hoped the men *had* escorted him to trouble; perhaps that would sort his priorities for him. It was time he saw his obsession for what it was.

Furious with herself, she pushed the thought aside. It was draining whatever energy she still had, besides allocating blame where none was due. It was no more his fault than hers. A car horn brought her back to herself in time to see headlights at the rear windscreen. Their foggy beams filled the glass and filled the driver's mirror to a white burning rectangle. 'Get back, you bastard,' she heard the driver complain beneath his breath as the vehicle behind pushed closer.

'Is that one of your cars?' Elaine said, although it was impossible to tell and irrelevant to ask. She didn't need the driver to confirm it for her: there was no doubt that this was the other taxi, the one the killer had taken.

'Who's ever it is, it's too bloody close,' the driver said then, and she felt the Datsun surge forward, pinning her back in her seat. 'Turn here,' she said sharply as soon as she realised where they were. They'd reached Rushey Green, almost overshooting their junction.

'Right here?' the driver said.

'Right here, right now!'

The driver braked, fought the wheel, and momentarily there was the shriek and the biting smell of rubber. Beyond the car a carousel of amber houselights revolved. Ahead, the side-street looked empty − cars abandoned by their owners, no dogs flitting to and from gateways, a token party flying past like a Doppler effect. Elaine eased forward as the driver smoothed the car along the road, lumping both forearms on the back of the passenger seat. 'Now turn here,' she said only seconds before the junction appeared on the right.

He swerved the car, nothing said, no questions asked. He would curse her all the way back to Lewisham, she imagined. When she told him where to drop her, his emergency stop nearly flung her over the seat to the front. 'Do you live like this all the time?' he wondered while she rooted her purse for change.

'Only when I'm trying to stay alive,' Elaine said. She may as well tell him that much: no doubt he'd already written her off as an imbecile or a neurotic alcoholic.

Fussing a note towards him, not knowing or caring what colour it was, she stepped from the car. 'Your change,' he called after her, but he didn't protest for long. She was already on her way.

The street was silent, and as yet there was no sign of the gunmetal Escort. The telephone was only seconds away, one flight up, and she started towards it. Could she have been mistaken about the taxi that had followed her, or its passenger? She hoped so, but suspected not. Her driver had turned so suddenly the car behind had missed the junction; there was another just past it, and any second now she'd hear the motor speeding along it and the headlights would bleach out the street.

She'd reached the gate opening on to the overgrown path when she realised she should have asked the driver to wait and watch her indoors. Too late to call him back. She groped for the cool reassuring feel of her key and strode forward. The Datsun was already branching along the next side-street. It had passed out of sight and the sound of its engine faded when she heard footsteps crisping across the tarmac behind her. She glanced back in time to see a man running clear of a patch of darkness under a broken streetlight and coming blundering towards her. 'Please,' he was crying, his voice a dry and exhausted rasp.

The shock caused her to drop the key. No time to think; no time even for dread to overtake her. She fell to her knees, scooped up the key, thrust it towards the lock, through the dark. 'Please,' the man cried, reaching the gate. He was as scrawny and tragic as she remembered; a mere wasted derelict of a man, but deadly for all that. 'Please don't; I have to – '

Have to what? she wondered. But by then she was inside, the door securely slammed in the intruder's face. She had no intention of hearing the rest, whatever it was, however urgent he'd like her to believe it was. Feeling his weight shudder the door from the other side, she ran for the stairs.

Have to what? she wondered, taking the risers in pairs. Have to finish what I began six months ago? As if he felt obliged to ask permission! No, surely it wasn't so: that wasn't what he'd been trying to tell her at all. Too late she thought, the plea was an innocent one: I have to talk to you, he'd been saying. Please, you mustn't go in.

It was an understanding which reached her as soon as she rounded the top of the stairs and burst on to the landing; as she raced headlong, breathless, into the arms of the shadow that waited there.

thirteen

This is no limo, Jim thought, it's a hearse. No one had uttered a sound from the moment they left the Psychic Dance-hall. The faces of his companions were set like granite, like the faces of mourners at a funeral. For a fleeting moment he half suspected they were delivering him to his own.

As they neared Notting Hill Gate, Max Beresford brightened. The effort of smiling seemed to strain his features to the point of splitting them apart; it was a smile as treacherous and as insubstantial as his touch, his moist handshake. He was holding a small pale token between forefinger and thumb, placing it now in the open palm of Jim's hand.

'Try some,' he said.

Jim could just about see the object in his palm; pale and slippery to the touch, a texture of used soap. 'What's this?'

'A little something to put you in the right frame of mind,' Beresford said. 'Let's just call it Acid from Heaven.'

'Sweet as Death,' the platinum punk remarked with amusement. He was sitting at Jim's right on the wide, warm, leatherette seat; on Jim's left was the smear-featured man, his stubborn silence larger and darker even than he. Beresford sat facing on a flip-down seat. As passing headlights searched through the limo, his features took on the phosphorescent glow of a novelty mask.

'If you're taking me to see Cora,' Jim told him, 'I'd rather keep control of my senses.'

'Are you sure about that?' Beresford's tone was faintly mocking. 'You may think you know what you want but you don't.'

'If you're expecting me to drop this you're out of your skull.'

'Then why don't you join me?' This time, the smoothly modulated voice was firm and sure and its message unmistakable: this was no offer but a command. 'Seriously Jim, you're not telling me that you don't accept freebies? That your principles won't allow it? Come now, loosen up. Compromise a little.'

At that, Jim sensed a sudden pressure from both sides. Beresford's two henchmen were beginning to dig; combining their strengths they might splinter his ribcage if Beresford would allow it, and at the moment it appeared that he would.

He'd write something about Beresford for this, the worthless fuck. Under the circumstances it was the worst he could hope to do. Thinking no more of it, he popped the Acid from Heaven on to his tongue and swallowed. Though his mouth had run dry, the delicacy slipped down like an oyster, tasteless and fleshy.

'A little something to follow?' Beresford said now. The cork exploded before Jim could register what it was, and he flinched. Colourless light glinted about the bottle's neck and the frothing contents. A wafer-thin glass was slowly levelled brimful towards Jim's lips while the two henchmen sandwiched his shoulders, pressing closer.

'I hate champagne,' Jim said to Beresford. 'And we've nothing to celebrate.'

'But we have, or will have,' Beresford answered. 'Aren't you aware how privileged you are?'

'Didn't anyone ever teach you about press relations? I'd bring in some people with a lighter touch, Max, if I were you.'

Beresford laughed and began parting Jim's lips, then teeth, with the glass. Seeing no point in struggling, Jim accepted the drink, took the stem into his fingers, began to sip without interest. The pressure in his sides relented at once. 'A toast,' Beresford said then, and raised his own glass. 'To the Queen Bitch herself.'

'The Queen Bitch,' the punk muttered.

Jim was beginning to feel he'd wandered out of his depth — into what he couldn't yet tell. 'Tell me, Max, how does a nothing company like Monolith — an indie without a track record and no signed artist — come out of nowhere to do as you're doing?'

'Foresight,' Beresford said. 'It's a matter of reading the signs and seeing what people are really looking for. We happen to have found what they need. I'll tell you one thing for free, Jim: it's nothing to do with music any more; it hasn't been anything to do with that for years.'

'Then what?'

'Whatever fires the imagination. The image, the promise and the mystique; that's what draws them to Cora, just as it drew you.'

'Yes, but there's something more. Anyone can put on clothes and put on make-up and pretend to themselves they're changing the world. Anyone can get themselves banned to help sell a few records. But Cora has something more than that — a power, a glamour, I don't know what. I know she isn't a hype, Max, but what is she?'

'You really haven't worked it out for yourself?'

'I really haven't.'

Beresford sighed as though amazed at Jim's slowness. 'When you meet her you'll know,' he said.

A less than comfortable silence elapsed. The tattered remnants of this year's Notting Hill carnival gusted across the streets — torn-in-two banners, food wrappers, reefer stubs. A dark coagulated patch sparkled on a passing pavement, reminding Jim of the cop who'd been stabbed near here on the Saturday. At the time it had seemed an isolated tragedy; the potential for something of the kind existed as long as the carnival did. But now he could see the night of the stabbing for what it was — part of a far larger, far broader, far more unsettling scenario altogether. If the riots had not been co-ordinated — it was hard to believe they hadn't — then how could one explain what had happened in Brixton, at Oxford Circus, in Birmingham and Liverpool and in Leeds, all in a matter of hours? Was it as Derek had said, symptomatic of a nationwide sickness? What kind of sickness promoted spontaneous acts of aggression, such unity of purpose?

For an instant the torched man turned over in his mind and collapsed yet again, thick dark smoke rising in plumes from his cooking limbs; onlookers stepped hastily aside or retreated, as though he were no concern of theirs. A girl swathed in tartan scarfs watched from a street corner as the limo cruised around on to Ladbroke Grove, then hurried on to her bus stop.

They crept along a row of white-painted houses, the paint peeling away in chips and the steps leading up to their solid front doors guarded by youths on their haunches. Ghetto music prowled the streets like mist, a never-ending dread beat which gathered in every doorway, in every lighted upstairs room.

As the vehicle eased on to Blenheim Crescent, the platinum punk and the smear-featured man began easing themselves forward on the seat. 'We're here,' Beresford said to Jim as the limo pulled over to the kerb. To the others he said, 'Better search him now.'

Jim had no time to ask what was happening before they seized his arms. The door was open, and they were flinging him out to the pavement and the orange sodium cast of streetlights; shadows stretched themselves as his legs were spread, his arms wrenched outwards, his palms pressed flat to the car's roof. The smear-featured man moved hands up and down him, checking pockets, armpits, the seat of his pants.

'What're you looking for?' Jim demanded. His stupefaction was turning to a small compressed ball of heat in his stomach. 'Do you think I'm an assassin for the music press, is that what you think?'

'Just checking for notepads, micro-cassettes, that kind of thing,' Beresford assured him. 'It's only a formality, but we don't want anything recorded. In this business, there's no discernible difference between a typewriter and a gun.'

'Later,' Jim began. A dull ache was slowly insinuating itself at the back of his neck, though no hand had put it there. 'What's to stop me writing about all of this later?'

'Only your better judgement,' Beresford said to his back.

'I met a few cranky press liaison officers in my time, Max, but you're the fucking limit.'

Beresford laughed appreciatively at that – apparently his vanity knew no bounds and he'd taken the comment for a compliment. Finishing his frisk, the smear-featured man stepped back, allowing Jim to turn. As he did, the wash of streetlight threw the man's face into sharp relief, and for the first time Jim was able to see what was wrong with it.

The man's face was cauled; cauled as though the entire

head had been polythene shrink-wrapped, distorting the nose and lips underneath. The eyes were grey and filmy, the upper lids smudged like dabs of pale pink gouache. He was staring at an underdeveloped photograph, void of life, a face glimpsed briefly in an outfitter's window. He must have been staring long enough to lose himself, for he jumped when Beresford said, 'It's time to go in.'

From the outside the Monolith building was unexceptional. Above the short flight of steps a solitary camera eye surveyed all-comers, and a chromium panel embellished the door with the company name and logo. As Beresford raised his eyes to the camera, the electronic door-lock buzzed. A palmed hand in Jim's back steered him inside.

Thunderous rock music greeted him – *The Dark Brigade* piped between the wide pale walls of an entrance hall and foyer altogether too large for the building. A buff-coloured carpet led past a door on the right marked RECEPTION, past another, unmarked door towards the chromium shimmer of a waiting elevator. Beresford must have been reading his thoughts when he said, 'I suppose you were expecting to walk into a squat, weren't you? Appearances do deceive. Don't you agree that too much product is packaging; all gloss on the outside, trivia on the inside? I think you'll find Cora has something more substantial to offer than that.'

'What's this if not packaging?' Jim wondered, looking around him. As he reached the elevator the caul-faced man stabbed a button and then leaned back against the doors, expressionless. The platinum punk stood with feet apart and eyes unfocused. 'Too loud for you?' Beresford wondered as Jim clasped his hands to his ears.

For a second he could have sworn the music was something inside him, not in the elevator at all. His head seemed to be swelling with it, or was that the first rush of Acid from Heaven, or the alcohol, or both?

'You don't look too good to me,' Beresford said; his forefinger and thumb mused at the cleft of his chin. 'Are you sick or just nervous?'

'I'll be fine in a minute,' Jim said, though he couldn't believe he would be. The fire in his gut had released itself to his loins, his chest, his throat. Even his eyes felt as though tiny, immeasurably small fingertips worked behind them, exciting the nerves. It felt much like the start of a severe headache, a migraine. But he wouldn't let it intimidate him, not now, so close to the prize. The prize was too precious, and the Queen Bitch was waiting.

The elevator opened on to a pristine but sparely furnished corridor. The usual paraphernalia of record company headquarters was nowhere in evidence: no framed front pages from the music press, no wall-mounted silver or gold or platinum discs. From a company yet to release a record, Jim thought, that might have been asking a lot.

There was no doubt in his mind, though, that this was the heart of the place; he could feel the tug and tow of its pulse as they bundled him along the corridor. A series of sealed offices eased by him. His head thumped like a dull chipping tool each time the caul-faced man dug fingers into his back. With an irritable flourish, Jim thrust the man's hand aside. 'Do you think I need to be pushed into this?' His anger rose sharply to displace whatever qualms he had. 'Do you seriously believe I'd go out on a limb for this interview just to turn tail at the last minute?'

'That's the spirit,' Beresford cheered. 'You came to see Cora of your own free will, isn't that right, Jim?'

'I would have done, given the chance.'

Two doors faced one another at the end of the corridor,

and Beresford stopped outside the one on the left. A plaque on the wall beside it caused Jim to look twice: it was embossed with symbols and icons, hieroglyphics perhaps, or some strange new language. At the last minute, as Beresford turned the handle, Jim wondered aloud, 'Why me, Max? You said that Cora chose me for this, but why?'

'That's something you'd better ask her,' Beresford replied, and then Jim was being helped over the threshold. No one followed him inside. The others backed away sharply. 'Welcome to the machine, Jim,' Beresford said as the door shut him off from the corridor.

A latch clicked solidly behind him. There was no handle on the inside of the door, no point in beating against the woodwork or raising his voice in protest. This was, after all, what he'd wanted and waited for. No need to be edgy.

Then why was he trembling? It was only another interview, he reminded himself, although he knew it was far more than that. It was a secret to uncover, a phenomenon to embrace; the beginning of something he desperately wanted to be part of.

The room was white, with black-curtained windows. Apart from the warmth, which felt tropical, that was the first thing that struck him. Everything here was two-toned. The white shag pile carpet, the black leather furniture, the white drapes drawn across an adjoining doorway, made him feel he'd wandered into a monochrome photograph, or a negative version of one. The black-leafed trailers of exotic plants tumbled from a waist-high shelf and from a sizeable plant pot set into one corner. The walls were adorned with op art prints, white on black gashes and chequerboard patterns and maddening spirals which tempted his eyes to their centres.

As Jim stepped further into the room he heard voices. Or one voice: a muffled monotone, a man's voice which may have been Beresford muttering in the corridor or a nearby office. He stopped, listened, willed his crowded head to be silent for a moment and let him hear. The voice was not Beresford's, nor was it outside the room.

It was accentless, completely impersonal, and seemed to be trapped beneath waves of white noise. What was it saying, and to whom? After a second the static cleared. 'The role of the dreamer is to accept his dreams,' the voice asserted.

What on earth could the speaker mean by that? Jim looked frantically around for the source, but could see none. 'Silence is twice as fast backwards. Repeat: silence is twice as fast backwards.' Then, 'The mirror would do well to reflect again. Repeat – '

White noise cut off the rest. Whoever the words were intended for, they surely weren't intended for him. They were meaningless, they simply didn't connect with his world. He wondered whether the stuff which Beresford had given him had mind-warped him into hearing them. He'd once been accustomed to writing on amphetamines before he realised they only made him produce garbage, and lots of it.

Flustered, he skirted the room, touching walls, touching furniture, a prisoner testing the limits of his confinement. But the answer was close at hand: the sprayed black fascia of a hi-fi tuner nestled amongst a tangle of foliage on a shelf. The red stereo beacon faltered off and on as the static peaked and troughed. What he'd heard was a radio voice then, but which station?

At least the tuner explained something, but not enough. For instance, where was Cora? He couldn't wait and sweat in this heat much longer. He'd be damned if he'd tolerate much more of this nonsense. They'd forced him away from Elaine to bring him to this, forced Elaine to trek home alone to an empty flat, something he'd promised himself he'd never allow her to do. Where was the reward for all this trouble? If he managed to lay hands on Beresford as soon as this was over he'd show him the meaning of trouble.

He twirled the tuner's dial idly back and forth along the scale, but it returned only static. The stereo beacon flickered and went out altogether. He was still trying to decide what options were left to him when another voice intruded, 'Out here on the perimeter there are no stars . . . Out here we is stoned, immaculate.'

He recognised the voice in an instant; it came from behind him, and this time it wasn't a voice from the airwaves. He turned, adrenaline shaking his body, and stared across the room. She stood in front of the drapes, in front of the adjoining doorway which gaped towards darkness. As soon as he saw her he could feel his breath steal away, and after a lull it was Cora who spoke first.

'Pleased to meet you again,' she said.

fourteen

She wasn't as the media imagined her, and she wasn't what Jim had expected — but then, how could she be? She was flesh and blood after all, not the disembodied dream he might have supposed. At first that was what most surprised him: would he have been less surprised by a flickering image on a screen, with nothing behind it? If Cora was in any sense a dream, she was a dream made flesh. Nevertheless, he imagined that if he should touch her she would burn like ice.

'Again?' he said. 'Did we meet before?'

'At various times,' Cora said. 'At the show. And in all the times and places you visited at the show.'

She didn't elaborate, and it probably wouldn't help if she did. His memory was a blank tape; he couldn't remember a thing. When Cora smiled and her eyes and the surface of her skin became aglow, remembering seemed hardly to matter at all. She was a natural — her beauty neither loud nor self-proclaiming, but of a gentle, insidious kind which drew his eyes back to her again and again. 'If we're going to talk we may as well be comfortable,' she said, stepping forward. She went barefoot, he noticed.

She was real enough, but her arrival had brought a kind of energy to the room, an electric charge to the air. She wore a Lycra jumpsuit the colour of raven's wings; a zipper

137

descended from throat to crotch, dissecting her, making him
as acutely aware of her body as his, making him feel
inadequate. Her hair shone like gel and was swept back from
her brow and behind her ears. A solitary ringlet unfurled at
her forehead, the curlicue of an Egyptian priestess.

She settled on a leather sofa with one leg hooked under
her, the other extended to the carpet. Her toenails, like
her fingernails, were painted black. Patting the cushion
beside her she said, 'I won't bite, you know. You shouldn't
believe what you read. Or what you write.'

When Jim had eased himself on to the sofa she said,
'But I'm forgetting. Wouldn't you like a drink before we
start?'

'No thanks. I think I had enough on the way.'

'I imagine so. Did Max take good care of you?'

'He made sure I didn't get lost. For a minute there I
thought I was under house arrest.'

'Trust him. Sometimes he tends to be a little over-
zealous, but he means well.' Her voice had the slightly
grainy aspect of other singers he'd known, those who gave
all when they sang. 'I expected someone like you, Jim. Did
you expect someone like me?'

'I couldn't say what I expected. Maybe someone a little
more distant, an ice-goddess Garbo, perhaps.'

That seemed to amuse her. 'Well, that's what I'm not.
I'm none of the things the press would have me be. I'm
not a saviour or prophet or poet. And yet I'm all of those;
I'm whatever the people make of me.'

'In most cases I'd say they've made you into an idol,'
Jim observed. 'You're something they want and can't have,
so they worship you. Doesn't that bother you at all?'

'No. Does it bother you?' She leaned slightly towards
him, the light delicately brushing her cheekbones. 'Am I
something *you* want and can't have?'

138

Even if she was he'd never admit it. He faltered, studied his interlaced fingers. 'Let's just say I'm curious.'

'Ah, curiosity. Sometimes that can be fatal.' She laughed — a light, free, girlish laugh — and reclined again to a whisper of cushions and clothing. 'Tell me what it is you're most curious about.'

He might have given her a list, but said, 'You, me — this. You could've gone to the dailies if you'd wanted, or *Life* or *Time* or the six and the nine and ten o'clock news. You could've spoken to millions instead of thousands, but instead you came to me. Why?'

'Because the others are interested only in copy,' Cora told him. 'To them, I'm a story. And I know you're looking for something more. You want to be more closely involved, and I respect you for that. There's no longer any room for impartial journalism. What we need are bold new voices on the roof-tops, in the streets, in the media; and I'd like you to be mine.'

White noise intersected the silence. She was asking him to act as her spokesman, a tempting prospect; and yet something about the offer jarred within him. Was this the reason they'd brought him here?

'Suppose, after this, I don't sympathise with what you're doing,' he said. 'I still have to do a reporter's job. Why shouldn't I express my doubts?'

'You should.' Cora's eyes glimmered. 'But you should use your better judgement.'

'Meaning?'

'Know what you're up against.'

Her words, or the way they were spoken, sounded final and decidedly chilling. If only he had a cigarette! — but they were still in Elaine's bag, in the central zipped compartment. He would have to cope without. 'It sounds as though you're in this for more than rock-and-roll glory,' he said. 'As though you're prescribing a militant uprising.'

'I'm doing that,' Cora said. 'And I'm doing something a little more than that.'

'Then why not make your approach through politics?' There were already too many soapbox lefties strumming gut-stringed guitars, attaching themselves to the political woodwork like lichen. 'Wouldn't that be a more direct way of effecting change?'

'If we appeared to mortals in the guise they expected, it would make our task far more difficult,' Cora replied.

At first he thought he'd misheard her. Whatever she meant by that, it was enough to cut him off in midstream. Something in his chest seemed to resonate like a snare. He heard static waves rise and fall and a voice trapped within them, not his, not hers, saying, 'I can't change the world, but I can change the world in me. Repeat –'

'Besides,' Cora went on. 'I'm not talking politics in the sense you think, nothing so trivial as that. What we're communicating lies just beyond the spoken word; it can be sensed if not understood. No one *understands* the rhythm, or why it does what it does – we just know that it *does*.'

While she'd been speaking, the room had taken on a soft wintry glow, its walls distant, its hard-edged two-tones blurry and indistinct. Jim blinked, though the illusion remained. The Acid from Heaven, no doubt, he thought, but the sensation was now almost pleasant, he was starting to cruise. Had he asked another pointed question? He couldn't remember doing so, but he must have done, for Cora was saying, 'Can you imagine how many atrocities, how many primitive acts of violence pass through the minds of the so-called normal each day? Or how many visions of splendour? The problem, Jim, is that so few people externalise what's in them – they're resistant to change. Their thoughts are buried treasures. Their potential shrivels and dies inside. Even the radicals, screaming for upheaval, turn and run when they see what it is they've been screaming for.'

'I see,' Jim said, though he didn't at all. He was far too preoccupied with the light caught in the dark of her eyes and the glossy gasp of her skin. 'But what are you prescribing?'

'Whatever's necessary. I'm saying that for some of us it would be as well to be toting machine-guns as guitars. That's really another way of saying I wish our followers would prepare for a revolution, not dress for one.'

'It's still rather an extreme way of putting it.'

'But Jim, we deal in extremes. Someone has to. You don't liberate men from their worlds, from their boxed-in, shrunken little lives, from themselves, unless you have something more than love songs to sing.'

Jim faltered as the walls rotated slowly about him. Would he be able to recapture this later? He wished there were a tape he could rewind and study before going on. 'You're talking about liberation, but what kind?'

'The kind you're experiencing now. From inside to out.' Could she sense what was happening to him; indeed, had she planned it this way? 'Nothing will change unless the people themselves are changed; a corrupted vessel in a corrupt world is worthless. To build a new state you first have to *enter* a new state – physical, mental, everything together. It's difficult at first – for some it's impossible – but you must give it time, Jim, you must give it time.'

The sickness, he thought. The sickness of which Derek had spoken as the riot shields formed a wall in Brixton. Had Derek welcomed it because he was already part of it? 'Looting, burning, gang warfare, the annihilation of order. Is that where you're leading us?'

141

'That's a part of it, but only a part.' She spoke calmly and matter-of-factly, without a tremor. 'You have to remember that order comes only through chaos. Those of you who've prayed for chaos will have thought no further than that. But see how the anti-establishment radicals run? Last year's subversive is this year's TV ad for hairspray, right? They're trying to resist what's happening to them, but the violence has always lived in the hearts of men, even in the supposedly well-adjusted. It has to be purged before the new vessel is complete, and once it's out it's out.'

She'd barely finished speaking when the dizziness rushed forward in his head, a capsule of air in a spirit level. He stood up sharply as if to catch it before it could escape – too sharply in fact, and the effort almost slewed his legs from under him. He hadn't realised how dreamy Cora's voice had been making him; her talk seemed to have drained all his strength. 'Don't fight it,' she said now, or he thought she was saying, but noise – a blur of static and electric distortion – drowned out her words.

He tipped forward and landed on hands and knees on the soft white carpet. In its way, his posture seemed oddly appropriate; the proper way to acknowledge the Goddess, down on all fours in subservience. There was no pain now, no threat of nausea or migraine. He was floating pleasantly on a calm sea. Who cared where the interview went from here? She'd soothed him, removing his discomforts. Of course he would be her voice; he'd serve her as he'd always imagined he would. Why should he have considered doing otherwise?

He noticed, as he raised his eyes, that the black-leafed plants were in flower. Pink fleshy buds nestled beneath the leaves and pock-marked the stems where the stems tumbled forward into light. It was probably the plants – it could hardly be anything else – which gave out such a sweet,

142

meaty fragrance. Though he hadn't noticed when he'd entered, the delicate scent was now unavoidable, whetting his appetite. He blinked as the room slowly turned.

'I think he's ready,' Cora said.

There was radio noise and a commotion of movement as a door was thrown open across the room. He glanced up to see Cora standing, and rounding her towards him were Beresford's henchmen. Beresford stood behind Cora. The room was mellow and soft, its stark tones merging to grey.

The punk and the caul-faced man caught him up to his feet, where he wavered unsurely, the carpet miles below him. 'There's no need for that,' he told the caul-faced man, whose stiff bony fingers were clenching his arm. He was perfectly capable of fending for himself. The fingers tensed again, though they brought no pain. His marshmallow senses made everything soft, remote as history. 'Take him inside,' he heard Beresford say, and then Cora said, 'Gently – don't harm him. He's special.'

His heart went out to her as they dragged him to the draped doorway. She was, after all, going to change the world. Why should she bother with him? 'You heard what she said,' he told the punk, forcing a smile. 'Don't damage the goods.'

They stalled in the doorway while the punk swept aside the drapes and nudged the door open. The adjoining room was in darkness; a muted phosphorescence burned somewhere inside, but from here he couldn't make out the source. 'You've been overdoing it again,' Beresford remarked, mimicking Elaine's voice. It was a fairly passable impression. 'You know what happens to people who backslide, don't you?'

'They return to their own vomit like dogs,' Jim said. For some reason he found that fitfully amusing. It was one of Elaine's father's favourites, that simile. 'I never could resist an exclusive though, Max. You know how it is.'

'Are you comfortable?' Cora said to Jim, and to the others she said, 'I think you'd better prepare him now and then leave.'

They steadied him forward into the black. What were the henchmen doing now, their hands fussing so precisely about him? They were working to loosen his clothing, that's what, undoing shirt buttons, undoing cuffs — and why shouldn't they? This was, after all, the great rock-and-roll mindfuck and, besides, the cloying heat was unbearable. His clothes were mere distractions, trappings he was better free of altogether.

Behind him, a zipper slowly ground or unground its metal teeth. Cora was readying herself for him. When the men tugged Jim's jeans and underpants to his ankles, he was surprised to find himself already at half mast, as though the gathering hardness were nothing to do with him. In his mind he felt no such eagerness; his body, by the looks of it, was better prepared for action than he. Seconds later the men were padding silently away and he was alone in the room with Cora.

'At last,' she sighed, her voice the mildest disturbance of air in front of him. 'Are you ready to come to us now?'

The sourceless light illumined a bed, whose taut clean sheets looked stretched like skin across a drum. He backed towards it as Cora advanced, nearly tripping over his bundled clothing. His jeans were still wrapped round his feet, and he absently kicked them aside as he moved. 'Us?' he wondered. 'Who do you mean by *us*? Who are you?'

Not that it mattered now he was close to the moment. He could feel the tempo increasing again. She was squirming from Lycra as a butterfly from its silken cocoon; shadow and light described the perfect geometry of her, emphasising slopes, shading valleys. Now she was helping him backwards and down through space and on to warm sheets. She settled over him, arms and thighs parting. Her breasts were like doves, and he was afraid for an instant they might suffocate in his hands. As she encircled him she said, 'Now you know who I am. I am the revolution. Repeat: I am the revolution.'

Darkness curtained the rest of the room, a darkness so complete the walls might have been miles apart, or tens or scores of miles. The space was anechoic, like a recording studio: as he touched fingertips to her body, note piled on note, distorting guitar pick-ups swept across uprighted mike stands. 'I am the revolution,' Cora repeated, and feedback bloomed, and noise overshadowed everything else.

'At last,' she murmured. At last his affair with the beast was to be consummated. He'd loved her before he'd known her, before he'd known she was in the world, and he was finally bedding the great whore, the Queen Bitch, as so many before him had done. She was turning him around and inside out, transferring her heat to him. She moved back and forth above him and then lowered herself, breasts crushing against his chest, her skin like vinyl and glossy as shrink-wrap in a supermarket. By comparison he was unremarkable – white and awkward, many boned, a body which restricted him, made him useless.

He gasped, placed open mouth to her flesh, tasted salt and salt-sea air, tasted blood. This, the warm and dark salt-sea blood, was the taste of her revolution. Its colours were red and black and shades in between. He should taste it and toast it and drink to it. He should embrace the danger as long as it wished him to belong to it. As she took him, one firm hand guiding him to the heat between her thighs, he sensed he was entering death.

That was the rock-and-roll game, of course; to flirt with danger and with death. The kick was to flirt, the trick to emerge from death untarnished, but this was far beyond flirting. In a moment's euphoria it occurred to him that this was the hit he'd been searching for with amphetamines, with booze, with all the paraphernalia of dangerous living. He bit into Cora's mouth, drawing blood, tasting and swallowing blood. A sweet pain took hold as her nails scoured his flesh, leaving tracts. She worked over and around him, her body clenching and then releasing him like a soothing hand, sapping his strength only to replace it with her own. She rocked him to the beat. Massed applause urged her on.

He saw colours mute and stars fall, felt deafened by colliding electric sounds, heard a voice like white noise whispering, 'Now we are one', heard primitive Afro acoustic rhythms and numberless palms patting down on stretched membranes and steel tom-toms. As the unstoppable rush possessed him, the face above him shifted into the light, and he saw that it was his own.

It was only a fleeting impression. Nothing lasted here, everything moved with such haste towards the end, from which there was no retreat. He blinked away the apparition, reached up to her face, touched a dewy softness too supple by far to be flesh or have bones.

A paroxysm seized him, and he was already jerking into her when he saw that Cora's face was hardly a face at all. It was too late to check what he was doing, but her mask was coming slowly apart in his hands. Her breasts, so full a moment ago, were sacks of white dead meat; her face was moist and as featureless as a slug's. He closed his eyes as the mouth opened, spilling its contents.

Now he was blind as well as deaf. He'd discovered her secret, the secret which had swallowed everyone else. He'd been fleeing this revelation for years, and perhaps because of that he'd always been pulling inexorably towards it. He'd remembered, finally, where they had met and why he'd needed to find her again. She was his very own Future Now.

He felt himself come and go, and his body slacken, and the soft weight above pressing him down into the bed of raw flesh. Beneath him, the sheets were tacky and coagulating with sweat and with blood: his blood and hers; the blood which her revolution would let. Radio voices thickened the air around him, repeating, repeating as a fusillade of drums and guitars and other sounds faded.

'The death of my cock gives life,' Jim Morrison, a dead rock hero twenty years removed by history, had said. Was that the exchange they'd made here − his stamina for hers, his life for her death? That, he thought, would be the roughest trade of all. Tonight he'd lost his virginity for the second and final time.

Something seemed to implode in him then, and there was only the salt-sea breath in his face and a tangle of foreign long-wave voices, shipping forecasts. He sensed Cora's weight lifting itself from him to roll clear of the blood-warmed bed. He thought, as his head cleared and his breathing grew even again, that what he'd been hearing all along was the sea. At times, it sounded uncommonly like static between radio stations, or like thousands of palms applauding in darkness. He was sure that the minute he opened his eyes he'd be back at the Psychic Dance-hall again. But when he opened his eyes he was not.

fifteen

The first thing he knew was that he was no longer inside the black room. This wasn't a place of voices and spoiling flesh two floors high above Blenheim Crescent — but then, had it ever been? Still thick with sleep, he turned on to his side and faced the small square uncurtained window several feet beyond his face. Outside, a crescent moon was snared in the tree's tangled branches, the forked tips of which scraped the glass. A booming bass riff downstairs helped him gradually awake.

Propping up pillows, he forced himself upright in bed. The sheets were damp and bonded to the hair of his loins and legs. Though his lungs felt heavy with dust, he was aware of a thick, now unpleasant after-sex smell whose meat-sweet fragrance reminded him for some reason of the black-leafed plants in the dream.

It had been a dream of course, hadn't it? Traces were still swirling behind his eyes like an Edvard Munch painting of a scream. It seemed too vivid, too real altogether to be anything other than memory. But whichever it was — vision or afterglow of some unthinkable act — how could he explain his being here, at home? He must have passed out at some point during the evening, and had been brought here by Max Beresford or possibly even Elaine. He only hoped it wasn't Beresford, that would almost

149

certainly mean the nightmare, or parts of it, were true. Surely not even a liberal dose of Acid from Heaven could account for such visions?

A plateau of bedsheets beside him described Elaine's sleeping form, patched with moon. There was a pang of guilt when he considered what he might say when she woke. She couldn't have known, but in her way she'd feared and tried to warn him about Cora's régime, and now it seemed that her fears had been justified. In search of greater and yet greater stimulus, he'd jumped Cora's bandwagon only to lose touch with everything he held dear. He'd stepped into something more intricate, more deadly, than even the street-fighting men had forewarned.

For the first time he was able to see, truly see with Elaine's eyes, how futile his position was, how senseless his quest. This whole shabby business had made him a moron; potential H-Bomb. And tomorrow, or the day after that, he was going to walk clear of it. He'd straighten himself out, raise his sights, turn his back on the r'n'r scrapyard and leave the rest of the pickings to the scavengers.

He turned and twisted towards Elaine through the dark, planting the softest of kisses between her shoulders, so as not to disturb her. The damp sheets clung to his chest and stomach as he shifted. Elaine did not stir, or emit breath, or sigh from the drugged depths of sleep. He rocked her gently by the shoulder, trying to coax a murmur from her, but the only reply was a straining of bedsprings, a sigh of linen.

Something was amiss here – she had always slept soundly, but never so silently. 'Elaine?' he said, and there was only the papery hush of his own voice coming back off the walls. His voice sounded no more alive than the tree at the window; it belied his concern. Groping for the bedside, he put on the light.

The bed on which they floated was a crimson lake. Warm red-brown estuaries clogged folds in the sheets and flowed down from the edges, on all sides, to the carpet. For one white silent second, Jim could do nothing — could not move, could not cry out. The room swam around him. One bright red hand went to his mouth, cupping it. The pulsing heart of this mess was the figure beside him, Elaine in her death's bed scene. He did not want to, but an involuntary rush made him pull back the sheets.

Elaine had been butchered. Whoever had done this had not merely set out to steal her life; they'd sent her out of this world as if determined to deny her even her looks for a passport. She must have been glad, in the end, to go free of her body, if only to escape its steepening layers of pain; but there was no coming back to it now, there was no use left in it.

Suddenly he could not look, he was too close to vomiting. He threw back the cover and thrashed his way clear of the bed; the sheets cleaved to him as he did, the carpet sloshed underfoot as he made for the bedroom door.

He was trapped in a dream, a dream which Cora had been spinning about him from the moment he had first laid eyes on her. None of it was real; he mustn't believe it or his sanity would leave him as a note from a tuneless guitar. Only the nausea was real — he'd only have to retch and the vision would end. But there was no time for anything to end or settle in him. He'd already burst into the lounge, hammered on lights, picked up the candlestick telephone receiver.

Once he'd dialled for emergency he realised it was the cops he should be asking for. There was no life left in the bed along the landing; an ambulance would be a pointless request now. Staccato clicks dogged the line, and he heard cross-connected numbers ringing and numbers being

151

dialled, wafer-thin voices mumbling. He hadn't managed to gather his thoughts when his connection came good. At the far end of the line a receiver was being lifted, and someone was saying, 'Hello, Jim.'

Although his nerves were shouting, he recognised Cora's tone instantly. He wasn't surprised by it, for surprise was beyond him now. In one stroke she'd shattered his security into small glittering fragments — to hear her now, so close, was only confirmation of that.

'If I were you I'd think twice about who you tell,' she said. 'You're as much a part of this now as I am.'

II

The Enemy Within

Texas Chainsaw Massa-cree
Took my baby away from me

– The Ramones

sixteen

In the bathroom, a stranger returned Jim Doherty's gaze from the silvered, toothpaste-flecked mirror above the sink. Naked, the stranger stood uncertainly on his feet, arms dangling loose at his sides. His ribcage was visible, his face blotchy and stubbled, the skin drawn too tightly across the bones. Jim baulked. How long had he been here? How many days had eluded him to make him so weary and yet so sleepless?

Having turned on the cold water and doused his face, shaken glittering beads from his brow, he felt no better. Briefly he visualised an insect, a spider perhaps, running loose in his brain, skilfully weaving a network of new and impossible thoughts. As yet the creature's work was incomplete, but its completion would enlighten him in ways he'd never thought possible. Soon he'd understand everything — why Elaine had had to be sacrificed, why even his body was turning against him. Until that time, he was helpless.

The scent of death hung over the flat. Nothing had changed in the bedroom and why should he expect it to have done? Elaine — what remained of her — was exactly as and where she had been before; a coagulating mass trapped half in, half out of the tangled sheets. One pale arm hung from the bed's edge, fingernails just fractions above the carpet's nub.

This time, he stepped no further than the threshold. Sooner or later he would have to do something about her; he would have to enter and retrieve his clothing from the floor, but not yet. He still remembered too well the bubble of blood her last breath had formed at one nostril, and he couldn't contend with that yet.

Pulling the door to, making sure the latch clicked firmly, he went to the kitchen, made coffee. When the kettle had switched itself off he stood listening to bird song and distant light traffic. As he did, a tingling, glowing sensation began slowly to rise in him, exciting the nerves at the base of his throat, the pit of his stomach, his balls. He was in possession of something almost terrible in its beauty, some strange and archaic gift perhaps, which had still to reveal its full purpose.

Suddenly elated, he laughed aloud. Goosebumps prickled his arms and chest. Perhaps this was how a woman with child must feel, all at once acutely aware of what had always been possible. So he was pregnant, a small miracle occurring inside him; but pregnant with what?

In the living-room, he sat cross-legged on the floor in front of the TV, the coffee cooling in the cup at his side. He studied his hairless chest and spindly arms and his small, shrivelled penis. He seemed to be shrinking back into himself, like a fearful child, retreating from the challenge of living.

The TV informed him that three days had passed, but was it possible to retreat so far in so short a time? It was as if daylight had never reached him, as if all his years had been spent above Seaborough, in the small attic room whose porthole window refused light. The skin of his forearms looked pale and transparent, beneath which a maze of lavender-blue stations connected, and traffic rushed, and fluid pumped. 'You're evolving,' he

156

remembered Cora saying, and instinctively he glanced at the telephone. The phone was ringing. It rang twice and then stopped.

The lines were jammed, or the atmosphere was playing havoc with them. Since the first day – the day he had tried dialling emergency – there had been only one incoming call: Martyn Sheppard sounding busily irate as usual. 'You're late,' he'd said as soon as Jim picked up the phone.

'Late for what?'

'For work, for everything. Most of all for this week's deadline. Do you mind telling me what's happening with the Cora piece?'

'It's coming along,' Jim had lied. 'It isn't as straightforward as I thought.'

There was a short muffled silence before Martyn said, 'Not straightforward? You spoke to her, didn't you? That sounds straightforward enough.'

'There were complications,' Jim began, and stopped himself short as something lurched in his stomach, a cartwheel of pain or uncontrollable pleasure; lately, it was nearly impossible to tell the difference. 'I can't explain now, Martyn. I should've called in sick before. I'll have to get back to you.'

'You do that. One last thing though,' Martyn insisted, and Jim heard a feverish intake of breath on the line. 'What was she like?'

'Something else.'

What more could he have said? He'd been duped, the piece would never be written. Indeed, the interview itself had never been the issue – it had only been Beresford's rather theatrical way of trapping him – and in all likelihood Cora had never intended her words to find print. To make her as real, as accessible as that would be to cheapen the legend somehow. After the hype, anything she might say would naturally seem final and dead.

As he toyed with the television's remote control a Russian woman gave slow-motion birth underwater; an old man whose face had turned yellow and mauve spoke from his hospital bed of the youths who had beaten and robbed him; a girl no more than eight or nine chased a dragon alone in a quiet backstreet. Madness held everything balanced in its palm. The day had begun with bird calls, but with what would it end?

He was trying not to think of Elaine, but every TV image seemed designed to remind him of her. If he could only believe what he wanted to; that for Elaine it was not an end but a new beginning. But she'd been stolen away before her time, nothing could alter that. Not even this condition, this feeling of newness and euphoria, could alter that.

Jim coughed dryly into a fist and his swollen throat complained; he would have wept if he hadn't been so utterly parched. Images rushed at him on the TV screen — infants being born dependent on junk, afflicted by incurable diseases; thieves stripping central-heating systems from houses in order to support their habits; riots breaking in Islington and in Camden and Hackney, further north in Leeds, in Liverpool, on Tyneside. Death moving north like a low pressure zone. Families dividing, children bleeding, old women weeping, shops boarding up their windows forever. All of these images from the world. The atrocities went on. The supply of new terrors was endless.

Enough, he thought, and got up sharply. His coffee went over as he marched from the room. Somehow he had to pull himself out of this; he was behaving as though the Acid from Heaven had never worn off. He mustn't submit so easily, that was just what Cora wanted. It was only his body that registered these new, bracing pleasures, but hadn't he learned his lesson yet? Where pleasure was greatest, there was death's pull at its subtlest.

At the bedroom door he hesitated, working the handle slowly back and forth. He resisted an impulse to knock before entering, as though at any moment Elaine would sit up from sleep to welcome him. He stepped inside, trying not to look towards the bed, gathering his clothes from the floor and from chair backs. Two scraps of paper fluttered to the carpet as he unhooked a jacket from behind the door. One was a weeks-old cinema ticket; the other, which had landed face upwards, read plainly: *Jim, I'm going to ruin your life as you ruined mine.*

He dressed hurriedly outside on the landing. His body felt aglow, but at least he was starting to see clearly again. Nothing Cora could say or do would convince him he was responsible; he'd woken with blood on his hands but that was as far as his guilt extended. Why should the Queen Bitch intimidate him?

Throwing on his jacket, he returned to the bathroom. He closed his eyes, counted to twenty, and eventually urinated. Flushing the toilet afterwards seemed a wasted gesture, a single point of order in the midst of chaos. This time he avoided his own ghosted self in the mirror. He didn't bother to wash his hands. Readying himself with every step, he headed for the telephone in the living-room.

An instant before he came through the door he realised he'd blundered. What he should have done was thunder downstairs and outdoors without so much as a backward glance. The room was tainted, its light heavy and oppressive. Motes of dust of an indefinable colour floated, trapped, in the pillar of daylight between the curtains. At the far side of the room Cora's face filled the TV screen. The image shimmered unsteadily as if through a smouldering heat haze. She saw him, he knew, at least as clearly as he saw her. Like the storms he had always feared and yet somehow belonged to, she was returning to claim him again.

'You don't mind if I come in, do you?' she said, and advanced. A dusting of TV snow fell from her like stars; as she entered the room Jim sensed the air around him expand and contract rapidly. Behind her the TV screen flickered and went blank. 'I couldn't let you desert me,' she said quietly. 'After all, there's so much you've still to learn.'

'I can't believe I had anything to do with what happened here,' Jim said. 'I've decided not to take your advice; I'm going straight to the police about this.'

Cora shook her head, half amused. She began to pace slowly back and forth in front of him, maintaining a close arc. Perhaps this was a tactic meant to pressurise him, to make him feel like a suspect. 'Do you really think that's so urgent,' she said, 'when what really matters is that we've found one another?'

Jim looked at her, bewildered. Her cool stare was draining his confidence.

'Don't tell me you've forgotten our first night together so soon,' she said.

'No,' he said. 'No, I haven't. How could I?'

'You wanted it to happen for so long. So did I, even before we met face to face. If you had but known it, I was close to you all those years, Jim; now we're closer than ever.'

She was speaking as though she had feelings. But she was a murderess, remember, and like everything else about her this lover's role was not to be trusted. He'd test her then; he'd finish the interview here and now. 'When were you ever close to me?' he wondered aloud.

Cora smiled, her eyes glimmered. She said, 'Remember a trip to New York, long ago, maybe a year and a half ago?

160

You'd hired a car for the weekend, you and the PR from Chrysalis, the one who was paying your way?' She stopped pacing and took a step nearer, and he sensed the cold inevitability of what she was going to say. 'Remember taking the wheel when you drove down to Philadelphia, and taking drinks of bourbon from a hip flask and speeding? Don't you remember who sat beside you, speaking to you in low tones, begging you to go faster, *daring* you to go faster?'

Jim nodded soberly. It had not been the Chrysalis girl, who had slept in the back through most of the journey. Yes, he recalled the day and the quality of light and minor details, such as which songs the FM stations had played towards noon. He'd always assumed the voice he'd heard had been his, however.

'Perhaps then,' Cora said, letting her fingers stray to his cheek, from there to his throat, to the buttons of his shirt. His flesh came alive at her touch; she was caressing him inside and out. 'Perhaps you remember the evening right here, in the city, when acquaintances of yours began fixing up after supper. You watched them heating up spoons and dividing the junk into neat little lines, and you felt yourself growing afraid, thinking No, I've tried everything else, but this is one step I won't take, I won't go that far —'

'I remember,' Jim said. She now had the front of his shirt half unbuttoned, which strangely distracted him hardly at all; it seemed to be helping him think more clearly.

'No one dared you or forced you,' Cora was saying. 'All that was needed was the squeeze of a hand and the softest voice. Someone to tell you, Once will make no difference at all; you only need try this once for experience. Remember who shared the needle with you that night?'

'I remember.'

Cora looked at him, her eyes not leaving his as she gently unzipped his jeans. 'So few get to know me as you're getting to know me,' she said and smiled, perhaps appreciating her own words in the Biblical sense. 'We're evolving together, Jim. We're exchanging something which, frankly, money can't buy.'

Scarcely able to contain himself, he pawed at her, blindly, smearing her face with both hands, seeking her breasts through her clothes. 'Slow down,' she told him. 'There's always time.' She was watching him fixedly and without expression, her lips slightly parting. What did she feel, if anything? He winced as she raked her nails down between his left shoulder and right hip. After a moment, blood filled the trenches she had scored. She began moving over them with her tongue.

No, he thought, as the pain and pleasure became one. It was such a small word, uttered in a voice soft enough to be lost beneath his own thudding heart; but the voice was clearly his own.

'You're becoming like us, Jim,' Cora said, 'just like Elaine. There's nothing to gain by standing against the inevitable. Elaine belongs to us now. Wouldn't you like to be with her again?' She was supporting him towards the door as she spoke. The door was open, the darkened landing lay ahead. 'Now we'll move through to the bedroom,' she said.

'No,' he retorted, withdrawing slightly.

She looked at him, not a trace of warmth in her face. Whatever it was he saw there now he wanted no part of it; her desires were entirely divorced from his own. What she intended, he realised now, was something forbidden; an act he hardly dare contemplate.

'We'll move through to the bedroom now,' she repeated. 'And after, we'll decide what to do with her.'

seventeen

Carolyn sat on the edge of the bathtub, mouth pressed firmly into the back of her hand. All around her the tiled walls swum, replaying the faint rustle of her breath until she could no longer bear the sound of it. She rocked back and forth, nursing the pain in her gut. Although this wasn't her time of the month — that had been done with a week ago — something told her she was bleeding inside. After what Derek had done, she wouldn't have been at all surprised.

He'd made her bleed from the nose and mouth too, by the looks of it. Raising her head just slightly, she studied the scarlet imprint her lips had made below her knuckles as if it meant something. Absently she dabbed at her face with a handkerchief and found that the flow appeared to have stopped. Her gums still smarted though, as did her eyes, from crying. This time there'd be no kiss and make up: things had been worsening between her and Derek for weeks, and this was the limit; this was the kind of weird shit that made headlines. For the first time in her life she knew what it meant to know fear. She knew, for instance, that if she unbolted the bathroom door, however carefully, she was dead.

Carolyn dampened her handkerchief with spittle and began to work at the red on her hand. A silence had stolen over the ground floor and over the rest of the house, a silence her ragged breath emphasised. Fifteen minutes ago, Derek had finally stopped cursing and buffeting the door from the other side, and his footfalls had faded away. Soon afterwards the dull hammering above her head, in Elaine and Jim's flat, had stopped too. The noise had been present all morning, but it was only when it ceased that she noticed it. It could have been the hi-fi, even if the beat seemed too designless and clumsy for music; more likely it was floorboards being prised up or laid down. If she could just forge a way past Derek, catch him unawares for a second, she might stand a chance of reaching Elaine or Jim, or both. All she needed was Derek to make a noise of some kind and she'd be able to locate him, visualise where he was in the flat.

Instead, silence. Sitting upright, she worked hard to regulate her breathing. Even her lungs felt clogged with blood. She looked wearily around the bathroom, but there was nothing here to defend herself with; not the loofah for sure, nor the soft sole of her one remaining flip-flop. She kicked it off with a sigh. A window would have helped enormously, something to scramble through, but the downstairs bathroom was an afterthought in the building, plumbed in during the great upheaval when the landlord had divided the place into two separate tenancies. It wasn't made for daylight.

Carolyn crossed to the medicine cabinet and opened it. No cut-throat razors, nothing but small, anonymous bottles of outdated capsules, a pack of Richard Branson's condoms, a bottle of Anaïs Anaïs, one of Aramis, a dozen miscellaneous ointments.

She wondered whether Elaine had witnessed a similar change in Jim recently. She must have done, if her suspicions were correct and Cora was in some way responsible for this lunacy. Jim was closer to the scene than Derek. Surely that made him more susceptible. She must warn Elaine. She could only hope Elaine had had the good sense to take notice of her previous, barely coherent warning; if she'd heeded it herself, acting upon what she'd feared, she mightn't be in this fix.

Twenty-three years, she thought, and slammed the cabinet door shut. Twenty-three years of peace, love and common-law marriage had brought her to this. It was more a bad trip than harsh reality. Had the bliss always been illusion, or had she always been as utterly, achingly alone as she felt this moment?

Suddenly and without warning she felt the tears wanting to come again. She took three paces to the toilet, flipped down the lid and lowered herself on to it, facing the door. The glamour poster which hung there was Derek's: a pouting, dark-haired girl in an Airtex vest held the zip on her jeans half open, promising to go even further. The image had never struck Carolyn as particularly erotic so much as deliberately knowing, a bold wink. But she still objected to the poster's situation directly opposite the loo. It was almost an invasion of privacy. Something as insidious as this had touched a raw nerve in Derek, loosening a quality in him she'd never known he possessed.

She sat perfectly still, waiting. Her hands clutched at her knees, her bloodied handkerchief floated down to her feet. She sniffed and made a face, wondering whether she really smelt smoke and, if so, where it was coming from. Then she understood why she was tense. Derek was stirring beyond the poster, padding about between the rooms. She moved to the door and settled against it, listening. A series of blows upstairs shuddered the walls and the door panels, making it impossible for her to hear.

She gritted her teeth, tried to focus on the movements

outside. After six or eight beats, the noise upstairs obligingly ended. If Derek would only go into the bedroom and close the door firmly and stay inside long enough for her to move. If only something would happen to remove this dreadful uncertainty. Then she realised that something *was* happening. Derek was charging the door.

The first impact rocked her back on her heels. She couldn't be sure she heard a splintering of wood, but Derek's whimper of pain was unmistakable. He would injure himself rather than let her remain in here. 'Carolyn,' he said quietly.

'Leave me alone,' she said, drawing her fingers into fists. The words hurt her tender mouth. 'Let's end it right here, Derek. Peacefully.'

'That's what *I* want,' he said.

'Then go.'

This time it was Derek's breathing, not her own — a dragged-out, asthmatic rustle she had never heard before. She pictured him standing on the opposite side of the door, stroking the varnished wood with both impatient hands. The wheezing sounded heavier now.

'I don't want to hurt you,' he said finally.

'Really?' Indignation swallowed her fear for a moment. 'After what you've already done? I think you've damaged me, Derek. Inside,' she said.

'That wasn't me. I didn't mean . . . I couldn't help . . .' This time, the voice outside was barely recognisable; more a confused gargle than a voice. 'You have to understand that what happened before — was a phase I had to go through, a doorway. I'm only glad I didn't hurt you any worse than I did. But I think I'm getting better now, I really do. Carolyn?'

'Yes.'

'I'm sorry. God I'm so sorry.'

Carolyn stood watching the door. The brunette pouted. She wanted more than anything else to believe what Derek was saying; wanted to be able to pull wide the door and face him, accept his apologies. Wasn't that what he wanted too? 'After what you've done,' she said, 'I'm not sure I can let you in.'

'I want a peaceful settlement,' he insisted.

'Don't make things any worse now, Derek, please.'

She wondered whether the lull meant he was contemplating a new angle or striving for breath. At last his reply came, softer and, she suspected, further away than before. 'Can I call you?' he wondered. 'Maybe we could meet on neutral ground to discuss this. I was hoping, just hoping you might accept me as I am, here and now, but maybe that's asking too much too soon.'

He was retreating further, taking soft steps away from her. She heard him say from the tiled kitchen, 'I won't push it. I'm not going to ask you to do anything you don't want. I understand how you feel. I love you, Carolyn,' he finished, and the sentiment sounded sincere and true; only the old Derek could have voiced it, and she had to suppress a sudden urge to chase after him, her heart ruling her head.

She heard the door between the flat and the hall closing softly, and after a relevant interval the main house door slammed. She closed her eyes as she fingered the bolt, her whole being seeming to contract, pounding, around the place where her thoughts were. If this was relief, it wasn't relief enough, and she needed a friend very badly. Taking one deep breath, she unlocked the bathroom and looked out.

A short, narrow passageway connected the annexe with the rest of the downstairs flat. Straight ahead lay the kitchen, its door half ajar; to her right, the lounge and bedroom, both stubbornly closed. Rusty smears the colour of blood marked the walls on both sides. The worst was on the bathroom door itself, where Derek had tried to force a way in. What damage had he done to himself, or tried to do?

Should she try and catch up with him after all, and telephone for an ambulance? A sharp twinge far up between her legs told her she could use one herself, come to that. Thank goodness he'd sounded fairly rational when he'd left: half an hour earlier he might have been capable of acts which would make an ambulance call irrelevant.

She strode half-way along the hall before halting abruptly. The linoleum floor was marked too, but not as the walls were marked. This wasn't a random smearing of hand or footprints but a smooth, unbroken trail, as if a seeping mass had been dragged from the bathroom as far as the kitchen. Keeping to one side of it, she took another step forward. An abstracted beat began again upstairs, startling her into motion. She stumbled into the kitchen.

Derek was there, leaning back against the tumble dryer, regarding her with calm, almost bovine eyes. His long frayed hair had been pushed rather than brushed back behind the ears, and his cheeks were flecked with minute drops of red. In his right hand he held an empty wine bottle by its slender neck, but his left arm looked worse than useless and sagged at his side. Surely he couldn't have done this while attacking the bathroom door? His shoulder was either missing or pulped, judging by the way his shirt had collapsed on that side. A stain spread darkly below it, between armpit and waist, and where his shirt was torn open at the midriff a solid blackness gleamed like snail skin.

'Oh no love, you're not alone,' he said. 'No matter what or who you've been . . .'

It took Carolyn several instants to realise the words were not his own. He was quoting flatly from 'Rock and Roll Suicide', knowingly or otherwise.

'Let me go, Derek,' she pleaded, starting forward.

His gaze fell on the door adjoining the hall just a fraction before her step took her towards it. He moved around to block her path, dragging one paralysed leg behind him.

'All the knives seem to lacerate your brain,' he murmured, still quoting, and waved the bottle. 'I'll help you with the pain.'

Twenty-three years of good vibes and good grass had not readied her for this. He was about to do something drastic, and it wasn't consistent with his philosophy of life, that was for damn sure. She saw the row of kitchen knives sitting in their rack above the sink, and dodged towards them.

'Why bother?' Derek wondered. 'I'm already going out in a blaze of glory.'

Glory, she thought: what glory? 'If that's what you want you should be out there with your friends in the mob, tearing the city apart.'

'That's where I will be,' Derek said, all too calmly for her liking. A bead of water divorced itself from a tap and landed in the sink. 'It's what I've always wanted, after all. It's the only thing that ever brought me out of myself. Are you sure you don't want to be part of the new age?'

'I'm sure.' She chanced a further movement to her left, towards the knives. Derek slid awkwardly around in front of her, at the same time swinging his good arm violently outwards. The bottle dashed against the work-top, spraying lethal shards across the kitchen in all directions. Derek was left holding a jagged stem.

'Please, Cal. I'd like us to be together.'

'Not like this.' The smoked-glass door was too far away,

and even with Derek incapacitated she doubted she'd reach it. The stainless steel knives shone lustrously on their rack, but had lost their appeal. She could feel herself deflating, the will to resist escaping her. 'She did this to you,' she whispered, thinking aloud. 'Didn't she?'

'It was for my own good,' he reflected, straightening up. She stared, fascinated and appalled, at the glossy blackness peeping between his shirt buttons just above the belt-line. Then Derek said, 'You'd appreciate it too, if you gave it the chance. Cal, do you remember the first time we dropped acid together? How we spent the day walking around Little Venice in the golden sun? How we broke into one of the empty houseboats and made it inside all afternoon? How it felt?'

Carolyn looked at him, venturing nothing.

'I think this is going to be better,' he said.

'No shit, Derek.' She could have struck him for that; for stomping over their shared treasured memories, pretending that what he'd become could ever compare with what he had been. Zoe had been conceived that same afternoon; she had been both conceived and delivered while together they sailed away, mind-warped on LSD. To think that after such beginnings, rage had swallowed Zoe out of their lives and returned, still hungry, for Derek.

'It would be better still if you'd join me,' he prompted. He must have been reading her mind, because then he added, 'You, me, and Zoe. What a threesome we'd make!'

'You won't have me too,' she said. 'I'd rather . . .' She was about to threaten him with suicide – I'd kill myself first – but under present circumstances what manner of threat was that? Suddenly she was afraid again, shamefully only for herself. Death was no escape, not if this sordid scene was what it amounted to. All options were closed. Fresh tears burned her eyes.

'Please don't hurt me again,' she said.

'No, I won't do that.'

He smiled, and his features appeared to settle, and she noticed a momentary flicker of decision in his eyes, a sudden presence then, just as suddenly, absence again. 'I love you, Carolyn,' he repeated, and smiled. 'Strawberry Fields forever.' Raising the shattered bottleneck to his face, he began to carve into himself.

Carolyn's first, involuntary reaction was to scream. The kitchen acoustic enlarged the sound, making it vast, fanning it outwards around her until she felt dwarfed by her cry. She covered her ears with her hands to cut out the noise, but was still unable to close her eyes. The fluorescent bulb faltered vaguely overhead. A quick pale light stuttered about Derek's flesh as he worked the serrated glass across both cheeks, around below his jaw, then upwards and into his mouth. The dark red flowed generously now; and beneath the surface, wherever his flesh parted, she saw the same hard, glowing blackness waiting. He wasn't so much destroying himself as making way for what had developed within him.

Too much, she thought, it was really all too much; just too Sid Vicious for words. Self-mutilation as the latest word in rock-and-roll hedonism. She wouldn't stay for another second of the performance.

He barely knew her at all now anyway, and he certainly didn't need her to go on with him. He was all the audience he required as he collapsed to his knees, not knowing her, still carving. She stepped neatly around him and around the pool he was forming, and was gasping for breath as she reached the door. Short painful clucks somewhere between sobs and shouts worked her throat. She couldn't be sure what she was trying to express, but words would never have put it better. She looked back

171

once before slamming the door after her. Once was more than enough.

She ran along the hallway, which her tears had unfocused and formed into soft muted colours. Everything seemed to waver at the wrong end of a lens. The front door tempted her straight ahead, but instead she turned to her left, up the stairs. In any case where would she go if she went outside; to whom would she run and tell?

The stairs drew the last of her breath. The air was suddenly thicker here, and she caught the edge of a fragrance she'd smelt earlier – not smoke but dust, perhaps plaster dust, and perhaps something else as well. She could hear the telephone ringing above her, and someone moving about in Elaine and Jim's living-room. Please, oh please! Whoever was there would help her get a firm hold of herself, show her exactly what she should do. As she reached the top and turned left the loose strip of landing carpet shied away underfoot.

She'd come this far almost to fall straight down again. Steadying herself against a wall, she moved on towards the ringing phone. Why didn't someone answer it? It didn't matter; she had reached the end of the landing, and was about to knock when Jim appeared at the living-room doorway, holding the door open no more than a foot.

'Oh,' he said. He looked wary. At first she couldn't be sure he recognised her. 'It's you.'

'Jim.' Dragging for breath, she cupped a hand to her breast to soften her heart. 'Jim, I need . . .' But what did she need? It was impossible, still, to purge herself of the words. 'It's Derek,' she managed.

'What about him?'

The telephone was still ringing and, past his shoulder, the air in the room looked chalky. Then this was where the noise had been centred all morning. 'Is there some

172

reason I can't come in?' she wondered, at the same time brushing past him and into the room.

She'd taken him unawares, as the room wasn't furnished for company and his attempt to stop her came a fraction too late. By the time he'd seized her sleeve she was already inside, looking speechlessly upon a residue of death.

Jesus God, she thought, and covered her mouth. What on earth had been let loose here? The living-room hearth had been topped up with rubble — piles of red bricks and brittle mortar, mounds of fallen soot from the walled-in chimney. Everything had been plundered out, then partly rebuilt. Old bricks had been salvaged, new mortar mixed. Here, too, was the fragrance she'd been unable to identify until now: the indefinable aroma of the dead. Far back in the recess was Elaine, propped in a sitting position, her pale head resting on her shoulder. She was half extinguished from view by the first two feet of new wall. Had she also gone out in a blaze of glory? Carolyn doubted it.

'Oh Jim,' she said, and found herself unable to speak or think further. 'Oh Jim, why?'

She only noticed the hammer because he was swinging it at her in such a wide, lazy arc. The blow chipped open a silent grey hole in her mind, deep and wide and fathomless, and she promptly entered in without further thought. If a second blow fell, she knew nothing of it. She knew virtually nothing at all, and her one remaining thought as she began the descent was a half-formed hope: that someone would answer the fucking phone.

eighteen

Jim let the hammer fall. It landed with a leaden thump he hardly registered. What he heard, instead, were sounds crowding in from the borderline of sanity — autumn waves breaking across a pebbled shoreline; hammers becoming hands becoming drums on a jukebox which never stopped, never ran out of new songs.

He let the hammer fall. It landed on the thin carpet, the faint reverberation a reminder of a distant, more physical world. He suspected he'd belonged to that world once, but of course he now belonged neither to one nor the other. He straddled the two, having stymied mortality; that at least was something he'd gained from the interview.

He blinked twice, listening to the thunder of waves, tasting the lightly salted spray for a second before the sensation faded. He saw the room again, the daylight excluded, its walls crawling with dust and decay. It was like the aftermath of the worst amphetamine party in the dowdiest squat he had ever attended. Time passed before he was fully aware of what he had done, and what he was still supposed to do.

In the centre of the floor, between the hearth and the ringing telephone, Carolyn lay spreadeagled on her back. She murmured once, and her head rolled to one side and settled. One hand slid limply from her ribs to the floor.

Jim put his fingers together as if readying himself for prayer, and felt the tenderness of new blisters rimming the palms of both hands. He stepped back, away from the hammer. He couldn't look towards the fireplace, for he knew what spectacle would greet him if he did. Habit, or perhaps only the need to mobilise himself, made him turn and collect up the telephone.

'Hello?' He was in no fit state to talk to anyone yet, but having started the ball rolling he repeated, 'Hello?'

'Jim? Jim Doherty?'

'Yes, speaking. Who's this?'

'I know what you're involved in,' the man's voice said flatly, so flatly it might have been speaking directly from the void. 'I saw them bringing you to your flat.'

'Saw who?' Jim's fingers whited out around the telephone's earpiece. 'Saw who?'

The line stuttered, and Jim found himself closer than ever to prayer. This morning's euphoria had passed as quickly as it began; in its place there remained only a deadweight sense of loss, of being neither one thing nor another. Whoever had promised to ruin his life had certainly honoured the promise spectacularly. Surely there couldn't be worse to come: this must be the barbaric end of it, not the beginning. 'Who are you?' he wondered.

'Please don't go any further with what you're doing,' the man advised, ignoring the question. His voice remained calm, firmly controlled – perhaps too firmly controlled, as if he were containing a scream. 'I know you've done . . . something you wish you hadn't,' he said. 'We've all done things we regret.'

'Would you mind being more specific?'

'You know what I'm saying. You wouldn't have listened this far if you didn't.'

There was laughter outside in the street, below the drawn

curtains. It faded when a car door slammed, and a radio turned on to a crash of white noise and a Cora song.

Jim said, 'I don't understand what it is you want. If I've done something wrong – if you're the law or something –'

'I can help you,' the voice cut in. 'I think we can even help each other. That's what I want.'

After all that had happened he could hardly trust the man, at least not so soon; but what more could he lose? 'All right,' Jim said. 'Just tell me how.'

'Well, we'll have to talk, but not like this. We should meet. At nine, say. Have you a pencil and paper?' Jim kept one beside the phone. The man finished dictating the address, in Soho, and said, 'Quickly. Whatever happens between now and tonight, make sure you're there. Don't let her do anything to prevent you.' He was rushing breathlessly on, without his former composure. A series of pips – he was calling from a pay-phone – dogged the connection. 'If I don't meet you there myself, someone else will. probably someone you know, who'll recognise you.'

'And you,' Jim wondered before the man could hang up, 'are you also someone I know?'

'I'm the one who sent you the letters,' the caller said.

Jim was still clutching the receiver when the dialling tone returned. He set down the telephone and moved around to stare out between the curtains, repeating the man's last words to himself, under his breath. Should he assume that the caller and Elaine's murderer were one and the same, then? That would connect him with Cora and Beresford, the Monolith in-crowd. For a moment he was tempted not to attend the meeting, which was surely another trap, though there was really no question of his not going: he had no choice. The man knew his name, and had implied that he knew much more. Chances were that he did; and what could he, Jim, provide in return? Where was his own security?

In the kitchen he picked up and put down several sharp, not-quite-sharp-enough knives; stared at a steak hammer for almost a minute; eventually settled on a silver skewer, eight inches in length and drawn into an elaborate loop at one end, a lethal point at the other. As a weapon, it hardly compared with his typewriter, which had always allowed him the privilege of cutting and thrusting anonymously, without fear of direct reprisal. But this involved personal risk: it was intimately physical. Its sole advantage was that it was easily concealable.

When he slipped the instrument into his pocket, it was as if he were conceding that he must go all the way, that the chips were down. Already one lay dead; probably two, if Carolyn's condition matched her appearance. How many more innocents had Cora swept before her? How many?

It was hard to believe, as he stepped outdoors, that what he was leaving behind was real. The South-East London street was a model of propriety, everything in its rightful place. A bald-headed man hosed down his car, whistling, while a cat leapt from a dustbin to a wall, startled by a closing or opening door. Had nothing been touched here at all? Did they sense nothing, fear nothing? Perhaps it was better never to know or care what was happening under the surface, or what was about to. Just don't let them find out, he thought. Don't let them answer for what I've caused.

He set off towards the bus-stop on Rushey Green. Overhead, the rushing clouds promised an end to the humidity, or at least a reprieve. A woman pushing a loaded shopping trolley turned to stare accusingly after him before turning in at her gate. But that was understandable; she probably saw no deeper than his appearance, his unclean clothing and hair, and judged him according to that. If only she knew the whole truth though, he thought bitterly, and continued on, hardly aware that with each new step he took his body was raising the tempo.

nineteen

He spent much of the late afternoon wandering in a daze from one West End street to another. Eventually he found himself slumped in a Haymarket cinema, attempting but failing to concentrate on the captions in a new European film. The actors seemed preoccupied with small things; small by his current standards, at least. Presumably there was much that was worthy about the film, but he was heartbreakingly separate from it, unable to lose himself. While the end credits rolled, he thought of Elaine, and hoped no one saw him red-eyed when the houselights came up.

He emerged into dusk and a rash of coloured neon. A light rain had fallen, and reds and greens flecked with blinding silver whiteness trailed over the streets and pavements before him. He was vaguely aware of traffic creeping along beside him as he set off to Soho, and of pedestrians running indoors to fluorescent fast-food places. They all moved in groups, or at least pairs. Everyone but him seemed to be with someone else.

Several windows on Shaftesbury Avenue had either been taped together or boarded up, and across one the letters F-U-C-K were sprayed almost flippantly. He turned on to Brewer Street and soon became lost as the sights and smells enfolded him, guiding his senses.

Night collected in all the doorways he passed. Litter breezed in the gutters. A jumble of music and voices swirled ahead of him, always ahead, never quite near enough to be tangible. As he rounded a corner a woman's stare nearly stopped him short. She leaned from a ground floor window, beneath which steps fell sharply away to a basement. 'Hello,' she said dreamily as soon as she spotted him, and put her hands together. Her thick make-up emphasised her age. 'Looking for company?'

All his best lines had deserted him. Tonight he wouldn't have been able to use them on her with conviction anyway. He hurried on as if he were easily shockable, slowing almost immediately when he saw the youth who was waiting for him.

The youth didn't seem to notice him at first. Pale-skinned and dark-haired and all in black, he leaned against an iron railing three basements along, smoking. His body looked rigid, too affectedly stiff to be a pose. Just tense perhaps, or half dead or, judging by the deep, furious draws he was taking on the cigarette, both. Closer, Jim realised he knew the youth. There was a slack-mouthed arrogance about him that was hard to forget, if not easy to place. As he approached, the youth looked up, startled.

'Jim,' he said, and tried to smile. 'Bloody hell, what happened to you? You all right?'

Jim nodded. 'I've seen better days.'

'Same here. You remember me, of course?'

'The face, not the name.'

'The name's Danny,' the rebel said. 'I used to do *Killzine*.' Licking his lips, he scrutinised what remained of his cigarette, then tossed it into the road. '*Used* to, I say, because the bitch stole my gift. She's taken so much away from me.'

There was no need to ask who he meant, but Jim was

nevertheless baffled. 'When we spoke earlier, why didn't you tell me who you were?' he asked.

The rebel looked at him, the lines taut across his face. 'No, that wasn't me. I didn't phone. The one you want is in there,' he said, indicating the basement above which they stood. At the foot of the concrete steps a door stood solemnly closed, and above it an electric sign – disused or broken – said, Shaman's Bar.

The name was enough to stir memory, and at once Jim knew where he was. A wave of nostalgia swept over him. The basement had been a makeshift rock-and-roll venue until the ownership changed hands in the late eighties. As a freelance for *Alter-Image*, before he landed the staff job, he had served several nights of his apprenticeship here writing three-hundred-words-a-throw reviews for the live pages. For groups still cutting their milk-teeth on the nightclub and pub circuit, Shaman's Bar had at that time been as necessary as The Marquee or The Nashville ten years before it. In more recent times, he had heard of it only in connection with illicit gambling and drug trafficking.

Danny led the way down the steps and inside. As they entered, set faces looked up in far-flung corners of the bar, in alcoves and booths. The years had not been kind to the place. Little had been done to upkeep it, and the immediate impression was one of dust swept into corners, of foul money tainting the air. Half the clientele looked like faded hookers. The old stage, no more than knee-high, was now a platform on which unused chairs and tables were stacked. To think The Fall had played here once, and jazzmen from James White to Courtney Pine; and look at it now.

At the bar, a man lolled on a stool and studied the depths of his glass for meaning; or perhaps only to remind himself how much beer he had left. His head moved in a slow, docile circle, like that of a novelty dog in a car's rear window. Danny held up a palm to prevent Jim from reaching into his pocket. 'No sweat. What's money anyway?' he said. 'You can't take it with you, right?'

Jim watched the bartender measuring out the whiskies, both large, and wondered, 'Where is he? I'm not sure I can take much more of this suspense.'

'Give me ten seconds.' Danny smiled, a little knowingly, Jim thought, and drummed his fingers on the bar. Perhaps he and Danny were in this, whatever it was, together. It was virtually impossible to see Danny conspiring against him — his face was too plaintive, his manner too nerve-wracked for that. Across the bar, someone had selected a yesterday hit on the jukebox. By the time Jim had remembered the vocalist's name, the drinks had arrived.

'He's in one of the back rooms,' Danny said, lifting both glasses from their ring marks. He took a hurried sip from one and handed Jim the other. 'It's all right. I know the manager. We can have the room all night if we want it.'

He started around the bar and towards a sign for the toilets. Past it, a passageway led between two facing sets of twin doors, and towards darkness beyond. The walls were faded, ochre, with square and rectangular ghost-marks where paintings or posters had been removed. The second door on the right was half open, and a dim light burned within. Fear and fascination welled up in Jim's chest all at once, and he was forced to steady himself, gasping for air, before following Danny inside.

The best that could be said of the room was that it lacked character. It was purely functional, emptied of anything that might distract the eye or the mind, or come between the cards which were dealt here and the men who gathered to deal them. Even the wallpaper had been stripped clean, the walls skimmed over with colourless matt paint. The only attraction was the small, circular table in the centre around which half a dozen chairs were drawn. The low-powered bulb above it had at least been blessed with a shade.

While Danny closed the door, Jim stood watching the man who had half risen from the table to greet him. The man's bony hands rested on the table-top, an untouched vodka or gin placed between them. As though the effort of getting up had exhausted him, he settled in his chair, gesturing for the others to sit. The haggard look, Jim saw, stepping closer, wasn't confined to the man's hands but extended to his sucked-in cheeks and pale, veined temples, to his frame inside his filthy clothes. Yet he wasn't especially thin, he looked neither anaemic nor undernourished. Just thinner, Jim realised with a shudder, than he ought to have been.

Suddenly he wanted to leave. There was a faint precognition of discovery, a horror of knowing what he would rather not know. He groped for a chair and sat, eventually finding the man's eyes across the table. In a moment he would place the stranger, put a name to the face, and know why his features should have been fuller and his eyes brighter. Was this the one who had slaughtered Elaine; the one who had made it his life's work to threaten and persecute? He considered, fleetingly, the skewer pushed deep in his jacket pocket. It seemed an embarrassment to him now, an idea he could push no further. This man, the one who had threatened to ruin his life, looked in every way a victim, not a perpetrator.

After a moment, the stranger's stare fell from Jim's. He moved one forefinger over the table, tracing a circle in the dust. 'Do you know me?'

Jim waited until Danny had joined them before

answering. 'I thought I remembered you from somewhere. You obviously know who I am.'

'Let's say I have a vested interest in your case. For a long time, I've been watching you.'

'And writing to me. That's what you meant when you mentioned the letters, isn't it? The threats?'

The stranger looked to be searching within himself for a hiding place. Lifting his drink, he took one trembling sip. 'Strange as it may sound, one of the reasons I wanted you here was to apologise,' he said. 'Right now, well, an apology must seem the least appropriate thing . . . But I'd like you to hear the whole story.' He glanced as if for guidance at Danny. 'There's so much to explain.'

'Perhaps,' Jim said, 'if you'd tell me who you are. That would be a start.' Wanting and yet not wanting to hear, he was surprised to find that he felt nothing for this man; not even hatred, least of all pity.

'Cigarette?' the stranger said, testing his pockets, flustered. Discovering a crushed box of Camels, he removed three and passed one to Danny, but Jim declined. 'Everyone's hooked on something,' the man smiled.

'Some of us are trying to cut down,' Jim said.

'Or even stop?'

'Even that.'

A match was struck and a blue-grey cumulus of smoke soon settled over the table. When he had taken one draw from his cigarette and one more sip from his glass, the stranger looked directly at Jim and said, 'It's about time you knew. It's gone too far as it is; everything's out of control now, anyway.' A burden of years seemed to have accumulated in his face. 'For as long as I can remember I've been wanting to get you, to hurt you – wanting to . . .'

'To ruin my life as I ruined yours?' Jim pre-empted.

'Exactly. And I was wrong, I know, I'll freely admit that. I wanted to punish you for something I *thought* you'd done to me. I'd convinced myself you were the enemy,' he said, and tapped his chest lightly, 'while the real enemy was in here all along. We were on the same side and I never — never knew it.'

'In case you thought you were the only one, you're not,' Danny asided quietly to Jim. 'When we met for the first time he thought *I* was to blame.'

The stranger went on, 'It was just that I needed someone to take to task, because of what I was turning into. Like yourself, Danny was such an easy target — we'd bumped into each other in a pub and he handed me a cassette, *The Dark Brigade* bootleg. You know all about that, of course, and what it can do.'

Jim nodded. His chest tightened. 'Think I'll take that smoke after all.'

'But it isn't the *cause*,' the man said. '*The Dark Brigade* simply releases what's there. When I finally traced Danny to South London, I realised he was suffering too. All the music ever did was provide the catalyst, accelerate the problem. I'd already done things — things I feel ashamed of — before I heard it. We're all here now,' he said, gazing wearily around the table, 'because we've all tasted Death. We're all heading there in our own separate ways. The difference is that Danny is innocent, and can do nothing about it; and you and I, Jim, we're partly responsible.'

If he had been standing, Jim would have been forced to sit down immediately. Without warning the room's four darkened corners loomed at him; there was a charge in the air, but not one he relished or took pleasure in. It was as though his mind was overloading, but here were the loose ends trying to make sense, here came the name to match the face. He thought of Elaine, crimson and lifeless behind bricks; and of Carolyn, perhaps better off dead than subjected to this. 'How could we ever be responsible? How could we ever *deserve* what's happening to us?' he demanded.

'We never deserved it, but we did invite the inevitable, Jim. We let it loose in the first place,' Colin Schofield said. 'Or have you forgotten Providence Street?'

twenty

It was another weekend, another October late afternoon. For three days the storms had blown in from the east, stranding the town's residents in their homes and pubs and closing the last of the outdoor amenities. Then the storms blew themselves out and the fine weather came, a cloudless haze of blue and gold warmth like a memory of childhood. It had never been so idyllic, of course. The hair of the slim blonde girl seen entering The Café on the Rock had never blazed so yellow; the seafood being sold from trailers and stalls on the promenade had never really smelt or tasted so good. It was just that by the time the fine days arrived, the wait had made them seem like Arcadia.

In the small attic room above the town Jim Doherty's story had seized up. Whenever he stared up from the sheet rolled into his typewriter he saw only darkness clinging to corners. He'd received an ultimatum, a threat of detention the English master fully intended to carry out, and had been given the rest of the weekend to finish the tale. That wouldn't seem so daunting once he'd begun.

A delicate pattern of lace curtain strayed across the page, and Jim got up from the table, cursing. He crossed to his bed and flopped down on it and stared at the ceiling. Downstairs, the hammering continued, as it did each Saturday, providing Jim with a feeble excuse for poor

189

productivity. But the genuine distraction was the shadow, the thing he'd been trying to fix clearly in his mind since its first appearance – and disappearance – on Hawthorne Drive. Neither he nor Colin had mentioned the incident yet. At first, Colin had wanted to say something – he'd seen that in his face – but in the end the question had proved insurmountable. So had the silence they'd shared, walking home.

Perhaps he should call. Now that Colin had had an opportunity to think it over, he might be able to provide something more constructive than futile, blocked questions. He lolled on his bed a minute longer and then swept himself up and swept up his jacket from its hook behind the door.

The hall telephone was wall-mounted in an alcove between the lounge and kitchen. The noise seemed to consolidate in the narrow space. Palming a hand over his ear to shut it out, Jim dialled. 'He isn't here,' Colin's mother apologised and then added helpfully, 'He's probably somewhere else. As far as I know he'll be doing his round. Shall I tell him you called?'

Colin did a newspaper round six mornings a week, including Saturdays, the day when the local free press came out. 'Never mind, I'll catch up with him,' Jim said and, thanking her, hung up.

Before he went out he turned in at the lounge. 'Shouldn't be more than an hour,' he announced, and Andrew Doherty swore loudly, the hammer misfiring, splitting a thumb. 'Make it five,' he called through his teeth, his glare hastening Jim clear of the house and its atmosphere of sawdust and linseed oil.

He found Colin on Levin Park Drive, perched on a wall in front of three modern beach-coloured blocks known as Cedarwood Dene; the flats overlooked a tree-lined descent to the park, where greenery flourished over the skeletal railings and gates. A canvas bag with the *Echo*'s insignia sewn on to it sagged at Colin's feet, and a gentle breeze turned a page of the newspaper he was reading.

'Oh, it's you,' he said, looking to see whose shadow had fallen across the print. As he returned to the paper, Jim asked, 'What're you reading?'

'What does it look like? A newspaper.'

'Anything of interest?'

'How should I know?' Colin said, turning another page.

Jim sat, holding his tongue. Colin was seldom so secretive or unsociable. Eventually he'd have to explain what his mood was in aid of. High above them, a solitary gull dipped from the sky above the park. To their right, a bottle-green Hillman Hunter laboured along the road, a trail of exhaust fumes boiling behind it. Nearing them, the vehicle slowed, then accelerated past. Watching the car grow smaller, Jim said, 'Is everything all right with you? Colin?'

Colin almost snapped at him. 'Of course. Everything's great. Everything's just – ' Unable to sustain the outburst, he let his shoulders sag. 'I haven't been sleeping too well, that's all.' Folding the paper neatly, he fitted it down in his bag and stared across the park to a clear horizon. Was he looking outward or inward? 'This bloody town,' he said quietly.

What changes had taken place in him since yesterday? Hadn't he been his usual self at school? Jim thought of his chat with Colin's mother, her curt, rather distracted manner. Possibly there was something between her and Colin, or between her and her husband. Colin had often complained, confidentially, of the bickering that went on between his parents. Now he was standing. 'I've still another estate to do. Are you coming?'

Jim immediately broke into a run to catch up, Colin having set off without waiting. The breeze ruffled their hair as they moved. Their shadows – they each possessed one today, glory be – strode out before them over the tarmac. It was with great relief that Jim found he could see what his silhouette was doing. Casually, so that Colin would not notice, he reached up to scratch his head, to make sure the shape was really his own. He glanced at Colin, whose face was set and mouth firmly shut, and was wondering what he could say to improve things between them when Colin said, 'Jim, there's something you've got to tell me. The day we visited Goatbeard's, when the rain came in, what did you *really* see?'

In all this time, Colin had thought no further than this stupid question. How could he expect Jim to answer with certainty? It was impossible to say what he'd seen. Something had been born there, that was all that he knew. He quickened his pace along the street, projecting his annoyance on to the shadow before him, and had taken six or eight steps before realising his shadow walked alone. This time, Colin's had vanished.

It was because Colin had stopped, petulant, intent on an answer to his question. As Jim turned, he saw Colin standing several yards adrift of him, the strap of his *Echo* bag trying to slip from his shoulder. There was more than curiosity in his trembling voice as he said, 'I remembered what happened, Jim. I stayed awake for hours last night thinking about something Goatbeard said – when he said, *He's the one*. Do you know what he was trying to tell me?' He moved towards Jim, mouth quivering, right hand working itself loosely into a fist. Was he about to lash out or weep bitterly? 'It might have been all right if you hadn't gone,' he was saying. 'Something's happening to us: I don't know what, but it's because you were there. It was *your* shadow, remember, you can't deny it.'

'And it was your idea in the first place.' Jim backed off as Colin advanced. Again, Colin seemed to be softening, his shoulders relaxing as if all his anxiety were spent. 'If you hadn't dragged me inside with you —'

'I'm afraid, Jim.' They stood, facing each other, fidgeting. The silence on Levin Park Drive was emphasised, not spoiled, by a rustle of falling leaves. Colin was staring at his shoes as if embarrassed, chewing his lip, shaking his head. 'What did you see?' he repeated.

He only looked up because of the sudden throb of an engine behind him. It was the Hillman again, returning the way it had come, scraps of paper and dead leaves gusting along behind it. Was the driver lost? Jim assumed that he was when the vehicle pulled up alongside. The window was wound down, and the man behind the wheel — his long hair and drooping, Puerto Rican moustache embarrassingly out of date — was leaning out. 'Hey, kid,' he said, twitching a forefinger.

The driver was addressing Colin, but Colin's expression told Jim he would move no nearer without him. Together they edged to the car, keeping an arm-span's distance from the door. 'What?' Colin said.

'Do you know the Highfield Estate?' the man said. 'Would you run me an errand there if I made it worth your while?'

'How much?'

The driver shrugged, smiling behind his moustache.

'It's near where I'm going,' Colin volunteered, patting his bag. 'But with wheels you could get there in half the time.'

'I know that, but I got things to do. You deliver me this,' the man said, and lifted a tiny brown paper bundle from

193

the passenger seat, 'and I'll make it worth your while. Do you know a kid they call Terry Mack?'

Colin took one cautious step forward. 'I know him well enough. What am I supposed to deliver?'

'This,' the man said, and tossed the bundle.

Jim caught it: a small silent weight, roughly the size of a Swan Vesta box. Handling the package thoughtfully, he passed it to Colin. Colin, in turn, made as if to return it to the driver. 'If you're not going to tell me what's in it,' he began, but the window was being rolled up and the driver was saying, 'Meet me back here in an hour and I'll have something for you. And remember I got your faces, just in case.'

There was no time for dissent: he allowed them none. The Hillman sped off along the road, backfiring once before it turned the corner on to sloping Seaview Terrace. After a wait, Colin dropped the prize in his bag with the newspapers. 'It *is* on our way,' he said.

They walked on in silence for a time. At least the errand had shifted the emphasis away from themselves. They would never discuss the fortune-teller's again, Jim privately vowed. Far better to forgive and forget, if that were possible; leave what had been left unsaid well alone. They could only make matters worse by accusing.

Ten minutes walk brought them to Highfields. Except for the perfect sky it was hard to believe they were still in Seaborough. The coastline was forgotten here: the estate, a drab brown complex of semi-detached council dwellings, had fallen to ruin long ago. Vandalism and natural weathering had systematically depleted the houses since the sixties, when they were built. More recently — echoing the headline-grabbing Lewisham riots of the summer just ended — the process of destruction had advanced noticeably.

Elongated grassy islands floated between the concrete blocks, in front of which toddlers could be seen dragging their plastic toys, or casting half bricks at streetlights. Those old enough to read would doubtless cull broad vocabularies from the walls outside their homes, where names from the new age – The Buzzcocks, The Slits – mingled with easily pronounceable obscenities.

If Indian Summer had brought life back to the streets, it had emptied the houses to do so. 'What if he's out?' Jim wondered when Terry Mack failed to answer. When Colin failed to reply he told himself, 'I guess we could check the arcade.'

'We'll try the back first.' Colin was already moving around the side of the house towards an excitement of overgrown lawn. A next-door neighbour gawked as she transferred a peg from her mouth to her washing line.

'What do you suppose we've got here?' Colin said, removing the package from his bag and testing it between his hands. 'Do you suppose it's legal?' The woman frowned beside her underwear, and now even her pigtailed daughter had joined her in gawking. 'Is something wrong?' Colin said, and hurled a copy of the *Echo* across the fence. 'Is this what you're waiting for?' Immediately mother and daughter shrank back, and a white bedsheet blustered on the line.

Colin knocked and waited. Jim stood a little behind him, rubbing his hands together though he felt no chill. Was Colin wary of him, afraid? Surely he didn't believe that the vision, and what was beginning to happen, could be anyone's fault.

There was movement inside the house – a door opening, a muffled rock song increasing in volume. After a short delay, Terry Mack appeared in shirtsleeves and rubbing his eyes, and behind him, in the hall beyond the kitchen, the face of a pretty girl was briefly glimpsed before vanishing into a doorway. In the instant her eyes met his, Jim knew he had seen the girl before; he was still trying to place her when Colin announced, 'We thought you weren't in.'

'Well,' Terry Mack said, 'I am. What you want?'

The parcel being proffered, Terry accepted it. He took it, Jim noted, with the scarcely concealed relish of a child. But his face was sleepless and nervy, and his frame looked faded inside his clothes. 'You've got company, I see,' Colin said, indicating the empty hall, and Terry said distractedly, 'Her? Oh, yes.'

'We brought that here for a guy who looked like Serpico,' Colin explained. 'Do you mind telling me what's in it?'

Terry Mack merely nodded his head and touched a finger to his nose. 'I do mind,' he said. Presumably this was where the money went; all the ten pence coins he'd lovingly groomed into fifties. Terry was sticking nothing up his nose, however.

He was sticking it in his arm.

Three days later he was dead. The heroin, a police forensics man later testified before the juvenile court, had been cut with an equal proportion of rat poison. Someone — Colin Schofield, it was also affirmed — had blended further quantities together with a household scouring agent for distribution throughout the town. The rest of the drugs — a little under two ounces in total — had been recovered from Colin's locker at school. The man behind the wheel of the Hillman Hunter was never identified.

Until their reunion, years later, in a back room at Shaman's Bar, it was the last Jim heard of Colin Schofield.

For Colin, the hearing was merely the start of a descent which had never ended. A summary conviction gave him a twenty-month stretch at a junior Borstal on Tyneside. The worst began there.

twenty-one

Colin lit another cigarette and drew longingly on it as though it were an accommodating teat. Head thrown back, eyes graduating shut, he exhaled. Jim watched him, too apprehensive even to breathe. The memory had touched off others in him like small, dim fireworks, but the picture they illumined was far from complete. He'd seen the monster at a distance, long ago, and until recently had managed to escape its wrath. Colin, apparently, had not. He now possessed the air of a man who had ridden deep in its belly for years.

'I remember spending my fifteenth birthday inside,' he recounted, 'and I spent it staring at the wall in front of my face, getting to know every mark on it, every flaw. A card arrived from my parents, full of cheer and encouragement, with none of the shame they must really have felt. It brought me to tears, if you really want the truth of it. If they'd sent me despair or outrage instead it would've been preferable, would at least have been honest — but I guessed they were avoiding problems of their own. They were, as it turned out. I was guilty of nothing, I'd been sent there by circumstance, and at home the people were making my parents suffer for it. The fact I'd been convicted was proof enough. Maybe they didn't care how much damage had already been done.

'Later that day, the day of my fifteenth, I was taken into the toilets by four older, heavier youths and – and sexually assaulted, each taking his turn. I think I can talk about that now: it was only the beginning of things, after all. I remember my palms slipping on the tiled walls above the urinals, and my ankles being grasped from behind and pulled firmly apart. They used their hands, as well as some object I never identified. They laughed in my ear while they worked. And I remember thinking I'd never pass another exam, or captain another school soccer team or athletics team. And I wouldn't know the success I'd dreamed of since the early days, the days when I believed I was destined for something.'

He faltered, moist-eyed, before continuing. 'Instead, everything ended there. Those bastards had learned all the tricks of rough trade inside. They'd entered the place as habitual petty criminals, and they were going to leave it wiser and tougher and trained in deadlier arts than I ever dared think of. They made me bleed that day, they made some part of me die, inside. The worst of the bleeding stopped, I suppose, after three or four hours, but I couldn't sit – or stand – comfortably for almost a week after that.

'Yes, I can talk about it now. It hurts less the further I get from it. Before the pain had stopped, two weeks before my release, I got word that my parents were separating. In my absence, I was to blame for that too.' He laughed, though bitterly, at the thought. 'My mother returned to Cumbria, the place of her birth; my father went back just as swiftly to the bottle. When I heard the news I understood that I'd never feel anything for anyone again, I really couldn't afford to. I knew I would suffer again – that was the role I'd been made for, if you like – but with the suffering I'd learn to endure. Like gold refined by fire, the hardship would make me strong.

'When I did return to Seaborough, I went to my house and stood on the doorstep and knocked; and my father opened up, holding the door but saying nothing. For a year we lived under the same roof, and we lived exclusively, never connecting, and there was never a time when I didn't feel the shame I'd brought into his life. After the first weeks I came looking for you, Jim. Your folks said you were at college in the south. I'd thought we might strike up our friendship again. More than that, I hoped we might find a solution — a reason for everything that was happening to me.'

Jim felt the cool finger of conscience skim his brow reproachfully, and swallowed hard. 'Colin, I'm so sorry. In all those years I never so much as gave you a thought. I left Providence Street and all the rest of it behind me; I thought it was over at last.'

Colin stared wistfully at his cigarette butt before putting out its glow between his fingers. Did he feel no pain, or had he mastered it? 'It hardly matters now,' he said. 'There was nothing for me in Seaborough. No one would employ me, for sure. The place was always a closed shop to outsiders, and now it was closing its doors on one of its own. The word was that Colin Schofield was bad news: everything around him soured and died. My touch was a stigma. In the end I could only wash my hands of the place and move on.'

As he reclined in his chair, darkness caressed his features, causing them to withdraw sharply. Seated opposite him, Daniel Zero scratched at the crook of his arm through his sleeve.

'Was that when you came to London?' Jim asked.

'London was later,' Colin explained. 'I spent years drifting between cities, in search of a life. There was no money, and a string of arrests for vagrancy and for shoplifting. I began to think of you, Jim, as my enemy. You know how easily a small, snap assumption can blow up into obsessive resentment. I began to imagine the success you were heading for: I imagined that whatever good became of you would certainly be at my own expense.

'I was in Chester, sharing a room and a bed with a girl I knew as Corinne, if that was really her name. She was sweet and easy-going and deserved better. I don't think I loved her exactly, but I do remember wanting to. We had an understanding, you might say: it was good while it lasted, at any rate. We were in a kind of half-furnished legalised squat, and there were four or five others in different parts of the building: a hooker named Ro and her pimp-husband, Tony — I forget all the names.

'It was Christmas, I remember, and I was heading back from the supermarket in the snow, and the snow was beginning to settle. I had a carrier of cheap bottles under one arm and I was half-way up the stairs to our room when I heard the scream. It was Ro; she was backing away from the doorway as I reached it, and had one hand cupped over her mouth. At first I couldn't tell whether it was fright or amusement, because her face gave nothing away. When I stepped inside, the carrier slipped from my grasp and landed; I don't believe anything broke. Corinne was on the bed with her face turned away from me and someone, mostly covered by sheets, was rutting away on top of her. Something about the scene turned me utterly cold: it was too unexpected, too rich to react to. Then I heard Ro again, screaming; and a door slamming somewhere downstairs.

'I could only do then what I felt I was supposed to. I moved forward and said, *Roll off the bed and put your fucking pants on*. I was angry, but not angry enough: I was managing not to shout. As soon as I'd done that the

figure on Corinne stopped moving and threw back the
sheet. It was a girl, naked and dark, with a tawny look
to her skin. She moved so casually as she got up, plucking
her clothes from the floor and moving to the doorway, it
hardly dawned on me what she'd been doing, or what was
wrong with Corinne.

'Corinne must have been dead for hours. There was
hardly a mark on her, except for a faint discoloration
where the girl had pressed down on her stomach and chest.
She was cold to the touch and her colour had blanched.
It looked as if the life and soul had been sucked right out
of her, but I didn't intend to wait for an inquest. I knew
my affliction by now: I'd be falsely accused if they found
me there. Already, Ro had gone running for help. I began
to run too, to save myself, and I haven't stopped running
since.'

There was a restlessness about him now; an eagerness
to finish what he'd started, or perhaps a dread of doing
so. 'I found myself here, in the city – it's easy to become
anonymous here – and I was bedding down on the
Embankment along with others like myself. Some were
losers by choice; others because fortune had never smiled
for them in all their years. With them, I was at home.

'And I slept under the stars and dreamt of a Doors song
we used to play – remember, Jim? *When you're strange,
faces come out of the rain*? I dreamt of it every night for
a year, it seemed. And I was close to my destiny now,
something was pulling me closer towards it. I started to
view myself differently – as a wondrous thing; a creature
singled out by nature, by fate. I'd been made for a purpose
after all.'

'Which was?' Jim said.

'To finish the great whore; the whore we invited into
the world; our Future Now.'

'Cora?' Jim said aghast. 'You're talking about Cora?'

'That's correct.'

No one seemed willing to disrupt the silence which followed. It felt almost sacred. Drinks were thoughtfully sipped, cigarettes were handed around and lit. The jukebox beat resounded through the walls, a mechanical, tuneless boom. 'The girl,' Jim said finally. 'Did you know her? Had you met her before?'

'We both had,' Colin replied. 'It was the day we delivered the junk to Terry Mack. There was someone with him, if you recall.'

Jim nodded. The dark-featured girl. 'But that was years earlier, and miles from where –'

'But think,' Colin interrupted. 'First Terry, then Corinne, now Elaine. Three deaths, and I'm close enough to come under suspicion each time. They put me away for what happened to Terry; they're probably still looking for me after what happened in Chester; and as for Elaine –' He trailed off.

'You had nothing to do with Elaine's death?' Jim said. The question had to be forced out, and there was genuine surprise in his voice. 'It wasn't you who did that to her?'

Colin shook his head. A thought-bubble of smoke arose from his nose and mouth. 'Believe it or not, I followed her to the house to warn her, but she gave me no time to explain. I'm not pretending I'm innocent – Good God, I'm anything but that. I've made headlines with some of the things I've done; she had good reason to be afraid.' Unable to meet Jim's stare, he studied his trembling hands. 'I suppose you'd like to kill me after what happened in Finsbury Park,' he added.

Jim could only shrug. 'I don't know what I want any more.'

'You'd be doing me a favour,' Colin said, 'because

strictly speaking, I'm still responsible. It was the same when I took the hooker back to her room: it was something I was compelled to do — it made me helpless, watching the whole thing take place outside myself. There must have been a part of me wanting it, a part that was stronger than anything I could muster to fight it with. I thought it might solve something, help me. If I tried to resist, it only made matters worse.'

'They should be punished for what they've done,' Daniel Zero said glumly, and the others turned to face him. 'Cora and Max Beresford, I mean. They made us like this. Look,' he said, drawing attention to the fingers of his right hand, which were absently drumming the table-top. 'I can't stop that. I'm no longer in control of my body. It isn't functioning as it should. I'm losing the war.'

'We're all losing,' Colin said soberly. 'The same goes for anyone who ever made Cora's acquaintance. And I think some of us have done more than just that.'

The panic was stealing Jim's breath, and he struggled to keep from gasping aloud as the truth came home. Yes, he had done far more than make her acquaintance, as Colin put it, and what did that make him? A messenger of the void, a carrier of its plagues and secrets? Perhaps that was what Cora intended when she'd asked him to represent her. She wanted him for a kind of glorified sales rep.

'What kind of virus are we discussing?' he wondered. 'Is there anything that can be done medically to prevent it?'

'I think it's safe to say this is terminal,' Danny said, and matter-of-factly began unbuttoning and rolling up his shirtsleeve. When Danny looked up, grinning, Jim thought he saw madness shine briefly in the rebel's eye. 'You want to see what became of the rock-and-roll dream, Jim?'

'Jesus God,' Jim heard himself exclaim as Danny

extended his arm. It was all too much. He had seen many strange sights already, but could scarcely look upon this dubious glory; nor, he realised, was he able to tear his eyes from it. The forearm, exposed from wrist to elbow, crawled with a shining blackness of root formations, arteries and tendons which had broken the skin to envelop the surface. Muscles and valves retracted, pumping a substance which might have been blood or might not. Except for the glossy blackness, this might have been part of any ordinary body flipped inside out. 'What in God's name *is* it?' he said.

'It's what you call wearing your cause on your sleeve,' Danny said. 'We've all prayed for change, but I don't think we ever imagined it looked like this.'

'And you?' Jim turned frantic-eyed to Colin. 'Are you the same?'

Colin's hand twitched. 'More or less the same.'

'Why don't you touch it?' Danny suggested then, smiling when Jim withdrew from him. 'Go ahead, touch it. It's either in you already or it's not − and Jim, it's in you, believe me. Go on and touch. Tell me what it reminds you of.'

Tentatively, with a forefinger, Jim did as Danny requested, and quickly recoiled from the cool, polished smoothness which met his touch. It was less malleable, less moist than he'd expected, which did nothing to lessen the shock. 'It feels like,' he began, but faltered, aware that what he was thinking was ludicrous.

'Feels like what?' Danny prompted.

'Like vinyl. It feels just like vinyl.'

Danny laughed indulgently and without humour. Re-buttoning his shirt, he leered at Colin, who leaned back in his seat in silence, then at Jim. 'So much for the fucking superiority of CD, right? I'm Daniel Zero, play me!' His laughter subsiding, he became subdued, his speech measured. 'Don't ask me what it is, but it has a hold on all of us now. In the early stages I came up with every pseudo-scientific diagnosis under the sun. I suspected a cancer of the lymphatic system, but we're going a sight further than that now, wouldn't you say?' He picked up his glass and drained it with a flourish. 'Colin had to see for himself before he'd accept he wasn't the only one. Knowing he wasn't alone was half the problem solved.'

'Let's say it healed my mind,' Colin said. 'I doubt whether the rest of me is quite so receptive.'

Slowly, uncertainly, Jim looked from Danny to Colin, and back again. Three condemned vessels together. At least there was comfort, of a kind, in the presence of fellow sufferers. At least the experience, however dreadful, could be shared. The beat was the gateway through which they'd entered this death; presumably it would provide their exit as well. Even as he considered this, he could feel the ceaseless momentum working through him, making his breathing short and ragged. 'So what do we do now?'

'What can we do?' Danny took to his feet, and began pacing in a broad semi-circle around the table. 'We can do as much as we can do. Raze Monolith Records to the ground, is my vote. We'll start by killing Beresford.'

'You're serious about that?'

'Deadly serious. Max Beresford and Cora both: we built them up, and they've bitten the hands that fed them. It's time for the backlash.'

'They left us no option,' Colin added, taking the initiative. A bead of perspiration made an unsteady descent of his temple and cheek. 'Besides Jim, what do we stand to lose? Haven't we already lost everything? The fortunate ones are the victims they've left behind. Think of that when you think of Elaine — she's better off now than she would be like this, like us.'

'Well?' Danny said, and stopped pacing. 'Are you with us or not?'

'Can I trust you,' Jim said, addressing Colin directly, 'after everything you've done to me?'

Colin's reply was merely another question. 'Who else can you trust?'

It was too late to inform the authorities, Jim thought: they had all come too far for that now, the malignancy was too deeply formed, the conflict too personal. There was nothing of the pregnant, almost sensual arousal he'd felt earlier today; in its place was the knowledge that whatever lived in him lived only to destroy. He watched a lump of ash drop from his burning cigarette, angled forgotten between his fingers, and knew the decision had already been made for him.

'I'm with you,' he said after a time. 'Just tell me what I have to do, and we'll begin.'

It was after midnight by the time they arrived on Shaftesbury Avenue. A group of teenagers waited outside a cinema, staring out passers-by, grabbing lazily for an old lady's hat. Because of what Jim had left behind on Laleham Road, and since Colin had no home to retreat to, it was agreed they would spend the night at Danny's place in New Cross. First thing tomorrow, the backlash would begin.

Jim dawdled behind, lost in thought, while the others waited for the lights to change at a road junction. Until the TV images in a showroom window drew him up in his tracks, what he'd learned tonight seemed too rich and too unreal to digest: it was hard to accept that Colin could have descended so far in the years since Seaborough, or that they should have been brought together again, such radically different people, so inextricably linked. He doubted they could ever be friends again — it was impossible to double back on the past, and too much had happened — but for now, they needed each other as never before.

It was Carolyn's face he saw first. He'd passed the domestic electrical shop's display before the after-image registered. Backtracking, he realised he hadn't been mistaken. Nor could a hundred FST televisions be mistaken. Carolyn, very much alive, her face discoloured and bruised, sobbed wordlessly into the newsman's wind-guarded microphone. Initially, all he could feel was blessed relief at seeing the woman alive. Cora had failed to push him all the way, thank goodness; he hadn't sunk to murder yet.

Then the inevitability of what she must be saying occurred to him. She must be telling the newsman who had done what, furnishing details, naming names. Behind her, an ambulance was being loaded with a stretcher, its occupant draped with a pale sheet. For a moment it looked as if the ambulance already contained a stretchered body. Stock shots of the building's exterior followed, but there was no photofit picture. Too soon, probably.

But now the authorities knew who they were looking for. He stood there, fixedly watching the banks of TV screens long after the image had switched to a report on a National Front march which ended in violence. From somewhere far beyond him, almost from beyond his conscious, he heard Colin Schofield and Daniel Zero calling. They were at the far side of the junction, signalling him to join them.

At last he tore himself from the window. The soundless report had left him curiously relieved, as if everything had suddenly fitted itself into place for him. At the very least, he knew there was no turning back from now on.

209

twenty-two

Posters of Cora adorned the walls at Danny's place like pages from the Bible in *The Omen*. Jim's first impression as he stood on the threshold was that she'd materialised again, or soon would. He hesitated before following Colin inside. 'Danny,' he said when he saw and smelt the mess, 'doesn't it bother you, living like this?'

'You can't get the help these days.' Danny closed the door and leaned back against it. The small room was a calamity of odd socks and soiled underwear and food left out to spoil on shelves and crumb-dusted plates. Coverless paperbacks and scraps of loose notepaper lay strewn across the floor and the bed, from which the creamy sheets had been pulled. The carpet was stained pale in several places. In the squeaky clean age of condom consciousness, it appeared that the champions of hygiene still had their work cut out for them.

Danny crossed to the sink, which was crowded with pots. Between the taps, a milk bottle crawled with green fur. From the drainer he selected two cups before taking a bottle of German white wine from the refrigerator. 'If you're hungry, help yourself to whatever you can find.' He handed one cup and the bottle to Jim, and the other cup to Colin, who had discovered the bed and collapsed on it, head pillowed on his hands.

'When was the last time you slept on one of those?' Jim said, scanning about for a bottle opener. 'Aren't you going to join us?' he said to Danny, and then froze.

Danny had moved to the table beneath the window, and was standing over the sealed briefcase which lay on top of it. A small automatic handgun, a .22 or similar, sat next to the briefcase. Danny picked it up, smoothing his fingers around the muzzle as if handling a talisman. 'I have to go out for a while,' he announced deliberately. 'Some personal business to attend to before we take care of Beresford.'

'Is that for real?' Colin wondered sleepily as Danny pocketed the weapon.

'Real enough for the job,' Danny said.

'You're not going to do anything stupid, are you?' Jim took a step towards Danny. 'Shouldn't we stick together? I thought that's what we arranged.'

'This is just security; don't worry about me. We need all the help we can get now.' Danny lifted the briefcase from the table. The weight took him by surprise, jolting his shoulder. 'Must be losing my strength,' he said, heaving it to the door. When the door was opened, he turned. 'If I'm not back by six, get yourselves moving. It probably means I've gone straight to Ladbroke Grove. Meet me at Beresford's office as near to seven o'clock as you can.'

'How do you know he'll be there at that time?' Colin wondered.

'I don't, but I'm prepared to wait. We're not going to save anyone's life or solve anyone's problems. But we might take a few of those bastards with us before we're finished.'

He went out, taking their collective energy with him, it seemed. Colin was already floundering on the edge of sleep. Unearthing a corkscrew in a drawer under the sink,

Jim took the bottle to the table. Above the roof-tops the night sky was a colourless mass, more smog than sky in fact. After a lull, a downstairs door slammed; seconds later Danny appeared below on the street, hurrying away into darkness beneath a fire escape, the briefcase held to his chest. He'd neglected to ask Danny what the briefcase contained, but perhaps he could guess.

He uncorked the bottle and half-filled his cup, sipping without interest or thirst. Cora watched from the wall, from whichever wall he happened to look to. It was alarming that such rare beauty should cover so many nameless terrors, such barbarism; but of course her beauty, like everything else he had grown to detest in the rockbiz, was no more than skin deep.

Yes, they could take the bastards out, they could bloody their hands and purge a hundred and more derelict souls, and Danny would be perfectly correct — it would solve nothing. They would still be leaving chaos behind. Elaine would remain in his thoughts as he'd seen her last: a crimson puppet behind bricks he had mortared together himself, a shape without a face on a hospital stretcher. 'What good is revenge going to do us?' he wondered aloud.

Colin muttered and turned on to his side. 'None whatsoever.' He sounded drugged, barely conscious. 'But there's a point where it stops being revenge and starts being something else.'

Jim twisted to look at him, bemused. His chair creaked. 'What?'

'You don't believe we can damage these people and their empire with pop-guns, do you? I mean, you've got to admire Danny's enthusiasm, but surely Cora has to be tackled on *her* terms. Let's go after her with guns by all means, but let's not fool ourselves it'll make any difference.'

'Then why bother at all?'

'Because there's a way, there must be. He eased himself up on an elbow, suddenly wild-eyed and animated. 'When you've been through what I've been through, you soon stop searching for answers in the real world. There aren't so many there, anyway. Besides which, Cora never came from the real world, did she? This isn't her natural habitat.'

What was Colin getting at? – or had he missed the point? Jim said, 'I'm not sure I understand,' and held the bottle aloft.

Colin declined it with a wave. 'I'm not sure I do. All I can say positively is that something happened at the fortune-teller's, something came into the world. I don't know what you saw, Jim – maybe it doesn't really matter now – but whatever it was, it brought misfortune on both of us, and on everything and everyone we ever cared about. Wherever it came from, that's where our war is; that's where our problems are.'

Jim placed the bottle carefully on the table. The liquid shimmered, catching a light from one of the buildings opposite. His hands were shaking, causing the cup to vibrate against his teeth as he sipped. 'And what do you propose we do? Isn't it out of our hands now?'

Colin settled again, allowing his eyes to close. 'Perhaps it is out of our hands, perhaps it is. But if there's a way through to the other side, we'll find it. And if we find it, Jim, we'll put an end to this jinx once and for all.'

'You really think there's –' What? A doorway? Jim frowned, attempting to picture what Colin meant. It was too much to contemplate, at least while he was relatively sober. He thought of the black room in which Cora had traded her gifts for his, and shuddered. He'd made her alive that night, if she hadn't been before. The thought shook him to the bones.

He stared from the window, scarcely daring to consider the consequences of that, and took another swallow from his cup. The wine was too sweet, but he would probably finish the bottle alone tonight anyway. Behind him, Colin's breathing was heavier, more regulated, as sleep snatched him away from the room. 'Even if we did manage to find a way through,' Jim wondered, 'what would we find when we got there? What would we do?'

Colin did not stir, though it didn't matter. The question was purely rhetorical.

twenty-three

The underground train was the first of the day, and when Danny alighted at Ladbroke Grove the streets were just beginning to wake. Two cars idled past him towards Holland Park, then the road was clear. There was activity behind the shuttered window of a greengrocer's he passed and at a newsagent's, further along, where a pre-pubescent delivery boy stood thumbing a sex magazine plucked from the racks. But a sense of morning torpor persisted, and he felt curiously out of sync with the world, as though seeing beyond its three dimensions. He enjoyed the feeling in a way, for it calmed him. Even the shrilling pain in his ribs and chest calmed him. He needed to be calm, because he was certain his body was changing again. The malignancy was entering yet another new phase.

Perhaps it would be the last. The struggle would soon be over, the torture would end, he would gain his freedom. He strolled along Blenheim Crescent, across the road from the Monolith building. There was no sign of life there, either at the office windows or in the street below. A white Saab was parked in front, but it could have belonged to anyone. Checking the reassuring bulk of the gun in his pocket, he set off across the road.

A pavement artist had chalked a huge butterfly at the foot of the office steps, between the steps and the Saab,

217

and Danny stopped to admire it. Thankfully last night's drizzle had not touched the image. The cobalt-blue eyes central to the creature's forewings looked pleasure-filled, stunned to behold the body they belonged to. He hoped to share their pleasure soon, as soon as his mission was done. It would take a lot, though, to top the sense of release he'd felt this morning as he tossed the loaded briefcase to the Thames, lingering to watch it go under. He'd dreamt of the moment for weeks, but no dream could match the reality, none. The craving had worsened since then, the pain wracking his body had discovered new heights, but it had all been worth it. He should have kicked the habit long ago.

Somewhere along the crescent, an early riser had switched on a radio or TV set: he couldn't tell which, for the sounds were too distant and distorted. He stood at the foot of the steps, looking up. Everything told him it would be better to wait until the others arrived, that he should keep a low profile until then. Maybe he could walk up to Portobello Road, see if there were any places serving breakfast at this hour, then take a leisurely walk back.

Who was he kidding? As if, so near, he could forestall the moment any longer. No, he was too far gone, he was going to make Max Beresford pay for everything he'd done, and if the others weren't here to help him they could wait their turn. Furious, he marched up the steps to the door, only hesitating when he noticed the video camera surveying him.

Who could be watching him at this time of day; who would expect him? Perhaps no one: the camera was a cheap psychological barrier. Like security system dummies on the walls of affluent suburban houses, it only functioned as a deterrent. Only an amateur would fall for so obvious a ploy.

He put his hand to the door, wondering whether Colin and Jim might be inside already, waiting. He doubted it, after Jim's insistence that they stick together. Again, he hesitated. The thought had just occurred that he was being drawn towards the office against his will. It would be sheer lunacy to go in without the others.

Immediately he snatched his hand free of the door, but it wasn't the thought which made him do so; it was the odd sensation he found there. Again, he recognised a peculiar indecision in himself, a sign that his mind and body were at odds, straining in opposite directions. What did he do now? Shouldn't he retreat and wait below the steps? Not really wanting to, he touched the woodwork a second time.

His hands, like both his arms, had been desensitised by the sickness, most of the feeling having left them. Nevertheless, he was aware of a thick, slow pounding, a displacement of air on the other side which was causing the door's solid mass to vibrate. It was as though the building itself were alive; as though he had somehow magically located its pulse. Surely all he sensed was the nervous, quickening beat of his own heart. He was bound to be anxious, so close to the showdown. Searching for courage, he pulled out the gun. As he did so the door gave an electrical buzz – he thought of a fly trapped in water – and opened.

Without another thought, he stepped inside. He had visited the Monolith building once before, when the upper floor had been laid open for the Cora launch, and remembered the place as rather faceless, perhaps more spacious and emptier than most record company HQs were, even with so many hangers-on crammed inside. In any event, the place had suggested nothing out of the ordinary to him at the time. He'd witnessed nothing then,

219

or since, or at any time, to compare with the scene he'd entered now.

His first impression was that he'd unwittingly happened into a bad heavy-metal video; that fire had gutted the place from the floor up. A multitude of rock songs thundered between the walls — classics from every age, coming at him all at once, 'Green Onions', 'White Rabbit', 'Satisfaction'. Every step he took brought another burst of nostalgia, another gem locked in time. 'Hey Jude', 'Rainy Day Women', 'God Save the Queen'. It was chaos, the way these anthems clashed and overlapped and merged; yet a pattern was emerging, a growing semblance of order. Was it this that made the house tremble as if alive? He thought not. Something else — something of immense power — had passed through here only moments before him. He could still feel traces of its heat on his face.

But there had been no fire. Everything in the foyer was intact, if tarnished. The panelling, vinyl-veneered, had melted in places and formed bubbles in others; the carpet crisped underfoot where extreme heat had singed it; patches of the high artexed ceiling were smudged black and brown; a chromium doorknob had lost its gleam.

Danny headed straight to the lift. The doors were already open, and he stepped in without delay. As he did, the temperature soared dramatically. The steel walls and floor were still conducting heat, enough to soften the rubber soles of his sneakers. The unexpected warmth made him dance on the spot. Had the power passed this way, or was it still here?

Perspiration broke across his brow. A deep-seated ache began either side of his chest, below the arms. He would have been screaming in pain if not for the Novocaine numbness which already filled him. Time to put an end to the misery, he thought, finger tensioning the trigger; and if he must go it alone, so be it. What could be gained in any event, by waiting for the others? He'd existed alone all this time, it seemed only fitting he should cease to exist alone. Groping for the lift's control panel, he saw that the top floor indicator was already alight before he selected it.

The doors closed, the lift ascended. More songs began. 'Paint It Black', 'Do the Strand', 'Love Will Tear Us Apart' — all these sounds from the world, everything crashing together. Danny cried out, or the cry was forced from his lungs by a pressure of hot air. He fell sideways against the wall as the lift reached the top with a shudder. Apart from the numbing pain below his arms, he was empty of feeling now. He couldn't even be sure he was still squeezing the trigger. Drum patterns were synchronising, all the songs of protest and revolt were becoming one definitive anthem; yet what he was hearing was not new at all: the song in his head was Cora's.

He had always known she would turn out to be a sham. Everything about her — the image, the wall of noise, everything down to the gloss on her lips — had been plagiarised, carefully sampled and remodelled to fit the times. The delirium she'd caused in the streets had been drained from previous rebellions, times when rock and roll had seemed to matter. Cora had absorbed it all, every morsel: a true counter-culture-vulture. Just when Danny thought he was close to understanding the rest, the music stopped and the lift doors opened.

He was facing a long, lean corridor, its pitted walls touched by the power he'd seen downstairs. A wind swirled in the narrow space, scented by decay, buffeting an unclosed office door back and forth against its jamb. Scraps of charred paper and paint tossed and turned. Striding clear of the lift, Danny moved into the face of it.

At the far end of the corridor, facing him, Max

Beresford stood flanked by two others. It took Danny a second longer to identify the punk and the heavier man whose face was incomplete. The instant he saw them he knew this was going to be easier than he'd thought. His trigger finger itched. 'Danny,' Beresford said, unsurprised. But of course he wouldn't be surprised, would he? 'I see you came prepared for an altercation.'

'You bet,' Danny said, advancing. There was no stopping now if he wanted to. The wind was too strong, stronger than his own free will as it ushered him forward. 'You're finished, Max. I'm here to see to it.'

Beresford's slow, unflurried manner only made him more loathsome, Danny thought. 'I think we've all just about finished what we started, haven't we? Do you really think there's anything to gain, toting that gun?'

'A clear conscience. After everything you made me do.'

'Really, Danny, to think you'd be so quick to shed your loyalties.'

'What loyalties? You had me on remote control, didn't you, delivering those fucking tapes for you. I don't think it had much to do with loyalty.' He had reached the first offices on the corridor. A door to his right gusted open, then shut again. 'Where's Cora?' he demanded.

Beresford shrugged. 'Back where she belongs — where we all belong. I trust you'll be joining us soon.' He lifted his hands, palms up, as if to make Danny welcome. 'There's no need for her to stay in the public eye now that her work's complete. You know what over-exposure can do.'

'Oh yes,' Danny said. 'Oh yes.'

'Our tree is planted, Danny, and now we can leave it to grow of its own accord. I wish you could see with my eyes; see what a marvellous thing . . .'

'Your tree,' Danny said, 'is a cancer. That's the *only*

222

fucking thing you've planted.' He was nearly speechless with rage. The adrenalin seemed to be swelling up in his face, dehydrating him. 'Where do you get the gall to go passing off your disease as a cure? — that's what I'd like to know.'

Beresford smiled. If only those worm-lips would betray anger or doubt, just once! 'Frankly, Danny, I'm surprised to find you rebelling against our rebellion. After all, we're only doing what you yourself advocated years ago in that half-arsed fanzine of yours.'

'Which is?'

'Changing things from the inside. Do you mind if I quote you? *To be truly subversive, we must be in the system, but not of it.*'

'Don't give me that old hat shit, Max. I —'

Danny was half-way along the corridor when a crippling twist of pain in both his sides brought him to a standstill. It took him completely unawares, and for a moment he imagined he'd been punched or kicked, except that no one had moved. Max Beresford and his aides were yards away. Help me, he thought, but he wouldn't give Beresford the pleasure of hearing him say it. The pain burrowing through his ribs, he was forced to bite into his tongue to stop the scream.

Something was trying to claw its way out of him. He managed another uncertain step forward. For some reason, Beresford looked further away now than he had to begin with. But what was more curious was the way the two henchmen were flinching, backing away. Probably that was because he was the aggressor this time; the one with the gun. Yet he was holding it pointing down at the floor — no force of will seemed able to make him raise the gun, level it, squeeze the trigger.

He squeezed the trigger. He did so involuntarily, the gun

going off without his consent, the noise of the explosion echoing off through the corridor. Then the sound was swallowed by the vortex. Looking up, he saw that the platinum punk and the caul-faced man had retreated further, to the last door on the left. Why were they watching with such awe on their faces? It was almost as though they were afraid of something.

Suddenly he thought he understood. The gun in his hand was weightless now, if indeed it was still in his hand. Never mind: it was no use anyway. As the song of pain in his body became a crescendo, he glanced down at himself. No amount of morbid self-absorption had prepared him for this, no drug had opened his mind widely enough to accept it. Daniel Zero could only watch, now with the same astonishment that paralysed the others, as the fury which had been in him came out.

It had belonged to him for years — he'd become quite intimate with it, in his way — and had, he supposed, expected it to be something like this in appearance; but he hadn't expected it to have fingers or nails which gleamed like steel, or such lightning speed as it emerged from under his arms and reached for his face. Even Max Beresford, smiling no more, lowered his head respectfully as the thing from inside Daniel Zero proceeded to tear him apart.

twenty-four

A four-limbed darkness, no more than a shadow, flitted into Codrington Mews as Colin and Jim reached the Monolith building. Jim saw the flicker of movement just as they crossed to the office. 'Could that be Danny, do you think?' he said. But he'd sighted nothing clearly; he'd only had time to register the figure's unusually low, huddled posture. It could easily have been a dog, scampering for cover.

There was no trace of it in the mews, so unless it really had been a dog, the figure had entered another building nearby. Turning away, Colin said, 'It wasn't Danny. He'd be waiting for us outside. He wouldn't be playing tricks.'

'No,' Jim agreed. A vast, multi-hued butterfly drew his eye as they turned back on to Blenheim Crescent. 'All the same, I'd like to know why he's late. He was behaving so urgently when he left. You don't suppose — '

A Mitsubishi transit rattled past, moving them on its tide of air, stealing Jim's words away with it.

'I'm ready and willing to suppose anything,' Colin said. 'If he *has* done something stupid, you can hardly hold him responsible for his actions. I'm amazed we've all been able to function as long as we have. What do you suppose this is meant to be?'

He was referring to the butterfly at their feet, but Jim

was already staring up at the door above them. It was open – not far enough to see inside, but sufficiently to coax Jim up the steps towards it. Colin followed. At the top Jim said, 'He's here already, I'm sure of it. Either he couldn't wait for us to get here or –' He stalled, suddenly unable to push the door all the way open.

'What are you waiting for?' Colin said.

'Nothing.' It was the memory of this place, the dim afterglow of a nearly, not quite, forgotten dream. Terrible things had happened here: all the worse because he'd been personally involved in them. Of course the hallucinogen they'd given him had altered his perception of events; but it hadn't altered the black and white, newsworthy outcome. Before he could prevent it Elaine's face rushed into his thoughts – a pristine picture of her alive and laughing and cheeks infused with colour. Her laughter made him buckle inside, but if there were more tears to come he wouldn't let them out, not yet.

'Are you sure we have the right place?' Colin's jaw sagged as they moved inside and through the hall. A charred fragment of paint or wallpaper floated down past his face. 'Is this where they brought you?'

'It couldn't have changed this much.' Jim was shaking his head in disbelief. 'Not in just a few days. How long *has* it been?' The large foyer looked like the aftermath of an accident: either that or vandalism had made it like this, or perhaps a fire. Gone was the aura of burnished chrome and piped, anarchic rock music. Instead there was darkness, and silence.

Several paces along, Colin banged open a door on the right, marked RECEPTION. Inside, the collapsed frame of a chair and legless coffee table were strewn in the centre of the bare floor; that was as far as the décor went. Another door across the hall opened on a similar scene.

This was no functioning office. It was a squat; an abandoned one at that. No one had lived here for years, let alone worked. Without another word, they turned towards the lift. If there had been a fire, it had most probably started in the electrical system. Most of the wall switches were blackened, one or two dangling free of the walls were still held by lengths of umbilical wire. The lift was broken too, its doors stubbornly refusing to open, even when forced. 'What do we do now?' Jim wondered aloud. 'Doesn't look as if he came in through here, does it?'

'No, but we ought to be sure. Is there another way up?'

The fire door was tucked away in the furthest, darkest corner of the foyer. Beyond it, a stairwell rose and descended. The down-leading flight terminated, probably, in a disused basement storage area, but there was little time to investigate there. Colin was already leading the way up.

Although the stairs had escaped the damage they'd seen elsewhere, they were in poor repair. Several risers threatened to give way underfoot, one near the top of the first flight already had. Because there was nothing else to hold on to, Jim flat-palmed the wall for balance as he climbed. The plaster was moist, surprisingly and unpleasantly warm beneath his hands.

A door which should have let on to the first floor was locked from the other side when Colin tried it. Rather than force it, he continued upwards. Nearing the top floor, Jim felt a familiar pressure beginning far back in his skull, a hazy forewarning of migraine, practically second nature to him now. For once in his life he actively welcomed the pain: it was a wonder, given his present situation, he could still feel anything at all. 'We're there,' Colin said above him, and seconds later the icy light flooded the stairwell.

The stairs brought them out near the upstairs lift. Ahead, the corridor, though empty, seemed caught in the act of settling after much physical activity; the air was still moving. 'Do you feel that?' Colin said, wild-eyed. He stopped to wipe sweat from his forehead with his hand. 'Someone *was* here. Maybe they still are.'

While Colin went ahead, throwing doors open either side of him, Jim dithered uncertainly behind. His eyes were on the last door to his left, his thoughts inclining to the black room behind it. Had Danny found his way in there, perhaps? If so, it was easy to speculate why he hadn't emerged again. The room was all there was up here, the very heart of Cora's mission, unless it had also been decimated. Suddenly the thought of what lay ahead made him want to turn about-face and run, and he was about to do just that when Colin's cry dragged him on.

'Oh my God, Jim, come here!'

The silence seemed devastating, once Colin's voice had faded. He stood in an open doorway, hands groping blindly at the jamb to support himself. From where Jim was, he looked ready to keel over. 'Here, Jim,' he said, but this time his voice was barely a whisper. His lip was trembling like a child's when he turned and backed away, allowing Jim to move forward.

All that prevented Jim from screaming aloud instead of deep in his mind was the notion he may never stop. Gathered at his feet, in the doorway, were the heaped, bagged remnants of Daniel Zero – or a collapsed outer layer of him. Steam rose from the gutted cadaver; the clothing, much like the flesh beneath it, lay open from throat to crotch. Rust coloured fluid flecked the door and the nearby walls, still damp.

Lesser details escaped him. Dry-retching, he reeled away. It only occurred to him as he did that Danny, defiant until the last, still held the gun in his hand and his finger on the trigger.

'Jesus, there's nothing left of him,' he managed to say. He looked at Colin, who had turned white, who seemed to be searching for somewhere else to look. 'It's just as if he − just as if he shed his skin. What happened to the rest? Where did the rest of him go?'

The question was unanswerable. Kneeling beside the mess, Colin set about retrieving the automatic from Danny's grip. Though he could bear to watch only briefly, it seemed to Jim that the hand still clutching the weapon was boneless, offering no resistance.

Wiping the weapon on his trousers, then pocketing it, Colin rose to his feet. For almost a minute he stood absolutely still, saying nothing, trying to regulate his breath. Ladbroke Grove, the streets teeming with life, the faces of the innocent, all seemed a world away now. Perhaps he was relating what he'd found here to himself, his own dilemma.

Colin came back to himself then, the light returning to his eyes. 'Death to the revolution,' he said quietly, and after a respectful silence Jim said, 'We haven't finished here yet. There's one more place.'

'Where?' Colin said.

Jim hammered open the final door. Within, the two-tone room had been reduced to a white walled, bare floorboarded emptiness. There were no curtains, no furnishings − there wasn't even sufficient to bring memories rushing in. Where Jim had remembered an adjoining room, the black room, there was only a blankness of wall.

Still staring aghast into the hollow space, he took a pace back from it. Had he ever really been here at all? Certainly: but his mind had not been his own, and whatever this place had been used for was over and done now. He'd given Cora all the power she needed, the night his future caught up

229

with him. Apparently she needed nothing more from him. She had it all.

'This is it,' he told Colin, exasperated. 'It must have ended here. They must have − I don't know − returned to wherever they came from, taken Elaine and Danny and everyone with them. There's nowhere left to look.'

Colin's response was spoken calmly and without enthusiasm. It was probably spoken in fear, in fact. 'Yes, there is, Jim,' he said.

twenty-five

The Café Bizarre was a basement off New Bond Street, all Mondrian prints and prints of Warhol's soup cans lining the bare brick walls. From midday through to midnight the turnover here was rapid, the rustic benches crowding with the fashionable new rich; but this early in the morning, service was given only reluctantly. After a ten-minute delay a demure waitress in a French beret brought teas to the corner table where Colin and Jim were sitting. She glanced critically twice at Jim before departing, or perhaps Jim only imagined she had.

'Is it really wise to be here?' he wondered, watching the girl back to her place behind the counter. After a moment, she reached for a telephone mounted on the wall. 'The police must have circulated my description to every TV newsroom by now. This place is making me nervous.'

'You're learning how it is to feel hunted,' Colin said gently. He scratched at his bristled jaw with four grubby fingernails. 'Remember, I was there years before you, running from crimes I never committed. Believe me, they've less chance of finding you here than if you were off in the wilderness somewhere. Here you're just another face in the crowd.'

On the table between them sat a new pack of Rothmans and a cheap Clipper lighter. Slowly and methodically, Jim

231

began removing the shrink-wrap from the cigarettes. 'How can you be so sure, though, that going back to Seaborough will solve anything?'

'I can't. But it might help us understand what we're caught up in, and why, that's all. It's time we stopped running from whatever happened there.'

'And if nothing in Seaborough can help us?'

'Then we're screwed.' Colin shrugged, and sipped his drink.

Jim sat back in his chair, massaging his eyes with forefinger and thumb, and for one precious moment the pounding receded completely. Thankfully the Café Bizarre management saw no necessity for piped new-age muzak at this hour. It was the nearest he'd been to relaxing in days, perhaps weeks. Unlike Colin, he hadn't been able to sleep at Danny's, and exhaustion was fast overtaking him.

At last he glanced at his wrist, only to find he was wearing no watch. 'It's hard to imagine anything will be the same at home. You know how it was with the fortune-tellers' places: open one year, gone forever the next.'

'And yet nothing changes there, not really,' Colin said. 'As I recall, we didn't lay eyes on Goatbeard's place until the day we went looking for shelter. In retrospect, you could almost believe he was just . . . well, waiting for us, for that day to happen. Do you think there'll be another day like that?'

Jim demurred. 'For all we know he's dead by now; he's taken the secret with him.' He was about to go on when the slow rise and fall of a siren cut him short. He put down the cigarettes he'd been toying with. At the far end of the café, the waitress was replacing the telephone. Couldn't she have recognised him and called for help? But it was surely too soon, there hadn't been time for a response to her call.

232

'Perhaps we should leave now.' Jim was getting up hurriedly. 'It's better we don't stay too long in one place.' He picked up and turned over the bill, which the waitress had left face-down under his saucer, and dropped two one-pound coins on it. Colin's face became hard and tight, and he stood a little reluctantly. 'You're sure this isn't paranoia speaking?'

But the siren was no longer distant, or even middle-distant, and its pitch was unchanging now; the vehicle it belonged to must have stopped outside. The waitress, now joined by a suntanned, dark-haired man with warningly folded arms, stared Jim and Colin all the way from the table to the exit.

As they emerged from the café Colin said, 'It's all right, they're not after you, just hitch up your collar and walk away.' From what? Jim wondered, before he saw the skirmish taking place across the street. A group of uniformed police were dragging apart two men who were struggling for possession of something that looked like a dog, or a cat. Behind them, the display window of a small portrait gallery had been smashed, the pavement before it flecked silver and crimson. Someone was screaming uncontrollably, a woman who was trying to join the fray, arms flailing. When the two men parted, the bundle they were contesting fell to the floor, rolled over, lay still. It was a child. One of the men had been using the tiny body to break in the window.

The screaming woman was, without doubt, its mother. Still screaming, she approached her child, throwing her arms theatrically skywards while at the same time collapsing to her knees. Behind her, one of the men was pulling away from the police, who were trying to restrain him. After a flourish of limbs he was free and breaking into a flat-footed run. When several onlookers converged on him from shop doorways, it seemed to Jim that they were stepping in to assist the police. Then he saw the glint of cold steel whispering down through the air, and the quick, silent sweep of a club or wrench. That was as much as he had time to see before Colin pushed him on along New Bond Street.

'Why are they punishing the defenceless?' Jim said. 'Children and women, men without weapons. Why?'

'They remind them of their own inadequacies,' Colin replied. 'The helpless are too much like themselves.'

So this is it, this is really it, Jim thought breathlessly as they went, as the sky above the city gradually bleached itself of colour, clouds drawing in and across it from the south. There would be more atrocities, smaller and greater acts of paranoid rage, but this was where the precedent had been set, this was where it became a way of life.

At the junction of Upper Saint Martin's Lane and Long Acre, the crowds had overturned an electric blue Capri and set it ablaze. Several passers-by were not, in fact, passing by but queuing to take souvenir snapshots. Thick grey smoke belched upwards above a war dance of flame, while numbers of Cora sweatshirts mulled around the periphery.

Jim stared hard and long into the depths of the pyre before moving on, and at some point he sensed something give in himself, a hard, clean twist of resolve. There was nothing to it, really; it was only a small moment, half-forgotten an hour or two later. Yet with it came the clear understanding that everything died with him here. If not quite dead, nor was he truly alive any more. But just think of the freedom that gave him! He had embraced Death once, and would do so again. This time he would go all the way if need be.

twenty-six

By the time they were travelling, the light had begun to fade. It was still too early for nightfall, but there were forecasts of storms from the south-west, the clouds having stolen the sun's warmth with its light, and they drove with the rented Sierra's heating system turned on.

Jim couldn't help wondering if further bulletins had followed the one last night, but there was nothing about him on the car radio. The Capital DJ seemed more concerned with what he called the overall picture, claiming the bursts of inner-city violence were becoming more and more sporadic, less organised. When the DJ cut short his monologue with a track from *The Dark Brigade* Colin reached across to twiddle the dial.

The north-bound traffic was denser and slower than Jim had anticipated, and after four hours they were still short of Birmingham. On the M1, a series of collisions had blocked the inside lane, causing a two-mile tailback while motorists sounded their tempers through their horns.

Several of the wrecks were roped off like exhibits. In one instance, the victims of a crash — two families with small children — were laid out on the hard shoulder like slabs of spilled meat, their vehicles welded together in ripples of metal, bellies upwards. 'What reason can she have for bringing this chaos?' Jim wondered aghast, tapping the wheel, and Colin said, 'What reason does she need?'

They pulled into a noisy motorway services station, and between mouthfuls of congealed shepherd's pie Colin went on, 'She's stealing what doesn't belong to her — the hearts and minds of good people like Elaine and Danny — but she doesn't need a reason. She's doing the only thing she knows how to do. Just as if she's doing her job.'

'Some job.' The notion took as much swallowing as the cool food they'd brought to their table on unscrubbed trays. 'But what *right* does she have? What right does anyone have to steal the souls of the living?' If he and Colin, visiting Goatbeard, had broken some unwritten law, then surely the forces they'd unsealed had been equally guilty.

Laying down his fork, Jim stared across to where a gang of young teenagers huddled around a bleeping, exploding video game. That's me, he thought; that's Colin; and the one on the far left, that's Terry Mack, the image of him, before he died.

Beyond the games machine a large window framed the services car park. Directly outside were three new-looking telephone kiosks. Jim stood, checking his pockets for change. 'I've a couple of calls to make. Do you mind waiting?'

'I'll meet you at the car,' Colin said before wandering in the opposite direction, probably in search of a toilet.

Outside, beneath a towering Mickey Mouse that guarded the entrance to a children's play arena, Jim slid into the first of the three booths and loaded a palm full of tens into the slot. After he'd dialled and the line had settled, a girl's voice said questioningly, '*Alter-Image*? Can I help you?'

It was Nina Fowles, working late for once. 'Nina, is Martyn there? This is Jim, Jim Doherty.'

'Jesus Christ,' she said after a wait. Temporarily, the ice maiden's image had cracked. 'Where are you?'

'Where I am doesn't matter. Is Martyn around?'

'You might reach him at home. The office is nearly empty now; just me and a couple of cleaners. What's going on, Jim? The cops were in earlier, they were taking your desk apart. They took your passport, I think.'

'That's all right,' he said, allowing himself a smile. 'Where I'm going I won't need it.'

'And there was something on the news: they mentioned your name, but it was all over so fast I couldn't −'

'You'll have the whole story soon,' Jim assured her. And put every second-hand word of it in your column, no doubt, he thought. 'Listen Nina, this is for Martyn. Do you think you can write it down or something? Tell him there *will* be a Cora feature on its way, and it won't be the one he's expecting. Another thing: I doubt I'll be coming in with it. Have you got that?'

'Jim, I −'

'Thanks Nina. See you around. Give my love to the smart set.'

Hanging up before she was able to utter another sound, he fed in his change and redialled. This time it was a Seaborough number, and the feeling of nostalgia as his father lifted the receiver forced him to close his eyes tightly.

'Dad?' he said, and his father said almost suspiciously, 'Jim? Jim, is that you?'

'Who else? How are you?' He had to clamp his mouth shut to avoid saying, How are you both? − but it was more than six years since the stroke had killed his mother. At least it hadn't caused her to dwindle away, paralysed, unable to fend for herself: no one would have preferred her to end up like that. 'I'm on my way home, Dad,' he said.

The news seemed to confound his father, at least at first. 'When? What for? But then, you don't need a reason, do you? You'll be staying, of course? I'll get a bed ready, shall I?'

'Better make it two,' Jim told him. 'I've someone else with me. Do you remember Colin Schofield?'

There was a pause on the line before his father said, 'I thought we'd all heard the last of him. Last I knew of Colin was when he came looking for you, after they released him from that place he'd been in. Did it really take him until now to find you?'

'Yes.'

'What's happening, Jim? What's this about?'

'I can't explain now,' Jim said, and blinked as the kiosk flooded with light and just as quickly emptied of it. He watched the car's tail-lights turn past the Mickey Mouse silhouette. 'Just wait until we arrive, and I'll fill you in on everything. In the meantime, see if you can get those beds aired and the bar open. We'll probably be home late.' Home, he thought; and in the last ten or twelve years he could count in days the time he'd actually spent there.

Speaking to his father again had filled him with a new sense of urgency, even hope. At least there was something unchanging and stable he could turn to in this world. He walked briskly across the parking area, roughly towards the spot where he remembered leaving the car, not noticing the white Saab creeping from shadows some distance behind him.

Because the night had settled while he'd been on the phone, the vehicle only became a Saab as it passed through the bars of light extending across the asphalt from the services complex. After that, it was swallowed by darkness again.

twenty-seven

Seaborough was almost a disappointment when they arrived, but that was because the night had made it vanish except for a scattering of houselights like fallen stars. Perhaps they had both, deep down, expected to find the aurora borealis, the town covered over with magic and lights. Instead, only the unmistakable sound of the ocean and the brine on the air told them when they'd arrived.

In the passenger seat, Colin's sunken face glowed amber as he set fire to another cigarette with the lighter drawn from the dashboard. 'Do you mind if we drive around for a bit first?'

Jim thought he understood why Colin would want that, and turned the car on to the coastal road that rose above and behind the town towards the cliff-top guest houses and large white hotels which looked down on it. More than ten years must have passed since Colin had been anywhere he could truly call home. As the tree-lined road climbed he shivered, either because of the cold air or the memories that were stirring. Leafy branches formed a thick canopy overhead, and he remembered running home this way one long-ago night, dodging the dappled moon on the road, telling himself he would die if the light ever touched him. There was no moon tonight, no light but the dipped beams of the car until the trees fell sharply away behind and the road began to slope downwards. As the road threatened to vanish into the black, Colin said, 'Pull over here.'

They were nearing the cliff-tops, somewhere above the pitch and putt and the crazy golf. A pale phosphorescence swarmed distantly at sea. Dropping gears, Jim eased the car off the road and on to the verge. The grass felt brittle underfoot, as if no rain had fallen here for weeks. To their right, a solid darkness the size of a bungalow turned out to be one of the cliff-side lifts, perched atop its steep track. 'Time was,' Colin said fondly, 'I used to run down the footpath and see if I could beat the lift to the bottom. Sometimes I came pretty close.'

'How did you fare coming uphill?' Jim wondered.

'Uphill? I took the lift. I know when I'm licked.' He moved to the edge, laying his hands on the iron safety rail. Standing beside him, Jim could see the lights on the promenade below, the lamps above the sea wall a blazing string of pearls, reflected once in the blackness beyond. The arcade and the other amusements were closed, though nightlights burned here and there, and there was activity of some kind at the Hippodrome and, further along, at the cinema.

After a lull, Colin tossed his cigarette to the wind and said quietly, 'Seems I spent half my life trying to escape this, and the other half trying to get back.' The stopping, starting rhythm of waves was soothing, as was his voice. 'Now we've come this far I'm almost afraid to go on. Feels like — I don't know — the town's waiting. Or something in the town.'

'Waiting for what?'

'For us. For everything to begin. Do you think we were wrong to come back?'

'Do you think we had any choice?' Jim closed his eyes, trying to savour the hush that followed and the feeling of dark, invisible spray on his face. For a moment he felt he'd never left Seaborough, that neither of them had. Was it wrong, he wondered, to be sharing this moment – or any moment – with Colin, when for so long he and Elaine had lived in fear of him? Perhaps it was necessary to forgive, if only because they must finish what they'd started together.

They stood for a while in silence – a silence that seemed to emanate from the muffled, blackened stars. Finally, it was Colin who turned back to the car. 'Ready?' he said.

Jim grew rigid as the car swept in through the gates and around to the yard behind the guest house, the headlights wafting across a tilting For Sale sign. The car park at the rear was empty.

Andrew Doherty, who had grown wider and balder and unaccountably shorter since Jim last laid eyes on him, swung the door open before anyone had knocked and stepped neatly aside to let them in.

It was more than his mother's touch that was lacking, Jim realised as soon as they'd entered; it was as if the life had gone from the house when she had. The walls were red and gold velvety eyesores, the paintings by local artists which adorned them were of the harbour and nearby cornfields and brooks. Half-way along the hall, a barometer's needle had stopped at Changeable. A thin layer of dust covered everything in sight.

In the lounge, a switched-on but soundless television above the bar was the only sign that the room was in use. White sheets draped over most of the furniture made everything appear moulded from dough. It wasn't until they were seated around three tall tumblers and a bottle that Jim's father seemed able to face either him or Colin.

His mouth trembled agape and then closed, as though whatever he had to say could never be adequate.

'I thought this was supposed to be the height of the season,' Jim said, waving a hand at the room, flabbergasted. 'How long has it been coming to this?'

Andrew Doherty shrugged. 'Just the last couple of years, I'd say. I've been losing the regulars ever since we lost your mother. I can't keep up to the place, never really had her knack. And they've found they can get cheaper on the continent these days.' He shrugged, and smiled philosophically. 'Well, if that's what they want.'

Jim said, 'You never let me know you were putting the house up for sale. Did you have to?'

His father gave a curt nod, took a mouthful of Scotch, and swallowed. 'I can't afford to keep it any more, and besides, can't you feel how empty it is? Last week we dropped the price for the third time. No interested parties, is what they're telling me at the estate agents. They're going to have drag people in off the streets to view the place.'

'But it's a valuable property,' Jim exclaimed. 'I don't understand why no one − ' He faltered, hardly daring to think himself further. He did understand though, he understood perfectly; yet how could he explain what he knew to his father? When his father changed the subject, he only wished he could feel more relieved.

'What about you, though?' his father was saying, and to Colin, 'And you? When I opened the door I smelt you before I saw you, but by God you're worse to look at. Didn't you bring a change of clothes?' Before anyone could stammer a reply he went on, gesturing towards the TV, on which English test match wickets were tumbling in slow motion. 'Jim, I want you to be truthful because − well, we're not so remote up here as you think. We still get the national news. That's enough to make everything that goes on down there real enough. There was a story tonight that mentioned your name, and showed your picture, and for the life of me I don't know what to think.'

'Then try not to think the worst,' Jim said, 'because the story isn't true. You'll have to take that on trust.'

'But the dead girl, the state she was in when they found her, that's true enough, isn't it?'

'Yes.'

'And the man downstairs. The one who was all messed up? You had nothing to do with that either?'

'You can either believe me or believe what they say on the news, Dad.'

'Yes, well.' His father was standing, patting the back of his chair, from which a puff of dust rose. Pocketing his hands, he seemed to sag and concede. 'So you're both innocent men, are you?'

'I don't know about innocent,' Colin said, and Jim said quickly, 'We're neither of us guilty.' He nodded at Colin, and even half-managed a smile: it was the nearest he was going to get to forgiveness, and when Colin returned the smile it seemed that Colin understood as much.

'Whatever's going on between you two,' Jim's father said, 'I have to believe you. I ought to know you well enough, Jim, to know what you can and can't do. And you couldn't have done what they said on the news. I suppose it wouldn't help me to know the whole story?'

'You suppose right,' Jim told him, 'but if you really insist, let it wait till morning. We've sleep to catch up on.'

'There's hot water for baths as well as warm beds,' his father announced as though addressing the guests he'd lost. 'Colin, there's a door open on the first floor — that's yours, I hope it's all right. And Jim, I took the liberty of putting you where you used to be, in the attic. It'll be just like —' Just like old times, he might have intended to say, and then the spark went out from his eyes like a snuffed flame. 'Anyway, I've tried to make everything the way it was,' he said, but by the time he'd finished speaking he looked almost shamefaced.

They parted outside Colin's room, Colin shaking hands with Jim's father and saying goodnight distractedly in a faint and dreamy voice. He could only be thinking of tomorrow, Jim decided, to have suddenly become so subdued. Better though the uncertainty of tomorrow than the certain knowledge of what had already taken place.

The more Jim thought of 1977, the more missed chances he saw. Memories were hurtful, angry things that accused him of having blundered, having fouled up. All the way up to the attic, he could sense the past closing in on him, the dim walls leaning nearer. On the last flight of stairs he stalled, dragging for breath, hardly daring to go on.

The room itself was exactly as he remembered. Jim stepped inside, closing the door softly in case the sudden disturbance shattered the illusion. But this was no illusion. The solid feel of the oyster walls and the rugged shelves as he skimmed his hands across them proved how real it was. Of all the rooms in the house, in fact, this seemed the best preserved, even to the dustless surfaces, the porthole window's freshly painted frame. Why had his father kept up this room when all else had been mothballed? Probably he'd hoped for this night, or one much like it. He'd hoped that Jim would eventually leave the city and return to stay for good. Well, in a way, he had.

Removing his jacket, he flopped on the bed and unfastened his shoes before noticing what else his father had done. Then he felt his heart warming, felt laughter wanting to scramble out of him. If he laughed aloud, though, would it sound like madness? Would he be able to stop?

On the stripped pine table under the window, his father had placed the old portable typewriter, purchased from Woolworths for Jim's thirteenth birthday, and next to the typewriter a new, sealed ream of A4 paper, a Reporter's Notebook, a cracked mug filled with pencils and pens. Closer, he saw that the pens were ordinary biros, not the fine-line felt tips he preferred, but his father couldn't be expected to know that. In any case, what had he imagined Jim would want to write?

It didn't matter. Jim already knew what had to be written before he could leave. He owed it to Elaine, to Danny, not least to himself. He owed it to others too, to the numberless consumers who had prayed for a goddess and found one; a murderess who seduced and spirited away what had never belonged to her.

And he was beginning to see why he must write it. If Cora were real, she would certainly wield less power. She had become all-powerful because her followers *wanted* the myth, wanted to fall down before it, and if he could do nothing else, if nothing came of tomorrow, he would make her real tonight. He'd remember everything, quotes and all. Then she'd be nothing; another inflated star, grown fat on glory and adoration. She wouldn't pass this way again.

Before drawing his chair to the table, he pushed open the porthole window, which tried to stick because of new paint. Though the air was chill, he imagined he'd need it to stay awake as the article progressed. For Elaine, he thought, and set to it. He tore open the ream and wound the first sheet into the platen.

Nearly three hours later the truth was out, and it read like the mutterings of a madman. Was this the best he could do? His first impulse on reading what he'd done was to tear the pages into halves and then quarters, but resisting, he clipped them together instead. Whether the readers believed him or not, he was telling the truth as he knew it, and that was as much as anyone could do. On a clean sheet he wrote in pencil:

> *Martyn –*
> *I know this is not what you'd hoped for but it's what you're going to get. Death to the sub that takes liberties with this copy because for once it's all too real, and it's important that people know. There are some who would have vouched for what I have to say but they lost their lives in the struggle. There may be more to follow, but I can't say for sure you'll be hearing it from me.*
>
> > *All the best,*
> > *Jim*

Finished, he turned off the light at the wall and collapsed on the bed. He'd meant to close the window in case of rain in the night, but he hadn't the energy for that now. Beyond the small capsule of his room, all sounds had blended into one serene rush, neither wind nor sea. He was wondering whether the sound would keep him awake in spite of his tiredness when deep, dreamless sleep closed over him.

twenty-eight

A sudden breeze caused the trees to flinch as Colin and Jim took the shortcut through Levin's Park. The spiky iron gates were rusting and stiff-hinged, their bottle-green paint flaking off when touched. Jim pulled them firmly shut and followed Colin down and along the winding path and around the lake's edge, watching himself waver across the surface. Soon his reflection was broken by a Mallard and its mate bursting helter-skelter into the lake from the concrete bank. Out in the centre, a lone canoeist dipped his oar once, and sailed.

'I thought,' Colin said, 'we'd start off where we were the first time. How do you feel about trying the arcade on the front?'

'And then McGonnigles?'

'If it's still there, yes.'

'I wish,' Jim said, 'I wish to God we'd gone there the first time instead of − of −'

'I know,' Colin said, 'I know. But I learned to stop saying "if only" a long time ago. It only makes matters worse.'

It had been Jim's first full night of sleep in almost a week. Thank God for hot water and clean towels! Having bathed, shaved, dressed in clothes that his father had kept for him, he not only smelt and looked better, but felt it.

His skin felt real this morning, his pores clear, his mind his own. He'd woken in readiness, mentally and physically prepared. For what, he had no idea.

They had breakfasted late and at leisure – coffee, eggs, waffles and more coffee – and by the time Jim had posted his feature to London the town was crawling with summer guests. They weren't out in summer clothing, however. All the figures at the lakeside looked faded to grey, sunken-eyed, overgrown by sweaters and coats worn with upturned collars. Nevertheless they were out in numbers. 'And you have to assume that business is booming,' Jim remarked. 'It's every bit as busy as it used to be, isn't it?'

'Your dad wouldn't say so,' Colin shrugged.

'But why?'

'Why what?'

'Why should his livelihood be in ruins because of something we did years ago? He never invited anything like this.'

'Nor did we,' Colin said evenly.

They were following the path away from the park's south exit, which led to the harbour. On the north side, past the public conveniences, a putting green was dotted with ankle-high flags. A diminutive blonde girl stood between the seventh and eighth holes, watching one mongrel dog mount another, pantingly, mindlessly. Until her parents called her away in panicky voices, she looked paralysed, unsure whether she ought to be laughing or crying.

The air, so sweet an hour ago, was suddenly cloying, its brine offensive. A gate on the north side brought them out on to Acacia Avenue. Some of the smells that greeted them on the promenade were foul, as though the fish the small shops sold had lain rotting for days in the humidity. One alley between two souvenir shops, in particular, gusted air like halitosis as they reached it. Deep in the alley, a man dressed all in blue denim stood urinating against the wall, unworried that his efforts streamed darkly down the slope to the promenade.

They strolled past a newsagent's, past a joke shop with wind-up teeth and plastic dung in its window, past a red and white ice-cream parlour whose walls were murals of James Dean and Elvis and which belonged, Colin said, in an American road movie, or a Pepsi commercial based on one. A number of boys in white shirts and with neatly combed hair and girls wearing ankle socks were chatting on stools at the banana-shaped bar. Advertising *what*? Jim couldn't help wondering. He was beginning to linger and stare when the first peal of thunder, far away and at sea, speeded him on.

The arcade was next door, its grim panorama of the front the same as ever. A greyness cloaked everything now, squeezing the daylight to a watery haze; fingers of foam came prying almost speculatively over the promenade wall, then withdrew. Standing just inside the arcade's wall-sized window, Colin inhaled deeply, folded his arms, shook his head once, and exhaled. 'They've made the games more sophisticated, the fashions have changed, but we're pretty much back where we were, don't you think?'

A cross-current of electronic battle noises drowned much of Jim's reply. He nodded instead, waiting for the warfare to fade. There was nothing in the arcade to keep them, and outside he said, 'What are you planning exactly?'

'Planning? I'm not planning anything. Just trying it on for size, that's all, second time around.'

'You think that all we have to do is retrace our steps? Begin again?'

'No, not begin again – this time it has to end.' Colin was quickening his pace, racing to leave the truth behind.

'Don't ask me how; I just feel we should do things in roughly the same order as before. If you've any better suggestions —'

'No,' Jim said. He had none; could think only of his fears, of all the things that might go wrong, the negatives. That Goatbeard had moved from the area or — even worse — died, was the first, most glaring, possibility. Certainly it was the most likely. But it was important, Jim rebuked himself, not to allow for such an eventuality. If he must, he would keep the old man alive by pure thought, until they had learned what they needed to. He couldn't allow him to be dead yet.

At the end of the prom they turned up on to Seaview Road. Several doorways along, Jim halted by a window displaying second-hand books, mostly paperbacks. The yellowed, faded covers of James Hadley Chase and Richard Matheson novels were like random fragments of his past, some sweet, some sour. 'How many Saturdays did we come here?' he wondered aloud. 'How many hours did we kill inside, browsing?' He shivered pleasurably, at last glancing up to see whether Colin shared the memory. There was no sign of Colin at all.

At the top of the street, where the road curved around past a barber's pole striped like a stick of local rock, a figure had just darted out of sight. That would be Colin, running ahead like old times. Jim set off in pursuit, straining uphill until his lungs began heaving and his armpits and chest grew unpleasantly warm. Though he couldn't remember the old-fashioned barber's shop, he could visualise what ought to be near it, two or three doors along: a confectioner's with baskets of cream fudge and hand-made chocolates in the window and a fat white-haired lady moving about inside. Neither the shop nor the lady were there.

Obviously he'd misjudged where he was. Instinct told him this should have been Providence Street, its gaily coloured shutters and window frames swarming ever upwards; but he'd arrived on a steep, cobbled side-street, so steep that a hand rail was bolted to the walls alongside. Somewhere — or was he only imagining this? — a track from *The Dark Brigade* riffled the air. At the top of the slope was a music shop with its many racks of second-hand records standing outside. Near them stood Colin, his hands aloft as if pleading ignorance. 'Where *is* this?' he said when Jim reached him.

Three concrete bollards plugged the entrance to a narrow alley beside the record shop. Colin squeezed through first, leading with his long, low stride, heels occasionally scraping the ground. Someone's washing flapped overhead, its dripping supplemented by the first spots of rain. A nameplate affixed to the wall at the alley's end said Rochefort Mews, but Jim couldn't recall having heard of it. Nor, Colin's frown said, could he.

All at once the air tasted of hops instead of brine, the mews adjoining a street of pubs and wine bars, many of which were dark and soundless. They were nearing a junction and a road that must have been adjacent to the cobbled side-street. Colin said, 'Notice it stops climbing here. We just lost our bearings for a minute, that's all, no sweat. It's easily done when we've been away so long.'

Jim nodded, but clearly Colin believed nothing of what he'd just said. There was a dry-mouthed edge to his voice, a twitchy vitality about him that suggested he was motoring not on this morning's breakfast, but on fear.

A car flashed by as they reached the junction, but there was no more traffic. A flash of sunflower yellow somewhere to Jim's left made him turn, but it was only a parked Mister Whippy ice-cream van, not what he'd expected to see: the colourful shutters of a palmist's house.

'Which way? Left or right?' he demanded. A sports shop, a Photo Mart – there was nothing remotely familiar here. A group of girls giggled their way in through the door of a small café. 'I thought you said nothing ever changed in Seaborough,' he said, but Colin retorted, 'It probably hasn't. It's simply the way we're approaching it.'

They turned uphill, to their right. The sea was no longer to be heard; there was a sudden disturbance of squealing gulls and, nearer a car horn bleating the first few notes of 'The Internationale'. Now the blend of seafront smells were being lost to a spicy fragrance of Chinese, Italian, Indian restaurants and the open doors of delicatessens. Where were all the street names, though? One, even one, would be something to go on with. 'Should we ask?' Jim said. 'Directions, I mean.'

Colin greeted the suggestion with scarcely concealed disdain. 'This is *our* town, *my* town, Jim. I grew up in these streets. I know them like the back of my hand. If we're lost, we'll find our own way back. I refuse . . .'

'Then what do you suggest, if we can't ask?'

'We're above the town,' Colin said. 'From where we are now, it all starts to level off. There's no sense going any further this way. We've only to find the right combination of streets to get back where we were. We overshot our mark, that's all.'

But he was unable to hide his frustration, or his mounting panic. The town was not large or particularly convoluted: how could it contain so many new and unremembered streets, so many misnomers?

Jim couldn't help wondering whether Providence Street did not want to be found. Surely, surely it couldn't be afraid they'd unlock its secret. Wouldn't that mean there might be a way to beat it; to reverse the jinx somehow?

The thought was overpowering. It was vital, now more than ever, that he hold on to Providence Street with everything he had, all the force of his will; that everything be real, untouched by time.

They continued past a shop selling bicycles, a junk shop, and further along, a hairdresser's with the nerve to call itself Blow Job. Many of the styles illustrated on the door looked like accidents, and one of the stylists flitting to and fro inside resembled the man from *Eraserhead*. Colin tugged up his collar as the first fork of lightning whited out the sky. By the time the rain arrived he'd already broken into a run.

Quite suddenly and without warning, there were no more shops. A boarded-up tattooist's was the last, after which the streets became narrower and darker. As yet the rain was only a drizzle, but there was no freshness in it, only a grimy unpleasantness that made Jim feel coated with smog, made him think of the sweltering city. Hopefully the storm would clear the air. For the moment, he was fighting for breath, even though it was all downhill from here. A twist of cramp in his abdomen forced him to clutch at his ribs as he ran.

Colin was lengthening his stride, increasing the distance between them. His hair flapped, his unbuttoned coat trailed loosely behind him from the waist. He was running, Jim thought, as he used to run at their inter-school sports meetings, when Jim had been relegated to the touchlines to cheer his hero on. And Colin had been a hero of sorts, hadn't he? Yes, he had once been a role model, someone and something to aspire to, not only gifted but born for a purpose. That, at least, was how it had seemed at the time.

One street led to another. All were strangely alike, their jutting, angled roof-tops dashed with mist. Here was another street name: Hutton Way. Again, Jim did not know it. The alley terminated in a pedestrian precinct of market stalls and milling shoppers, many of whom were huddling under the canopies draped over the stalls to keep off the rain. No one smiled, or doffed their hat, or said good morning, although a woman in thick-lensed spectacles did turn to glower at Colin, then Jim, as they tried to ease by her. 'I thought the market was on the other side of town, above the harbour,' Colin said, and then added, 'Maybe that's where we are.'

'Maybe,' Jim replied. 'We could be anywhere.'

Nothing was real any more, yet he had to believe that the town hadn't changed, that Providence Street remained as it was. Every plodding step he took seemed another step beyond hope somehow. Perhaps all his fears were slowly becoming one, and what he'd always dreaded most was this weird and unaccountable loss of direction. What if Providence Street had never truly existed, except for one moment, long enough to trap them within its spell? What solution was there if the problem itself lay out of reach? Was there no going back?

The lightning shocked him back to himself. The storm was repeating itself, the rain dashing into his face and body and dashing across the pavement before him. Some short distance ahead he saw Colin slowing, breathless, and turning his back on the rain, which was suddenly loaded with hail. He was slumping against a window near the brow of the hill as Jim caught him up.

'The jinx is doing this, sending us round in circles,' Jim managed at the top of his voice. He raised a hand to protect his pink, raw face. 'Who's to say we'll find the guest house again if we ever get back there? If we could just — '

'Just what?' Colin was holding himself and staring at the ground, gasping for breath. A clump of hair plastered itself across his brow as he lifted his face. 'What's wrong?' he said when he had Jim focused. 'What's wrong?'

Jim was wiping the water from his eyes and mouth with the back of a hand and gazing past Colin's shoulder at the small bay window that hadn't been properly cleaned in years. 'We're there,' he said, putting his fingers to the pane. 'We're there.'

The sign above the window was missing, but the blurred surface of glass was enough to bring everything else flooding back. The grime inside the window was not grime, but a darkness that had grown tangible over the years.

It had always been, as Colin had said, a matter of finding the right combination. And here they were, everything falling into place around them. If they should glance uphill, back the way they'd come, there would be Hawthorne Drive; and below them where the road took a dog-leg would be McGonnigles. Indeed, there was a handful of customers now, fumbling down their umbrellas and pressing forward into the shop, out of the rain.

'I suppose this means Welcome Home,' Colin said, and reluctantly turned towards the alley beside the house.

'Did we find it by accident, do you think?' Jim said. But he knew the answer already. The house had always existed. There had never been any such thing as coincidence. They were here because it had once been prophesied.

twenty-nine

The alley was exactly as Jim knew it would be. Some of the old new-wave names had vanished, time having washed them from the brickwork, but otherwise they might have been stepping into '77 again. Even the plaque on the door was still there, its message, YOUR FUTURE NOW, the same. Only the lettering had faded, perhaps for want of being read.

Just as they reached the door, Colin stopped and swung himself around at a noise. But the movement behind him was only a cat departing a burst-open dustbin liner, through which it had been foraging. Garbage flowed wetly out from the hole in the plastic, liquefying in the rain.

'All right now?' Jim said.

Dragging for air, Colin nodded once to show he was ready. Ready as he would ever be, anyway.

The doorbell no longer worked. At least no one came hurrying to answer it. Testing the door, Jim found it wasn't even latched. It pushed open easily, without a sound. Giving fear no opportunity, he stepped inside.

'Fuck me,' Colin said as soon as they reached the kitchen. 'This is just too disgusting for words. Who could *live* in this?'

The light was scarce and visibility poor, but that in itself was nearly too much. Almost as bad was the regular, sourceless sound of dripping which seemed to be coming from upstairs somewhere: probably just rain from the gutter, Jim hoped.

To their right, where the sink had been, a creamy-coloured fungus had swarmed up the wall to chest height. The sink itself and the drainer lay smashed on the floor and, above them, the small window was draped with a curtain that looked like moist, rotting parchment.

A small ripple of movement low and to Jim's extreme left made him turn, then just as quickly put a hand to his mouth. In the corner lay the carcass of a small animal, unidentifiable now, swarming with grubs, a massed, frenzied family of them. Colin swore and turned away, towards the curtained doorway at one end of the kitchen. As he reached it, a milk bottle collided with his foot. In one motion, he picked up the bottle and smashed it against the wall, releasing a little of what had developed inside him.

'Wait till I get my hands on that bastard,' he said.

'Steady,' Jim told him.

The front room with its vista of Providence Street was empty except for the seats in front of the hearth. No sooner had they entered than the air seemed to thicken dramatically. There was a sour tang of decay, as if death itself were at work here. As Jim grew accustomed to the light he realised there was more to it than that, far more; the air in the room was literally alive.

Unless his mind had finally collapsed, there were sparks before his eyes — quick, white flashes of energy cracking the air. In less than a second a chain of a dozen or more tiny flames raced up the wall and across the ceiling above the fireplace. Jim flinched as their heat reached his face.

A charge of static bristled his hair. Swirling motes of dust glowed brightly, albeit briefly, before expiring. When Jim put out a hand to steady himself against the nearest wall, the plaster collapsed, and his fingers sank into a mushy coolness that made him cry out.

In the same instant thunder shook the house, or perhaps more than thunder. It seemed that with their arrival here the power had consolidated, releasing itself to the full. What were these sparks of energy if not the dregs of second-hand prophecies? Suppose other, earlier horrors too numerous to count had entered the world through here, and this was their residue?

'Well, he isn't here,' Colin announced simply, as though he saw nothing out of the ordinary. 'Looks like we're wasting our time. I suppose it was too much to expect that we'd find him. What now?'

'There's still upstairs,' Jim said, withdrawing as soon as the wallpaper over the mantelpiece bulged, threatening to split itself open. 'We may – may as well try up there.'

The miniature electric storm seemed to recede as they doubled back to the stairs. Fourteen noisy wooden risers climbed towards a dim, stained-glass skylight. Above, on the landing, a row of four doors stood firmly closed. The first of these were the bathroom and toilet, the stench from which was worse than sewage. The interiors looked blackened and charred, where they weren't smothered with moss. The bath was a haven for spiders.

The third door along was blocked from within. Colin shouldered it, tentatively at first, and it gave slightly. He glanced at Jim, hot-faced, ferocious-eyed. 'Here,' he said softly, and shouldered the door. 'Here,' and the weight budged further, and a quiet voice gasped aloud in the room.

Finally Colin threw what must have been all his force behind it, and the door swung open, the half-light from the landing rushing into the room.

Jim took three long strides to the threshold. He heard the figure topple back into the room before he saw it. The man was little more than a shadow; but if his cramped and withered gait was anything to go by, Jim would be pleased to see no more. The man stumbled backwards two or three steps, too shocked or too physically inadequate to keep himself upright. Colin advanced on him, grabbing the man with both eager hands and dragging him to the doorway.

'Now, you old fuck,' he hissed. 'Now.'

'Don't,' was all Jim had time to say.

Colin ignored him, thumping the man twice, three times against the doorframe before relenting. Now his breathing was thicker, less regular still; he sounded on the verge of an asthma attack. 'You,' he said.

The goatbearded man's gaze strayed as far as Jim. At first he looked merely disorientated; then, in the silence, everything seemed to make sense, and he brightened. 'You,' he returned. 'I was hoping we'd seen the last of each other.'

'I imagine so,' Colin said.

'Don't,' Jim pleaded, too late to prevent Colin from mashing the man's nose with the heel of a hand.

There was no reason for it. The man gave a muffled cry, reaching to claw frantically at the pain in his face. Colin stepped away from him, gasping. He had made it this far, but now his defences were shot, the rage was winning. Any minute now, Jim thought, he's going to lose control altogether, do something even he'll regret. His thoughts turned to Danny, the smouldering mass of flesh he'd become: it could easily be himself or Colin, at any time. They had to remain calm, avoid giving the sickness free rein. 'For Godsakes give him the chance to talk,' he said.

'Now then,' Colin said to the goatbearded man, 'you have some explaining to do, I think.'

'Please,' the man said. A single bead of blood trickled from his nose to his lips, his tongue emerging to lap it away. 'I don't,' he said, 'I don't have to explain *anything* I see to you. It's *there*, that's all. Do you think that by hitting me you can stop what's happening to you? It wasn't my fault, I didn't make it happen, I never made anything happen.' After a pause he said, 'What I saw in your future, I wasn't mistaken, was I?'

'No, you weren't mistaken.'

'And I gave you fair warning. Don't you think I wouldn't prefer to see everything come out right in the end, all candy-coated and happily ever after? But I have no control, I see what's there. I only provide —'

'Go on,' Jim said, stepping nearer.

'I only provide a way in. If I weren't here to do it, then someone else —' He stared at Jim until Jim felt the need to avert his eyes. ' — someone else with the gift probably would. Someone like you, perhaps.'

'Me?' Jim said, alarmed, but Colin said, 'He's trying to fuck us over, can't you see what he's doing?'

Then he was wrestling Goatbeard to the stairs, and had already descended two steps with him before Jim realised he hadn't intended to throw him down. 'Come on, keep moving,' Colin was saying as they passed into darkness below. 'You're going to look into my future again.'

In the front room, Colin bundled the fortune-teller into the chair before the fireplace, then flopped on the couch opposite, resting his hands on his knees. Jim waited uncertainly at the doorway before entering and sitting beside Colin. Though the air still had an electric charge, he was relieved to see that the wall above the mantel had restored itself, that the paper's floral design was just that, a confluence of vines and flowerheads. Even so, he was unable to look past Goatbeard to the window. The memory of what he had seen there was as strong now as the vision itself had been.

'Shall we begin?' Colin said, and Jim said, 'Why were you hiding?'

'Afraid of what we'd do to you?' Colin said. Then, as if he were actually relishing this, 'We still might, you know.'

'I thought you were someone else,' Goatbeard replied.

'Who?'

'Someone else. The ones who did this to us.'

'Who might they be?'

'They've already taken everything away from me,' Goatbeard reminisced as if the question had never been asked. His face, now that Jim could see it more clearly, was a skull covered with tawny, flabby skin, with troubled eyes frantic for somewhere to hide. So this was what a thousand futures bearing down on you did. His hands worked together ceaselessly, unable to settle. Finally he wiped the back of one over his bloody nose and said, 'They've taken my life. But they won't have what's left of me. They won't have my soul as well.'

'Who does he mean?' Colin said.

'Were you expecting them to come here?' Jim said to Goatbeard.

'They always come here. They come and go as they please. I have no choice but to let them.'

'Why don't you leave?' Colin wanted to know. 'Why not just get out of this hole?'

'Because this is what I was made to be. A doorway is

a doorway: it can't choose to be what it's not. And this is as it should be — just me and my dreams together.'

'Nightmares, more like. He's cracked,' Colin asided quietly. 'We're not going to learn anything here.'

Jim put a restraining hand on Colin's shoulder. 'Why us, though?' he said to Goatbeard. 'Why were we singled out?'

'You weren't singled out. This kind of thing happens all the time.'

'You know what I mean, though.'

'You're talking as though you're the only ones who ever had to suffer. If it makes any difference, I'm sorry for both of you. But you're not alone.'

'I realise that,' Jim said. 'Perhaps I could handle it if we were. Friends have been hurt, though, family. Innocent blood is being spilt.'

'Innocent blood is always being spilt,' Goatbeard shrugged. From a breast pocket he retrieved a cigarette that had crimped and curled, and pushed it between his lips, letting it dangle there. 'In Israel they used to stone their prophets for bringing bad news. Couldn't bear to hear what God had to say about them; the truth was too painful. But can the messenger help his message? Can he change what it says, even to save his life? What can I do?'

'You could begin by telling us what *we* can do,' Jim said. While he spoke, Colin enclosed one hand with another and began cracking his knuckles, one by one. 'Like you, we've nothing to lose you see; its already been taken from us, everything.' He paused, listening for a moment to the storm brooding about the house and the rhythmic pattern of rain at the window. 'So we need to know what options we have, how we can fight what's happening to us.'

'Someone has to be made accountable,' Colin said.

'We came here in the hope you'd help us,' Jim added.

Goatbeard sighed, clutched at the unlighted cigarette in his mouth and hurled it aside with disrelish. 'If I could do that, would I be sitting here now? If I thought for one moment I could alter your lives or mine for the better don't you think I would do it?'

'You're just weak,' Colin said.

'Wouldn't you be? With such a gift as this? The years have made me this way; the years and the storms.'

'You've resigned yourself to this — this Hell you're in.'

'Each to his own abyss,' Goatbeard retorted.

'You're telling us we don't have the power to change the outcome,' Jim said. 'That we may as well accept our fate and curl up and die peacefully.'

'I'm not telling you that,' Goatbeard said, and a shadow crossed his face. 'I'm telling you *I* lack the power to change anything. There's nothing I can do to help you. I'm old, and I began to be old once I'd learned how to be submissive — believe it or not I decided to stay alive as long as I could, in spite of this burden. So I gave up the fight. But you,' he went on, turning to Colin, 'You've heat in your blood. There's an anger about you, a kind of madness. First, you need to learn how to use it constructively before it destroys you; turn it against the ones who did this.'

'But how?' Colin wondered, sitting forward, fingers digging whitely into his knees. 'What chance do we have of finding them?'

'There's a way, but you won't find what you're looking for this time around, in this life.'

'Then where?'

'You have to start over again. You have to become like the powers themselves by entering their world. Then you'll fulfil what was foretold.'

'Jesus,' Colin said, as the fortune-teller's words began

slowly to dawn on him. 'I think I know what you're saying.'

'I don't —' Jim started and stopped, but perhaps he understood too and, somewhere deep down, had always understood. As lightning searched the room, throwing a ripple of wallpaper into sharp relief everything began to make sense. 'You're saying we have to die,' he said. 'You'd seen our deaths in the future, and now's the time.'

Goatbeard smiled and slowly nodded, and his face was a mask of years, timeless and beyond numbering. 'After all, you're more than half-way there already, aren't you? In your condition, death should barely touch you; I doubt you'll feel a thing.'

Colin said, 'If we're dead, what good are we?'

Goatbeard merely shrugged, this time addressing Jim directly. 'More good than you'd know since you'd be amongst the powers themselves. You must remember, Jim Doherty, when you thought of yourself as a rebel, your talk of changing the system from the inside.'

'I remember,' Jim said fondly. It was a dream he'd once shared with both Colin and Daniel Zero at different times. They had all been young and idealistic and marvellously naïve once, and clean-bodied, not riddled with sickness and death. They'd believed that walls and barriers were there to be overcome: if you couldn't go through, then over, under, would serve just as well. Hopefully that was what Daniel Zero was doing this very minute; rebelling against Cora's Underworld, fighting the good fight even in death.

Colin cleared his throat. 'And wherever we go when we die, is that where we stay? Is there no coming back?'

'Certainly not as you are,' Goatbeard said. 'But would you want to come back as you are? And anyway, I wouldn't want to give you false hope. Where you're going, nothing is final and nothing is decided.' He closed his eyes, touched his temples. 'But your future here is virtually used up, your bodies are decaying rapidly. Rest assured, if you find another way back to the world, this is where you'll enter. It doesn't matter how or where you go out, but this is where you come in.'

A silence elapsed then, a silence broken only by the beating rain. Thunder boomed in the chimney, and somewhere in the room, wallpaper tore with a damp, pulpy sound.

'But what kind of death?' Colin wondered, later, outdoors, walking home. 'I still don't know whether we're meant to go looking for it or whether it's coming for us.'

'When the time comes, we'll know,' Jim said, and blew warm air into his fist as they climbed towards Hawthorne Drive with its array of dowdy shops. However death came, it would be soon, he was in no doubt about that.

No sooner had they reached Hawthorne Drive than the clouds seemed to part. A steady rain rebounded from the pavements and the multicoloured canopies which dangled over the shopfronts, but the thunder had moved slightly inland, and the air was less oppressive than before.

Thank goodness, too, that the streets and alleys made sense again, connecting where they should, bearing names that Jim knew from childhood. Further ahead, above the sex shop which was now a video rental shop, he saw the familiar face of the Kodak billboard girl. Her smile seemed to have faded in the rain. Above her head and the newsagent's door, a huge carton of Rothmans billowed back and forth at the end of its chain, and as they passed underneath Colin gave two firm tugs at Jim's arm.

'Do you see what I see?' he said.

Jim didn't, at least not immediately. His first emotion was one of fear – fear that if he turned he would see his shadow, the shadow that had left him near here all those years ago, returning.

Then he saw the headline on the dripping rack outside the newsagent's door. THE FACE OF EVIL IN BRITAIN TODAY, the tabloid's header exclaimed, rather hysterically Jim thought. Perhaps evil was the word for what had been gripping the country just lately. But when he unfolded the paper from the rack to examine the story more closely, he was surprised that the face staring up from the front page was his.

thirty

They weren't content with Elaine's murder, it seemed. The journalists or the police, or the journalists *and* the police — he scanned the item too hastily to be sure — had also managed to blame him for Derek's death, the assault on Carolyn, and for several other attacks in the Lewisham area. The story was sectioned into headed paragraphs, presumably for the sake of the sensation-starved: Mutilation, Psychotic, Drug-Crazed, the paragraphs began. He couldn't argue with anything they said about Elaine or Carolyn — he remembered only too well what he'd done — but Carolyn's statement to the media, printed bold and underlined for good measure, suggested she'd lost her wits.

'She claims it was all premeditated,' Jim said. 'She'd been afraid I was going to do something rash ever since we moved in.' He folded the sopping paper and replaced it on the rack. 'And what's this about Derek? Anyone would think I'm the only guilty party. In fact, that's exactly what they think.'

'Well, if nothing else, it fits the pattern.' Colin was steering him clear of the doorway. A man behind the counter inside was staring. 'Everyone needs someone to blame: you ought to have gathered that by now. If it's any consolation, we've both passed the point where what people think makes any difference.'

'That's no consolation at all,' Jim said.

'Still, it's better we keep a low profile for the moment. It won't take long for the cops to make the right connections and trace you here.'

'As long as they leave my father out of it. He's been hurt enough as it is.'

'I know,' Colin said, 'but haven't we all?'

They followed Hawthorne Drive until it veered right on to Campbell Street, where the houses were terraced and gardenless. A bitter row was in progress between a woman on her doorstep and a man on the pavement outside, presumably her husband. It wasn't so much a row as an exchange of abuse, the rain making the couple sound somehow more urgent and hateful. In the gloomy hall behind the woman, a child was crying. Further along, the shops ended abruptly with an off-licence into which Jim briefly vanished, emerging with a large bottle of Remy Martin wrapped in red crêpe paper.

'Something to celebrate?' Colin said, and Jim said, 'Maybe, when the time comes.' He might have added that if death came soon, he would like to accept it without fear, or at least without pain. The less he knew of it, the better. At least he wouldn't be going out alone; but there was no consolation in that, either. Oblivion was still oblivion, whatever the company.

Nearer home the rain hardened again. The crêpe wrapping became a soggy mess in Jim's hands, clinging to his palms in tatters. Puddles overflowed the gutters, the grates blocked with ice-cream and sweet wrappers. One or two clothes lines in neighbouring yards sagged from the weight of forgotten washing. At Jim's father's house, someone had parked a white Saab in front of the gateposts, blocking the drive.

A distant sound of thunder followed them to the door.

The air was thick with salt and static. A smell of fresh blood wafted outwards only an instant before Jim stepped in. Get back, a small voice warned him, but he couldn't be sure whose voice it was. 'Dad?' he said to the silence.

Two or three paintings had been knocked from the walls; others, askew, were still hanging. The barometer, stepped upon and shattered, lay on the carpet amid a sprinkling of glass. 'Dad, are you there?'

As far as Jim could see, nothing had been disturbed in the lounge: white sheets covered everything, and he was unable to blink away a sudden image of Elaine, butchered, the linen being swept from her lifeless body.

Nearer the foot of the stairs the wallpaper was marked with a smeared red handprint, dark as blood. Though Jim's first instinct was to turn back, Colin had planted himself solidly in the doorway behind him. After a moment he stepped forward, touching Jim's shoulder. Was that pleasure in his eyes, or just relief? 'This may be it,' he said quietly.

'I know,' Jim said, and swallowed.

Get back, the small voice warned, but he found himself advancing even so. At the far end of the hall the kitchen door was slightly ajar. It creaked, probably because of the air the front door was letting in. Jim was striding towards it, gripping the cognac bottle by its slender neck, when a movement to his right made him stop and twist round.

It was on the stairs. A shape, three parts shadow, squatted half-way up the first flight. Jim's first thought was that the enemy had found him — he was face to face with the physical summation of all his fears, the presence he'd always been running from. Then, as the shadow rocked its upper body forward into the light, he was able to give it a face and a name. The bottle fell from his grasp, but did not break.

271

'Go back,' the figure said. 'Get out.'

'Oh my God,' Jim heard himself gasp.

It was his father, both hands spread firmly over his abdomen, the long fingers extended and rimming with blood. 'Get out before it's too late,' he said.

But Jim had already started up towards him. 'Dad! Who did this? Who did this to you?'

His father made a sound and was silent. There was blood on his lips as well as between his hands; only the whites of his eyes were visible between their narrowed lids.

'Who was here?' Jim insisted. 'Where did they go?'

'They didn't —' Jim's father managed. 'They didn't —'

'Didn't what?'

'Didn't go.' Raising one dripping red hand from his stomach, he pointed downwards, past Jim, past Colin, who remained below in the hall, staring up. The front door gusted shut with a slam which rocked the house. 'They'll come again. Please get out while you can,' he breathed.

Jim couldn't be sure whether it was fury or fear that turned him away and back down the stairs. He'd been wrong to assume his terror was all used up, that nothing could touch him now he'd accepted his fate. Now he wanted to kill and be killed in one fell swoop, take whoever had done this with him. If he must enter death then he'd enter it tasting justice, by God. Filled with murder, he pushed past Colin and trooped along the hall.

'Where are you?' he cried. 'Come here and let's finish this once and for all! First Elaine, now this! I promise I won't rest until I've repaid you for everything you've done.'

'Jim,' Colin said. 'Maybe he's right, though. Maybe we should —'

'What? Run away now we're so close? Come here!' Jim

spat at the hallway. 'Come here and finish what you started, why don't you!'

To begin with there was only silence. The house might have been slumbering, his shouting in vain. All he could hear were thundering waves, the wail of a gull that wasn't a gull at all but a siren. Then he realised these sounds were gradually shaping a reply: the siren was nearer, the ocean an almost tangible presence whose salt he tasted, whose spray touched his skin. The huge sound filled the house.

'Jim,' Colin said then. In front of them, in the lounge, one of the white cotton sheets was slowly collapsing from its chair to the floor in a pile. Above the bar, a mouldering damp patch was weeping into the room through the wallpaper.

Unable to check himself, Jim stepped through to the lounge. Something was finally taking shape, and to retreat from it now would be futile. It would only reform, reappear somewhere else. There had never been any escaping it.

The damp patch was more than just that, of course. It was expanding rapidly — rapidly enough to have half-filled the wall by the time Jim understood what it meant.

It was the great storm he'd been waiting for, the one he'd anticipated and feared all his life. Perhaps he had always been one with the storm, and that was why he'd been living in fear. Just seconds before the wave exploded into the room, he imagined the smell of the ancient dead coming in with the tide. There was a moment of quiet tranquillity. He closed his eyes as the water broke into his face.

It moved through the room as a solid mass, as a wall that kept pressing forward. The force of it knocked air from his lungs and sent him back against the doorframe. One of the sheet-draped chairs overturned. Water gushed into his eyes and mouth, and he was choking on water, breathing it, tasting the grit and the salt in it. Behind him in the hall, Colin was skittled from his feet as the wave fell across him.

It was more than just a wave. Jim grasped the doorframe with both hands to keep upright. Purblind, he could vaguely make out Colin's shape in the hall and the shape that was pressing down on him, more solid than water should be.

Had something lurched out of the rain, determined to take Colin with it? It had, he thought, a man's shape – four limbs, a substantial trunk. He couldn't determine whether it had a face, he only knew it was vital he help Colin before they were separated. He was letting go of the doorframe when a dull warmth began to insinuate itself beneath his left arm.

He was sure he was bleeding. Something that felt like flesh was slashing and pawing at him from the midst of the rain. He grabbed at it, seizing what he thought was a wrist, though it proved too insubstantial, too soft for skin and bone, and his fingers met as though moving through putty. Then he realised why: his assailant had not quite arrived yet, he was still midway between here and beyond.

Jim jerked his hand away. A surge of electricity tingled his flesh, he recoiled from the touch of incredible power. All too briefly, he glimpsed the dark that was coming; he understood it as if from experience. Help me, he thought, in the hope an anonymous someone might hear him and act. Give me the strength to go through with this.

Somewhere behind him, Colin and the man who had latched on to him were struggling. Jim was past helping now; he had troubles of his own. Fresh pain whispered across his collarbone and his open palm as he raised a hand to shield himself. Wherever the pain landed, wounds the thickness of hairs opened up. Soon he would be a web spun in blood. Soon he would know how it felt when pain ran out.

The downpour slackening, he blinked water from his eyes. The creature emerging from the storm was Beresford's sidekick, the blond punk, who was wielding a cut-throat razor. His hair and clothing were drenched and his skin beaded, and he came at Jim with both hands – both solid hands, no longer soft as clay. A moment ago he had been water. Now there was weight in his limbs; bone as well as fluid.

The razor gleamed, came down, sleeked at an angle across Jim's belly. Jim fell aside from the door. To his right, Colin was on his feet and stumbling for the stairs. The caul-faced man was giving pursuit, thumping up the first few risers before throwing himself full length after Colin's ankles. They tumbled downwards together. Jim lost track of what happened then. The hall turned sideways as the punk looped both arms around his waist, bringing him down.

All at once, daylight collapsed to dark. Water dripped like diamonds from the walls. He had landed heavily on his back, the weight of the punk bearing down on him, straddling him at the waist. There was no need to resist – he should be welcoming death, not fighting it – but he found himself fighting nevertheless. He punched the air above him, reaching with both eager hands for the punk's face, or wrist, anything he could seize to advantage.

Instead, he grasped the blade. The punk drew it back so neatly it had parted Jim's palm like lips before the numb shock registered. Grabbing Jim's wrist and turning it over, the punk sliced again in the other direction, slowly, across the knuckles.

Jim struggled, to no effect. He was a small lost soul, an insignificant dot on a vast map of pain. Both sides of his hand were coated red. Now the blade fell again, first across one cheek, then the other, then skimmed almost casually over his brow. Why was the punk taking so long over this? Why not end it quickly, if that was why he was here?

The smile on his face told all. The bastard was toying with him, enjoying every minute of this. 'Pain,' the punk said, 'and pleasure . . . are one and the same where I come from.'

'Fuck you,' Jim told him. 'You murdered Elaine. I'm going to repay you for that.'

'You are?'

'Damn right I am. I'm going to — going to —'

'Do what? Kill me?' The punk was snickering, eyes brimming with madness. The razor flashed up and then down. 'Looks like your work's cut out for you then. Before you know it you'll be just like the rest of us, and then where will you be? What do you think you'll do then?'

'At least I won't be damned,' Jim said, but how could he be certain he wouldn't? The blade descended, parting his shirt and the nipple beneath it.

Death was close; he could taste its nearness. Straining with both arms and legs at once, he tried to lever the punk off him. The effort was too much, loss of blood had weakened him. The punk grimaced and fastened his free hand around Jim's throat, steadying the razor in the other.

This is the end my friend, Jim thought. He resented the anti-climax, the clumsy melodrama, the fact it was playing itself out in the hallway of his father's house, of all places. He'd hoped for better. Where was the glamour, the street credibility in this? He closed his eyes, anticipating the kill, and realised he'd missed the point entirely.

There was so much noise inside and outside his head it took him an age to hear Colin's cry. Even then, he could make little sense of the words. 'Jim, they're like us,' Colin was shouting. 'They're exactly like us.'

Jim let his eyes open. Everything was happening upside down, far too quickly. Colin and the caul-faced man were banging into walls and tearing at each other with bare, clawed hands. Both men were tattered and bleeding. The caul-face looked by far the worse for wear.

'They're exactly like us, Jim,' Colin repeated, and it was then that Jim understood what he meant. These assailants were damageable; the punk could be damaged. But of course, Jim thought; of course. They'd made themselves real as soon as they left the storm. All flesh was like grass.

The realisation gave him new impetus. The power he'd touched just a moment ago was fading: the punk was taking him on with mortal strength, nothing more. So long as he walked in the world, flesh and blood, he was vulnerable. Let's see, Jim thought, *how* vulnerable. Thrusting both hands upwards, he found his assailant's eyes with both thumbs, and pressed.

It seemed to take all his strength, all his concentration. The punk choked up a soundless scream and dropped the razor, which tumbled harmlessly to the floor.

Jim was only distantly aware of what he did next, or why. But he'd passed the point of reason long ago. The revulsion he felt as his thumbs collapsed inwards soon passed. Rage did the rest. He let his anger come forth in small, easy steps. This was for Elaine, this for his father, for Terry Mack – a virtual shopping list of innocent dead. He ticked them off one at a time.

Somehow he managed to sit upright, launching the punk back against the nearest wall. He slammed the creature's head twice and again against the doorframe and then let go, unhooking his thumbs from the skull. Then he rolled free, leaving the punk to slide down the wall, to claw at the darkening voids where his eyes had been.

Where was the end to this horror? Perhaps, he thought, and then wished he hadn't, this was really the start. He turned just in time to see Colin yanking something from his pocket – Daniel Zero's gun – and thrusting the muzzle almost casually into the caul-faced man's mouth. Without a second thought, he pulled the trigger.

The shot sounded as a muffled slap in the narrow space. No one moved for a moment or two. Leaving his mark on the wall above what remained of his head, the caul-faced man tumbled sideways.

'Why bother?' Jim said, stepping clear of the punk. 'Why on earth did we bother?'

Colin looked up as if the words had taken him off guard. He stared at Jim as he might have stared at a stranger. 'What's that?'

'Nothing,' Jim said. 'Just that our deaths came to collect us and we refused to go. I thought we'd agreed that we had to. I thought I *wanted* to until the time came.'

Colin cradled the gun in his hands, then pocketed it. 'If we were meant to go this way, there's nothing we could have done to prevent it. I don't know about you, but I'd like to finish things *my* way, not Beresford's way, or Cora's.' Stooping over the caul-faced man, he began searching pockets. At last he rose, holding aloft a wisp of silver: a key. 'In fact,' he said, 'if I have to go at all, I'll go in style, thanks very much. How do you feel about taking the Saab for a spin?'

Jim said nothing as he collected the unbroken cognac bottle from the floor and followed Colin outdoors. Though his body wanted to turn and run to his father, he didn't even look back. After all, what help could he give? What had he ever given anyone besides death?

The sooner he went to his own, the better, he thought. Somewhere near, somewhere soon.

Still at Colin's heels, he ran out and into the grey rain, stamping his feet impatiently while Colin unlocked the car. Inside, a Japanese hi-fi was built into the walnut-veneered dashboard. A selection of cassette tapes were scattered over the seats and the floor. Jim brushed them away and settled into the passenger seat. The sound of the thunder of waves had vanished, but the siren was louder and nearer still.

'Now then,' he heard Colin say as the engine came to life and the Saab moved smoothly, silently along the street. 'Now then.'

And through the rain that made the rear windscreen appear to melt, Jim caught his first glimpse of the police car, taking the corner behind them.

thirty-one

Even if it were possible to go back and begin again, Jim thought as Colin eased the car on to Levin Park Drive, I would surely make the same mistakes, perhaps at different times and perhaps not in quite the same order, but the outcome would never change. I would still lose everything I ever loved, because that's the way it was written and nothing so final can ever be changed. And I would find the road leading me this way wherever I'd meant to turn that; and my death waiting ahead of me whenever I thought I'd left it behind.

'Dreadful, isn't it?' Colin said. 'All the dreams we used to share going to waste. All that pie-in-the-sky shit. To think what we'd planned to do after leaving this place.'

'We were never meant to leave, though,' Jim demurred, his fingers absently plucking at a matchbox he'd picked from the ashtray. It had Cora's name upon it, and inside was a creamy, glutinous substance he remembered at once; he touched it, then tasted his finger. 'Here,' he said. 'Try some.' Separating the blob of Acid from Heaven into halves, he gulped down one and proffered the rest to Colin.

When he'd swallowed the drug, Colin licked his lips and said, 'What is it?'

'You should've asked me that first. It's our ticket to

wherever we're headed. I've a hunch it'll make the passage easier.'

'Huh?' Colin said.

'The last time I dropped it Elaine wound up dead, and I caught a glimpse of where Cora comes from. I saw — I *think* I saw her true face.'

'Sounds like good shit to me,' Colin said. 'Put on some sounds, why don't you?'

Jim selected a Suzanne Vega cassette from the pile and prodded it into the dashboard player. Then he set about the cognac bottle. With his first swallow, which burned his stomach, everything settled into place — the Acid from Heaven, the car, the thrill of the chase. 'Small Blue Thing' merely completed the picture. They were heading, unless he was much mistaken, for the kind of r'n'r suicide others jerked off dreaming about. The police car was still within sight, though it was rapidly shrinking to a dot in the near-side wing mirror. There was no going back, and because there was nothing to go back to it was just as well.

'Jim,' Colin said, and took a deep breath as though preparing to summarise his feelings. 'Jim, I know what I said about saying "if only" but I wanted you to know that —'

'Don't,' Jim said quickly. 'Soon it'll be over. That's one thing about death; it means never having to say you're sorry.'

'I was only trying to say,' Colin murmured.

'I know,' Jim assured him.

He settled for a while and watched the town cruising by through the rain-smeared window, his heart skipping beats at a memory here, one there. To his left was Cedarwood Dene, its rows of garages like pigeon holes. In front was the knee-high brick wall on which he and Colin had sat, moments before their errand took them to Terry Mack's.

Further ahead, Colin swung the car right and on to the gladed walk sloping down beside Levin's Park. Shadows flitted by, some retreating up steps to the doors of the houses opposite the park. Jim had received his first kiss somewhere down here past the brow, in the shade below the trees and bushes overhanging the gates. The girl's name was Heather, he seemed to think, and one evening after school he had joined a queue of fidgeting, hand-wringing boys his own age in waiting almost twenty minutes for the privilege. Moist-eyed, he wondered what Heather was doing now, this minute. He hoped she was happy.

He was seeing the town go by for the last time, but could find no rhyme, no meaning in any of it. Everything seemed only half-formed, agonisingly inconclusive. He'd lost sight of the cop car altogether now, which at least was one less thing to worry about. His head was aching from the pressure of loss; his body felt lumpen, a deadweight growing soft and rotten around him. He'd soon be rid of it, though. Leaving his body might be all he had to look forward to yet.

A tangle of masts pierced the sky as the Saab swept around past the harbour. A whiteness swelled on the horizon. Because of the rain it was hard to tell whether the whiteness was incoming mist or light beyond the storm. Jim took one more drink as Colin accelerated towards the prom.

The promenade road was straight and flat, the lanes intersected by bollards set on concrete islands. Shops and alleys travelled by to the right. Colin upped the speedo to sixty. Ahead, the cliffs rose hugely above Seaborough like clouds, their defiant, immovable mass declaring that nothing ever changed here, or would.

As they tore past the ice-cream parlour, the spray condensed, shortening vision to three or four car lengths.

Even with the wipers set at top notch, the front was scarcely more than a smear. 'Here goes,' Colin said, and accelerated.

The town closed in; everything was reduced to this place, this point in time. There went the cinema, there went the arcade where all of this started. Jim watched it go, his heart a knife in his throat. For one disquieting moment he thought he saw two boys staring out from the arcade's large front window, watching the storm: himself and Colin.

As he turned back to the road, Colin pulled violently at the wheel.

The police car was heading straight at them, in their lane. The siren rose and fell languidly. It hadn't abandoned the chase at all but had doubled back, anticipating their every move. But then, it should have been easy to calculate. All roads led here. There had never been anywhere else to go.

Instinct made Jim grab the door handle as the car careered across the road. He didn't know which was stronger: the impulse to survive or the rage, the will for revenge. The Saab's offside glanced against a bollard, bending it back on its metal spine. Ahead, two cars were parked eight or ten feet apart. The driver of one, fumbling to open his door, stepped neatly aside just in time.

Maybe Colin had accepted his lot, for he never so much as touched the brakes. Accelerating, he torched the Saab through the gap between the cars and over the kerb. At the last, before the vehicle plunged into the Magical Mirror Maze, Jim felt himself gasp with relief. At last, he thought, at last, thank God.

Goodbye old world, hello new.

And Oblivion opened its arms.

III

Hell Games

There is a land beyond the spoken word
Communication only some have heard
And if I tell you the highway turning to take
Keep it a secret or all of your mirrors will break.

— Doll By Doll

thirty-two

The image had cracked.

Even beyond the point of impact, a thousand rippled mirrors reflecting their multiple auto-deaths, the Saab was accelerating. As far as Jim was aware, there was no actual moment of transition, no grande finale and new beginning; only a distant impression of light collapsing and glass shattering, glass as fine as spring rain. Each spinning fragment brought a fresh perspective to the crash. Death was not an end, but another stark chapter in the great continuum.

In the depths of the Maze, two mirrors faced each other, one laterally distorted, the other vertically. In the first, a man's head was compressed as a pancake, his arms foreshortened to fleshy stumps. In its twin, positioned opposite, his screaming mouth was a blackened spine which opened his body from crown to crotch.

Then he was gone, and pain closed over everything. Blood streaked the windscreen, though Jim could not remember having collided with it. Then he saw that the blood was outside, the smearing caused by the wipers at work. The car was gliding across a bottomless darkness, the road gone from under it. Ahead there was light, hazy and flat. Another collision caused him to jolt forward and back in his seat several times.

The last thing he was even remotely aware of was an image which caught in the corner of his eye: Colin being propelled forwards and up by the impact, pelvis crushing against the wheel, head thumping the windscreen to form a perfect, instantaneous spider's web across the glass.

The web was still there when Jim came round – he didn't know how much later, though it was dark and presumably late – in what seemed to be the entrance to the Mirror Maze. In the distance he could hear the unambiguous throb of traffic noise, and nearer, the dripping of moisture in black empty spaces. Perhaps he'd expected to emerge somewhere else; not here, in this wasteland.

At first his head felt overloaded – a waveband into which too many stations were cramming themselves. Too many thoughts, all of them confused, were trying to reach his tongue. When he spoke, his voice came as a shock to his senses.

'Colin?' he said.

The door on the driver's side lay open, the seat was empty. Colin must have dragged himself clear of the wreck or even thrown himself out at the last minute. If so, chances were he hadn't wandered too far.

What was this place though? Jim budged the door open, fragments of glass tinkling from the roof to the bonnet and the ground. The front of the vehicle had concertina'd against a concrete pillar just inside the entrance. As he climbed out, an impression of asphalt and darkness was compounded by one of emptiness. The Mirror Maze should have been situated midway along the prom, facing the sea; but here was a steep, lightless backstreet whose buildings were blanks. Colin was nowhere in sight.

The street was black as a midnight lake; shadows had claimed it. Jim started down the slope to his right, towards the traffic noise. There was no moon, but the distant horizon looked a splendid mauve, illumined by something more than stars or sunset. When Jim looked back to where he'd been, he saw that the building above the Maze was totally gutted from the first floor up. The row to which it belonged had been decimated.

There were no roofs or chimneys, and the upstairs windows were boarded or bricked up. Doors had been torn from their hinges, affording views of further destruction within – heaps of rubble, ransacked furnishings, limbless tables and chairs. He was passing, he imagined, through a war zone, a zone once bombed, now forgotten. Perhaps these hollow shells had been munitions factories once, before this. As he reached the last house on the row, a shape somewhere along the hallway leapt from a wall.

Dry-mouthed, he twisted around, but the sudden movement was his own; when he stopped and waited, so did his shadow.

The side-street adjoined a dual carriageway, which vanished two or three hundred yards to his left into darkness as vast as a country; to his right, however, there was activity. A convoluted flyover busy with traffic and, beyond, the flaming lights of a city.

There was no traffic heading this way. The confluence was far ahead – impossible to estimate how far – and he was able to cross to the central reservation with ease. Litter gusted towards and past him: food wrappers, paper cups. He stood for a while, trying to collect himself, neither hot nor cold, neither anxious nor unwilling to continue. It was, he thought, a three in the morning feeling, the first awakening of sobriety. Without doubt Colin had travelled this way, to the city, either voluntarily or not. But whatever the circumstances, why had he taken off – or been taken – alone?

At last he set off for the lights and whatever the city held in store. He was still some way short of the intersection when he noticed the city brighten and fade. The lights that illumined the sky were more than just rivers of neon, he understood then. From where he was, it seemed that the buildings themselves were on fire.

thirty-three

The longer he toured its busy streets, losing himself in its darkest sectors, the closer Jim came to understanding the city that had taken him in.

It was a troubled place, strife-torn, a composite of cities from the world he had left — Belfast, Beirut, the English metropolis in the days of the riots. Violence reared its head at street corners, beggars clutched blindly at passers-by with heartfelt requests for money or sex. In one doorway, a kneeling girl pressed her face to the groin of a man whose stance and whose stiff, jerking climax made her whole body rock. When the man was done he collapsed backwards panting against the door, and the girl turned, licking her lips, towards the light. Though her eyes were mascara'd, her cheeks rouged, she couldn't have been more than ten years old.

Street by street, alley by alley, the city unfolded itself for inspection. To Jim, it seemed nothing so much as a vast, ever-expanding red-light sector. Vice was openly displayed, not hidden away in brown paper bundles. A toothless teenage boy, gums crawling with rot, propositioned Jim as he entered the green neon haze outside a nightclub. Not daring to reply, Jim hurried on. The traffic converged thickly at every junction, windscreens so dark they might have been painted. What hope did he have of locating Elaine or Colin amongst this?

Above him, and as far ahead as the eye could see, the buildings were blazing. He'd learned by now that the fire at the roof-tops was unreal; spectral, even. The destruction never ended, yet never worsened. Glass burst outwards from yellow burning upper rooms while, below, the air thickened with smoke and the faint aroma of cooking flesh.

No one seemed to mind. The spectacle was as much a part of the scenery — ignored by those in the street — as the bars and casinos and clubs that lined every pavement.

At the far side of the next intersection was a market square crowded with stalls. The illusion was that of a normal world filled with normal things, traders here, tourists there, children and grown men haggling. Further inspection informed Jim there was more, far more to it than that; certainly more than he was prepared for.

The stalls were literally dripping with horrors. From hooks above them depended sections of human anatomy, arms severed between elbow and wrist, whole hands and feet and, in one case, a still-beating heart. Arranged on the counters were trays of entrails, lungs and livers; offal of every description competitively priced, a sign said. At another stall, blue-grey embryos were bought and sold in sealed demijohns whose labels claimed 'No Preservatives'. A nearby linen stall boasted bath towels with razors stitched into their linings.

Jim had reacted before he knew it. He turned, bent double, retched. His stomach was empty though, and nothing came. No one paid him any attention. He straightened up and walked to the edge of the market square over cobbles that were slippery underfoot. Beyond the square the neon lights, burning in sympathy with the pyres at the roof-tops, made him think of Piccadilly Circus, Times Square.

This was the city's secret. It was a mockery of the real world, an assembly of ill-fitting parts. Its architecture was cobbled together, the old standing uncertainly with the new. There were elements of Seaborough here, but also of London, Paris, New York; of all the great and varied capitals of the globe. Apparently the dead had each brought a small piece of home when they came here, founding their Mecca with mementoes and keepsakes.

Jim was waiting for a gap in the traffic when he noticed a figure, white-clothed from head to foot, watching him from across the road. At first he thought the figure's attire was what drew his eye. Perhaps it was; but it was also the way the man remained perfectly still as the crowd flowed this way and that around him.

He took a step back, allowing Jim to pass, as Jim scurried across the road. High above the street was a tower fronted with a handless clock; a surrealist detail of no use to anyone. As Jim pushed through the crowd beneath it, the man in white took a firm hold of his elbow and said, 'Forgive the intrusion. Can we − ?' He gestured. 'Do you mind if we walk together awhile? I was watching you at the stalls.'

As soon as they were clear of the roadside, Jim turned. The man was inches shorter than himself, and far older. His disorderly hair, pure white and spilling forward over his brow, was the only thing about him that didn't look perfectly ordered. His suit and cravat, the handkerchief forming an inverted V at his breast pocket, suggested careful grooming; an eloquent *film noir* villain.

'You were watching me at the stalls,' Jim said, 'but so what? I wasn't the only one there.'

'You were the only one who reacted,' the man said in gentle, measured English. Gesturing ahead, he began leading Jim towards quieter quarters. 'That's why I noticed you. It set you apart. The others, of course — they never react, but why should they? They know the score. They understand that anything's possible, anything's permissable. They're all dead here.'

'And you're not?'

The man fluttered a hand, palm downwards, and smiled. 'Touch and go really. At this very moment I'm at the mercy of two very reputable surgeons; I'm lying anaesthetised in a hospital operating room. Blocked arteries, would you believe.'

Jim was flabbergasted. 'You're in two places at once, is that what you mean?'

The man in white smiled.

'You're out of your body?' Jim said.

'Just temporarily, I hope.'

'Has this happened before?'

'Several times. I'm getting to know this place like the back of my hand. I've got the knack, now, of finding my way here of my own free will.'

'I wonder,' Jim said, 'why anyone would come here by choice.'

'For the girls, of course,' the man in white said, and touched his nose. 'The twelve year olds are the best thing I've seen since Taiwan, and here, as I say, anything goes. If *they're* not worth damnation, nothing is.'

Jim had already started away, the man in white hurrying to keep up. 'Then that's your problem, not mine,' Jim said. 'If screwing under-age dead girls is what turns you on, then go ahead; but don't try and drag me into your scene.'

'They're not,' the man was saying, waving his hand at the clocktower. 'They're not under-age, that is. You have to understand there are no laws here; the anarchists have taken over. The authorities have different values. For one thing there's no such thing as time, there's no old or young.

It never rains, the sun never shines, and so on and so on; there's so much you'll have to learn.'

But Jim was hastening away. Better that than turn his growing anger against the man. Better to save it for Cora, if he could. He said, 'I don't know what you want from me.'

'I want to help, if I can. I approached you because I could tell we had something in common.'

'Such as?'

'We're both passing through. We're not like these others. But you have to be careful. If they see that you're different they'll catch you and keep you.' After a pause he said, 'Do you mind if I ask why you came here?'

'I'm looking for someone. Is it possible, do you think, to find what you want in a place like this?'

'With the proper assistance,' the man said.

They were outside a bar whose closed doors and windows were buzzing in sympathy with the music inside. Far away, in the absolute dark beyond the square, a bell was chiming.

'I hope I didn't give you the wrong impression,' the man in white said, watching the market crowds. 'There are good things here as well as bad. You'll discover that for yourself. There's a war going on, and it's vital you find yourself on the right side. Otherwise you're here to stay.'

'I don't understand,' Jim said, and the man in white said, 'You will.'

There was a sudden commotion along the street to their left. While they'd been speaking, something had bolted from the midst of the crowd at the junction, halting the flow of traffic. Vehicles were sounding their horns. Four youths armed with clubs and sticks were chasing what, from here, looked like a black, hairless dog. Its coat shone moistly in the green and red light. As it scuttered across the pavement, pedestrians drew back from it, perhaps in fear.

Now the youths were surrounding it. Someone was shouting, though the words were unclear. An axe was raised and brought down. Jim blinked; felt the blow shake the ground and echo through his body. When he looked again the creature appeared to be scampering away in two separate directions at once.

'What the hell,' Jim said.

'In here,' the man in white said then. 'It's better not to get involved.'

Taking Jim's arm, he led the way inside through the doors, then down to the bar at the foot of the steps.

thirty-four

It was all, very nearly, too much.

'What kind of crazy fucking place *is* this?' Jim demanded, once they were safely inside. 'Why did you bring me here?'

The man said nothing until comfortably sited on a high stool at the bar, which stood on a dais. 'Steady on, don't make a scene,' he said, and touched Jim's elbow. To the bartender he said, 'Two of the usual, if you please.'

The bartender, a Rastafarian whose shoulders and chest strained his white and red Jah Wars T-shirt, laid down a towel on the bar and began slopping unmeasured tequila into two tall glasses.

Jim stared around the bar while they waited. With its thick, fumy air and its low ceiling, the place resembled a film set – *The Blue Angel* perhaps, or *Cabaret*. At its tables were Mods, Punks, Hippies, speed freaks, acid heads, junkies, winos, pushers, a gallery of the world's garbage. Seated in one corner were several young girls whose drinking and soliciting would have been illegal in a city beholden to laws. On stage at the far side of the club a shapely half-naked girl was dancing to Killing Joke in a fog of violet light. Between the stage and the bar was a large, illuminated Wurlitzer.

When the drinks arrived, Jim turned to the man in white

who was opening and closing a gold cigarette case. 'I thought the horror might end here, but it never ends, does it, it just goes on. Would you mind explaining what was happening on the street just now?'

The man hunched his shoulders. 'Nothing out of the ordinary. For this place, that is. Sometimes it's better just to turn a blind eye, let the troubles work themselves out.'

'Seems to me there's no difference between this and the world I just left,' Jim said.

'That's not strictly true,' the man in white said. 'For one thing, the residents of the city never die: that's the privilege of the dead. Nothing dies here, no matter what you do to it.'

Jim tried to blink away an image of the creature in the street as it scurried away in two halves. 'But the buildings, the people, and the bars, and the traffic: it's as if this place is just a poor reflection of the world. Everything that happens there happens here also.'

'On the contrary,' the man said, 'the *world* is the poor reflection of what's really going on. I said we're at war, and we are. Everything that happens here has its counterpart there. What's Life after all but a preparation for Death? Life's a trifle. Death's where it's at, young man.'

Jim was watching the man with fascinated horror. He was close to an understanding, yet afraid of where it might lead him. The anarchists ruled Oblivion; must the world automatically follow? To steady himself he took a shot of tequila. 'You're saying the violence in the streets in the world is because of what's happening here, outside?'

The man said nothing, but gazed placidly at the group of young girls, who were laughing amongst themselves, and waving.

Jim stared at his glass, turning it carefully on its ring-mark. 'And the war?'

'Yes, the civil war. Frankly, I see no sense in it. Everyone's trying to kill everyone else, but where's the point when there's no death any more, just greater and greater agony? The true struggle is spiritual,' he added. 'That's the only kind there is.' Suddenly he brightened, began slowly to dismount his stool. 'Relax, will you? There's more to life than death, you know. Are you planning to go soon, or will you stick around for a while? I was going to say why don't you live a little? – but that's hardly appropriate, is it?'

Jim did not share the man's high spirits. 'I thought you were going to help me.'

'But I already have. I brought you here, didn't I? As long as you're here you're amongst friends.' Cocking a thumb towards the girls at their table, he grinned broadly. 'Are you sure I can't encourage you to join me?'

'I'm sure,' Jim replied. 'But don't let me stop you.'

'Oh, you won't, don't worry about that.'

The girls were clearly well acquainted with the man in white, fussing to make space for him as he approached their table. All were smoking; a couple were laughing into their hands. None looked anywhere near the age of consent; but again, he was thinking of world-rules. Nothing was strictly illegal here.

Jim turned back to the bar. The bartender faced him, and was leaning forward on his forearms and chewing a toothpick which travelled from one corner of his mouth to the other. 'Do you come here often?' the Rasta said.

Jim could find no ready answer to that and instead looked away to where an ageing obese woman, seated in the thick of the crowd, was dragging a child towards her distended breast. At once he was aware of other, more sordid sideshows elsewhere in the bar – two figures copulating in darkness just beyond the stage; a woman sprawled on the floor beneath a broken Toilet sign, weeping and masturbating; a young magician producing a crimson, skinned rabbit from his wide-brimmed hat with one clean flourish.

Jim shook his head at the scene. He'd wandered into someone's nightmare, and what was worse was that he couldn't be sure it wasn't his. Everything in it was a sham; it wasn't even that the patrons took pleasure in what they were doing. It was as if this were something they were forced to go through with.

The Killing Joke number faded, and a new song began, a Sam and Dave bygone classic. Now the dancer, dressed only in a basque and stockings, was leaving the stage to indifferent applause. Jim saw her sweep up her robe from a stage hand as the stage lights went out, and looked away as she reached the bar and eased herself on to the stool the man in white had vacated.

'Fuck,' she sighed, and shook her head. After a silence she looked quite purposefully at Jim. 'This scene.'

Jim turned his glass anti-clockwise on its mark. 'If you don't like it, why do it?'

'What choice do I have? That's the difference between us: when you're living at least you can try to do as you want. Here you just do what you have to.'

Jim looked up at her then; took in the girl's close-cropped auburn hair, her tapering chin, the mark like a faded tattoo on her forehead. He tried to avoid a glance down at her cleavage, but failed; facially she was sweet sixteen.

'What makes you so sure you know all about me?' he asked. 'How do you know there's a difference between us?'

'Don't worry.' She clicked her fingers at the Rasta behind the bar, and the Rasta shook his mane and reached for a bottle. 'I'm on your side. I saw you come in with that fellow — that creep. Which told me as much as I needed to know. You're new around here, aren't you?' Leaning forward, she guided a fold of hair from Jim's brow. 'Are you permanent, or just passing through?'

'That depends.'

'On what?'

'On where I am. And on whether I find what I'm looking for —'

He was about to go on when the girl put a finger to his lips, silencing him. Someone behind him was screaming. Deep in the crowd there was a sudden, violent disturbance. Before he could register what was happening the dancer took hold of his arm, dragging him from the stool and clear of the dais.

Everywhere in the bar, people were standing, making for exits, skewing glasses from tables and overturning chairs in their rush. The song on the jukebox died as a plug was pulled and lights, one by one, began to go out. The man in white stood abruptly, his arm looped around a young hooker, a diminutive thing who stood no higher than his chest. One of the girls at his table was wailing; she was joined now by others.

At the top of the steps by which Jim had entered, the door lay open. Standing there, peering down, was the first of an army of uniformed men. His helmeted, visored head was a black gleaming shell concealing his face; at his side, in one gloved hand, was a truncheon around whose girth was a decoration of nails. By the time he and the mob began to move down, the floor of the bar had virtually cleared.

'Bastards,' Jim heard someone exclaim behind him — the bartender probably. 'They've no right in here, it's off-limits.'

Jim was aware of little else for several seconds: only the

scene being played out before him. Someone, knowingly or not, had jarred on the stage lights, though the stage remained empty of drama. Patrons swarmed every exit. The girl with the man in white was clawing to free herself of him. He only let go when she slapped his face: his arm fell away, and he watched her go as if dazed, his fingertips travelling to his cheek. At the last minute, as the uniformed group reached the foot of the steps and began their advance, he seemed to awake. He turned, but too late. A club was swung, felling him.

'The Dark Brigade,' the dancer explained, and tugged at Jim's sleeve. 'That's what we call the authorities. It's their duty to arrest the souls of the living. They don't need warrants. Come on, quick, before they see you as well.'

As she bundled him clear of the bar towards a door that seemed to materialise from the shadows, Jim glanced once behind him. For a moment he was back on the London streets. Some of the uniformed men had separated, wafting their weapons – clubs appended with blades, skewers, hooks – and were dragging innocents from the crowd to be beaten at random. In the centre of the floor, the man in white was no longer white; bloody patches were swelling all over him. He rolled over and lay still, his whole body shuddering when a polished leather jackboot met his skull.

The surgery was killing him, Jim thought then, barely coherently. The man was dying at the hands of two trusted surgeons. The operation was failing to save him. Because the authorities had laid claim to the man in white, he would never return to his body.

'This way please, out the back,' the dancer told Jim as she guided him through the dark behind the bar. It was spoken casually, so casually it sounded like practised routine; a scene she had been through time and again.

* * *

302

Seemingly miles high above the city, her bedsit was dominated by its view. Some distance below, the streetlights flared harshly, but beyond the flaming roofs the sky appeared mellower, a pale azure tinged with mauve.

'Would you kindly explain where I am and what's happening to me?' Jim said, chomping the ice she had plopped in his drink. He turned slightly away while the dancer, whose name he had learned was Julia, changed in the open doorway of an adjoining bathroom. 'You could also try explaining why you do what you do for a living.'

'I'm not sure living is quite how I'd put it,' Julia said. Finished dressing, she stood in front of him in a T-shirt and slacks, took a sip from his drink and returned it. 'I never deserved anything better from life, I suppose. I never aspired to anything better. Sometimes I wish I had.'

She watched while Jim inspected the book-lined walls of her room, brushing his hands across the spines of classics. There were many to choose from – *Ulysses*, *Tropic of Cancer*, books he had always promised himself he would read. He selected one at random, only to find the pages were blank from first to last.

'Are the others like this?' he wondered.

'We have to keep up appearances,' Julia said. 'But as you've seen, most things are illusions here.'

'Then will you tell me where I am? In Hell?'

'Hell?' She clapped a hand to her breast like a Southern belle. 'You have to be kidding. What do you take me for?'

'Well, whatever you are, you're not alive, you're not real. Nothing I've seen here so far is real.'

'Alive, well no. I never said I was that. But I'm real enough. Here,' she said, and taking his free hand clasped it to her breast. She was firm, firm but soft and warm, and he retrieved his hand sharply, embarrassed by what he was thinking.

'But you're right,' she said, 'it may not be Hell, but it isn't exactly Utopia either.' After a pause she said, 'You saw what happened to your friend in white?'

'He wasn't my friend.'

'Well, you nevertheless saw what happened. He didn't have the good sense to practise what he preached; by which I mean keeping a low profile. He was under the impression that what he'd discovered down here was freedom, so he flaunted himself. He thought he could have everything he'd lusted for in life.' She made a face, clearly disgusted by the thought of the man. 'There may be no law against it, but that doesn't make it right. But the plain fact is, everyone knew him by sight. Even here, you can quickly gather a reputation. He laid himself open to the authorities.'

'The Dark Brigade.'

Julia nodded. 'He's a slave like the rest of us now. Just make sure it doesn't happen to you. You'll be safe, Jim, only when you accept that nothing is safe here. It's better if you trust no one.'

Jim finished his drink, which now seemed peculiarly tasteless. 'I can trust you, though, I hope.'

'I'd like you to. The place where I work is a kind of no-go zone for the authorities. They broke an unwritten law when they burst in tonight. In doing that, they destroyed everything we'd been trying to build.'

'Which was?'

'Security for the partisans; people like you and the man you came in with.' She softened then, smiling as she took Jim's glass and began to refresh it. 'Did you ever see *Casablanca*? Bogart and – Bacall, wasn't it?'

'Bergman. Who didn't?'

'Well, that's our mission. We support the rebels. We do what we can. It's not for honour or glory – there are easier ways to achieve that – but it's right that we help you in any way we can. Look,' she said then, pushing back her fringe from her forehead. The tattoo at the hairline was a sequence of numbers — a code of some kind, presumably.

'What does it mean?' Jim said.

'It means I'm here for keeps; it's supposed to make me a conformist. Everyone has one. You can't buy or sell or do anything without. You can't work or eat or — you get the picture? Most new arrivals are branded as soon as they're found.'

Her bag was draped over a chair in a corner of the room. In a moment she had produced a mascara stick and scribbled a series of digits across his brow. She took a pace back to admire her work. 'That's just in case anyone looks at you twice. Try not to smudge it.' After a pause she said, 'It's time we talked about you. Don't tell me you came here because you chose to.'

Jim stood with his back to the window, took a swallow from his glass. 'I'm a journalist working on a story,' he said. 'It's sensationalist and trashy and I hope the right people get hurt by it. To be absolutely truthful, I'm looking for someone. Someone I — love, I think.'

The girl let her gaze fall from his. 'I see.'

'The people that took her were out of line. I'm the one they should have taken. I came here to do what I could, to see if I could get her back.'

'It would help if you had names.'

'Her name, at least where I came from, was Cora. Cora De Ville. She was this year's rock-and-roll model. There was a Max Beresford too, her mentor.'

'In that case,' Julia said, joining him at the window, you're on the wrong side of town.'

The faint aroma of scorching flesh rose from the busy streets, displacing the customary stink of cities: dust and petroleum. They stood side by side for a time, teetering over the dotted lights and the dark, letting the silence rush in. At last Julia indicated, through the small window, past the roof-tops, the pale horizon.

'There is where you have to go. I can see you as far as the border, after that you're on your own.'

For a second or two, he was lost. He heard the faint opening and closing of her lips, caught the glimmer of light in her eyes as he turned. 'What is that place?'

'It's the Pleasure Zone,' Julia said. 'The nearest you'll see to Heaven down here. That's where you'll find who you're looking for. The rich and famous hang out there. The stars you grew up worshipping.'

Elaine as well? And Colin? He could only wonder and hope. 'How long will it take to reach?'

'As long as it takes. Did you bring transport?'

'I've a car a few miles back. I thought it better to leave it and walk until I knew where I was. It's the one I –' He wanted to laugh at the understatement. ' – the one I drove here in.'

'And it's still in working order?'

'I don't know. I hope so.'

'Then we'd better find out,' Julia said.

thirty-five

Because the clocks had no hands, Jim was not aware of time passing as he steered the Saab past the market square. There were no signs or street names, and soon the ruined inner-city blocks were swept away behind and the lights at the roadside were gone. On the radio, a voice from another time, seemingly years ago, recited, 'The voiceless bird has no song to sing. Repeat. The voiceless bird has no song to sing.' There followed a silence, a burst of static and then, 'Eternity takes longer for those in a hurry. Repeat. Eternity takes longer –'

'You're listening to Radio Death,' Julia explained. 'That's as intimate as broadcasting gets around here. It goes on like this all the time. Personally, I miss the rock and roll and the panel shows, don't you?'

'I never thought I would, but I'm starting to.'

'Turn here,' she said then, without warning, and that was the last he saw of suburbia.

They were crossing a wide, bleak expanse of lightless landscape. Ahead, the sky was suffused with twilight. After a while the lulling, almost cushioning sense of the road beneath the car began to make Jim dreamy. Drifting, he imagined he and Julia were traversing fields of swaying black corn, the corn growing rotten and fetid from the ground, and scented by death.

It couldn't be far now, he was nearer than ever to grasping his future in both ready hands. Ahead — perhaps miles ahead yet — was the source of the terror he'd been meant to confront since Providence Street.

'Silence is twice as fast backwards', the voice on the radio recited before Julia switched it off with a huff.

The light improving, the flatlands they were travelling opened up like a palmed hand. Arid brown desert stretched outwards in all directions as far as the eye could see. Vast relay transmitters were planted across open spaces, miles, perhaps hundreds of miles apart. Morse code riffled the air. Clumps of tumbleweed fluttered across the highway like cutaways in a counter-culture road movie.

Several miles on, if distance could still be measured in miles, the roadside was littered with burning cars. Smoke rose vertically from the carnage, untroubled by any breeze. Several burning and bloody corpses were dragging themselves about, rising to their feet or else falling to their knees, unable to cease to exist.

'If they could only die,' Jim said, slowing the Saab to a crawl. 'If only they were able to die.'

'Keep going,' Julia said. 'There's nothing we can do to help. Soon we'll be at the border. That's our priority.'

'Why not come with me?' Jim wanted to know. 'Wouldn't you be safer across the border? Isn't it the next best thing to Heaven; isn't that what you said?'

'Don't think of it as Heaven, think of it more as a great big waiting room. And don't expect it to be any easier over there. You may meet James Dean and Marilyn, but there are unhealthy influences everywhere. Cora for one.'

'So you're staying. There's nothing I can say to change your mind?'

'That's correct. There are plenty more souls where yours came from.'

Jim could only shake his head, impressed by her courage. 'You know, you're remarkable, Julia. I wonder –'

'Yes?'

'I wonder how it would have been if we'd met while we were both alive.'

Julia laughed. 'You would have been too young for me, is my guess. Didn't I tell you I topped myself back in '71? OD'd on booze and barbiturates the night I heard Janis died? I used to be so irresponsible.'

'It seems death changed you, then.'

'For the better.' Again, she laughed. 'I found my vocation at last; that's why I can't cross the border. I'm sorry.'

There was no checkpoint. A barbed wire fence marked the perimeter, but this was in disrepair and the road ahead lay open. Jim brought the car to a standstill and stared at the city he was soon to enter. It looked, he thought, like a place the world had once been – or would one day become.

Elegant verticals, high rising towers, craned their silhouettes up from the horizon. Silent white flashes danced across the sky, an electric storm signalling the energy at the city's heart. That energy, Jim knew, was Cora's.

'This is where I say goodbye,' Julia said, and pushed open the door on her side. She was wearing a khaki army jacket, and it was now that Jim saw the badge – an anarchy symbol – stitched on to one lapel. As she got out she made a fist. 'Go for it,' she said lightly, 'do what you can.'

She slammed the door and leaned in at the open window for a moment, saying nothing. Some distance behind them Jim could hear meandering sirens; or perhaps only static on the dusty air.

'Whoever you are and whyever you're doing this, thank you,' he said. 'Take care of yourself.'

Julia nodded, brushed hair back from her numbered brow. 'Don't worry about me. There's nothing the authorities can do to me they haven't already done.'

He watched after her as she turned and started back along the highway, the immeasurable distance stretching before her, and then he saw the haze of blue light at the horizon's tip. The light was a regular, recurrent flash, like that of an ambulance or police car back in the world. Were such things called for here? In any case the light was coming this way; coming for Julia, perhaps.

He wondered whether he should rush to her aid, or at least wait and see. He pressed the accelerator, then the brake, at a loss which direction to take. But Julia was turning, a silhouette in the desert, and waving him on: 'Go,' she cried, and again for good measure, 'Go! I know what I'm doing!'

Ahead was his destiny. Behind him his life; and all the souls who had suffered on his behalf. He hoped that Julia wouldn't be one of them. He waited a little longer, until she was smaller and the blue hazy light larger, and at last he drove to the Pleasure Zone.

thirty-six

Legends came and legends went. In the world Jim Doherty had departed they were ten a penny, created, loved, and then murdered as soon as times changed. Oblivion, though, was another matter: a place in which nothing changed and where permanence reigned; where the legends who came stayed for ever.

They came here, the majority, like the song about Marilyn, as candles snuffed by the wind. Others came in a blaze of glory, hyped up on chance and amphetamines, hitting the mainline, driving fast cars to inevitable conclusions. But however they came and from wherever they came, these r'n'r gods and goddesses, they came to the Morrison Hotel.

Here it stood, alone in its glamour, a many-floored city at the desert's edge, upper storeys enveloped by electric storms. Here was where the power was − in this refuge of the dead, the once rich and famous; in this luxury complex with its bars and casinos, its pale gleaming walls and its broad sombre halls, its silent lifts.

As soon as Jim saw it, as he sighted the fork of lightning at its summit, he knew there was no need to drive further. This was the end of the journey, no question.

He parked the car away from the road, on a junction half a block from the hotel, and walked to reception. There was no receptionist. No one moved in the burnished, thickly carpeted foyer or lounged in the lounge. Instead of investigating further indoors, he retreated outside to skirt the building.

The main street was dusty and wide and empty of traffic, the buildings like parched Spanish villas. A shutter flapped at a window across the street, breaking the silence, though nothing else stirred. As he walked, his footsteps amplified; above their clatter there was only the sound of desert wind, the warble of radio morse.

Was that all though? Still on the main street, he stopped and listened, quieting himself. His mind still sounded like too many arguing voices, but wasn't there music somewhere? – a radio or a jukebox perhaps? Not a radio, for the sound had a liveness about it; the bass notes could be felt as well as heard.

He turned the corner towards the rear of the hotel. The side-street was deserted. Ahead, the corner of a poster flapped beside a casino with graphic palm trees above its door. He could make no sense of the poster's hieroglyphics, but its images were unambiguous: high cheekboned faces as pale as ghosts, electric guitars on fire, a drumkit standing on a darkened stage.

Behind the hotel was the car park, its many spaces taken by classic American cars of the '50s: T-Birds, Plymouths, brand new Cadillacs. Beyond this extended the asphalt tennis courts, and between the courts and the building an oval swimming pool.

The pool looked inviting, even in light as dour as this. Empty chairs and tables with parasols were arranged around it, and a high board towered above water that glittered, turquoise, reflecting the light of the storm. Jim looked up and shivered, suddenly cold, though his palms were tacky. More than ever he longed for a cigarette. Unless he had lost his mind, the electric storm was not only gathering outside the upper rooms; it was emerging from there.

As he neared the pool the music became louder, more vivid. Snare drums were sharp as his breathing, as his pulse, as the rhythmic sickness that had grown up inside him. Past the tables and chairs at the far side of the pool, twin patio doors stood open. Judging by the sounds there was a party in progress. He hurried towards it.

Just as he reached the doors, a lanky bouncer, flat-topped and wearing sunglasses, stepped from nowhere to block Jim's path. He studied the numbers marked on Jim's brow carefully before nodding and stepping aside.

'What is this place?' Jim said, and the bouncer said, 'You mean you don't know? The Last Whisky Bar, man, that's where you are.'

'There's a show going on by the sounds of it,' Jim observed. 'Have I missed much? How much is left?'

The bouncer shook his head, grinning. 'This show,' he said, 'goes on for ever.'

As Jim edged inside, the darkness rushed at him. He'd taken no more than a dozen steps when the floor seemed to fall away beneath his feet, throwing him forward. Instinctively he flashed a hand out to his right, finding the panelled wall there, then the railing. In his haste he'd overshot the first few steps of a flight leading down to a basement. Steadying himself, he started down again slowly, letting his eyes adjust to the light.

It was not a large place, The Last Whisky Bar; nor was it unbearably crowded. It couldn't compare with nightclubs in London, New York, or Paris. But its clientele set it worlds apart: no eye had witnessed gatherings like this, no mind had dreamt them. By chance – no, not by chance; by hook or by crook, by the finger of fate – Jim Doherty had found himself in ligger's paradise.

Here they were — some seated, some standing in shadows, some leaning against columns that supported the low-beamed ceiling — the legendary dead of rock-and-roll history whose names he'd absorbed, whose music he'd lived and breathed for. The walls were all Rothko prints. Smoke formed a greyish-blue fog overhead; glasses clinked in celebration. The mood was almost jovial, the guests chatting quite happily amongst themselves. On a small cramped stage, above which the ceiling pressed like a coffin lid, a jam to end all jams was in progress. Mistrusting his eyes, Jim took a step towards the beat.

Gripping the mike stand with both pale-knuckled fists and tossing her lion's mane from side to side, Janis Joplin was wailing 'The Ballad of John and Yoko'. *Don't let me dow-ow-own: don't let me down.* Beside her, Jimi Hendrix worked away at his famous white Fender with admirable restraint, finger cocked at his tremolo arm. To say he had choked on his own vomit, he looked in the peak of condition; he hadn't gained a year or a line or a pound since the tragedy. Jim caught the briefest glimpse of Keith Moon at the drums before the crowd at stage-front blocked his view.

Astonished, he turned away through the smoke. His mind was throbbing, threatening to split with the sheer force of the visions; he had to look at everything twice. At a table to his left Buddy Holly, Richie Valens, Eddie Cochran and Gene Vincent were seated. Elvis Presley was squeezing in at their elbows — thank God, though, this Elvis was the man in his prime, before he turned into a vast bloated beefburger. When Presley spoke — there was too much noise for his words to carry — he spoke as rebels were supposed to, from a corner of his mouth. When he listened, his upper lip curled.

At the bar, Ian Curtis, who had taken his own life in

1980, stood chatting with Jim Morrison, the mystic. Both were drinking beer from bottles. Morrison was wearing a 'No One Gets Out of Here Alive' T-shirt under his jacket and blinking his heavy eyes as if they were filled with moisture or smoke. It had once been said that Morrison, the shaman, was really alive and well and living in Ian Curtis: and then Curtis had pointlessly ended it all. It was only fitting, Jim thought, that the two kindred spirits should spend eternity drinking together, sharing their tortured thoughts in this way.

Not everyone here had attained legend, though. Many were punters who had killed themselves for a pose or a laugh. Many had died stupidly and in ignorance, bloodstreams polluted, noses rotted away by the white stuff they'd breathed. Might Terry Mack be here somewhere? Here were two more burnt-out cases brooding in a corner, Sid Vicious and Nancy sneering and shaking their fists at a bartender, their table cluttered with empties.

Wherever Jim turned he saw stars. There was Bob Marley, another tragic loss, enjoying a spliff. Marc Bolan, who had driven into a tree; Brian Jones, who had gone out like a loser on *Sunset Boulevard*. Jim watched them all. Surely he had seen everything now. His mind had imploded, and this was its residue: the ultimate trip. For a while he wandered in a daze, unsure whether to laugh or clench his teeth in an effort to hold in his panic, and managed to do both by turns.

Shouldn't he be celebrating like everyone else? Perhaps a drink would help, he decided, and squeezed in beside Tim Buckley's elbow and called for a Tom Collins. As he did, a face jutted forward into candlelight somewhere to his left. Jim did a double-take and then squinted to make sure. The face he had seen was Colin's.

Colin was in a booth on the other side of the bar. With

him was a man who was leaning forward polishing his round-rimmed spectacles. Between them on the table was a half empty vodka bottle. Both men looked up as Jim approached their booth. When Colin's companion replaced his glasses on his nose, Jim recognised him as John Lennon.

'I don't believe any of this,' Jim said, and flopped down beside Colin, his legs no longer supporting him. 'I don't believe anything I'm seeing.'

'Well, you'd better,' Colin said. His eyes were wild and pink from too much booze, and his teeth were bared in an almost canine grimace. He was squeezing the glass in his hand so tightly it might break at any moment. After a moment he said, 'Jim, allow me to introduce –'

'I think I know,' Jim said.

'When he talks he sounds just like one of the Beatles,' Colin added, smiling.

Lennon nodded modestly and extended a hand. Jim shook it. 'The world misses you greatly,' Jim said.

'Likewise, I'm sure,' Lennon said.

'You're the only one I ever wept for, you know. When I heard the news . . . I thought it was the end of the world. I couldn't speak to anyone for days after, just stayed in my room and cried.'

'Thank you.'

'You were only fucking forty years old,' Colin put in, perhaps a little more loudly than intended. 'I hope Michael Chapman, the one who gunned you down, I hope he gets cancer. I hope he bleeds to death slowly.'

'Relax,' Lennon said mildly. 'You're only making yourself feel worse inside, talking like that. I wouldn't wish cancer on anyone.'

Colin nodded, seeming to deflate. His hand went involuntarily to his gut. 'I'm sorry.'

'The two of you are together, I take it,' Lennon said to Jim.

Jim nodded, and Colin took up his glass, took a drink, and set it down. 'That's right. Jim's a journalist.'

'Ah.'

'I'm working on a story right now, Jim said.

'One hell of an exclusive, I'd guess,' Lennon laughed.

'A Cora De Ville exclusive,' Jim said, and then fell silent as Colin's hand enclosed his.

Madness or anger or both — whichever it was, there was heat in it — rose to Colin's eyes for a second, then was gone. Withdrawing his hand from Jim's, he pushed it firmly into his pocket, and Jim remembered the gun. Surely a gun was of little use here. 'It's all right,' Colin said. 'There's no need to look further. The Queen Bitch is here.'

'Where?'

'Somewhere upstairs, I believe.' Colin glanced at Lennon for confirmation and when Lennon nodded he said, 'As far as we know she and Beresford are on the thirteenth. We can take a lift straight to them.'

'We can get to them as easily as that?'

'Of course,' Lennon said. 'As far as the Morrison Hotel is concerned they're just regular guests. The least welcome guests, mind you. Don't think I don't know what they're doing to the world just because I'm here and not there; the utter mess they're making. They still think the rock-and-roll game is all about sucking life and power from the masses; they've got themselves drunk on power. It's enough to give revolution a bad name.'

On stage, Janis Joplin was taking a breather while Hendrix embarked on a bluesy solo: feedback soared and fell as he drew the Fender's pick-ups this way and that across the mike stand. Some of the crowd responded by

317

cheering and clapping their hands above their heads in unison.

'Those were the days,' Jim said fondly, not thinking, and Lennon said, 'Yes, they still are.'

'I think we'd better be going,' Colin said finally, standing, fist still buried in his pocket.

As Jim rose to join him Lennon said, 'Good luck, I hope there's an audience for your exclusive. I hope you get to finish it.'

'I hope so too. And I hope you stay happy. If the story happens, is there anything you'd like to add?'

'Tell Yoko I love her. And tell the world I haven't sold out; I'm still angry.' He laughed warmly. 'That's how I keep going.'

Colin was turning away, but Jim held his ground just a moment longer. 'One last thing, John. Who *was* the walrus?'

Lennon laughed, and took a sip of his vodka before answering. 'The walrus was Paul. Didn't you figure that out yet?'

Leaving Lennon to his booth, they walked from The Last Whisky Bar and started up the steps. Seconds later, nearing the top, it was Lennon's voice they heard as the band in the basement segued into another old song: 'Helter Skelter'. At least that was appropriate.

Thunder cracked the atmosphere; dust rose from main street like a lifting dream as Jim followed Colin up the steps to the Morrison's entrance.

There was still no activity at reception. As they crossed the foyer to the waiting lift, the floor seemed to tremble underfoot as if the foundations were laid over a subway system. Presumably someone had cranked up the PA downstairs. Rhythms shook the walls with blows as regular and mindless as a hammer's, and a huge chandelier, sparkling as champagne, trembled overhead. It wasn't until he pressed for the thirteenth floor that Jim sensed the greater power was above.

It was waiting for him upstairs, waiting to fulfil everything he'd glimpsed in his future. What he sensed was not just the music but Cora herself, as much a part of this place as the décor.

The doors closed, the lights ticked away floors while Colin leaned back against the chromium wall, gun in hand. 'I haven't decided what I'm going to do when we get there yet. Have you?'

'Not yet.'

'But there's no way I'm going to be on the losing side.'

'We're already on the losing side,' Jim said, watching the lights.

'How can you be so defeatist? What would John Lennon say if he heard you say that? We haven't come through all this just to – just to –' Colin shook his head, sighed emphatically. 'I've a question, Jim. Why am I still aware of my body? Why can I see it and why is it solid? That's more than one question, I know; but why is the sickness still in me, in here? Can I have died and still feel?' He was chewing his lip to hold back the tears when he should have been letting them go. There was more than anger flushing his face now, there was confusion and terror as well, a terror to match even Jim's. 'Where do we go if we ever get out of this mess? What chance have we got?' he finished.

Jim could find no reply. Dry-mouthed, he watched the level indicator jump from the ninth to the tenth. As the lift moved silently upwards, it seemed to him that the air grew dense and the light murky, that every part of him pounded and strained to tear itself free. Sweat drenched his arms and his chest, a pulse lodged at the roof of his mouth. He didn't feel capable of breathing or even thinking without effort. Could he make himself move?

The lift doors were opening on the thirteenth. Colin was first out, gun levelled before him as he went. Jim followed unsteadily. An odour of decaying meat greeted them, and the light in the hall seeming to falter, rising and falling. Sparks of power ignited the air like tiny flashbulbs going off.

'Thank God, we're home,' Jim said under his breath, and then wondered what on earth he meant by that: in any case, what was to celebrate? Perhaps he meant that here, at last, was an end of a kind. All his nightmares had brought him to this. His thoughts should be thoughts of relief, not fear.

Doors without numbers were closed on both sides of the hall. One on the right stood fractionally open, incandescent light shivering between door and frame. They started towards it, Colin a couple of paces ahead. Placed at intervals between the doors, and on wall-shelves, and in every spare corner, were flourishing black-leafed plants whose moist, dewy stems and shoots had the appearance and smell of tainted flesh. They grew more thickly nearer the open door, in some cases sprouting from the walls themselves.

Colin was holding the gun pointing idly up at the ceiling. A bead of sweat depended from his nose. He had stalled at the door and was watching Jim closely, his expression a blank. Jim tried to swallow dryness. The pressure between his ears was almost unbearable now.

Everything seemed to be slowing, or speeding up; he couldn't tell which. He inhaled deeply and tried to hold on to it. 'Ready?' he said, and Colin, turning his shoulder to the door, said, 'Yes, ready.'

Together they tumbled inside. The room opened up before them. A bolt of lightning described it in detail, emptied its corners of darkness, lit up its shapeless furniture. Everything became still for a second. To Jim, it seemed ludicrous that his first impressions should be so mundane: the open window with its desert vista, the TV set with its screen of snow, the dishevelled bed.

The shock was too great for anything else to make sense. There was nothing here for his mind to take hold of; the rest was just too far removed from his experience. Nothing in life had prepared him for this. He couldn't respond. Somewhere deep down inside, he sensed his sanity give like the softest intake of breath.

The room was constructed entirely in flesh. Ceiling, floor, walls, chairs; all were of the same jaundiced, veined complexion. Books bound in skin stood on pale downy shelves; tattered strips of flesh hung in adjoining doorways like sick-joke plastic walk-through. The chairs, the bed, the walls of the room, all were pink and moist, expanding and contracting to the beat. Wisps of fine dark hair grew in corners.

Jim took three paces into the room. The floor was soft underfoot and his soles made clear white impressions which faded gradually. Because the room was alive, because he sensed he had just stepped beyond the realm of the sane, he didn't immediately see the pale figure rising from the bed, pushing aside the fleshy sheets.

Then Colin was grabbing at his arm, unable to prevent him rushing into the heart of the room. 'Jim,' he said, but in any event, Jim ignored him. The figure he was striding forward to greet was Elaine.

She was naked and pale and barely able to stand, her stomach and breasts still streaked with multiple bloody wounds. She was crying, and he felt himself wanting to cry too. Wordlessly, he removed his jacket and helped her into it. She watched as if only half awake while he tugged the zip to her chin.

'Where am I?' she said then. 'Jim, where am I?'

thirty-seven

The thunder faded, and the only sound then was the distant desert wind. Twilight closed over the chamber, corners refilled with darkness. Exhausted, Elaine fell into Jim's arms, and immediately he felt her body stiffen and tense against him. Past his shoulder she had caught her first clear sight of Colin. '*You*,' she said.

'What's done is done,' Jim said. Knowing how inadequate that sounded he added, 'Colin and I were friends once. We couldn't be again, too much has changed. But we started this together and we have to see it through.'

'Words won't make anything come out right,' Colin told Elaine. 'I can't even apologise, because it isn't enough. That's why I'm here, to do what I can, to make amends if I can. When I followed you to the flat, before they — did *this* to you, I was trying to warn you. You must understand I'm as much Cora's victim as anyone else.'

Whiteness stammered outside, less dazzling than before and further away. After a moment Elaine released herself from Jim and looked blankly at Colin, saying nothing. Forgiveness was out of the question; this was neither the time nor place for it anyway. The thing was to leave, if there was anywhere to go.

And if there was any way out. She had taken two strides to the exit before noticing there wasn't one. She staggered backwards and put a hand to her mouth, from which a petrified cry was trying to emerge.

Colin, who had been standing with his back to the threshold, turned and stared at the place where it had been; then stared at the gun in his hand as if it had lost its usefulness. He looked at Jim. 'This is what you saw on Providence Street, isn't it?'

'Something like this.'

The doorway was sealed off, but not by the door. Instead, a sheet of membrane stretched tight as a drumskin shut off the corridor. At the window too, curtains of flesh were slowly unfurling, closing out the desert view, closing in the stench of decay.

The last of the light was fading. Cora's trap had been neatly sprung, Elaine as its bait. Do something, Jim told himself, but he was dry of ideas, had nothing more to give. The true death, the eternal death he'd feared more than anything else was something that happened the instant the soul surrendered, the instant he stopped saying no. He must resist, even to the last. But something was happening; a subtle but quite real change in the atmosphere, the room, or himself.

Colin was fidgeting, stroking the gun for comfort. Elaine was muttering incoherently. Here and there, at strategic points around the room, contractions and swellings were developing in the walls, the floor, in the bed between the tangle of sheets.

It was only a matter of seconds before Jim was able to identify the faces forming themselves out of the room. He wanted to laugh, though he felt no amusement. He had once seen these visions in wallpaper flora; now, literally, he saw them in the flesh. Was he supposed to change with them, transform himself as he entered some strange new existence?

The first face he saw was severely disfigured; it was that of the platinum-haired punk, returning without eyes to his homeground Underworld. Next came the caul-faced man, half his head blown away. Why had he thought he would never see either again?

And here, now, was Max Beresford, whose smug thin smile he wanted to mash away with his fists. Others followed, slithering in through moist, mouth-like gaps in the walls, some entering crippled and lacking limbs, some wounded past repair, all victims snatched from the riots. The last to appear was Cora, rising to her knees on the bed, staring before her, stepping down in complete silence.

All in black, glowing like the icon she was, she melted the others into insignificance. When she smiled, at first, her teeth seemed unnaturally white. Then it became clear that the whiteness was a blazing inner light, the energy she'd stolen, the power of souls.

Jim felt her strength draining his. It took his limbs first, and he was forced to struggle to stay upright. Queen Bee, Queen Whore, Queen Bitch: whatever her name, one look reminded him why he'd desired and worshipped her. He'd fallen under her glamour once but he wouldn't again — not this time or ever.

'So this is where you come and go,' he called above the mounting pressure in his skull, which pounded like the band in the basement. 'This is where you suck life from the living. You *are* the Dark Brigade: you're the law and the order down here.'

'Correct,' Beresford said. 'All flesh is consigned here. It's where what's mortal becomes immortal. But why should you find it objectionable, Jim? Where's the harm in a little immortality?'

'I've seen what it leads to. Endless suffering, incredible pain; people trapped in holes they can't escape. At a market stall I saw a man's heart still beating because it couldn't die, didn't know how. I saw human eyes packed in egg cartons. There's plenty wrong with immortality, Max.'

'You'll see things our way eventually,' Cora said, advancing. Infinitesimal lights plagued her body, leaping here and there as sparks from her pores. 'You'll come around because you've no choice. You're one of us now. We accept you.' She smiled faintly and shook her head. 'How long did you think you could ward off the inevitable? You caused it to happen, remember. You wanted a change and you got it.'

'I won't buy what you're selling, Cora. Nor will anyone else when they know the truth.'

'Which truth is that?' Beresford wondered.

'That you're all growing fat and loathsome at their expense. They think you're returning their love but all you want is their strength and their anger. We're leaving, Max, we're going back where we came from; your audience is going to know the truth.' No longer able to contain himself he pushed Elaine, almost violently, towards the caul-covered doorway. 'Colin, shoot a fucking hole in that thing,' he said.

'You won't get very far,' Cora remarked as he turned. 'The bodies you're wearing are finished with, they'll serve you no purpose in the world.'

'Then we'll go without.'

She seemed both amused and annoyed by that. 'What's the use in a world you can't fit back into? Where's the pleasure? Here at least there's a physical aspect. If you went back, you'd forever be on the outside looking in.'

'We'll find other bodies. Alternative bodies. You won't have our souls to keep, that's all.'

Jim turned fully away just as Colin, wild-eyed, levelled

the gun at the doorway and fired. Elaine flinched, smoke rose, and a wound at the barrier's apex began to bleed copiously. Behind them Cora uttered a shocked, submissive noise. Now the power was rising to her eyes, the frosty light escaping her mouth in bursts like witch breath.

In one motion, Colin swung around and fired again, twice. He had lived for this moment — and died for it. The first shot hit Cora somewhere about the ribs, the misdirected second blew out the TV screen in a hail of glassy shrapnel. From somewhere — perhaps the room itself — a single guitar note ascended to feedback like a cry. Beresford's mouth ticked. A pale phosphorescence rose from Cora's wound, slowly encircling her, re-entering her by the mouth. No, Jim thought, she would never perish, however badly damaged she was. She had absorbed too much energy for that.

All around them, blood seeped from wounds which were opening randomly across the walls. Colin fired once more, emptying the gun, and cast it aside. 'Let's go,' he said.

'Fetch them, boys,' Max Beresford told his henchmen then. They advanced without thought — the caul-face, the riot victims, the punk who stumbled blindly, feeling his way forward with outstretched arms.

'Go,' Colin yelled as the caul-face descended on him. 'Don't try to help, just go.'

Jim could hardly decide what to do, which way to turn. All his faculties had deserted him. He was as close to Cora as to Elaine, who had uncovered the silver skewer from Jim's coat pocket and was gouging away at the membrane-sealed doorway with it. He looked at Cora, and Cora, in spite of everything, smiled quite passively in return. He could set about her while the others were occupied, but what good would it do? If he tore her to pieces she'd be a hundred icons, not one. Instead he joined Elaine at the door, grabbing at the screen of flesh. As he seized his first handful, Colin, behind him, began to scream.

The caul-face, the punk, and a man whose face had been burnt mostly away were towing at Colin's limbs in an effort to subdue him. The strain showed in his face, which was distended and blue, the eyes bulging. Both his arms were being held. After a flurry, they grounded him. Perhaps they intended to cripple Colin so as to make him useless against them.

'Go Jim,' he shouted again, 'for Godsakes take her and go!' He was unable to say more, for something was forcing itself from his mouth. The moment Colin's scream was cut short, Jim's began.

It was no longer possible to tell horror from hallucination. All Jim knew was that he couldn't make himself keep looking. Even Cora had retreated in awe, while Beresford cleaved to a freckled section of wall, searching for the place by which he'd entered.

The shining vinyl blackness wasn't only leaving Colin's mouth: his whole body was surrendering to it, opening itself up like a vast fleshy grape. This was what had happened to Daniel Zero. Everything Colin had allowed to build up in himself, all through the years, had begun to come out now. Rising from his shell was something halfway between man and spider and the size, perhaps, of an infant. They used to say it was better, Jim thought, to let out frustration than bottle it up, but here was an end to that argument; this was too much altogether.

Even Cora looked paralysed with fear, and no wonder; the creature's arrival had defused her power. The light faltering about her, she tottered backwards until the bed jarred her legs, then tried to work herself around it.

The creature was almost too quick for the eye to catch, yet beautifully intricate in its movement. Numerous spindly limbs carried it upwards and forwards, away from the mess on the floor. The caul-faced man rolled aside and out of its path, leaving the punk stranded, unseeing and unsure what to do.

In any event, there was nothing more to be done. As far as Jim could see, it all ended here. The rage had come home. Unlike so many before him, Colin had learned to cage his feelings, had stored them up, ready to turn them against their creator. Cora had generated the malignancy in the first place, and it was only fitting it should consume her too. By the time the sleek head had snapped open and latched itself on to her face, and the shining, many-mouthed body had moved over hers, Jim had seen more than enough. If rock and roll had never quite died for him in the past, it was certainly doing so now with this crazed blitzkrieg bop. He ought to feel privileged to be witnessing the end of an era, but for now he couldn't feel anything.

'Don't look back,' he said to Elaine after a time. 'Don't even think about what's going on.'

'I don't understand,' she said. 'Is he — did Colin sacrifice himself, to help us?'

'No, there's no sacrifice about it. I doubt he even knew what he was doing.'

The corridor was visible through the largening hole in the barrier. It was almost a shock to see normal doors, solid walls, and a carpeted floor waiting ahead. As they stepped into it, Jim noticed that the black-leafed plants, the scent of their flesh fading, were already reforming themselves into wallpaper.

'It's over,' Elaine said dreamily as the lift doors opened. Then, after a moment's thought, 'It *is* over, isn't it?'

'Nothing's ever over,' Jim replied. He'd learnt that much here, if nothing else.

thirty-eight

No nothing was ever truly over, Jim thought, but each moment of each day was a new beginning, a new hook-line. All flesh was grass and temples came and went, but all things changed, became dust, moved on. And change was revolution. A mortal condition. And the mortal tent would be torn down, his body broken, and in the blink of an eye he'd be new again.

That, at least, had been Jim Doherty's dream; that was the revolution he hoped lay ahead. Dogs might return to their vomit and scoundrels to their vices but not me, he resolved secretly, not ever again.

They were returning to the city of lights, across the blond desert. There wasn't much further to go. Automobile wreckage still blazed away either side of the highway, sending thick palls of smoke to an empty sky. Here and there, mutilated crash victims wandered aimlessly about like sleepwalkers.

Elaine touched Jim's hand on the steering wheel and sat back, her eyes closing. 'I love you,' she said, and Jim replied rather awkwardly, 'Me too.'

'Could we ever be the way we were before?'

'Would you want us to be?'

'I don't know . . .' She shook her head wearily. Then, 'I don't know where we're going.'

'Neither do I.'

'In that case, wake me when we're there.'

There was a lull, nothing more spoken, until they reached the outskirts of the city, when Jim began pressing the radio pre-sets one by one. Radio Death was no longer on air and there was nothing on the scale but pink noise. The few inter-station sounds were distant, reedy voices, unwelcome reminders of shipping forecasts.

Now the city lay before them, and they were cruising its rubbled thoroughfares towards a distant point of light, brighter than all the rest. There went a Hard Rock Café, there went the bar where Julia danced. Streets rushed by like fragments of dreams, like great neon waves storming the asphalt peninsula. Salt filled the cloying night air. As they passed the market squares Jim felt a strong compulsion to slow for a view of the stalls, to check that the horrors he'd seen there were real. Instead he accelerated.

All right, he thought, with his foot pressed down hard and the speedo ascending, we are going to get there. Whatever it takes, whatever becomes of us, however many deaths we must enter first.

Traffic clogged the flyover, a train of slow moving lights, but the intersection below was easier to negotiate. Beyond this point there was only the dark at the town's furthest quarter and the narrow extended tongue of central reservation. Gradually, while he drove, Jim's mind became focused. He thought of the fortune-teller and Providence Street and suddenly understood what he was speeding towards. Now then: what was it Goatbeard had said about entering and leaving the world?

But he couldn't control the thought or follow it through. The light was all at once in front of him, whiting out his vision. Braking slightly, he raised an arm to shield his face, and in the same instant saw he had fooled himself. The brightness was not the waiting world but a pantheon of headlights. He was accelerating towards a road block.

'Elaine!' he said, budging her awake with an elbow. Elaine murmured and started from sleep. 'Get ready, you hear me, take off your seatbelt.'

'Why take it off?'

'To do the job properly.'

He might have known they'd be waiting. Why should he have thought they'd submit without a struggle, without even contesting his soul? Yes, he might have known, after what they'd done to the man in white; these people meant business.

But perhaps they had miscalculated too.

At the last, before he turned the wheel, he sensed that time had stopped, had begun to recycle itself. Events were beginning again, in a way he couldn't yet determine, and he was filled with a sense of *déjà vu* more powerful than fear. The authorities had cordoned off the dark side of town, but had neglected the small steep junction immediately before it.

Jim swung the wheel. The Saab bounced over the road, cornering smoothly, yet throwing him forward into the wheel and Elaine against the dashboard. The moment he looked up he thought he'd junctioned into the face of another barricade, for the headlights in front were harsher than those he had turned from, and were rushing straight at him. Then he knew where he was: racing towards the reflected crash; towards the Mirror Maze.

It was then he sensed the power of choice at his fingertips. All the power in the world was here, as much as he needed. He could save Elaine and himself, or go on, explore. He heard shots behind him in the night, and sirens and startled cries, amongst them Elaine's and perhaps even his own, he couldn't be sure.

It may never be the same again, he thought. I'll never be what I was, nor will she. Will I even know her or need her when this barrier is down? Will I even know myself?

No, nothing was ever truly over. Nothing was ever resolved.

And death was a never-ending party.

Epilogue

On Providence Street

The light was all too much. The girl knew instinctively it would blind her if she stared for another second. Even when she'd averted her eyes she could see, imprinted beneath her lids, the shapes coming in with the storm.

It was almost as if they'd formed out of the rain and the lightning. In a moment, in the blink of an eye, the vision had risen in radiance before her. The walls had fallen away and there was only the whiteness. Now she dared to look again, face upturned, hands prayerfully held in front of her.

The two shapes were sexless, she could tell. Perhaps the light covered such details, or perhaps they were past the need for procreation, above it. Either way, it was impossible to tell which was male, which female. Their movements were graceful and gradual and small, the movements of creatures at peace with themselves. Surely they were human, or had been, or would be, and briefly the girl willed to join them, willed with all her heart to be like them.

She wouldn't be, though, wouldn't ever be. She would never possess such glamour or burn so brightly. As the light diffracted and changed and the rain at the window softened, the girl came slowly back to herself. A feeling of peace overwhelmed her. Though she felt no chill, she was trembling.

She was back in the room with the dingy wallpaper. Had the others shared her insight? Given the way they were muttering together, she doubted it. But how could they have avoided seeing?

The man with the red tuft of beard was lighting a cigarette, leaning back in his shabby chair after speaking. Kerry, too, was relaxing and fumbling in her purse. When Kerry saw the way the younger girl was looking at her she said, 'What's the matter with you then?'

But the man with the beard like a goat's looked pensive, and after a silence mused and nodded, as if in some way he understood. The girl rose, still trembling. The lime-green floor seemed a long way below her. Now that the vision had faded, it was hard to believe she had seen anything at all. Perhaps it would mean something later, when she'd had time to consider. For the moment, she only wanted to leave. When Kerry had dragged her in from the rain, the girl had been convinced the man would be a fraud, but now she was less sure.

'What a filthy old man, though,' Kerry decided five minutes later, wobbling slightly on her heels as they walked down Providence Street. 'I don't know how he manages to stay in business in a place like that. I wouldn't go there again if you paid me.'

'So you didn't get what you wanted?' the younger girl said. 'Didn't you find anything out?'

'Are you kidding? You know they're all the same, this lot. They're all in the same racket. What was wrong with you, though? You weren't even listening. You were miles away.'

'I was thinking.'

'Ah.' Kerry was slowing to check her reflection in a window and ruffling her hair with both hands. With a lick of the lips and a swish of clothes, she moved on, this time with haste. 'Hurry. I'm supposed to be meeting Darren at four at the arcade. You can come, if you want.'

The invitation sounded more like a threat, and the girl managed to bite her lip rather than accept. She was always made to feel so alone when Kerry and Darren were together. Sometimes she suspected they liked having her along just to make her feel — what was the phrase? — like a gooseberry, as if her being alone made them more secure.

At least the air was refreshing now, and she felt more alive than for days. Perhaps what she'd seen had helped raise her spirits, if she really had seen it. Did it have any bearing on her own future? She couldn't imagine how. When the time came, she'd calmly refuse Kerry's invitation; she'd walk home filled with pride and with a spring to her step, nobody's sidekick.

'Would you just look at that,' Kerry said, the moment they turned the corner on to the prom.

A grey mist covered everything, reducing the front to a queue of dulled lights. A wave hung in the air for a succession of instants before collapsing forward over the sea wall. Just beyond the arcade there were several parked vehicles, one of which was a police car, another an ambulance. A handful of uniformed policemen were trying to disperse the few pedestrians that were gathering.

Somewhere along the coast, a fog warning sounded. Two bodies were being stretchered from the pavement to the waiting ambulance. Fragments of glass gleamed everywhere like rain touched by sunlight. At the height of the storm, the driver of the car which had torn through the front of the Magical Mirror Maze must have entered a skid, or lost sight of the road ahead. Not surprising in weather like this. The girl hoped the two, whoever they were, would survive, but their faces were already covered with soiled white sheets. Perhaps it was too late to hope. She hoped not.

After Kerry had turned in at the arcade, where Darren was waiting, the girl stood a while longer, shivering, forgetting the time, until the ambulance doors were secured. At last the siren rose and the light on top began to revolve. The ambulance sped away from her, shrinking into the distance, and within seconds she lost sight of it in the grey.

Acknowledgements

'Chainsaw'
(The Ramones)
Chappell Music Ltd
Reproduced by kind permission of Warner Chappell Music
Ltd

'More than Human' and 'Hell Games'
words and music by Jackie Leven
© 1980 Virgin Music (Publishers) Ltd
Lyrics reproduced by kind permission of Virgin Music
(Publishers) Ltd

**AN EPIC NOVEL OF TERROR – WINNER OF THE
1990 BRAM STOKER AWARD**

CARRION COMFORT

DAN SIMMONS

'Dan Simmons is brilliant'
Dean R Koontz

They are 'mind vampires' – creatures with the psychic
ability to 'use' humans: read their minds, subjugate
them to their wills, experience through their senses,
feed off their emotions, force them to acts of
unspeakable violence.

Each year three of them, Melanie, Willi and Nina, meet
to discuss their on-going competition of vampirism and
slaughter. But this year something goes wrong and they,
and their innocent victims, are plunged into a struggle
that will determine the future of the world itself.

Ranged against them are a handful of normals: Saul
Laski, psychologist and concentration camp survivor,
who has devoted his life to tracking down the Nazi
vampire von Borchert; Natalie Preston, whose father
inadvertently and fatally crossed the path of the
ancient and deadly Melanie; Sheriff Bobby
Joe Gentry, dragged in while investigating a series
of bizarre murders.

Together they create a strange and vulnerable alliance
against evil.

'*Carrion Comfort* should be a mind-bogglingly successful
bestseller. [Dan Simmons] is one of the new masters of
modern horror' *Locus Magazine*

'*Carrion Comfort* is, in my humble opinion, the best
horror novel, the best SF novel, and the best suspense
novel of the year' Edward Bryant

'A compelling thriller' *Publishers Weekly*

FICTION/GENERAL   0 7472 3405 1   £4.99

More Terrifying Fiction from Headline:

STEVE HARRIS

ADVENTURELAND

The funfair's hoarding cries out to the brave and the foolhardy, 'Die a thousand deaths and live to tell the tale!'

During the hottest summer in living memory the AdventureLand funfair comes to town casting its dark shadow before it. At one of the sideshows young Tommy Cousins becomes separated from his mum and dad and vanishes without trace. Tragic, but kids get lost at funfairs all the time. As the summer scorches on Dave Carter and his girlfriend Sally realise that when AdventureLand arrived it brought more than just safe thrills with it. Something worse than nightmare lies concealed behind the fairground's enticing exterior and it is beginning to break out. When Phil and Judy disappear inside the Ghost Train, Dave starts to ask questions to which there are no answers. He and his friends discover that the evil at the heart of the fairground is spreading.

Only Dave and Sally can stop it but to do so they will have to ride the Ghost Train to the terrifying Limboland that lies beyond the screams and the laughter . . .

'A superb book ... Harris's imagination is impressive and breathtaking ... definitely a name to watch for the 90s' *Starburst*

'It's bold stuff that grows on you' *Fear*

FICTION/HORROR   0 7472 3394 2

THE NEXUS
MIKE McQUAY

'McQuay's best book to date' Roger Zelazny

Denny Stiller is a cynical TV reporter, once a star on the Washington circuit, now reduced to covering 'human interest' stories. Until the night, in a rhinestone cowboy bar in Texas, he meets Tawny Kyle, working miracles – literally – for small change.

Denny sees the business opportunity of a lifetime and spirits the alcoholic Tawny and her autistic daughter Amy away. But Denny has misunderstood what he's seen and bringing the story to the networks may be the biggest mistake of his roller-coaster career. For once the world understands the truth, there are those who will stop at nothing to control – or destroy – it. And Denny finds himself riding a tiger that could change the world . . .

THE NEXUS

'A strong and colourful story, an extended parable, a meditation on mankind, morality, the media and madness' Roger Zelazny

'Grabs you on the first page and hurtles you to a daring, visionary climax . . . It takes on serious issues with honesty and guts. A terrific job!' Lewis Shiner, author of *Deserted Cities of the Heart*

Dan Simmons

SONG of KALI

Calcutta – a monstrous city of slums, disease and misery, clasped in the fetid embrace of an ancient cult.

Kali – the dark mother of pain, four-armed and eternal, her song the sound of death and destruction.

Robert Luczak – caught in a vortex of violence that threatens to engulf the entire world in an apocalyptic orgy of death.

The song of Kali has just begun . . .

"*Song of Kali* is as harrowing and ghoulish as anyone could wish. Simmons makes the stuff of nightmare very real indeed."
Locus

0 7472 3044 7   £3.99

A selection of bestsellers from Headline

FICTION

A WOMAN ALONE	Malcolm Ross	£4.99 □
BRED TO WIN	William Kinsolving	£4.99 □
MISTRESS OF GREEN TREE MILL	Elisabeth McNeill	£4.50 □
SHADES OF FORTUNE	Stephen Birmingham	£4.99 □
RETURN OF THE SWALLOW	Frances Anne Bond	£4.99 □
THE SERVANTS OF TWILIGHT	Dean R Koontz	£4.99 □
WHITE LIES	Christopher Hyde	£4.99 □
PEACEMAKER	Robert & Frank Holt	£4.99 □

NON-FICTION

FIRST CONTACT	Ben Bova & Byron Preiss (eds)	£5.99 □
NEWTON'S MADNESS	Harold L Klawans	£4.99 □

SCIENCE FICTION AND FANTASY

HYPERION	Dan Simmons	£4.99 □
SHADOW REALM Wells of Ythan 3	Marc Alexander	£4.99 □

All Headline books are available at your local bookshop or newsagent, or can be ordered direct from the publisher. Just tick the titles you want and fill in the form below. Prices and availability subject to change without notice.

Headline Book Publishing PLC, Cash Sales Department, PO Box 11, Falmouth, Cornwall, TR10 9EN, England.

Please enclose a cheque or postal order to the value of the cover price and allow the following for postage and packing:
UK: 80p for the first book and 20p for each additional book ordered up to a maximum charge of £2.00
BFPO: 80p for the first book and 20p for each additional book
OVERSEAS & EIRE: £1.50 for the first book, £1.00 for the second book and 30p for each subsequent book.

Name ....

Address ....

....

....